PRAISE FOR

"A complex but joyful tale of family, food, love, and restaurants, *Bitter and Sweet* by Rhonda McKnight tells a poignant story of sisterhood, motherhood, and new love found in old places. McKnight's writing is as delectable as the Gullah cuisine at the heart of the novel, but the beautifully written characters, prose, and dialogue make this story memorable. *Bitter and Sweet* by Rhonda McKnight is women's fiction at its best and a must-read journey you won't forget."

—DENNY S. BRYCE, BESTSELLING AUTHOR OF *The Other Princess* AND *Wild Women and the Blues*

"*Bitter and Sweet* was intensely raw in so many scenes that my emotions were all over the place. McKnight deftly wove the dual time between the past and present of three generations of women. I was immersed in the history and the food, and impatient as I waited for the secrets to be revealed. The characters wouldn't let me go until I finished the last page and even then I felt compelled to pray for people needing healing from trauma. The moments of celebration were a reason to praise God."

—VANESSA MILLER, BESTSELLING AUTHOR OF *The American Queen*

"An unputdownable dual timeline story spanning generations, infused with Gullah culture, rich with themes of resilience and redemption, reconnecting family, leaving you with renewed hope. Masterful storytelling at its best!"

—MICHELLE LINDO-RICE, BESTSELLING AUTHOR OF *The Bookshop Sisterhood*

"Rhonda McKnight's *Bitter and Sweet* is a meditation on what it means to be family. To love beyond dislike. To mend seemingly broken bridges and forge a bond beyond blood. In her deft hands, Rhonda's characters navigate broken hearts and betrayals, the delicacy of depression and find grace for grief to push them into purpose. The woven stories of Tabitha, Sabrina, and Mariah are reflections of the past in the present and how by sheer determination they can propel themselves into a life they love that satisfies the soul and entices the sweet tooth."

—NIKESHA ELISE WILLIAMS, TWO-TIME EMMY AWARD WINNING PRODUCER AND AUTHOR OF *Beyond Bourbon Street*

"*Bitter and Sweet* is a delicious layered cake of a story that's compulsively readable. The history woven through the story enhanced the flavors of the low country cooking sprinkled through the pages, and I could smell the she-crab soup and taste the desserts. McKnight is a master storyteller, and I can't get enough of her books! Don't miss this one!"

—COLLEEN COBLE, *USA Today* BESTSELLING AUTHOR

The Thing About Home

"Rhonda McKnight has written the perfect southern story—warm, sweet, and full of hope. McKnight captures the heart and soul of Casey's journey to self-discovery and love."

—PRESLAYSA WILLIAMS, AUTHOR OF *A Lowcountry Bride* AND *A Sweet Lowcountry Proposal*

"In this zippy outing from McKnight (*All She Dreamed*), a humiliated social media influencer rediscovers her roots . . . McKnight lays out some vivid low country history, and her fully realized characters—especially Casey and her sometimes superficial, sometimes serious trials—ring true."

—*Publishers Weekly*

"*The Thing About Home* is a beautifully written story about family, self-discovery, secrets, and forgiveness. It is a truly wonderful and most enjoyable read!"

—KIMBERLA LAWSON ROBY, *New York Times* BESTSELLING AUTHOR

"Rhonda McKnight has written a gorgeously vivid, heart-felt novel that stirred my emotions from the first page. I loved getting to know the characters and wanted to stay in their lives forever. Through a dual-timeline, parallels in the women's stories were expertly delivered in contemporary and historical voices that will have readers exploring their own lives and legacies. I tried to slow down as I came closer to the last page because I didn't want this book to end. I've loved every book by Rhonda McKnight, but this one is her best!"

—VICTORIA CHRISTOPHER MURRAY, *New York Times* BESTSELLING AUTHOR OF *The Personal Librarian* AND NAACP AWARD–WINNING AUTHOR OF *Stand Your Ground*

"Southern writing at its best, *The Thing About Home* is a warm, atmospheric reminder that *home* is more than just a physical place—it's family and friends and safety and unconditional love."

—EMILY MARCH, *New York Times* BESTSELLING AUTHOR

"In *The Thing About Home*, Casey Black's shiny world of New York fashion and always-on social media implodes. Finding her roots allows Casey to heal and calm the chaos that has consumed her life. In *The Thing About Home*, Rhonda McKnight pens a safe place, a Lowcountry boil that's soup for the soul. Expertly weaving a dual storyline of a rich matriarchal past with the tumultuous present, McKnight builds upon her women's fiction repertoire with a fresh perspective on grief, forgiveness, and finding oneself in the midst of the storm."

—VANESSA RILEY, AWARD-WINNING AUTHOR OF *Island Queen* AND *Queen of Exiles*

"McKnight's beautifully rendered tale of a social media influencer heroine, distanced from the world through her constant engagement with social media, is a well-woven sweetgrass basket of a story. Family, history, heritage, and legacy all combine in the tightly woven warp and weft of love in *The Thing About Home*—a must read.

—PIPER HUGULEY, AUTHOR OF *By Her Own Design*

"In *The Thing About Home*, Casey Black's perfect life has just crashed and burned, forcing her to seek refuge in South Carolina. Ms. McKnight does an excellent job exploring not only what coming home can represent, but also the importance of family history and legacy. The reader is not only given a captivating story, but also a lesson in life. A well-written exploration of love and acceptance."

—JACQUELIN THOMAS, AWARD-WINNING AUTHOR

"Rhonda McKnight has written a story chock-full of Southern comfort. It reads like a Lowcountry recipe that's seasoned with just the right amount of family, love, history, culture, and self-discovery. As her characters become deeply rooted in culture, you'll find yourself longing for the same connection to home."

—TIA MCCOLLORS, BESTSELLING AUTHOR
OF THE DAYS OF GRACE SERIES

"You will get lost in this book. Every moment, every step that Casey takes to finding herself is magical. Rhonda McKnight is a masterful storyteller. Hands down, *The Thing About Home* is the best book I've read in a long time."

—VANESSA MILLER, AUTHOR OF *The Light on Halsey Street*

Bitter
and
Sweet

Also by Rhonda McKnight

The Thing About Home

Bitter and Sweet

RHONDA McKNIGHT

THOMAS NELSON
Since 1798

Published in Nashville, Tennessee, by Thomas Nelson. Thomas Nelson is a registered trademark of HarperCollins Christian Publishing, Inc.

Thomas Nelson titles may be purchased in bulk for educational, business, fundraising, or sales promotional use. For information, please email SpecialMarkets@ThomasNelson.com.

Library of Congress Cataloging-in-Publication Data
Names: McKnight, Rhonda, author.
Title: Bitter and sweet / Rhonda McKnight.
Description: Nashville, Tennessee : Thomas Nelson, 2024. |
Summary: "From the beloved author of The Thing About Home comes a dual timeline tale of family, grief, secrets, and the sweet redemption that lies within the bonds of sisterhood"-- Provided by publisher.
Identifiers: LCCN 2024003857 (print) | LCCN 2024003858 (ebook) | ISBN 9780840706577 (paperback) | ISBN 9780840706607 (epub) | ISBN 9780840706867
Subjects: LCSH: Female friendship--Fiction. | LCGFT: Christian fiction. | Novels.
Classification: LCC PS3613.C56817 B58 2024 (print) | LCC PS3613.C56817 (ebook) | DDC 813/.6--dc23/eng/20240202
LC record available at https://lccn.loc.gov/2024003857
LC ebook record available at https://lccn.loc.gov/2024003858

Printed in the United States of America
24 25 26 27 28 LBC 5 4 3 2 1

For my maternal grandmother, Laura Wilson Kennedy,
and the three beautiful children she gave the world.
We'll see you in heaven.

Prologue

Grandma "Gail" Cooper Holland

My expectations were too high. That's what I'd been telling myself as I exited the hospital. It repeated in my mind as I started the car and pulled out of the parking lot.

The sun had been swallowed by the dark of dusk by the time I parked behind the restaurant. I reached for my purse and stepped from the car. The keys jangled in my free hand as I walked to the back door. I inserted them, releasing the locks one at a time, and then pushed the noisy door open. Lingering citrus from the oil cleanser I'd used on the floor rose to my nostrils. I was impressed that the scent was still so strong. It'd been a week since I'd mopped. Maybe it was always strong, but this place wasn't always so empty. Usually, the tiny kitchen was in use. The smells of spices and coconut and sounds of searing meat and pots of seafood gumbo rolling to a boil always met me at the door— that is, unless I arrived before the cooking began, and that was rare. I was never here alone. I never considered I'd have to be here . . . alone.

I looked at the tables, their chairs atop them. The glass door to the bakery case glistened with a haunting emptiness. I stepped to my left and walked into the kitchen. It was small—much too small, I'd always thought, for all that we'd done here. But today it felt huge, like it was swallowing the nothingness that had erected itself and rested in every corner.

Nothing had been cooked here in weeks. Nothing had been served to the community who had depended on us for almost ninety years. We would reach ninety. Forever was the goal, but we couldn't end at eighty-seven. It was too odd of a number. It came up short. Eighty-seven was unfinished.

I walked to the wall across the room. I called it the "Wall of History" because it included pictures all the way back to 1937 when my grandmother opened this place. There were pictures of every cook, every celebrity and politician who ever visited, our family and friends—this wall contained lifeblood. A lot was shed to open this place, and even more was shed to keep it. My eyes roamed the many framed award certificates and settled on one in particular, a presentation from the mayor of Georgetown. I was proudest of this one. Etched in gold script, it read: GAIL AND ODELL HOLLAND FOR RESTAURANT OF THE YEAR. We had rivaled fancier establishments and shined.

I reached into my purse for my phone and placed a call to my granddaughter Mariah. Her voicemail encouraged me to leave a message. Coincidence? A reprieve? Maybe I wasn't supposed to ask. I pushed that thought away. Ask I would, because it was the season for shocking statements and questions. I knew that well. Three weeks ago, the doctor had let my husband's condition slip from his mouth as easily as raw oysters slipped from the shell.

"Your husband has had a massive stroke."

"He will need full-time care."

"A skilled nursing facility is your best option."

The doctor's report stabbed me, wounded me in a way I was wholly unprepared for and destroyed by.

And then Odell's words: "Gail, keep oona promise."

A tear slid over my cheek as I fell back against the wall. I was tired. My sixty-nine-year-old body was exhausted. It was time for the younger ones to relieve us in the same way I relieved my mother.

I went to my contacts again. This time I called my other granddaughter, Sabrina. I got her voicemail too. She didn't listen to voicemail. None of these young people did, so I sent a text to both of them with the simple message:

I need you to come home.

Chapter 1

Present Day

Mariah Clark

Find a way to survive.

I bolted up in the bathtub, water sloshed over the side. I coughed until my lungs were cleared of the water that had slipped down my throat and then pinched my nose.

I had to find a way, or I was going to die from heartbreak, disappointment, betrayal, and this migraine I couldn't shake. But I couldn't manage to find air anymore. Even though oxygen was all around me, breathing was not just hard but impossible.

Regretting I hadn't brought the wine bottle I'd opened into the bathroom, I reached for my empty glass and raised it to get the final drop out. Muscadine wine. My grandfather's creation. Low in alcohol, high in sweet, rich in love. The taste usually conjured up feelings of comfort and safety—memories of better days or at least not days as bad as these. But it wasn't working tonight. Not working because drinking it made me sad. My grandfather was sick. He might never make this wine again. A sick grandfather was the last thing I needed in my messed-up life right now. The life I didn't even know if I wanted to live. But I had zero permission from heaven to die. My grandmother had enough stress. She didn't need to bury her granddaughter.

And if I died, I'd be chum in the ocean for gossip. Everyone in Hendley was already talking about me. Again. I could feel the wind from their whispers. It wasn't hard to be the subject of gossip. In a town as small as Hendley, South Carolina, where the population was twenty-two hundred, including children, gossip was served with the grits in the morning and the cracklin' corn bread at night. However, I didn't think I would receive the honor of being the subject of conversation so soon. It didn't seem fair that it was my turn again.

The first time people let my name fall off their lips was because Vince Clark, one of the city of Hendley's golden boys, got married to someone other than Callie Humphries, the head cheerleader/prom queen in his kingdom whom they expected him to propose to after college. Callie had been waiting at his house when he brought me home. There was disappointment that their story hadn't ended in a happily ever after, but folks got over it fast. The cash bar at our wedding helped.

The second time my name was caught up in town gossip involved my mother-in-law, Sylvia. When the grapevine caught the news that she was sick, people were surprised I was taking such good care of her. Everybody knew she didn't like me. The Callie thing was a source of disappointment to her too, and liquor at the wedding had not changed that. Sylvia's aggressive form of bone cancer carried the prognosis—dying. The accuracy—right on, nearly to the day the doctor told her.

Sylvia refused a nurse until one was absolutely medically necessary. As she had no daughters, the assignment to care for her fell on me. In truth, I could have been a full daughter if she'd only embraced me. I'd lost my own mother at age six, had a horrible stepmother, and even as an adult, I still wanted that sacred relationship.

Still, I did the right thing. Even with our complicated relationship, I did all I could for her. What I did was right in the sight of myself and God, certainly my poor husband, who couldn't take care of himself, forget another person.

You would think I would have been appreciated by the wagging tongues and certainly by my husband for my charity, but I wasn't, which was why I was in my current state of depression. I couldn't unsee his horrible behavior or unhear his words. They pounded against my brain like a temporal migraine.

"I'm leaving you."

I stood over a boiling pot of sausage and kale soup, a new recipe I was attempting to perfect. I wasn't listening to him, not really. My head was full of basil, onion, garlic, and the scent of bay leaves, but I heard him say he was leaving. "Where are you going?"

"You're not paying attention, Mariah. I want a divorce." The words hit me from behind like a bat pummeled against my spine. I turned toward him and found he'd been waiting for me to look up from my pot, which I did before he clarified his statement with, "I'm taking a divorce."

Taking a divorce? *Who says it that way?*

After eleven months of date nights, new perfume, and five new lingerie purchases, this man was still standing here telling me he was leaving.

"You can't just give up."

"I've tried. I'm not built for this."

I really didn't know what he was talking about. "Not built for what?"

"Unhappiness."

A little sound escaped through my lips, something like a muffled grunt. I uttered, "Unhappiness? What does that even mean?"

"If you can't define unhappiness, then you're probably not happy either." Vince walked out of the kitchen like he hadn't thrown a meat cleaver at my heart.

I reached across the tub for my bottled water. Through the open bathroom door, I caught sight of the manila envelope I'd put on the table near the door. It held legal papers. Vince delivered them personally the evening after he'd spoken of his unhappiness. It was a temporary order issued by the Turnin County Court that gave him ownership of his family home and the diner. It also instructed me to vacate far too quickly for it to be legal. It included an Order of Separate Maintenance and Support that required him to pay my rent and my medical and car insurance. The document was signed by his second cousin once removed, Sharon Clark, justice of the Turnin County Court. One of the only two justices in the county.

Sharon had never liked me. She didn't even like Vince much. But if she'd been even a decent human being, she would have had more empathy. I didn't deserve to be made to leave the home I'd lived in for nine years and helped Vince renovate and pay the taxes on with only a two-week notice. Or maybe she still would have done just what Vince asked—protect the Clark family assets, mainly land, and in Vince's case the house his great-great-grandfather built and the restaurant Vince inherited from his grandparents. The restaurant that was in bankruptcy when I married him, and which I not only saved from ruin but made into the success it was today. Success that included it having been listed on just about every top list of diners to visit in the Southeast and a few spots on the Food Network. It was also the new location for my upcoming weekly cooking show for ABC Upstate Daily Television.

I didn't want his property. I wanted my show. The show that had been my plan, my pitch, my dream, which was disappearing in his newfound happiness. All I had now for nine years of marriage and the work I'd done to save the diner was anger, regret, and a paltry ten thousand dollars.

"An advance on the divorce settlement," Vince was quick to say as he handed the check to me. "I don't want you to be broke.

That wouldn't be fair. I know you have to buy food and clothes until you find a new j—" *Job* was on the tip of his tongue, but he didn't say it. "I'm sorry you have to leave the house."

Just the day before, he'd said he was leaving, but I supposed the word *leaving* was only a metaphor for breaking the covenant of marriage. *He* didn't have to go anywhere. I was the one in this tiny little apartment. My moving out was convenient now as he'd moved his girlfriend in. I hadn't seen her at the house, but the rumors were true. Small-town talk never failed to deliver. My attorney assured me that Vince would regret committing adultery. South Carolina courts took fidelity seriously. Maybe that was true—that Vince would reap what he was sowing—but today the only person paying for our separation was me.

It had been three months since I'd moved. I was still trying to get the knife out of my back, but my arms—they weren't long enough.

I stepped out of the chilly tub water, toweled off, and changed into my new favorite clothing—yoga pants and a T-shirt.

The doorbell chimed. I knew who it was before I peeked out and saw the little boy from next door. I pulled it open. "Hi, Jordy." I took care to use the name he'd asked me to call him. Jordy, not Jordan, because he didn't want to be called a river—not one the Bible said had dirty water. He was a smart kid.

"Hello, ma'am. My mama says you shoulda got her box."

The delivery companies couldn't get the addresses for these duplexes right to save their lives. Every week I received a package that was meant for Jordy's mama or one of my other neighbors. I walked to the dresser and picked up the small box. Before I handed it to him, I asked him the same question I always did. "Do you want something to eat?"

Jordy was a slip of a child. Small for nine and as dirty as a full-grown ditchdigger. He made good use of the playground behind our units. But I wasn't sure if that was the reason he looked so unclean. I'd seen him board the school bus a few times, and he didn't look much better in the morning.

Jordy nodded in the affirmative, his long sandy-brown hair moving with enthusiasm that suggested he very much wanted something to eat. He was always hungry. What his mother was ordering when she couldn't seem to keep one child fed, I didn't know but wanted to. Our nosy and gossipy landlord told me she had a public housing voucher and EBT benefits. How he knew the latter, I don't know. Based on the hours she came and went, I assumed she worked full-time or close to it, but still her kid needed a meal. Either Jordy had a tapeworm or there just wasn't enough food.

"Close the door." I put the box down and walked to the kitchen area with Jordy following me. It was a tiny place. We didn't have to go far to reach our destination. I tossed him the last apple from my fruit bowl, and I swear I heard the crunch before it could possibly have settled in his hands. I reached into the cabinet for one of the many empty plastic storage bowls I kept there and scooped out ham and potato corn chowder. The chowder was more of a winter soup, perfect for the leftover ham bones from Thanksgiving through Easter, but I continued to make it because children liked corn and potatoes and ham. I'd made this pot with Jordy in mind, so I scooped out most of it and pressed the lid closed. Next, I slathered butter on the yeast rolls I'd kept in the warmer and wrapped them in tin foil. I double plastic-bagged the bowl and put the bread on top before handing it to him. There was enough to last them two or three days.

"Thank you, ma'am," he said. He was the politest child I knew. No child deserved to feel the growl of their belly at night, but this sweet one doubly did not.

I opened the door and, carrying his mother's package, followed him outside. I put the box down on the cement stoop in the space that separated our units and left before Jordy could push the slightly ajar door open. I didn't want to see or speak to his mother. Apparently she didn't want to see or speak to me either because she never did, not even to say thank you. In a few days, I would find the same plastic bag hanging on my doorknob with the washed bowl and lid inside. She and I understood each other. I had more and she had less. There wasn't much to discuss. Jordy connected us and his thank-you was enough.

I'd barely locked my door when my phone pinged. A text message from my best/only friend, Hope. The preview line for the message read: Therapy is an opportunity to get strategies. It doesn't mean you're . . .

I'd have to swipe to see the rest. Hope was continuing the conversation we'd had earlier when I hinted not so subtly that I had nothing to live for. Did she think the idea of going to therapy was something to live for? It wasn't. Therapy looked painful. I was in enough pain.

I put down the phone and dropped onto the couch. Therapy wasn't going to give me my TV show. I'd really wanted that. After all I'd put up with from Vince and his family, I deserved it. He could have at least let the show start before putting me out.

My phone rang, and I ignored it. Hope didn't like her text messages to be ignored. The second time the phone started ringing, I ignored it some more. I picked up the remote and turned on the television. I glanced at the phone and saw two missed calls from my grandmother's number. My heart locked in my chest. I closed my eyes and prayed, "Please, God. Don't let anything have happened to Grandpa."

I tapped the screen and redialed my grandmother's mobile number. It went to voicemail. I left a message. "Grandma, this is Mariah. I'm sorry I missed you . . ."

The ping of a text message interrupted my message. I looked at the sender. It was Grandma. I ended the voicemail message and opened the text.

I need you to come home.

Chapter 2

GREENVILLE, SOUTH CAROLINA

Present Day

Sabrina Holland

Tap. Tap. Tap.
"Hey in there. This is the Greenville Sherriff's Department."
My eyes popped open. I pushed my body forward, fighting to climb into the front seat. Gear shifts and knees were not meant to collide. Jesus heard my cry. It was difficult, but I managed to sit.

The sound of the Velcro zipping free as I detached my window coverings was usually welcome. It signaled a new day, a quest for sunshine after a night of securing my privacy. But this morning, the tearing grated against the surge of fear I felt. Cops were scary for many reasons—chief among them being that it was illegal to sleep in a vehicle. My system went into fight-or-flight mode when I heard a tap on the window. I lowered the window, then locked my hands at ten and two on the steering wheel before peeking out at the officer.

I recognized him. For that I was grateful. At least I could hope for some kind of grace from one I kind of knew. I hoped, but I still followed the drill.

Keep your hands where they can see them and ask permission to do everything.

"Good morning, officer." A rebellious yawn slipped through my lips.

"You can't sleep here, miss."

"I'm sorry. I didn't know. I got tired last night . . ."

"No point in that. I know you live in this van," he said, scrunching his nose as he took a sideways glance at it. I knew what he saw—faded paint, a rusted bumper, dented wheel wells, and balding tires. "I talked to you when you were parked in the Home Depot lot a few weeks ago. We have a list of you grifters."

Grifters. What was that even? And I was on a list.

"License and insurance."

I swiveled my neck to glance behind the passenger seat and spotted my purse. "Is it okay if I get my bag? It's behind the seat."

The officer looked around me, behind the passenger seat, and replied, "Slow and easy."

I forced a closed-mouth smile despite hearing blood thundering through my ears. I removed my right hand from the wheel and reached for my well-worn hobo bag and pulled it to the front seat before fumbling around for my wallet. Once I had it, I used both hands to work the license free from its holder.

"My insurance card is in the glove compartment."

He nodded again, and I reached over and opened the glove compartment and removed my insurance card and registration just in case he wanted that too.

The officer's radio crackled to life. He reached up to his shoulder and pushed the bottom for the walkie-talkie and spoke.

I caught sight of myself in the rearview mirror. Ugly bags stole the beauty of my amber-colored eyes. It was eight o'clock. I hadn't fallen off to sleep until after four.

"I'm giving you a verbal warning this time, Miss Holland. You can't sleep here anymore. None of you can."

He didn't take my documents. He walked back to his car and got inside. Relieved he'd gotten summoned to a more important call, I released the tense breath that was lodged in my chest and raised the window, leaving only a crack for some fresh air. I'd lived to die another day.

I looked to the right. The parking lot of the Walmart was filling up, but not enough that shoppers would need this space I'd parked in. The assistant manager must be on early duty this morning. He was the only one who called the sheriff to report us "grifters" sleeping in the lot.

Once upon a time, all Walmart stores allowed people to park their cars overnight. There was an urban legend about Sam Walton having been homeless once, therefore having empathy for homeless people. But it wasn't a company policy. In the Greenville stores, permission depended on who was working.

I pushed the seat back, climbed across it to reach for my cell phone, and plugged it into the charger. I hadn't been able to pay the bill that was due two days ago, so the service was disconnected, but I had a few things downloaded that I could listen to while I made my morning cup of tea.

I unlocked the door and stepped out of the van. After a long stretch and another yawn, I reached into the cargo space and removed the caddy that held my morning routine items, put it on the passenger seat, and slipped back inside.

I plugged in my portable electric kettle and poured water from a bottle of water into the metal cup and pressed the power button. Then I reached into the caddy and removed my toothbrush and paste. I did a quick brush, rinsing with the remaining water from the bottle. I ran a disposable wipe over my face. Once the coating of night was gone, I looked at my reflection in the rearview mirror. The luggage under my eyes carried my exhaustion. I looked way too old for twenty-seven.

I tapped my phone until I got to the recording I kept in my files. Most days I didn't listen, but on mornings like this one—mornings that started rough—I needed to remember that I'd been happy once. I pressed the app.

Hey, Rina, it's me. I'm sorry about earlier. I . . . You're right. It's time. I'm not afraid of what I have with you. You've never hurt me. You've always been there for me, and I love you. Silence for a moment. A tear leaked out from under my eyelid. My insides ached. I wiped my eyes and sat up straighter.

Let's do it.

We'd be married for almost five years. Losing him wasn't as fresh as it had been, but still, how had five years passed so fast? A better question was, how had I let it all fall apart so quickly?

I swiped at my eyes again and tapped the phone for the music player until I found my favorite morning worship song. Then I dropped a tea bag into the hot water, added a packet of honey, and pulled out of the parking lot. It wouldn't do for me to be sitting here when the cop came back around.

After a quick trip to the gym for a shower, it was time to go to work at Kakes, which was a bakery. The interior boasted a state-of-the-art commercial kitchen that produced goods, but there were also four mini kitchens they rented out to independent bakers. I worked in the rental center a few days a week, signing people in and out, cleaning—whatever was needed. I also got to use one of the kitchens when I had a job. A job as a cake decorator using fondant flowers, icing, and colors to create show pieces. I was a baker too.

I was off from Kakes today, but I had a birthday cake due to a customer tomorrow. My plan? To deliver it early this evening so I could collect my money, get my phone turned back on, and buy some food other than ramen noodles. My last three paychecks had gone to my quarterly insurance bill on the van. I'd only had a few cake jobs. Those paid for my gym membership and put gas in my tank and noodles in my stomach, but little else.

The lemon-flavored cake I was decorating had been cooling overnight, so it was ready for the magic. I ran an offset spatula around the layers and released them from the pans and onto wax paper on the surface of the woodgrain island.

"What masterpiece are you turning that into today?"

Kevin Rose's voice cut through my peace like a housefly beating its wings near my ear. He happened to be the owner's son, so I couldn't tell him to mind his own business like I wanted to. However, I didn't have to meet his eyes. He was an okay guy, but eye contact would only invite him to linger. I liked to work without an audience. I reached for a serrated knife to level the cake's layers. "This is for a twenty-ninth birthday party."

"Twenty-nine seems like a silly year to make a big deal out of."

I sighed, standing upright to inspect my work from an elevated view. "All birthdays matter. There's an alternative, you know."

Kevin chuckled. Real throaty like he had spring pollen lodged in his throat. I could feel him moving closer.

"I'm just saying . . . most folks do a big deal for twenty-five, thirty, and then forty."

"I think people do what they want." I sliced the top off the second layer and put it aside.

He leaned across the island. He wasn't wearing a hair net, and he was sure to open his mouth again. I raised the knife sideways like a weapon and said, "Back up. No spittle on my cakes."

He did as I told him but kept watching as I worked. "You're fast."

He was right. I'd learned to work fast. You do that when you pay for space by the hour. I sliced the caramelized sides off.

"And always the perfectionist," he added, admiration in his tone.

I appreciated the respect, so I finally looked at him. "Your mother should hire me to bake for her."

"She will as soon as she gets an opening," he said.

The promise of a full-time baking job had been in the plan, which was why I kept a foot in the door with the part-time work, even if it was cleaning up. This kitchen—any kitchen—was my happy place.

When the cake was done, I loaded it into the van and drove the ten-mile ride to my customer's house in Simpsonville, praying the whole time she would be there to receive it, especially since I couldn't call first. Fortunately, I pulled into the driveway at the same time as Mrs. Halstead. She was the one paying the bill.

I followed her into the enormous kitchen, placed the box on the oversize marble island, and pulled the top open. Her inspection was slow and thorough, but satisfaction lit her eyes immediately. "This is beautiful, Sabrina." Even I marveled at the elaborate five-layer masterpiece. It was pink and green—sorority colors. I'd alternated round and square cake layers. Pearls and flowers trimmed the seams of each layer. I created an open jewelry box for the topper. The box held a handkerchief with "29" etched on it and was surrounded by more pearls spilling over the inside. It was all fondant. All art. "It'll be the hit of the party."

"Do you want me to transfer it to your refrigerator?" I asked, knowing they had one on the back porch for such things as this. She'd purchased several cakes from me.

Mrs. Halstead was busy with her phone. "If you will," she asked, finally giving me her attention. "Is a check okay?"

I cut my eyes to the clock on the microwave. It was already four-thirty. If I had any delay, I would miss the bank and not have my phone for another night. That was not safe when you slept in a van. "I'd prefer Zelle."

I opened the back door and the fridge doors and then came back for the cake.

By the time I finished, Mrs. Halstead turned her phone around and showed me the transaction, which included a nice tip.

"Thank you, ma'am," I said. I was grateful her phone rang, because she took the call, giving me an easy escape out of the house and back to my van, where I peeled out of the driveway three hundred dollars richer.

Minutes after I paid my phone bill, the familiar sound of life came to it. I went to my favorite café and ordered a sandwich. Just as I was about to place a call, a text message came through.

It was from my grandmother. It simply read: I need you to come home.

I called her and got no answer . . . over and over. *Is something wrong with Grandpa? Is he worse?*

The emotions of fear and worry collided in my chest. I slid out of the booth just as the server was delivering my food.

"I need it to go," I said.

Once I had my food, I made the drive up to the eastern part of Greer. Traffic wasn't a problem in this section of the city. I made lefts and rights until I reached my destination. The sun had set, and the large Magnolia trees outside of the house were giving sleepy Southern vibes like they always did.

I pulled in the driveway, not sure how I would be received, especially since I'd skipped calling first, but my giving Ellen a heads-up would be a mistake. I needed the element of surprise, even if it was selfish of me to use.

The front door of the house opened, and a familiar figure appeared on the porch. I exited the van and walked to the bottom of the steps.

Ellen Guthrie wrapped her arms around herself. Seeing the van always made her sad. She hated to see it coming, dragging with it memories of her dead only child. It had been his before it became mine.

"I have to go to Georgetown."

"You should have called." Ellen dropped her arms. "I'm about to plate her dinner."

"Would you wrap it up?"

"You're going tonight?"

"It's my grandfather . . ." I pushed through the words. "I want to get there as soon as I can." Tears pricked the back of my eyes. I struggled to finish my thought, which was to make sure Kenni got to spend time with him in case he didn't live much longer.

A small figure appeared in the screened door and then flew onto the porch. "Mommy!"

My heart exploded with a burst of happiness. I took a few steps closer, but Ellen grabbed Kenni's outstretched hand. "Slow down before you fall and bust your teeth out," she said letting Kenni's hand go.

I opened my arms and my four-year-old flew into them.

"I was making a picture, Mommy."

I never tired of hearing that name. My baby's warm body melted into mine. I stroked her arm and kissed her. "Is the picture for me?"

"No. It's for Nana," she said, looking over her shoulder at Ellen. She whispered conspiratorially. "But I cou' give it to you."

"That would be nice," I said, glancing over Kenni's shoulder to meet Ellen's wary eyes. "I need to get on the road as soon as possible."

Ellen shook her head and went inside. Ellen didn't like this. Didn't like me not calling. Didn't like me taking Kenni. The last few months had been rough, and our interactions had become strained. So rough and so strained that I'd been thinking this area might not be the right place for Kenni and me anymore. Kenni had been spending more nights with Ellen than I wanted because I'd been working a second job in a warehouse during the evenings. Sometimes I did a double shift. I was trying to save up for another apartment. Being evicted from the last one meant I needed a hefty down payment. At first Ellen was happy to help with Kenni, but more and more she kept asking if I wanted her to take guardianship of Kenni while I figured things out. The conversation always went the same.

"I'm not giving up my daughter, Ellen."

"I'm not asking you to give her up."

"I just need help," I said.

I softened the no she was hearing between the lines by mentioning the fact that she already had her hands full. Ellen ran a personal care home for the state. Her extra bedrooms housed elderly clients who couldn't live alone. She'd hinted more times than I wanted to hear that she would downsize her client load to make a bedroom for Kenni, but she'd never explicitly extended that offer to me too.

"You know you would need to go to training and have a background check and a drug test."

She mumbled the list without making eye contact. I could read between the lines. Ellen didn't want me in her house. She still blamed me for Kendrick's death. We had that in common. I blamed me too.

"Mommy, am I going whif you?" Kenni asked.

I kissed her again, this time on the forehead. "Yes."

"For how many days?" The child held up her hand and raised three fingers.

The most time Kenni had spent with me in recent months had had been two days at a time, and that was only when I could rent a motel room for us. Kenni wanted more. She always wanted three days.

I took Kenni's hand and kissed her pudgy little fingers. I looked up at the intimidating two-story Cape Cod that had everything a child needed to be comfortable. I'd been forced to leave my baby here while I chased normal, but this wasn't the only house that would welcome my daugther. I thought about the timing of my grandmother's text. The way she worded it: I need you to come home.

Georgetown wasn't technically home. I spent summers and some holidays there. Although I'd lived in Greenville my whole life, Grandma always considered her home to be my home. I'd been praying for God to fix my living situation. I looked at Kenni, remembered her question: *"How many days?"*

I said, "I'm not sure, baby." I thought, *Maybe forever.*

Chapter 3

March 1915

Tabitha Cooper

Tabitha Cooper measured herself against men. 'Specially, their height. She was tall for a woman, five foot nine by eighth grade, and that was where her height settled. There weren't many tall girls in her school, so she was seen—all the time. Seen enough for a nickname, which she didn't need. Her family already called her Bitta. Still, one of the boys in her seventh-grade class called her Giant. She was probably about five foot seven then. Taller than all the girls and most of the boys whose voices were still squeaking. She knew about squeaky voices. She had a brother close to her age. Anyway, Giant stuck at school. The kids said it to tease her, but her mama taught her to accept the power of the word. Mama was big on words and their meanings. She said giants were taller than everyone else, and because of their tallness, they had a unique view of the world. They saw things others didn't. Giants were feared, and people fearing her a little was a healthy thing. It kept folks in line the same way it kept them in line with God. So, Tabitha learned to be proud of her height. It was a gift from God. But on many days, it seemed like the only one she had. Until she met Joseph McCoy.

Tabitha had been working her after-school job at the North Market, a general store and pothouse when she met Joseph McCoy for the first time. She'd cooked a rice, oyster, and okra purloo that day, and he could not get enough of it. He kept coming back. She'd gotten used to him stopping in. They only had food on Fridays and Saturdays, so when he came in on a Monday, Tabitha could tell he hadn't walked in for no good reason. He rarely purchased from the store, and today he hadn't stopped to look at anything.

"You are looking mighty fine today, Miss Tabitha."

He had asked her for her name the first time she had served him.

"I've got to know the name of a woman who can cook this fine."

He smiled, and Tabitha didn't think she'd ever seen anything more beautiful in her life.

Joseph was tall, and she appreciated being able to look up to him. If she didn't have to hitch her neck back a little to look a man in his eyes, she wasn't interested in him. Tabitha believed God had a man for her who would be her giant. She didn't want to be the only one with vision.

She lowered her eyes and busied her hands with the garden pruner she'd just taken out of the box. Putting inventory on the shelves was one of her jobs.

She avoided his eyes when she replied, "That's fine of you to say, Mr. Joseph. What can I get for you?"

He didn't like that she called him Mr. Joseph, but he looked to be about thirty years old. She couldn't help it.

"I need whatever that is in your hand," he replied.

She looked at him now. He was being too direct for her not to. She observed him in his brown suit and shiny shoes. He wasn't working on a farm. His smooth hands made Tabitha think he'd never worked a day in his life. "If you don't know what it is, sir, how you know you need it?"

His eyes danced with amusement, and he raised a hand to stroke the shiny black hair of his mustache. "Tell me what it is."

"It's a pruner. It cuts stems and leaves on plants. This one is new. We just got it in from A. Fields. They are a German company. This one is made of cast iron."

"Do we not make cast-iron pruners in this country?"

"We do, but this is the best." Tabitha dropped her eyes again. Selling like this wasn't in her nature. The customers who shopped here didn't need someone selling to them. It was a small general store with inventory for the Negro customers who didn't want to travel downtown to the larger general store. Everyone who came in here knew what they wanted before they entered. Tabitha cleared her throat and finished sharing her knowledge of the thing. "At least the catalog we order from says it's the best."

"If you believe it, I believe you." One side of his mouth lifted lazily like he was smiling inside. "I'll take it."

She was confused by his purchase. "What did you come in here for? You weren't looking for a pruner?"

"I came in here to ask you if you would have dinner with me."

Tabitha looked away. Shyness overtook her again. "I don't know."

"You don't know if you want to eat with me?"

"I do not, sir. I don't know you." Tabitha said the words more firmly than she felt them. She wasn't sure how she felt. He made her nervous, but it was an excited tickle in her belly that made sweat break out on her forehead and back.

"Dinner is for getting to know each other."

"I can't keep company without asking my papa's permission."

Joseph frowned like he'd never heard of such a thing. Of course he had. He just wanted what he wanted. That's what Mama said about men when she warned her to be careful.

"You're almost twenty-one now, aren't you?"

"I'm seventeen. I'll be eighteen in a month," she replied, suddenly wishing she was older so Papa would be less ready to say a direct no.

"Seventeen. I wouldn't think you could get so pretty in seventeen years."

Joseph slipped his hand in his jacket pocket and removed a bill. "For the pruner."

Tabitha reached for the cash box to make change. He interrupted her fumbling.

"You keep the extra, pretty lady." His index finger was on her chin, lifting it so her eyes met his again like he wanted. He smiled, slowly and nice, like one of those handsome men in a picture show. "Buy yourself something."

Tabitha moved her chin away from his warm fingertips. "I cannot." She slid the change—five dollars—back across the counter. Her fingers trembled as she clumsily put his purchase in a bag and handed it to him.

Joseph took the bag but not his change. He walked backward as he spoke. "You talk to your father. I'll stop by on Friday to find out his answer. If he says yes, we can have dinner and go to the show." He was confident, and she didn't think he had a reason to be.

She looked down at the five-dollar bill, pulled it across the counter, and slipped it into her pocket. She wasn't sure this was proper. She didn't know what to do with it except keep it until she saw him again.

Once she finished at the store, she got on her bicycle and rode home. Her best friend, Dot, was sitting on the porch talking to Mama. Dot lived a piece down the road and visited most days when her mother didn't need help with the wash and folding. Like Mama, Dot's mother took in laundry for white families on the other side of Georgetown. Although Mama didn't do nearly as much as Dot's mother. It didn't seem Mama needed to, and that was because Papa made enough.

People complained about the pay for Negro men at the mill. Most of the men who worked at the mill didn't have much of anything. Tabitha's family did. Their rented house was nicer than most of the houses the Negro families lived in. Papa had a new wagon, and they had two bicycles. Their stove was the best Tabitha had seen. It was better than the stove some white folks had. Sometimes Tabitha helped Mama tote wash. She'd seen their kitchens. Some of the Negro mill workers thought Papa had better pay on account of his nearly white skin. Papa was the whitest Negro man in the city of Georgetown. But it wasn't true that Papa had better pay at the mill. Papa and Mama managed their money better than most. At least that was what Mama said was the reason they seemed to have more.

As Tabitha got closer to the house, Dot stood and leaned over the porch railing and waved. Tabitha waved back. She could tell by the movements of Mama's hands that she was shelling peas. Mama liked to have Papa's dinner on the table when he came home from working at the lumber mill. Mama, however, did not cook. It was Tabitha who prepared all the meals, so if she was just getting the peas ready, Papa wasn't going to be home before nightfall.

Tabitha stopped at the steps and got off the bicycle.

Mama looked up at her but then down at her work. "Reverend Clydesdale told me to tell you that he liked the catfish stew."

"I saw him. He came in the store and told me so."

Mama liked to give Tabitha's food away. Tabitha thought it was Mama's way of showing the world that Tabitha was worth something.

"You want me to help?" Tabitha asked, looking at the peas Mama had yet to shell.

"I offered," Dot said.

Mama looked at Tabitha again. "No. This clears my mind. You girls go on. I'll let you know when I'm done."

Dot followed Tabitha into the house. They went to Tabitha's room. Behind the closed door, Tabitha told Dot about Joseph and showed her the five dollars.

"I don't think I can keep it."

Dot did not agree. Her eyes were as big as saucers when she said, "He gave it to you."

Dot dropped down on Tabitha's bed and opened one of the fashion magazines Tabitha's sister, Retha, had given her. Retha lived in Columbia with her husband, Clifford, and their twin boys. Clifford made a good living as a federal land surveyor, so Retha had money for magazines and books. Those things were her sister's passion. Retha gave Tabitha all her old magazines and brought her novels whenever she came to visit.

Nervous to hear Dot's thoughts, Tabitha asked, "What will Papa say?"

"He might think he's too old. That's what my daddy said about Isra's first man." Isra was Dot's older sister. "Your daddy is older than mine. He gon' be old-fashioned. I say you need to start somewhere, or you'll never get yourself a husband. Plus, you have to be careful about your daddy. He might not . . ." Dot's words trailed off. She shook her head, but her eyes said she was sorry she'd started words she couldn't finish. "Never mind."

Tabitha didn't have to think hard on what Dot was being coy about. Papa might not care because Tabitha wasn't always on his mind.

Charles Cooper, the man Tabitha called Papa, was not her father, and everyone knew that. Tabitha sensed something was different about her from an early age. Papa and Mama looked like most any white people Tabitha passed on the street. Tabitha's brothers and sisters were the same. Only Tabitha was dark. By the time she was seven, she knew . . . Papa wasn't her father. She just needed someone to tell her. One day Mama did.

"You behave," Mama said. "Your daddy . . . he has hard days sometimes."

"He's not my daddy," Tabitha said.

Mama's eyes were scary. "No. He's not."

"Where is my daddy?"

"I don't know."

Tabitha cried.

"You stop crying. You don't need your daddy. You got me. Women hold up each other. You gon' learn that one day. You let your sister be your best friend."

Tabitha was confused. Didn't all children need a daddy?

"You hear me?" Mama asked.

"Yes, ma'am."

Then she said, "Retha, y'all go down to Miss Fran. Stay there for a spell."

Retha, four years older than Tabitha, nodded with knowing eyes.

Miss Fran's house was where they went when Papa was sick from shine. His drinking meant the house wasn't safe for anyone until he fell asleep. That included Mama, but she stayed and managed to survive his temper.

When Tabitha was older, it was Retha who told her the whole truth. Papa and Mama split once. Papa went away. He traveled north a few times a year to tend to some business. None of the children knew what or where the business was, but they did know Papa was estranged from his family. Everything about his trips was secretive. But one year, after an ugly argument, he told Mama he wasn't coming back, so she took up with a new man who put Tabitha in Mama's belly. Then Papa came back to an expecting wife and the shame of it. It was that year that his drinking started—or so Retha said.

Papa called her Bitta, supposedly short for Tabitha, but she always felt like it was short for bitter because she was a bitter reminder that Mama had been another man's.

Dot's voice got her out of her thoughts. "Anyway, I think you should go to dinner with him. We have to think on getting married." That was all Dot had thought about since they were little girls. Marrying and raising children. She didn't have any other thing that she wanted to do, and she was already keeping company with one of the boys in school. "It's not easy to find a husband with so many Negro people leaving to go north."

"The Good Book says, 'He who finds a wife finds a good thing.' It's not the other way around. Women aren't supposed to find husbands."

"The Good Book will have you be a virgin praying in the temple."

"Don't blaspheme the Word."

Dot rolled her eyes. "You don't go nowhere but school, the store, and church. So how he gonna find you?"

"That's not for me to decide."

Dot's smirk was long and full of expected disappointment. "You won't even go to bingo or dance at the hall."

"I'm not going to meet a good man in the dance hall."

Dot pursed her lips. "You met exactly who you gonna meet in the store. An older man. You could do worse. At least you say he's nice-looking, and he's not poor if he's got five dollars to give away."

She was right about both. Joseph had a carriage. He wasn't from Georgetown. He told her his people were from Atlanta, but he lived in Charleston. He traveled to Georgetown for business.

"I need a dress," Tabitha said, realizing she'd decided that if Papa said yes, she would have dinner with Joseph.

"You have time to go to Hudson's and pick out one." Dot popped off the bed. "I'll go with you tomorrow."

"How much is a tea dress?"

Dot walked to Tabitha's closet. "Hudson's has afternoon dresses for five, six seven . . . eight dollars."

Tabitha thought about the five dollars Joseph had given her. Spending it all on one dress that would be for one outing seemed wasteful.

"I know you been saving." Dot's words interrupted her thoughts and reminded her of the money she'd saved.

Mr. Wilson said he would pay Tabitha fifty cents a week to work in the store after school. Some weeks she got all the money, but other weeks she didn't. Everything depended on what he sold and which customers paid their bills. He had a lot of customers who ran up credit and some that never really seemed to do anything but add to what they owed. Mr. Wilson was good-hearted, but he wasn't a good businessman—not all the time. But he always gave Tabitha an extra fifty cents if she cooked on Friday and Saturday. He was sure to make money on the meals he sold. People paid for her food.

Tabitha had saved sixty-two dollars in the two years she'd worked in the store. She still made her church dresses, and she didn't spend money on things like makeup, perfume, and fancy shoes and hats. She did her own hair too. Even Retha told her she was going to be an old maid if she didn't start being more feminine sometimes.

But now she had a man calling on her—a full-grown man. She just hoped his age wouldn't have Papa running the poor man off with a shotgun—or at least that was the dream, that Papa would care that much.

"Do you want to go buy a dress tomorrow?" Dot inserted herself in her thoughts again.

"I'm thinkin' on it."

Dot rolled her eyes. "What are you saving for anyway? You don't need a dowry. You need to give in to the beauty of the romance."

Dot was in love with a love story. It made sense. She wasn't a giant. *Petite* was the word people used to describe Dot. Petite, fair-skinned, with long hair and pretty legs. It didn't matter how many men moved north; with Dot's looks, marriage would find her. Her future was set. Tabitha had to figure hers out.

Chapter 4

Present Day

Mariah

I didn't drive at night if I could help it. When I couldn't reach my grandmother, I called my cousin LaWanda to find out what was going on. LaWanda lived in Georgetown. She was also a nurse practitioner, which was helpful for decoding the seriousness of health emergencies. She advised me that Grandpa was still in the hospital but nothing had changed. He was stable, therefore she didn't know why our grandmother sent me the mysterious text.

"Must have to do with something else," LaWanda said.

I couldn't imagine what the *something else* could be. After talking to LaWanda, I tried calling my grandmother a few more times, but when she didn't answer I packed a bag. I got on the road first thing in the morning. Four hours later, I pulled into my grandparents' driveway. I welcomed the sight of the old craftsman-style house with its wraparound porch and hanging flower baskets. The thick stone columns with brick supports were covered in ivy. The steps, also brick, were lined on both sides with potted plants. Grandma grew lemongrass, citronella, and catnip in those pots to keep mosquitoes and other annoying bugs away. And it worked. Their porch had been a source of bite-free enjoyment for my whole childhood.

I parked in front of the detached garage next to my grandfather's pickup truck, and sadness washed over me. My grandfather was not here, and since I didn't see my grandmother's car, she probably wasn't either. They didn't keep their cars in the garage.

I eased out from behind the wheel, stretched my arms over my head, and shook the stiffness out of my legs. I spotted their neighbor, Mr. Sweat, moving about in his yard. The May heat burned warmer than it did in Greenville. It sucked the strength right out of me. After popping the trunk, I pulled my suitcase out and placed it on its wheels.

"The key is under the mat."

The voice came from the other side of the hedges. Mr. Sweat appeared in a small opening between the shrubbery and the fence. As always, a strange hat was perched on his head—it was more like a bucket—and he wore thermal underwear as cringeworthy gardening clothes.

"She don' gone to the hospital already. Told me to tell you guls how to get in." His baritone voice rumbled like a truck idling at a traffic light.

"Thank you, Mr. Sweat."

He threw a hand up to indicate no bother and disappeared into his yard again.

I retrieved the key and entered the house. I dialed back the anxious thoughts that I'd been fighting with all morning. My emotions rolled into a massive ball of knots, and it had nothing to do with my grandparents. This house reminded me of my mother. Memories of her in tangible spaces were limited to their home. That reality hit me every single time.

I stepped into the living room. The room was filled with puffy floral furniture in varying shades of tan, orange, and brown. The drapes on the window blended nicely with the furniture, and a bowl of nuts and fruit sat on the coffee table.

I walked through, passing several rooms off the hallway. Grandma's presence was everywhere, but so was my mother's. In the sitting room, Grandma still had the writing desk that my mother used when she visited. Grandma promised me she'd never get rid of it.

I dragged my suitcase to the stairs and entered the kitchen where I found a roast in the sink.

This is defrosted.

I wished Grandma would defrost meat in the refrigerator, but she was old school. The sink it was. I washed my hands, removed the packaging, washed the meat, and seasoned it before putting it in the Crock-Pot.

At the end of the day, we'd be grateful it was already done. Once I was finished, I placed a call to Grandma. I'd been calling her on and off for hours, but she hadn't answered. I was shocked to hear her greeting on the other end.

"Grandma. I've been calling you."

"I'm sorry. I forgot to charge my phone last night and then forgot my charger today. One of the staff loaned me one. They're transferring your grandfather to a rehab center." She let out an exasperated breath. "Today, I think."

"I just got to the house. I'll come over there."

"No need for that."

My eyes drifted to a family portrait over the fireplace. My father was a teenager in that photo, and my grandparents weren't much older than I was now. I pulled my attention back to the conversation. "I don't want you dealing with that alone."

"I'm not alone—or I won't be for long. LaWanda will pass through here soon. I need *you* to go to the restaurant for me."

"The restaurant? Okay. What do you need me to do there?"

"Everything," Grandma said. "The contractor is stoppin' by around four. Just figure something out with him." Someone interrupted on her end, and she responded to them. Something about a scan and some tests. I listened but couldn't make it out.

"Okay, baby. Do you understand?"

I understood nothing, but I didn't want to add to her stress.

"You have the key?"

"I know where it is."

"Good. I changed the alarm code last week." Grandma rattled off the new number just before someone interrupted her again. "They're taking your grandfather for a test. I need to go. I'll see you tonight."

She was gone, and I was still without an explanation for the urgent text she'd sent. I went to the kitchen and rifled through the drawer for the keys.

Twenty minutes later, I pulled my car into the rear parking lot of the restaurant. I wasn't the only one here though. I recognized the old junky van in the first parking space.

I got out of my car and walked to it. The sound of music blared from speakers too powerful to be inside of the rusty old tin box. The driver's seat was empty, so I walked around to the side where I found my sister standing over a table and some kind of camping stove, stirring a pot.

Sabrina's hair was an enviable big afro. Her almond skin glowed with sweat that she was unbothered about. Her attire— ripped denim shorts and a purple T-shirt that looked faded from many washes. Abandoned flip-flops were on the grass next to her. I think they were the only footwear my sister owned.

"Sabrina," I called to her.

She kept swaying to the soulful lyrics of the late Bob Marley.

I stepped closer and repeated myself. "Sabrina."

Still, she did not hear me. Finally, I tapped her on the shoulder. She turned. Shock filled her eyes.

"I called your name twice. You literally could have been kidnapped." Before she could reply, I asked, "What are you doing here?"

Chapter 5

Sabrina

If I had a hundred dollars for every time my sister greeted me with that question or any other disdainful "why are you, what are you, why must you" kind of question, I'd be driving a two-hundred-thousand-dollar luxury RV. She never, ever just said hello.

Mariah's hair was bone straight, like she'd just walked out of the salon. Her dark brown skin shined like she was using a high-quality shea butter all over. Dressed cute as always, she wore a pink sundress with a white T-shirt underneath. She looked fashionably cool. Wedge-heeled sandals made the three-inch difference in our height six inches. A to-die-for leather bag hung off her shoulder, and I could smell money in the rose and jasmine notes of her perfume.

But I could not process a statement to convey all that I saw when I looked at her, so I said, "You changed your hair." Last month when we'd come after Grandpa's stroke, she'd been wearing her hair the way she always did—in braids. The change in her appearance was drastic.

Bob Marley's voice got louder. I looked through the window and saw the top of Kenni's head. She was in the front seat playing with the stereo buttons.

"Kenni, turn that down," I yelled.

"Maybe off," Mariah added. "You know Grandma would not want all this noise."

"There was no one here though, except you now."

"I heard it all the way on the main road."

"I doubt that. These are the original speakers." I laughed to brush off her foolishness.

"I did," Mariah insisted, because of course she didn't joke or exaggerate anything. Well, she did the latter, but she'd never admit it.

The offending music was gone. Kenni had done her job.

And then we stood there, in a standoff of sorts. After the first words of disagreement, my sister and I always assessed each other—or rather, she always assessed me, determined me unfit, and sighed. Five, four, three, two . . .

Mariah released a long breath and pulled the shoulder strap of her bag tighter.

"It's good to see you too," I said.

Kenni popped into view and then dropped to her belly and scooted backward out of the van. She grabbed Mariah by the legs.

"Auntie!"

Mariah dropped to a squat, opened her arms, and let Kenni in for a deep, loving hug. "Hey, Kenni girl. How are you?"

Kenni pulled back out of her grasp. "Do you have McDonald's?"

Mariah stood. She eyed the pot on my camping stove suspiciously and then asked in the most condescending voice she could possibly have in her body, "Have you fed her?"

"It was a long drive. We're about to eat."

Mariah frowned. "Why are you cooking on that?"

"Because I don't have the new alarm code. Grandma gave it to me, but then once I got over here, I forgot it, and she didn't answer my text." Grandma only sent text messages. She did not answer them unless she had to.

I watched my sister's eyes travel from my stove to the inside of the van. Mariah's eyes widened, then widened some more as she took it all in—my twin mattress, makeshift sink, cooler, and other storage containers. It was a mess right now. I felt like an uninvited guest had caught me with a dirty house.

"Are you living in there?"

I turned off the stove and reached for one of the bowls to spoon soup into. "Sometimes," I replied, purposely being vague.

"Sometimes. Is she"—Mariah cast her gaze toward Kenni and lowered her voice as if my daughter wasn't going to hear her—"living like this?"

"Kenni, would you get your spoon, please?"

Kenni climbed back into the van and disappeared again. I could hear the squeak of the rusty drawer that held my dishes.

"She lives with me and Ellen sometimes. A lot of the time, but that's only because I'm working. Ellen likes to babysit her so she can spend time with her." I was whispering, hoping my sister would take the hint and do the same when she replied.

"So she's living with Ellen?" Mariah whispered, but it was still as breathy and bothered as it had been when she was speaking in a normal tone.

"Yes."

"Why not your own family?"

"Like who?" I cocked my head. "You?"

"Here, Mama!" Kenni said, joyfully holding the spoons out to me.

"That is too hot for her." Mariah reached for the bowl, and I yanked it back, feeling the sting of hot liquid on my thumb. "I know. I'm not giving it to her like this."

Mariah and I locked eyes again. We mirrored our emotions with furrowed brows, tight lips, and tense jaw muscles. How dare she even imply that I would give my daughter a bowl of hot soup?

If I could get up the nerve to cuss her out one good time, she'd stop disrespecting me, but I didn't have any four-letter words in me, and my sister could out-shade the best of them, so I didn't even get my feelings hurt.

Mariah gave my setup another once-over. Still dissatisfied, she said, "Mr. Sweat would have told you about the key to the house."

"Grandma wanted me to meet you here, so I figured I'd wait."

Mariah broke eye contact, turning her attention to Kenni again. "I have an idea. Let's go inside Gran's place so you can wash your hands and sit at a table."

I growled under my breath. "Her hands are clean."

"Let's go in anyway." Mariah reached for the bowl of soup again. This time she waited for me to release it.

Kenni climbed out of the van and followed my sister to the back door. After a minute, the door closed behind them. I rolled my eyes and packed up everything, leaving the camping stove on the table to cool.

My sister had snatched my appetite, but I took my bowl and went into the restaurant.

I stepped inside the quiet, somber, vacant space and instantly missed my grandfather. Although they were in their usual formation, the tables and chairs were unoccupied. The countertop was clear of menus, dishes, and plastic to-go cutlery. To the far left, a heavy black curtain hung, similar to the kind you'd see on the stage of a theater. It separated the existing space from the area Grandma told me they were building out as a part of the restaurant's expansion.

I put my bowl down on the counter next to the one that held Kenni's soup and followed the sound of my daughter's voice to the kitchen where I found Mariah standing in the freezer.

I'd never seen this kitchen empty. It was always busy and bustling. My grandpa and his help, be it some other cook or my grandmother, were always at the grill station cooking meat or at the fryer station. Someone was in the prep area slicing and dicing vegetables and other ingredients. At the sauté station there were sights and sounds of sizzling, chopping, tossing, and spooning over the open flames. I missed the sweet and savory smells of slow-cooked ham hocks and smoked turkey combined with peppers, cumin, garlic, and onion. All of that was missing. The kitchen was as cold as the items in the freezer.

"Grandpa keeps meals in here for quick grabs. You want some meat and rice?" Mariah was asking. I watched her pull a small container out. She examined it. "I think this is chicken."

Kenni bobbed her head yes. "Good. I'm hungry too, and it'll go good with your soup." Mariah closed the freezer door and put the container in the microwave. She turned around and looked startled to see me as if she'd forgotten I was just outside. I ached a little inside. That was the story of our sisterhood—Mariah wanting to forget me.

"It's weird seeing it like this," I said.

Mariah looked around. "Well, I'm used to the early morning and late night quiet of a restaurant."

I nodded. Of course she was, but this wasn't her spot. "Did Grandma tell you to come here?"

Mariah nodded. "She told me LaWanda had it handled at the hospital."

"I mean *home*." I raised my phone. "I got a text."

Mariah scowled. "Georgetown is not your home. You only lived here for four months."

It was on the tip of my tongue to tell her I knew my history. Dad sold the house after Mom died and moved us to Greenville. I spent summers here with Grandma and G-Pop too. Memories tethered me to the area just as our grandparents' love had, but

Mariah didn't want to hear that, and I didn't want to light the match that would result in fire between us. Not yet.

Mariah removed her leather bag from her shoulder and reached in for her phone. "She asked me to come home," she said, finally answering my question. "But I don't understand why she would tell you to come *here*."

I shrugged. "She told me to help. I have no idea what she wanted me to help with."

Mariah's look of confusion deepened. She groaned and walked through the rear of the kitchen to the back office.

I walked to Kenni and took her hand. "Come on, baby girl. Let's take a look out front."

We left the kitchen and moved through the dining room, venturing toward the dark barrier that stood between us and the unknown. I stepped forward and slowly pulled back the thick veil of fabric. Treading lightly, we stepped through the door.

The space was a cavernous, two-story event room, with upper windows that overlooked the grassy field that ended with a pond behind the building. The beams of the ceiling and the heating and ventilation pipes were exposed. Dust covered everything, even the ceiling. The door and windows were boarded up, and splotched paint dotted the floor. Drywall dust and a hint of musk hung in the air. It smelled like sweaty workers had just vacated.

"What's this?" Kenni asked.

"Grandma and Grandpa are making the restaurant bigger."

"Why? There's already nobody here."

I chuckled, picked her up, and planted her on my hip. "There are usually people here. It's closed right now while Grandpa gets better."

"This is messy," Kenni said.

"You don't know the half of it, baby," Mariah said, and it was obvious she was bothered by all of this. Nothing new there.

"It's a mess that can be cleaned up." I stepped over a two-by-four to walk farther into the room. I could see my grandparents' dream for this place and was proud of them. Even at such an advanced age, they wanted to expand and do more with Tabby's.

I felt Mariah before I heard her.

"I told them not to do this," she said.

I gave my sister a sideways glance. Here I was being proud of them, and she was disappointed in their efforts. If two people never agreed on a thing, we were the two. Glasses were always half full in my world, but to Mariah they were bone dry.

I looked up. "I like the two-story room. The windows will let in a good amount of light."

"I'm not sure that will matter. Most events are in the evenings."

I disagreed. "Not baby showers or other afternoon receptions. Work meetings."

Mariah grunted. "If they attract that kind of business."

"They'd market to do that."

"Oh, and you know so much about restaurant marketing from doing what . . . cooking on a butane camp stove?"

Irritation rolled through me. "I happen to run a small business too."

"One that affords you the luxury of living in your automobile."

I couldn't hold my temper. I no longer wanted to. "You don't have to be such a . . ."

Kenni screamed, cutting into my words. "There's a man!"

Mariah and I turned, and sure enough, a man was standing behind us.

"Sorry to scare you, but do you know you left the back door open?" he asked, removing his well-worn painter's cap.

The man was bald, and his brown eyes were tired. He looked like someone who kept a smile handy, but his disappointment over the door had stolen the pleasure. His hands were rough, with calluses and age spots. He'd seen his share of hard times. I could see that because he was missing a pinky finger.

"An unlocked door doesn't mean come on in," I replied.

"Unfortunately, it does, miss," he replied firmly.

Mariah didn't seem alarmed at all "You're?" She waited for his answer.

He gave Mariah his full attention. "Abel One, ma'am."

Kenni giggled. "That's a funny name."

I shushed her and waited for an explanation, but my daughter wasn't wrong.

"It's Abel Oner Wilson. Folks 'round here call me Abel One seein' as though when I'm not doin' this kind of work, I'm a handyman."

Mariah shook his hand and said, "You're early."

"I finished up a job down the road and thought I would stop by and see if anyone was here to meet with me."

"You're expecting him?" I asked.

Mariah pressed her lips together and looked at me like she didn't owe me an answer. "Your soup is getting cold."

I blinked a few times, wanting to fight for my right to stay for the conversation, but Mariah was right. My daughter was hungry, so I stepped back through the curtain, put Kenni down, and pulled a few chairs off a table for us to sit in. Kenni climbed and moved around until she was seated, and I grabbed our bowls off the counter and put them on the table with the spoons. I tested it to see that the food was indeed well cooled.

"Say your grace while I get the rice."

I walked into the kitchen, removed the plastic container from the microwave. The rice and chicken were warm. I could see and smell the stewed chicken seasonings Grandpa used. Garlic, thyme, onion, okra, and tomato. I grabbed two paper plates from one of the shelves. As I was headed out, I got curious about the office and took a detour into the room. Mariah had busied herself quickly with records. Several accounting logs were open, and a contract for Abel One Contractors was on top of it all.

What was my grandmother up to? If us being here was about the restaurant, what did I have to do with that? Restaurants were Mariah's area of expertise. The last thing my self-esteem needed was to be overshadowed, outdone, out-knowledged, and outranked by my sister.

I returned to the dining room and settled into my chair just as Mariah and Abel One appeared from behind the curtain.

"You have my number. The sooner the better," he said. He turned to me, slapped his cap on his head, and nodded. "Take care of yourself, and enjoy that good-smelling lunch." He smiled at Kenni, and she waved to him.

He walked out, and Mariah followed him to the door, turning the dead bolt behind him.

"So, what was that about?" I asked. I put a pile of the food on plates for Kenni and me, leaving some in the container just in case my sister intended to eat.

"The build obviously," she replied, reaching for the fork, sliding it under some rice and taking in a mouthful. "That's good."

She'd dodged my question with the full intention of not telling me.

"What about the build?"

"The timeline, remaining cost . . ." Mariah shrugged. "It's all bad news. She walked back to the kitchen door and reached into her purse. She returned with a key, which she put on the table on the counter. "You and Kenni should go to the house. I'm going to spend some time with these books."

I was dismissed on day one. "Okay."

"I put a roast in the Crock-Pot. I thought Grandma might be hungry when she gets home."

Glad to have something to contribute, I replied, "I'll make some vegetables."

"Yell to me on the way out so I can lock the door." Mariah turned to go back to the kitchen.

"Bye, Auntie." Kenni's voice squeaked. She was sure to feel the tension between Mariah and me, and I hated that. I hated it so much.

Mariah turned. Her face read disappointment in herself for forgetting her niece. She walked over to the table and kissed my daughter on the top of her head. "I'll see you in a few hours."

She raised her head and our eyes caught. Hers were sadder than they'd been just a minute ago. I looked from her to Kenni, and she looked from me to Kenni. I felt a heaviness radiating from her. She'd been married nine years and had no children. Was that by choice, or was something wrong?

I pondered this question over the meal, and then after cleaning up and washing the silverware, I let Mariah know we were leaving. Kenni climbed into her car seat and waited for me to strap her in.

I removed my phone and sent my cousin LaWanda a text. I had no details for Grandpa's rehab center.

She called me right back. "He's not going today. It might be tomorrow or the next day."

"Why?"

"His blood pressure isn't where they need it to be to transport him. Sometimes a patient's blood pressure goes up when they're moving. Stress. They have to get it under control."

"Okay. I want to see him."

"Grandma is going to say it's not a good day."

"Seeing us might cheer him up," I said. "Besides, we haven't seen him since he first got sick. I'm coming."

LaWanda understood. I felt she should. She lived in this county, so she got to see them all the time. I didn't, so I didn't want to hear someone tell me to wait.

I cranked the engine and drove to the hospital.

Chapter 6

GEORGETOWN, SOUTH CAROLINA
April 1915

Tabitha

Tabitha looked at herself in the mirror.
"The dress is nice," Dot said.

Tabitha agreed. She'd used seven whole dollars for it. She raised a hand to her chest. The gloss from her manicured fingernails caught the light in the mirror. Her nails were pretty and so was her makeup—rouge and lipstick. Dot helped with that.

"I'm going to wait right here until you come back," Dot said, stretching out on Tabitha's bed with one of Tabitha's novels.

"I can't believe you talked me into this." Tabitha walked by Dot and smacked the bottom of her foot. "You best be here praying no one sees me." She had never been so nervous in her life.

Tabitha hadn't had to ask Papa for permission, and Joseph didn't wait for it. She found herself lucky that Papa and Mama went to Columbia to pick up Retha. Her husband had gone to Atlanta for a week for some training for his job. Scared from a young age, Retha didn't like to be alone, so she was going to stay with them.

Tabitha didn't go because she had to work at the store. With Dot's urging, Tabitha decided to meet with Joseph.

Dot swung her legs over the side of the bed. "Nobody gonna see you. Besides, your Mama and Papa don't talk to nobody no way."

Tabitha considered that, but it wasn't true. You didn't have to be friendly with people to learn something bad about your child. Folks were more than happy to carry that kind of conversation. "I'm dressed. I'm going to go," she said, picking up the small handbag she was using for her lipstick and compact. She didn't even know how to use a compact, but Dot made her buy one.

Dot stood and gave her a hug. "You're gonna have the best time ever. You'll see."

Tabitha rode the bicycle to the diner Joseph had selected for them. She rode slowly, grateful for the little breeze the drop in temperature gifted her. She didn't want to be sweaty when she met him. The restaurant was all the way on the other side of Georgetown. Still, she was afraid someone would see her and tell Mama.

Joseph's carriage was parked outside. She stepped off the bike. Once Tabitha's feet were on the gravel lot, she felt unsteady for a bit. The shoes were new and tall for her. She didn't like high heels, but Dot said she couldn't wear plain shoes.

Joseph's driver tipped his hat. "Good evening, ma'am."

Tabitha greeted him back.

"He's inside," the driver said. "I'll look after your bike."

Tabitha leaned it against the side of the carriage. "Thank you." She turned and hobbled to the door. Once inside, she fidgeted, wringing her hands.

"There she is." Joseph's smooth voice warmed her entire torso. He extended a hand toward her, and she stepped, nearly falling. She'd forgotten the height of her shoes.

"Are you all right?" Joseph looked concerned about her footing.

Attempting to excuse her clumsiness, she lied. "I'm fine. I only wear shoes like this to church." She didn't wear these kinds of shoes to church either.

"You look fine in them."

Heat filled Tabitha's face, and she forgot her little toe was pinched. They entered the part of the diner where the tables were. A woman walked toward them with annoyance filling her face. Tabitha reckoned Joseph ate here often and the woman was jealous. She couldn't think of any other reason she'd be so pinch-faced. A man came from the kitchen, and he and Joseph exchanged a hearty greeting and a hug before the man noticed Tabitha.

"You have a dining companion this evening."

"This here is Miss Tabitha."

"Nice to meet you, Miss Tabitha. Welcome to my place." He instructed the young woman to seat them. She relaxed her face and escorted them to a table near the back windows. It was a little darker in their corner, and there were candles on the table. Candles weren't on the tables in the front. Tabitha looked up to see if there was overhead lighting, and she could see there was, but the whole area was filled with large candles instead.

Reading her mind, Joseph said, "He puts courting folks back here. It's more romantic and private."

Tabitha blushed again and was glad for the dim light that might hide it, although with her dark skin, he probably wouldn't see it anyway.

Joseph picked up the paper menu. "Order whatever you like."

Tabitha picked up her menu and read all the choices before settling on barbecued chicken. Joseph chose the ribs. The gal took their order, left, and returned with sweet tea.

Tabitha was already having a really good time. Joseph was nice. He explained things to her in a way that didn't make her feel dumb or country. He'd traveled all over, even New York City once. He operated a business and had even buried a wife.

"You might not want to be with me. I seem to be unlucky for women."

Tabitha pinned him with a serious look. It was easy to do that when she had something sure to say. "I don't believe in luck."

He cocked an eyebrow.

"The good Lord giveth and taketh away." She placed her hand on the table and pulled on a thin piece of the lace that frayed on the edge. Concentrating on her pain enough to be empathetic, she said, "My brother Hank was killed in a wagon accident. It wasn't even that bad of an accident, but he died anyway."

Joseph covered her hand. The heat of his touch soaked into Tabitha, ran up her arm, down her back, and pushed into her heart. She liked him. She liked his eyes. "We all lose people. It doesn't make us unlucky," she said.

His eyes pressed into hers, causing her stomach to flutter again. "I want to take up with you, Tabitha."

She frowned through her question. "You don't think I'm too young for you?"

"Most women my age are already married. The ones who aren't are sorrowful for one reason or another. I have my own demons to fight. I don't have the inclination to fight someone else's."

"I'm not going to college." Tabitha thought it was best to be honest with him.

He laughed. "Is that a requirement for a wife? The new standard for people of the race?"

Tabitha smiled again. He squeezed her hand *again*. "Tell me, Tabitha, what do you want to do with your life?"

She withdrew her hand. Her pulse was racing so fast she thought he'd feel it. Tabitha was unsure of herself. Was it okay to tell him what she really wanted? He might think of her as country. She hesitated to answer.

"Tell me the truth. I like the truth, whatever it is."

She pushed her silly fears out of her head and reached for her tea to take a sip before answering. "I want to own a small farm with a restaurant at the front. I can grow my own food to cook."

Joseph looked at her curiously. He frowned, and she knew right away, he didn't want a farm girl. She pulled her hands down into her lap. Shame enveloped her. Why couldn't she just want to be like other women? The uncomfortably slick feeling of her painted nails reminded her that attempts to be feminine were wasted on her.

"My grandmother had a gift with herbs," Joseph said.

Tabitha's heart quickened with new interest. "Really?"

"She learned it from her mother. She sold herbs and tonics in Atlanta."

A little relief washed over Tabitha.

Joseph pushed his back against the wood frame of the chair. "A restaurant, huh? Well, I know you can cook what you serve on weekends at the store. Can you cook other things?"

"I can cook most anything I try. Everybody likes my rice and chicken. I make a good stew from vegetables and whatever meat we have. I do most of the cooking in our house and at the church for functions. I have since I was twelve."

Joseph grunted like he wasn't sure about that. "You are so skinny, it's hard to believe you eat."

Tabitha raised her hand to her hair and felt her face warm. She was not skinny. Nobody ever said that. "I eat fine."

Joseph smiled. It was a nice easy smile that disarmed her. "I want to keep company with you."

"You said that already."

"I mean it."

He was good-looking. He had class or sophistication—maybe they were the same. They were words Tabitha had read in books about white women in England having romances with dukes and earls. In addition to his looks, he had a business that afforded him a carriage and driver. She did not understand his attraction to her. "Why do you like me?"

His eyes sank into hers again. Not that they'd ever really left her, but he had a way of making her feel caught in a web. He shook his head. "Why do we like anyone?" He cocked his head. "You're pretty enough. Smart enough. Tall enough."

Tabitha pursed her lips. "Tall?"

"I'm a tall man. I like a tall woman. Always have." Joseph placed his open hand on the table.

Tabitha pulled her fingers apart and raised one of her hands from her lap and placed it in his. Joseph smiled again. Her heart smiled back. God had sent her a man who liked a giant.

Chapter 7

Present Day

Sabrina

Room 310 at Georgetown General Hospital was small but comfortable enough. Kenni and I stopped along the road and picked a bunch of wildflowers and tied them with some craft string I kept in my junk box in the van. Then we went to the Dollar Find for a vase and a few bags of pistachios. They were Grandpa's favorite nuts.

Grandpa reminded me of a much-aged version of my father. He had no hair on top, and his skin was the same tan as Daddy's. His once-plump body was now paper thin over bone; the wrinkles in his hands and his shrunken frame showed his age. He looked so different than before, yet his eyes were still piercing— they said he was stronger than he seemed.

Kenni and I did exactly what I'd hoped we'd do—put a smile on his face. Grandma was there too, and she was more than happy to gather her hugs from us as well. We watched a few episodes of *Family Feud*, laughing at Steve Harvey while we guessed the winning answers to the questions. Grandpa struggled to eat his dinner. A sharp pang of fear over the thought of losing him added weight to every breath I took. Hospitals had a way of making everyone seem more mortal by the hour.

I hated this. I hated to see him sick.

He kept up conversation with Kenni, telling her a story he'd told me every summer as a child. But I could see he was growing weaker. The pauses between his sentences grew longer.

"You need rest, so we're going to leave, Grandpa." I stood, placed my drowsy daughter in the chair, and walked to the bed. I took his hand, and he clutched mine, his hand trembling uncontrollably and stealing my happiness.

"I want you to know. I'm proud of oona," he said.

I kissed his forehead, taking in the familiar smell of patchouli and cocoa butter. I could see from the shine on his skin that he'd been rubbed down by someone, probably my grandmother. She wasn't going to let her husband be ashy. "Tell me all about it when you're out of here."

"I'ma tell you now." He released my hand. "Oona is strong, Beanie. Don't let none of 'em tell you different." He turned his head in Grandma's direction and said, "She should read on the letters."

Grandma nodded. "I planned on it."

"What letters?" I asked.

Grandma stood and joined me at Grandpa's side. "Letters Grandma Tabitha wrote."

"We have letters from Great-Great Grandma Tabitha?" I couldn't believe what I was hearing. "Why haven't I seen them before?"

"You didn't need them before. Now you do." My grandmother enveloped me in a hug, and I was filled with an immense sense of warmth. Her scent was familiar: she'd been wearing the same perfume since I was a child. It added even more comfort to the embrace. She released me, letting her eyes sink into mine as she rubbed my arms just below my shoulders. "It's the right time."

Usually the idea of reading something old was unappealing, but letters from my great-great grandmother—that was exciting. I kissed Grandpa on the forehead again, gathered my sleepy daughter, and left them there with their fifty years of love.

I settled into my favorite guest bedroom and washed my daughter's face and hands before changing her into a nightshirt. She barely stirred from her sleep. Poor little thing was exhausted from the trip. I was pretty worn out myself.

The smell of something good drew me back down the stairs. I removed the lid from the Crock-Pot and inhaled. I pulled a bag of frozen broccoli-cheese casserole out of the deep freezer. My grandparents always kept food they brought home from Tabby's in the freezer. I defrosted it and then stuck it in the oven.

I'd missed a call from my father while my phone was off, so I FaceTimed him. After we caught up a bit, I told him about my visit with his father.

"Dad, you should come." I made a slow trek down the foyer hallway to my grandmother's parlor. "Grandpa looks weak."

"I FaceTimed with him today. He doesn't look weak. He looks what he is, and that's old, honey."

"I just remember him always being so solid," I said, dropping onto a chaise.

"I know," Dad said. "Aging is a part of life. Sometimes it happens overnight, and a stroke . . . baby, it speeds the process up."

He was right, but I still made my plea. My father coming was not just for Grandpa; it was for me. "I still wish I could see you."

"You are seeing me right now," he replied, smiling.

I frowned. "You know what I mean."

"How's your sister?"

"Mean as a snake."

My father didn't even argue about that. He knew Mariah's personality and temperament.

"One day you and Mariah will come to an understanding."

"We've done that. We don't like each other."

"That's not what I mean . . . That's not what your mother would have wanted."

"Tell her. She's the one who turned us into enemies," I said.

"Your grandmother told me she was expecting you two to work together."

"I don't know what Grandma has in mind, but Mariah's not going to stay for more than a week. She has Clark's. Then it's going to fall on me. I don't know anything about running a restaurant."

My father was suspiciously quiet before he spoke. "You and your sister will come up with a plan."

I sighed. He was surer than I was.

"How's the baking?" he asked, changing the subject.

"Slow, but I did a great job yesterday."

"Oh, yeah." He smiled. "Tell me about it."

"I'll send you a picture." I zipped the pictures I took to him and then told him about the client.

"Wow, baby, this is really something, and to think you taught yourself everything you know."

"YouTube University."

He chuckled. "You're a natural. You got it honestly." The light left his eyes for a moment, and my heart ached a bit. My mother baked. He'd probably thought about her.

"The job paid well too."

"That customer is sure to tell someone else about you. That's how the word gets out."

"I know. It's just, I don't get more than two or three cakes a month. It's not enough."

"Things like that take time. It's only been six months since you've been putting yourself out there. Did you put those business cards around town?"

"No."

"Social media?"

"You know how I feel about that."

I could see Dad's chest rise and fall with a heavy sigh. "I know it's a necessity for a business, so make an Instagram reel and a TikTok video and do what people your age do to get their things poppin'."

He amused me. "Poppin'?"

"Yes, poppin'. That's what we used to call it. On and poppin'."

I laughed. "I'll do it. It'll be fun to bake here. Grandma has the best kitchen."

"You could make those sweet cakes to get started." A momentary flash of sadness filled his eyes, and then it was gone. Sweet cakes, my mother's cakes, reminded him of her. He cleared his throat. "The ones in mason jars."

"I know what you mean, Dad." I gave him a supportive nod.

"Make a few. See how they come out," he said.

"I don't have to do a trial run. I'm pro at those."

"Okay, so be a professional at selling them too. Find some local stores or farmers markets."

"I'll think about it," I said, lying, but not maliciously. I was already talking myself out of it because . . . budget. My father didn't understand how broke I was. I was tired of borrowing from him.

"I need to jump on a video call with a client. Let me know if you need anything."

"I will. Thanks."

We ended the call just as the front door opened. I stood and greeted Grandma. I took her handbag from her and put it on the

57

foyer table while she kicked off her shoes. "I see you're in my favorite room."

"It's still my favorite too." Grandma's parlor was small but cozy. During my childhood, she and I spent many late evenings reading in this room. The walls were lined with built-in bookcases that held a large collection of novels and some Christian-living books. Grandpa's collection of Bibles and various concordances took up three shelves. He even had the Gullah New Testament.

"I didn't see your sister's car outside."

"That's because she's not here."

Grandma grunted. "I'm going to give you the letters now. I'll be rushing to bed and rushing in the morning." She walked into the room to a painting that covered their wall safe. After turning the knob back and forth, the electronic lock released, and she pulled a metal box from the safe.

I joined her at the desk she placed the box on. Grandma opened the lid and removed the contents. The stack of old letters tied with a ribbon were an unexpected treat. "I can't believe you have these."

"I didn't know about them until we cleaned out Mama's things."

"She didn't share them with you?"

Weariness came down on Grandma, and I regretted asking the question. "You know Mama's mind wasn't good in the end, but I don't know why she didn't give them to me before that."

"Are they going to make me sad?"

Grandma raised her hand to my hair and stroked it. "Heartache has a birdlike spirit. It soars, searching the earth looking for a place to land. It finds all of us at some point. It found Grandma Tabitha more than it should have, and she wrote about it." She was quiet for a reflective moment, and I wondered if her thoughts had shifted from Grandma Tabitha to Grandpa. She sighed and looked back at me. "These are a family heirloom."

"I'll return them as soon as I'm finished."

"No. Share them with your sister. I want her to know you've read them too." She closed the box. "I need to eat so I can get some sleep. I have early morning prayer before I go to the hospital."

Grandma walked around the desk and pulled a drawer open. She removed a key ring. "Leave your van here so you don't have to drive that gas guzzler all over the place."

"Grandpa's truck is expensive."

"Then don't wreck it," she said, pursing her lips. She kissed my forehead, leaving the imprint of her heart behind. "I'm going to get out of these germy hospital clothes." She left the room.

"I'll fix your plate," I called behind her.

My phone pinged. I checked the message, and I had a cash deposit from my father with the message: Bake.

Tears wet my eyes. My dad knew me. He could probably see how broke I was right through the phone screen.

I started to call him, but then I remembered he had a meeting with a client, so I sent him a thank-you text. Dad had always been my champion. He encouraged me in all things baking for sure. He was right about me needing to use social media. If he was willing to invest in me, I needed to put forth better effort.

I dropped into the desk chair and opened my phone to Instagram. I'd deactivated my page over a year ago. I tapped until I came to Kendrick's page. I looked at each of the pictures, reading the humorous captions he'd included. He hadn't posted all the time, but when he did, it was mostly scenes from his day, meals, and things he saw—a dog, a cool pair of sneakers, an odd building, a hot car . . . me. Our pictures together were the best ones. I reminisced on all I could and then, finally, I went to the last picture he'd posted. It was a selfie. Him smiling with the caption: *Things are about to change. I'm ready to wife my love.*

And then it was the comments. Over a hundred of them.

We miss you, man.

RIP.

Sorry for you, Sabrina.

Dude, your daughter is beautiful.

I remembered Grandma's words. *"Heartache eventually finds us all."*

I disagreed. Heartache wasn't birdlike. Not in my life. It set up camp in the nest of my heart on the day I was born, and it hadn't flown away since. I closed Instagram and looked at the letters. I reached for the tissue holder, stuck my hand in for the last one, and wiped under my eyes. Careful not to transfer moisture to the old paper, I picked up the stack.

I'd been hearing stories about my courageous great-great grandmother my entire life. I untied the ribbon and pulled out one letter as the question about what I might have in common with Tabitha Cooper pressed into my mind. I placed the first envelope on my chest and said a little prayer to honor her; then I looked at it. It wasn't addressed to anyone. It simply had a date written in the upper right-hand corner. *May 1915.*

My goodness. That was over a hundred years ago. I pulled the letter from the envelope. It was written on yellow parchment that though a little stiff had held up over the years. I read.

> *Dearest Mama,*
>
> *I am writing with barely any expectation that anyone will read this, so I address it to you, hoping and praying that one day we will be reunited and these stories I am putting on paper will be stories I can tell you over tea and biscuits and some of your muscadine jam.*
>
> *Although I was wrong, I still wish I could share these days with you because something wonderful has happened.*
>
> *I've fallen in love.*

Chapter 8

Mariah

L ove had created this place.

My eyes roved through the restaurant, taking in all of its details, from the vintage items to the modern ones. Everything blended, yet it never failed to feel like an embodiment of the Cooper and Holland families' rich history and culture. Nevertheless, with all this stirring my emotions, I couldn't help feeling it was time to close it.

I walked into my grandfather's office, dropped into his chair, and picked up my mug. The coffee inside was bitter but warm and rich enough to keep me company for a little while longer. I glanced out the small window. The sky cast yellow and lavender ribbons in a postcard-perfect pattern as the sun disappeared. The sunsets over the foggy Blue Ridge Mountains in the Upstate blessed me with their own unique depth and beauty. They contrasted with the vastness of low-country skyline in the evening. Both stole my breath, slowed me down, made me aware of God's omnipresence, even in moments when I felt alone.

A long yawn followed by a stretch reminded me that I was exhausted. I organized the mess of strewn papers, file folders, and stacks of loose paperwork before washing out the coffeepot and mug. I'd done all I could do today, and what I found weighed heavily on my shoulders.

As I passed through the restaurant's construction drape, levelheadedness overrode sentiment. The place was a wreck with Sheetrock residue, sawdust, and wires everywhere. Still, the financial mess was bigger than what I was looking at on the walls and floor.

I walked back through the drape, set the alarm, and stepped back to look up at the sign above the awning. *Tabby's Meats & Sweets*. Who would we be without it?

Fifteen minutes later, I walked into my grandmother's house. The only reason I didn't peel off my clothes and climb into bed was because I could see Grandma and Sabrina sitting at the kitchen table. Both had their hands on mugs.

Grandma stood and opened her fluffy arms to me. I folded myself into her waiting embrace. Grandma's hug held a comforting warmth like a soft blanket of security and love. I took it in for the seconds it lasted. "It's good to see you," I said.

She pulled back and inspected me for a moment. Her eyes reflected love, always had. "I was going to send a search party out for you, miss," she said, sitting again.

I hung my bag over the back of a chair. "Once I get started on something, I can be kind of hyper-focused."

"How ever you have to be to get your work done." Grandma raised her mug and took a sip. "The pork was delicious. Your sister heated a broccoli and cheese casserole to go with it. I put a plate up for you."

I walked to the refrigerator, removed the plate Grandma had filled, and stuck it in the microwave. "How is Grandpa?"

"He fussed a lot today about all the tests they did on him."

"What kind of tests?" I asked, washing my hands and reaching back into the refrigerator for the pitcher of lemonade I'd spotted.

"All kinds. They're making sure he can be moved to the rehab tomorrow."

The microwave dinged. I reached in for my plate and slipped into a chair.

Grandma and Sabrina resumed their conversation about the prices of flour and vanilla extract and other ingredients. Then they moved on to the happenings on Grandma's soap opera. Sabrina had always enjoyed watching those with Grandma in the summer. Me, not so much. I preferred to find my stories in novels.

When I put the last of my food in my mouth, Grandma turned her attention to me. "So, what did you find in our books?"

I picked up my glass and took a long drink, savoring the cool, tart taste. "There's no easy way for me to say this . . ." I delayed with another sip from my glass.

Sabrina's eyes flashed caution. She'd been at the hospital today. Maybe she knew something I didn't know, so I retreated. "It's late. I'm worn through. We can talk about it tomorrow."

Grandma shook her head. "We need to talk now, or I won't be able to sleep. Tell me what's not easy to say."

I sighed, wishing I'd used more discernment before opening my big mouth with that statement. But I hadn't, and now Grandma wasn't going to let me put her off. "The restaurant is in trouble. Real trouble. It's been operating in the red for a few years. And now with the loan for the build . . . it's . . . not salvageable."

Grandma frowned. "Not salvageable. That sounds like a word you use when you're talking about junk."

Grandma didn't seem to understand reopening the restaurant would include a thorough inspection of the books and that I would find out how much debt they were in. "I didn't say it was junk."

"Well then, tell me what you mean by 'not salvageable.'" Grandma's hands were on her hips now. Her eyes were communicating disbelief and disappointment. She was doing everything but rolling her neck.

"I mean you should close."

Grandma stared at me for a moment, unmoving, not showing expression, and then she laughed. "Close?" She stood and picked up my plate, walked it to the sink where she put it in sudsy water. "Whatever would make you utter a thing like that, Mariah?"

The disappointment in her tone picked at the rough edges around my fatigued brain. I looked at Sabrina again, gaining nothing from the blank expression on her face, and replied, "The condition of the finances."

Grandma turned in our direction, and falling back against the sink, she said, "I called you here because I need your help reopening it and finishing the new part." Her eyes cut to Sabrina's. "It's why I called both of you."

"Grandma—"

She sliced into my protest. "You need to figure out a way to fix the issues and reopen before we lose all our customers."

"You don't have enough customers."

"We'll find some more," Sabrina added, inserting her optimism where it wasn't wanted.

I pinned her with a look and through clenched teeth said, "Don't."

"Don't what?" she whispered like our grandmother wasn't in the room.

"You know nothing about this."

"Tell me what there is to know so I can do what Grandma asked and help."

I sat back, marveling at her gall. "You can't even manage yourself. How are you going to help with a restaurant?"

"Don't say that to her," Grandma interjected. "She manages herself and that baby upstairs just fine."

I rolled my eyes and took another sip of my lemonade. "Not really."

Sabrina froze. It was her turn to put the word *Don't* in the air.

Grandma cocked an eyebrow. "You girls are a mixed bag of secrets. What don't I know?"

I waited for Sabrina to answer that question. It took her a minute, but then she finally said, "I've been having a rough time lately."

Grandma's eyebrow hadn't come down. We both knew when she was waiting for more of a story.

"I lost my apartment."

"Where are you living?"

I watched Sabrina's Adam's apple shift like she'd swallowed all her courage. "I converted my van to a camper-like house."

Grandma dropped her arms. "You're sleeping in your car?"

"Yes, but it's—"

Grandma's eyes narrowed and widened with each question she asked and each answer she received from Sabrina. "You have your baby in a vehicle? How do you stay cool? How do you stay warm? Why didn't you tell me what was going on?"

When Sabrina finally got a word in, she said, "Ellen helps while I work, which has been a lot lately."

Grandma had been happy or at least content when I entered the kitchen. Now the worry on her face made me wish I could take back my words.

"We're going to get back to Kenni staying with Ellen in a minute. You need to explain to me how you live in a van."

Sabrina was slow to speak again. "I converted the back to a little living space. I have a bed, a little kitchen, my clothes . . . most of them. I have some things in storage."

"You don't have a bathroom. How do you clean yourself?"

"I shower at the gym." She shrugged. "It's a thing. If you look up 'van life' on YouTube, there are a lot of people that make this choice, and some aren't homeless even. They're trying to save money."

"I don't know nothing about YouTube, so you can tell me, which are you since your daughter isn't with you? Homeless or saving money?"

"I'm not earning enough to pay rent."

I knew grandma would take this personally. She would wail on the wall like a professional griever if she could. "I don't understand. How have I failed you that you would sleep in a vehicle rather than come here and stay with us?"

"Because I have a job . . . two if you count the temp work. I live in Greenville."

"You mean you roam the streets in Greenville. Hollands have always done better, not worse, and we've never slept in vehicles." Grandma reached across the table for Sabrina's hand. "I'm not judging you, baby, but I'm trying to understand why you wouldn't have brought your child here and just started over with our support."

Sabrina pulled her hand out of Grandma's. "I'm not ready to leave the Upstate."

"Why?"

"Because everything about . . ." Sabrina stood. She walked to the sink, washed her cake plate and fork, and put them in the dish drainer. When she was done, she turned around to face us again. "I wasn't ready to leave that area. I'm sorry you don't understand, but it's not about you and Grandpa. I know you love me and Kenni. My memories of Kendrick are there. My business may not be much, but it's there." She pushed off the counter, picked up her water glass, and moved to the door. "This has been an emotional day, so I'll say good night." She walked out.

Grandma turned her attention to me. "Why didn't you tell me about your sister?"

"I just found out."

"How is it that you just found out?" Now it was time for my inquisition. Why is it that all the children in the house were guilty no matter who upset the adults?

I slipped out of my chair and added a little more lemonade to my glass. "You know things haven't changed between us. That's why you sent us separate text messages. You made sure I didn't know she was going to be at the restaurant and vice versa."

Grandma pursed her lips. She was caught.

"We're never going to be close."

"Don't say that."

"It's true. And it's also true about the restaurant. Unless you've got some windfall of money to invest, it's going to fail."

Grandma loomed taller than me, and she did not like what I said. "Your grandfather doesn't have much family. Between the flu and hurricanes and just being poor, they died off, so I can't say much about them, but I can tell you this—the Coopers don't fail. You can save Tabby's the same way you saved Vince's place."

"The addition is a money pit."

"No, it's not. It was my mother's vision that we would have a banquet hall in the area. God gave me strength, and I won't let it not be fulfilled in my lifetime."

"I understand, but you have so much on your plate right now with Grandpa's care."

"Which is why I sent for you. *You* no longer have a lot on your plate." Grandma gently reminded me that I was no longer tied to Clark's Diner. "You've spent all this time helping Vince. It's time to be focused on your own family's legacy."

Grandma walked out of the kitchen, leaving me with the cost of my words.

Chapter 9

GEORGETOWN, SOUTH CAROLINA

April 1915

Tabitha

Heavy gray clouds blanketed the sky with darkness that wouldn't lift until the sun came up tomorrow. The wind rustled the trees down the way, their limbs bobbing with each light gust. A storm was coming. There was no doubt about that.

Tabitha decided to close the store. She always did when there was a threat of heavy rain. She had not remembered her umbrella or even her bonnet.

Tabitha put the *Closed* sign on the door and turned the lock. She turned when she heard horses approaching. Although it was unlikely, she hoped it was Papa's wagon coming to fetch her in the rain, but there was no mistaking Joseph's carriage, even from a distance. Still, she walked toward home.

The carriage rolled to stop. Joseph stepped out. "Miss Cooper. I feel lucky to have caught you. I gather you're on the way home in this weather."

"Church. It's Bible study tonight."

"Why yes," he said. "What church do you attend?"

"What church do you attend?" Tabitha asked.

Joseph hesitated for a moment before answering, "NorthStar."

"I've never heard of it."

"It's in Annadale. It's a church my former pastor suggested to me."

"Annadale is almost in Charleston County."

"I guess he wanted to keep me close."

The sky opened up and drops of rain came down—large ones that made a loud splash against the tin awning on the store.

"Let me give you a ride."

Tabitha shook her head. "I can't."

"You can't walk in this weather." He opened the door.

She heard a pop and looked up to see that Joseph's driver had opened an umbrella for his own head.

Tabitha hesitated but then felt the rain droplets on her hair and shoulders. She stepped inside and sat with Joseph following her in.

"It's not proper for me to be in here with you."

"It's not proper for you to get soaked either."

Tabitha had not entered Joseph's carriage when he had taken her to dinner. She had ridden on the back because inside she would be unchaperoned. Now that she was inside, she noticed how fancy it was.

"May I ask you something?" she asked before she realized how rude her next question was going to be.

"You may ask me anything," Joseph replied. The gentle quality of his voice sounded genuine.

"What do you do to own a carriage and driver?"

"I have investments in many things. My family has always been in sugar, and I have interests in lumber. That's why I'm in this county."

"I thought only white men owned the lumber mills."

"My family owns half of a mill in Sumter County, and I have interest in the Gardner Mill here in Georgetown."

The rain became heavier, and the carriage stopped. Tabitha looked out and saw they were off the road, near the woods.

"It's raining too hard," Joseph said, answering the question that was on her mind. "We don't like to drive the horses in it. It'll stop soon."

"What about your man?"

"He is prepared."

Joseph leaned forward. "I haven't been able to stop thinking about you." He planted his elbows on his knees and reached for her hands, cupping one in each of his. "I hope you thought about me some."

He set her heart to fluttering. The scent of rain and aftershave made her warm all over. "I have."

"Good." Joseph let go of one of her hands and crossed to her side of the carriage. "I'm going to Sumter for a few weeks for business. I won't be able to see you."

Tabitha hesitated, thinking about how much she'd miss him if he was to be gone for weeks. "Maybe you could call me."

"You have a phone?"

"Yes."

"Well, that's good to know. We'll have to be exact about it. I'll call when you're expecting me to. You can make sure to be waiting by the phone."

"That sounds fine."

Joseph stroked her forearm with his index and middle finger. "I want to hold off on you asking your Papa about me."

Tabitha looked down at his fingers and then back up into his hazel eyes. "Why?"

"Because if he says no, I'll be upset, Tabitha. The way I feel about you is special. I don't know that I felt this way about my first wife."

"Don't say that."

"It's true. Our marriage was an arrangement between our families. I want a love match this time, but I'd like to be sure we are . . . compatible." He emphasized the last word.

Joseph leaned in and put his lips on her cheek and then moved to her lips. The sound of the hard rain on the roof of the carriage was drowned out by the beating of her heart. She liked everything about how her heart and the rest of her was busting with feelings.

Joseph did not linger long on her lips. He whispered, "You are as sweet as a peach in late July."

Tabitha was in love when she stepped out of that carriage. Joseph and she decided he would call at 5:00 p.m. on Thursday. Papa and Mama weren't home from work on most days at that time. Tabitha never worked on Thursdays, so she would be in the kitchen preparing dinner.

The next week, Tabitha hovered over the phone from 4:55, and it rang at 5:00 exactly. She picked it up before the ring finished sounding. "Cooper home. This is Tabitha." Joseph had told her to identify herself in case he didn't recognize her voice.

"Hello, Peach." His voice was as smooth as the butter in the bell crock.

She got warm on the inside just hearing it. "You have made a name for me."

"I can't get the taste of your lips out of my head." He was quiet for a moment before saying, "I'll be back by tomorrow night. You didn't mention me to your parents, did you?"

"No, you told me not to," she said, gripping the phone.

"Good. I wanted to make sure we agreed. It's important for a couple to have the same ideas about things; otherwise they quarrel," Joseph said. "I don't like asking you to keep a secret, but I couldn't stand for your father to say no to me."

"You shouldn't be so sure Papa will say no."

"I'm sure he wants you to marry someone he's already got in mind for you."

"He doesn't have anyone in mind for me."

"He does. All men do, even if they don't tell you." Joseph laughed. "I'm sure he doesn't want some city boy from Charleston taking you way. I plan to move back to Atlanta. He'll hate that all the more."

Tabitha looked out the window. She could see Mama coming up the road.

"I have to go."

"I'll be in town on Saturday for a haircut before noon and then at BeBe's Diner for lunch, if you can meet me."

"I'll see. Bye." She hung up the phone and went back to stirring her pot as Mama entered the door.

"Who was that?"

"Someone looking for peaches."

"Peaches?"

"The operator connected the wrong number, Mama." Tabitha walked to the ice box and took out the deer meat. She didn't like deceiving Mama, but Mama didn't keep secrets from Papa. If she wanted to keep seeing Joseph, she had to keep their relationship to herself.

Saturday came, bringing Retha and Clifford to town in an automobile Clifford had purchased. Everyone on their street gathered to see it. Retha invited Tabitha to lunch. Clifford dropped them in front of BeBe's Diner. Alarm filled Tabitha. Joseph was planning to come here.

"Maybe we can eat somewhere else," Tabitha said.

Retha frowned. "What's wrong with here?" She didn't wait for Tabitha's reply. She pulled the door open and walked inside.

Tabitha spotted Joseph immediately. He sported a fresh haircut, which enhanced his looks. He read the newspaper and sipped from a coffee cup.

The clinking of silverware against glass and conversations at tables filled the crowded restaurant with noise. The scent of coffee, bacon, and grease wafted from the kitchen pass-through. Excitement teemed in Tabitha's blood. This outing made her feel less like a country girl and more like a grown woman. She liked that feeling. She liked the freedom of moving about in the world instead of wondering what other people were experiencing. Even if Retha and Joseph were in the same place.

They were seated. Before they could order, Joseph was at their table expressing a warm greeting. He introduced himself to Retha, the rich timbre of his voice drowning out the competing noise and causing heat to spiral from Tabitha's throat to her lower belly.

"Good day," Retha said, looking from Joseph to Tabitha. "I'm Retha Donovan."

"Nice to meet you, Mrs. Donovan. Tabitha has told me quite a few complimentary things about you."

Tabitha thought her eyes would fall out of the sockets. She had not told Retha anything about Joseph. She couldn't believe he said that.

Retha's smile tightened. "I wasn't aware that you knew my sister so well."

Joseph cleared this throat. He seemed to catch his folly. "Not well at all. I'm new in town, and I frequent the store."

Retha inspected him from his polished shoes to his handsome, expensive suit. He did not look like someone who shopped at the store, and Retha saw that plain and simple. "Will you sit and have another cup of coffee with us?"

Was it her intention to interrogate him? Tabitha would die if she did.

"I wish I could, but I have some business down the street with the tailor." He opened his billfold, removed a five-dollar bill, and put it on the table. "But please enjoy your meal."

Tabitha fought to breathe through this entire conversation. If it didn't end soon, she was going to faint. She stuck her clasped hands between her legs.

"Why thank you, Mr. McCoy," Retha said. The tight smile from before was still held at the corners of her mouth.

Joseph's eyes moved from Retha's to Tabitha's. Retha was so much prettier than she was. She considered he might think he had the wrong sister, but then his lip ticked up in the corner like it always did when he said something sweet to her, and Tabitha melted into a puddle right there in her chair.

"Tabitha," he said, nodding.

"Thank you for lunch," Tabitha replied.

Joseph pressed his eyes into hers one more time, put on his summer fedora, and disappeared through the door.

"Well, that saved us five dollars," Retha said, picking up the menu. "I'd like to know why."

"I can't say I know." Tabitha took a deep breath. She hated lying, and she was no good at it.

"Does he come to the store often?"

"Sometimes."

Retha looked curious. "He appears to be interested in you."

"He didn't sit with us."

"Of course not," Retha said as though Tabitha was silly for thinking he should. "Inviting him was a courtesy. He wasn't going to say yes. I'm married, so I can't be seen with him. You'd be the only other attraction, and that would get back to Mama and Papa."

"Or maybe he had business to attend to." Tabitha inspected the menu, but she'd already decided on what she wanted.

Retha pushed her back into the padded cushion of the seat and asked, "Have you spent some time with that man?"

"You promise not to tell Mama and Papa."

Retha's eyes widened. She hadn't expected a yes answer. "I don't know."

"Retha, you're not much older than me."

"Which means I remember how foolish I was at your age. I remember very clearly."

"I had dinner with him when Mama and Papa came to see you."

Retha pulled back her head. "Well, I can't say I expected that."

"I wanted to see what it was like to be out with a man." Tabitha pushed the nervous tickle out of her voice. "It was just the one time."

"It only takes one time for many complications in life," Retha said. "That man is much older than you, Bitta."

"I know."

"Was he a gentleman?"

"Very much so."

Retha sighed. "I won't tell Mama and Papa, but if you want to go out with him again, you must ask Papa's permission. You are a lady, and if he has honest intentions toward you, he will behave like a gentleman should and do things properly."

Tabitha agreed, but she was also swept up by the romantic secrecy. She wanted to hold on to Joseph and the private moments she had with him. The waitresses attended their table. They ordered and ate their food. When they were done, Retha went to the ladies' room. While Retha was gone, the waitress dropped off the bill. She handed Tabitha a paper. "The gentleman that was here before asked me to give this to you."

Tabitha nodded and accepted it. It read: *Meet me. My carriage will be on the street.*

Tabitha folded the note just as Retha came out of the restroom. "I swear I should have waited to use the one at Vera's shop. That one needs tending."

Tabitha sat there staring, so shocked that he'd gotten the note to her.

"Why are you looking so odd?" Retha asked.

"I was just thinking, you're right about Mr. McCoy. I need to talk to Papa about him. I don't know how to begin."

"You just tell him. You're near eighteen. Papa knows you're going to want to be courted."

"Do you think he has a man in mind for me?"

Retha laughed. "No. He didn't have a man for me, but he'll try to hold on to you as long as he possibly can. You are the cook in the house."

The waitress came back with the change, and Retha left a tip for her and pushed the other dollar to Tabitha. Tabitha's mind had not let go of thoughts of Joseph for a moment. For the first time in her life, she wondered what was beyond courting.

"What's it like being married?"

Retha pitched an eyebrow. "What do you mean?"

"I mean between you and"—Tabitha blushed—"at night."

"I can't tell you anything about that."

"It must be something special. No one wants to talk about it but the boys at school."

Retha was thoughtful for a long moment. "It's special, but it's meant for marriage. You come together in a way that's a gift from God." Her sister twisted her lips into a smile before adding, "A gift for being married. You need to talk to Papa if you have this kind of curiosity."

"Don't tease me."

"I'm glad you're growing up, but be careful around him. Don't make me regret keeping your secret."

They stood and walked out of the restaurant. Retha stopped just on the other side of the door and raised a hand to clutch Tabitha's chin. "You be careful. There are some things a man can't put five dollars on the table for."

"Yes, ma'am," Tabitha said, forcing herself to look into Retha's eyes.

They walked until they reached Vera's Beauty World. Retha always let Vera do her hair when she was in town. Tabitha picked up a magazine and busied herself with it for a few minutes. Once Retha's hair was wet, she said, "I'm going to the Five and Dime."

Retha nodded, and Tabitha left. Once Tabitha was on the street, she looked for the dark brown carriage. She spotted it on the side of King Street and walked down. The street was busy but not at that end. She turned the corner and Joseph's driver said, "Mr. McCoy is inside."

He tapped on the hood, and the door opened.

Tabitha looked around, making sure she saw no one before climbing inside.

"Hey, Peach," Joseph said.

She liked her nickname. "I can't stay. My sister is always curious."

"I'm sorry to put you in an awkward position. I assumed because we agreed to meet that she was your chaperone."

"She came to town and offered to take me to lunch. I couldn't say no."

"Will she tell your parents?"

Tabitha shook her head. "She promised not to."

Joseph crossed the seat, and once again she was in his arms, with him crushing her lips for a few seconds. The heat from outside was on his suit and her dress. Their bodies were hot from the outside in.

"I miss you," Joseph whispered.

The words on his lips vibrated against her ear and added to the jackhammer that was her heart.

Tabitha pulled back from him. These feelings were too much all at once, and his body felt too close.

"What are you thinking, Peach?"

She loved when he called her that. Everything in her loved it.

"I . . . we can't meet this way. It's not proper."

"Attraction to each other is human. Affection for each other is natural."

Tabitha's eyebrows knit together. Her emotions were confused. "I know it's natural, but—"

"God gave us these feelings." Joseph raised a hand and stroked her face. "Read it in the Bible . . . in the Song of Solomon. Your pastor probably skipped talking about that book at church." He ran a hand down her arm and clutched her hand.

"I've read the whole Bible for myself. That text is for married people."

"How do you think people get to marriage? They first have to have that hunger for each other." He stroked her face, this time with his eyes. "I have it for you."

It took Tabitha a moment to speak. He'd stolen her voice. "You have to meet my father."

"Charles Cooper?" He chuckled. "I think we both know that man is not your father."

Shock stung Tabitha and glued her lips shut.

"I would think you'd be glad to get out of that house. I know he drinks, and he's not nice when he does."

"How do you know about—"

"This is a small county. Small town." Joseph took her hand, but she pulled it away. "I have made some inquiries about your family."

"Why would you inquire about my family?"

Joseph sat back. Removing his hat, he said, "I have money, and people with money make inquiries."

Tabitha shook her head. "I'm embarrassed that you would say such hard truths about my life like you're talking about nothing."

"I don't care about your family situation. That should tell you something . . . that I care for you regardless of your parentage or the drunk who raised you."

Tabitha was still ashamed of what he'd said. Her parentage, as he called it, stung more than the fact that he knew Papa drank.

Joseph put a finger under her chin and tipped up her head. She hadn't even realized she'd dropped her eyes so.

"Peach, I'm too old to be meeting daddies. I seek no man's approval, especially not one who gives in to strong drink."

"So, you don't want to . . ." She paused, considering her words carefully. "I have to ask Papa to take up."

"You'll be eighteen soon. You don't have to ask anybody anything. You are not a piece of furniture or land."

Joseph tapped on the roof of the carriage. "My man will make sure it's all clear for you to step out." Seconds later, his driver opened the door.

Feeling the heat between them cool, she asked, "When will I see you?"

"I have business in Charleston. I'll call again, same as last week."

The tightness in her belly eased some. She nodded and turned to step down. Before she was out, Joseph said, "Give me a little more time. I need to get used to the idea of having to ask for you when I already feel like you're mine."

Tabitha stepped out of the carriage and hurried back up the block to the hair salon.

Weeks went by with Joseph and her meeting in the same way. Tabitha's birthday came and included a large celebration with her family and church members. She'd invited Joseph, thinking this would be a good day for him to meet Papa, but he didn't come, even though he said he would.

Tabitha could not hold her secret anymore. Asking Mama about Joseph made sense to her. Tabitha approached Mama while she was in her flower garden. With the sun burning down on their necks and sweat on their foreheads, Tabitha remembered Joseph's words about being grown, and instead of asking the question, she made a statement. "Mama, I plan to take up."

Mama craned her neck to look in her face. Her expression was complex. She stared at Tabitha like she'd just said there was no Jesus; then she turned back to the plant she was working on and snipped four long leaves. "Take up with who?"

"A man I—"

"A man." Mama's eyes were back on Tabitha. "He's not from school?"

"No, ma'am. His name is Joseph, and he comes to the store."

"Joseph who?"

Tabitha got down on her knees so Mama didn't have to keep twisting her neck. "McCoy. He's from Charleston and Atlanta, but he's here in Georgetown now."

"Atlanta. Charleston." Mama shook her head in disbelief. Tabitha had not said he was from another planet. "What kind of business does he do?"

"Lumber."

Mama looked at her again before returning her attention to the ground. "He works in the mill . . . with your father?"

"No, ma'am. He owns part of it."

Mama stabbed the earth with the hand shovel she'd been working with and pulled a rock out of the soil. "Owns part of it." She chuckled bitterly. "Colored men don't own none of the mill. He's lying to you."

"He has his own carriage and his own man. He has money."

Mama slowed her movements. She seemed to be considering that.

"I like him," Tabitha added.

Mama paused from her digging. She wiped sweat off her brow and sighed. "That's plain to see. You come here telling me what you gonna do rather than respectfully asking."

"I'm sorry, ma'am."

Mama continued to ask her questions about where he lived, worshiped, and more that Tabitha couldn't answer.

Mama dropped her head back and rolled it, trying to loosen the tension Tabitha had no doubt brought on. She didn't know how any of this worked. She didn't know she was supposed to know these things before. "Aren't these questions I'll have answers to when we court, ma'am?"

Mama stood, and Tabitha stood with her. "These are questions your father will have the answers to before Mr. McCoy sits down good." Mama wiped her hands on her dress and used the towel over her shoulder to swipe her forehead. "How old is he?"

"I'm not sure. I think about thirty. I didn't ask."

"But he knows your age. He knows you're just now eighteen, and I'm sure he was more than happy about that." Mama looked Tabitha up and down. The beads of sweat burst and spiraled down her face. "Why doesn't a man that age already have a wife?"

"He's been married before. His wife died."

Mama considered that too. It seemed to be a reasonable answer to her. "Does he have children?"

"No, ma'am. He didn't mention any."

"Bitta, you can do better than these answers."

"Mama, I like him. I never liked anyone before, and no one"— Tabitha swallowed against the painful words—"no one has ever liked me."

"You are my last daughter."

"I'm aware. Are you aware that you used all your looks and pretty hair on the older ones?"

Mama truly looked shocked.

"I'm lucky someone wants me. I'm the giant one with my *real* father's skin."

Mama sighed and did not meet Tabitha's eyes at first. "When did those two things start bothering you?"

"Always. I just don't talk about it, and I didn't much care because I didn't think anyone would like me anyway, but now that someone does, I care."

Mama put her hands on Tabitha's arms. "And you're sure he hasn't said something to you to make you feel this way."

"No. He's only said kind words."

She released Tabitha's arms and let out a long breath. "I'll talk to your father about inviting him to supper, but I cannot promise he will allow it until he knows more about his family in Charleston."

"Yes, ma'am." Tabitha wasn't sure Papa would care as much as Mama thought. She was someone he tolerated. Tabitha knew that, even if Mama believed differently. She hesitated before adding. "Please make sure he's in a good mood when you ask him."

"I don't need your advice on the when or the how, Bitta." Mama grabbed a hoe. "You go and start supper. I need a minute to gather myself."

It was plain to see Mama was not up for more testing. Tabitha wiped the dirt off her skirt and walked into the house.

Days went by. She kept waiting for the when and the how to happen between Papa and Mama, but then a telegram arrived, and Papa left early to catch the train. Again. As always, Mama fell apart emotionally when he left, so when she asked Tabitha about Joseph, Tabitha didn't want to burden her. She told her she was no longer interested in him.

By the time Papa was due to return, Tabitha realized she'd missed her time. She'd gone farther than she meant to in Joseph's carriage. Tabitha had so many voices in her head . . . Mama's, Retha's, God's, but still Joseph's was much louder. Joseph made her feel special, and she wanted the happiness he gave her.

When she told him she was having a baby, he looked satisfied. Tabitha couldn't imagine why. They'd dishonored themselves, the Lord, and her family.

"All that can be fixed once we marry, Peach," Joseph said. "We can do that in Charleston."

Tabitha thought that was a fine plan when he first suggested it—or at least that's what her mind told her—but for some reason she did not understand yet, her heart was not in agreement.

Chapter 10

Present Day

Mariah

Grandpa had been moved to the rehabilitation center. Grandma got up early, had a half cup of coffee before putting a full one in an insulated cup, packed her Bible study materials, and left to go be with her husband. That was love. Love transcended marriage. I don't care what anyone said. I had been devoted. I had been committed to it forever. But my husband and I weren't friends. I couldn't imagine a scenario in which he was in a rehab center and I would want to go *every* morning and read the Bible with him. We weren't that close. We were never going to get that close. No matter how long we stayed married.

Shuffling noises came from upstairs. The sound of Sabrina moving about in her bedroom over the kitchen.

Moments later, shoes padded on the steps, and then seconds later, Sabrina entered the kitchen. Still in her pajamas, she grumbled a good morning and went right to the coffee maker, poured a cup, sweetened it, and plopped down in one of the chairs. "What's on the agenda for today?"

"What do you mean?" I asked.

"The restaurant. I know you've got a plan. You always do." She took a sip of coffee.

I did always have a plan, but this time I did not. It had been three days since I'd arrived, and even with further protest, Grandma was adamant that closing Tabby's was out of the question.

Sabrina's voice broke my concentration. "Grandma asked me to help. I want to help."

"I will *find* something for you to do. I just have to figure some things out." I stood. I was ready to let her have the kitchen to herself. I thought better when I was alone.

"Maybe we can figure it out together. Why don't you tell me what you're thinking so we can talk about it?"

"What I'm thinking is what I've already said. I wish you would be on my side with this instead of encouraging Grandma to keep dreaming for a magical save."

Sabrina took a long sip of coffee and frowned. "It's been in our family for too long to give up on it."

"I understand it's a holy artifact, but I care about the grandparents who are here. They've worked their whole lives. They deserve a decent retirement."

"The restaurant is a part of their retirement. Grandpa said he was going to cook until we put him in the ground."

"Yeah, well that was before he had a stroke," I said. "I don't know if you know anything about this, but that rehabilitation home is probably five or six thousand a month. Grandpa has insurance from his retirement, but these things only go so far. Insurance has changed, and Medicare is either a nightmare or a joke. Trust me. I had to deal with my mother-in-law." I took my last sip of coffee and put the mug in the sink. "They have to think ahead. Grandpa could have health issues for a long time."

Sabrina looked bothered. "Grandpa could also recover beautifully."

There it was. She was *always* so whimsical and hopeful. She was incapable of anything else. That difference between us drove me nuts. "I know he could recover." I sighed just thinking about the alternative. "I want nothing else but to see Grandpa at his best again, but that's going to take a long time. Grandma wants it open right away, before she loses her customers. There's a big problem with that."

Sabrina frowned. "Okay. What is it?"

"Great-Great-Grandma Tabitha was a cook. Grandma Margaret took after her. She was a cook. Grandma and Grandpa together are cooks. We don't have a cook."

Sabrina drank more coffee. I could see she was considering everything that I was saying. "I know managing things is a job, but you cook."

"I'm a potager, Sabrina."

Sabrina twisted her lips. "If you're going to make me google, at least spell the word."

"It's a cook who specializes in soups and stews. I don't cook Gullah food."

Sabrina grunted. "Well, can we find a cook with an ad or something?"

"Do you think good Gullah cooks grow on muscadine vines?"

Sabrina pursed her lips. "You're looking for reasons to quit."

"I'm not."

"Maybe it's time to have a conversation with Daddy and 'nem to see if they're willing to pull some resources together to try to keep it open. I obviously don't have any money, and I clearly don't know what you may have, but . . ." Sabrina hesitated, the wheels in her brain turning. "We can't just let it close. Not without seeing if we can get the family involved in some way."

Kenni came running down the stairs. She bounced against her mother, nearly causing her to spill her coffee.

Her mother should have scolded her for that, but Sabrina did nothing but put her cup down because the worst had not happened; therefore there was no need for a conversation about it. She hugged Kenni and gave her a kiss. "Morning to you."

Kenni scooted in my direction and hooked her arm around my hip. "Good morning, princess," I said, tilting her head up so I could look in her eyes. "Somebody got all the sleepies out."

Kenni smiled. "I slept with Mommy."

"I know. That must have been nice," I said, thinking about how she lived with Ellen. Kenni twirled away from me and took a seat at the table.

"I'll look at the books again this morning. I'm going to dig all the way in . . . look at the inventory and equipment, look at the tax returns for the last couple of years . . . pray they don't have any debt I haven't seen yet. Once I know all the details, we can have that family meeting."

Sabrina clapped and gave me a huge smile. "Thank you for considering my idea. If you need me to set the meeting, I can take lead on that."

"Mommy, I want pancakes," Kenni interjected.

Sabrina nodded and popped up. She asked, "Did you want pancakes too?"

"I'm not a breakfast person."

"Some things never change," Sabrina said, half smiling at me. She'd obviously been remembering how I skipped breakfast in my teens.

I pushed off the counter. "I'm going get over there."

Sabrina's next words slowed my exit, caught me as I was walking out the door. "You look great. I've been meaning to tell you that. The change in your hair made you over."

"Thanks. I did it myself."

Sabrina shrugged. "You can fix anything. Hair, restaurants . . ." Her words trailed off as she rifled through the cabinet for a griddle.

I left the kitchen. As I climbed the stairs, Sabrina's words swirled around in my head. *You can fix anything.* I realized I'd been here before. Looking at a restaurant that was failing. Why did I think Tabby's was any different from Clark's?

Running Clark's was the only plan Vince ever had for himself. He wasn't big on trying to figure out a new path, so once we found out Clark's was in trouble, we decided to save it—first with an updated look. We drove to Spartanburg and visited several restaurants in that area. We took pictures of the décor and then came back to Clark's to implement the changes. With less than a two-thousand-dollar budget, we completely spruced up the place. Paint and lighting went a long way.

Sabrina was an artist. I could put her in charge of figuring out how to refresh the restaurant on a shoestring budget. She'd love that.

I went back down the stairs. Sabrina was flipping pancakes while Kenni played with her phone.

"I had a thought," I said.

Sabrina waited for me to go on.

"If you're up for it, we could do some of the work at the restaurant."

Sabrina frowned. "What part?"

"For one, we can paint. A room that large would cost a few thousand dollars. We can help put in the flooring. I've done it before, and we can also do the refresh on the existing space. We don't need to pay someone for that."

Sabrina nodded, and I tried to read the meaning. She scrunched up her face. "Legally, aren't there like code rules or something?"

"Not for cosmetic changes. I was thinking you could come up with some ideas for a new look. We could buy the materials and work on the old space while Abel One works on the new part."

"While you're coming up with your designs, I'll switch up the menu. It's almost the same as it's always been."

Sabrina's questioning tone was back. "People like the menu."

"People also like variety. Older people like things to stay the same. Younger people like change. We have to do both. We can have weekly specials. We'll use social media, some local advertising, and with the new look inside, it'll be nice."

"That sounds great. Maybe we can get local artists to play on Saturday nights."

I shook my head. "I don't think we should be adding line items to the budget until there's some profit, but we'll see. I like the idea of maybe incorporating some events that don't cost money. I had a Tuesday night book club, and we had a Wednesday morning veteran breakfast. The vets love dining together, talking about their days in the military. If you have events, people will come in just to have something to do." I envisioned the addition. Once it was done, we could do so much with it. "My wheels are turning now."

"I guess I'd better get my sketch pad and start my wheels to turning too." Sabrina flew to my side and pulled me into a hug. "Thank you for including me."

I backed away from her. She'd jarred me. I wasn't used to us embracing like that, but I could see the disappointment in her eyes. I looked down at Kenni and could see confusion in her eyes. Attempting to release tension, I cleared my throat and said, "The sooner we start fixing it up, the better." I nodded, and Sabrina nodded back.

I walked back through the kitchen door. I felt bad about the hug thing, but I couldn't make myself be someone I wasn't. I couldn't make myself feel close to her that way. She'd have to accept that.

I put my boots on the ground in Georgetown. I visited the actual vendor locations my grandparents shopped at and the ones they didn't. I went to the county office to get a copy of the county codes for restaurants to make sure I was right about Sabrina and me being able to make changes ourselves. Then I did a drive-by quickie tour of all the restaurants within a five-mile radius of Tabby's to size up the competition. There weren't many.

I spent a good part of the day looking at all the records, and my initial assessment was wrong. Things were worse than they appeared because my grandparents owed back taxes.

We weren't rich people. There was no way we were going to be able to convince our relatives to dig this restaurant out when they weren't invested in it. Like me, they would take Grandpa's being sick into consideration. It was time for him and Grandma to retire.

The telephone on the desk rang. The setting was so loud, it banged against my heart. I picked up the receiver and answered, "Tabby's Meats and Sweets. How may I help you?"

"Hello," a gentleman's voice said. On the end I could hear even in the hello the slight twang of a Gullah accent. "This is Dante Kershaw. Mrs. Gail asked me to call. She said her granddaughter would be there."

"This is her granddaughter, Mariah Holland. What can I do for you Mr. Kershaw?"

"Mrs. Gail says you need a cook."

Grandma must have been anticipating my reservations. Either that or the house was bugged. "When did you talk to my grandmother?"

"Just this past weekend," he replied. "She said that she was going to be getting some help to open the place again."

"I'm not sure that's exactly what we're going to do."

"You're not sure you need a cook, or you're not sure you're going to open?"

"Both."

"You can't just not open. It's been in your family for over eighty years, right?"

I pitched an eyebrow. *Okay, so now a stranger is telling me what I have to do?* "My grandmother didn't mention that anyone would be calling."

"Check with her. Tell her that Dante called."

"I'll do that. Let me have your telephone number. Once I confirm what you're saying, I'll be back in touch directly."

"Sounds like a plan," he said. He gave me his number. "I'd like to take a look at the kitchen this afternoon, so if you go ahead and talk to your grandmother and get back to me, I would appreciate it."

I pitched an eyebrow again. *Bossy.* Good cooks often were, and they were hard to find. I didn't need to run him off if he was a potential employee and certainly not before I talked to my family about what we were going to do.

I sent Grandma Gail a text, and sure enough she confirmed that Dante Kershaw was the person they wanted to work at the restaurant. She added that he had an excellent reputation. He was a great cook, and he would be flexible. Whatever that meant.

At two o'clock, Dante was at the door.

"Thanks for letting me come by. I'm headed out on a flight to Atlanta for my cousin's wedding. I'll be gone until next week. If we're going to get things going, I wanted to get my head around it prior to leaving."

"I'm not sure when we'll be ready to open," I said. "I still have to have a talk with my grandparents about some things."

He said, "Sounds like money business. Did your grandmother tell you that you don't have to pay me?"

I reared back my neck. "Why wouldn't we have to pay you?"

"Because I don't need the money. I'm looking for something to do with my time."

Now I was even more curious. Work for no pay. "Don't need the money? Looking for something to do with your time? What are you—independently wealthy and bored?"

He chuckled, his eyes sweeping the kitchen's interior again before landing back on mine. "Something like that."

I was joking, but he was serious, and now I wondered which *that* was he referring to. The elderly were victims of con artists all the time. For all I knew, this guy was planning to walk out the back door with all the equipment. "Where do you know my grandparents from?"

"My parents attend their church. I visit when my mother begs me. I prefer a service that doesn't take three hours." He chuckled again. "I'm willing to help them out. Your grandmother said the restaurant would open back up for the same hours that it had, Thursday through Saturday."

He walked through the kitchen, making an exhaustive mental inventory of everything that was there. Every pot. Every pan. He went into the pantry and inspected all the seasonings and the supplies. He looked in the freezer at the foods that were stored there. He did exactly what any cook would do if they were taking over a kitchen. I knew because I'd seen it several times at the diner. This man was ready to work.

"Well, I don't know if you have time before you go to Atlanta, but one thing I need before I can hire you is to see you in action. When can you cook for me?"

Dante smiled, and I wasn't sure what it was about, but it almost looked like he thought I was kidding. He crossed his arms over his chest. I couldn't help but notice what a nice chest it was. He was nice-looking, period, in the most clichéd way ever. Tall, dark as ebony, with short locs and a big smile that was framed by dimples. He was thick muscled. Kind of like I liked a man's physique. "What do you say?" he asked.

I cleared my throat. I hadn't heard the man. I was too busy checking him out. "Say about what?" I asked, embarrassed.

He smiled like he knew my secret, and I blushed as red as burgundy wine. "When I come back from Atlanta."

"Sure," I said.

A reminder pinged on my phone. I'd forgotten my meeting. I was glad to have a way to transition out of this embarrassing moment with the hot chef. Dante left. Although I had a feeling this was a waste of time, I got on a video call with my father and my aunt and uncle. Aunt Deborah was willing to pitch in some money to help lower the line of credit, but only if they sold the restaurant. My uncle David was a hard no on everything. He was off the call right away. Neither had children to pass it down to, so I think they felt like it was my father's issue.

"Dad," I said, continuing to talk with him and my aunt, "even if keeping it is a bad idea, I think the timing is horrible. It would break Grandpa's heart if he knew we were letting it go."

"Sometimes I think Daddy is more invested in this than Mama," Aunt Deborah said. "This is Cooper business. Can we see if more family members are willing to help keep it in the family?"

"I've done that," Dad said. "I put feelers out and didn't get anything positive back."

Disappointment enveloped me. We weren't a large family, but most of my relatives were successful. There was enough money in this family to keep Tabby's. "Help or no help, I'm going to abide by their wishes."

"You're a good girl, Mariah," Aunt Deborah said. "Good luck with it, and give Sabrina my love."

We said goodbyes, and she left the call.

"How are you doing?" Dad asked.

With a hand at the back of my neck, I demonstrated my answer before I spoke it. "Stressed."

"What about the situation with Vince?"

I'd called my father after Vince asked for the divorce and filled him in on everything that was happening. I also swore him to secrecy. I wasn't ready for everyone to know what I was going through. People loved giving advice. I wasn't in the mood to stomach a bunch of well-meaning Christianese about God hating divorce, praying through our issues, and the like, when Vince put me out. I couldn't save our marriage by myself, but making people understand that would require me to tell what the issues were.

I shrugged. "We have attorneys."

"Have you told your sister?"

"No."

"Mariah, you're under the same roof. You—"

"Whatever you're about to say about Sabrina, I don't want to hear." I sighed heavily, and I wasn't being dramatic. My father was always riding hard for Sabrina. He knew our issues, and he knew how *his* issues had exacerbated our problems. He was in no position to tell me how to navigate our relationship, and I never let him do it.

Dad looked regretful, as if he'd just read my mind. When he spoke, his voice belied disappointment. "Your grandmother asked Sabrina to be there for a reason. Let her be a part of this process."

"I already have."

"And your sister is still grieving, you know. She could really use a friend."

Now he was concerned about someone grieving? I counted to ten in my head. "I'm not good at the friend stuff."

"Just care. Caring goes a long way."

I nodded.

"I love you," he said. "We'll talk soon."

We ended the call. I signed out of the app and gathered my things and walked outside. My phone rang in a call from Hope. I realized I hadn't replied to the text she'd sent me. The one about therapy. Again.

After we got our greetings out of the way, I told her I was in Georgetown and why. We talked for a few more minutes before we ended the call. I walked around to the front of the restaurant and stood there staring at the building for a few minutes. *Established in 1937* was etched into a plank of wood below *Tabby's Meats & Sweets*. My great-great-grandmother risked a lot to open this place. Jim Crow laws and all the oppression that came with them were in full effect, and they'd opened on the back end of the Great Depression. Everything was a risk then, especially a restaurant.

If they could do all they'd done, I could save it.

I walked back to my car and slipped behind the wheel. Georgetown needed to get ready for the new and improved Tabby's, because once I was invested, there was no stopping me from succeeding.

Chapter 11

Sabrina

I was tired and apparently my child was too, because we slept in. By the time we got up for breakfast, Grandma and Mariah were both gone. Kenni and I had pancakes, dressed, and hopped in Grandpa's truck singing to Kenni's favorite Kidz Bop track as it played from my phone.

I was headed to my happy place, a craft store. I'd googled and found there was one downtown. I was tempted to send my father his money back, but after reading my great-great-grandma Tabitha's letter, I felt empowered to make the cake thing happen for myself. I needed supplies—four dozen mason jars, ribbon, tags, labels, and a new calligraphy set among other art supplies.

"Are you making cakes, Mama?" Kenni asked.

"I am." I'd taken her to the bakery with me a few times to watch me work, and I'd made a cake or two in Ellen's kitchen.

She smiled as she stroked her doll's hair. "I like making cakes."

What she liked was being with me. Although I saw her more days than not, it still wasn't the same as us having our own house and spending all our evenings and nights and mornings together. Ellen did some things differently from me, and Kenni was quick to let me know with statements like, "Nana does this" or "Nana does that." Ellen babied her more than she needed to. I believed in stretching children's limits, giving them assignments and chores early. Ellen was in the *let kids be kids* camp.

Next, we went to bakery supply store and picked up all the items I needed for four of my favorite cakes—red velvet, birthday cake, caramel, and chocolate.

I took a picture of my purchase and sent the text to my father. He sent back a thumbs-up.

My mother made cakes in mason jars. She called them sweet cakes. Baking them created warm feelings of connectedness to my mother, which I had to imagine because I'd never met her. All I had was her recipes and this flour, butter, sugar, and my imagination. I'd share it with Kenni when she was older, but right now, my little helper was bored with my errands. I still needed to go to the bank and open a business account.

Thankfully, we were not far from my grandparents' church, which ran a small daycare for the parishioners. Grandma had already called and set me up in their system. I was glad to give my daughter somewhere to burn off her energy, and Kenni was happy to finally get some kid time, barely saying bye before she was wrapped up in painting with a new best friend.

I traveled down Black River Road to South State Bank to get a cashier's check for my business license application. I'd never gotten one in Greenville, but that was because I was just contracted to make cakes. Now that my goal was to make sweet cake jars and try to get them in markets around the city, I needed to be official.

I went through the line, and just as I was pushing the door to exit, I heard my name. I turned to see who was calling me.

The guy looked familiar, but I wasn't sure where I knew him from. I fought the desire to stare until I figured it out, but then it didn't take long for that. "Quinton?"

I had spent summers in Georgetown until I graduated high school, and Quinton Rainey had been my crush for all those years. His family attended my grandparents' church, and he and I volunteered to help at vacation Bible school and attended the teen Bible study program and the camp the church had. I basically spent my summers with him.

His smile was as wide as the double doors that led out of the building. He walked toward me. "Sabrina Holland." He pulled me into a hug that was all spicy cologne and masculine muscles. "How long has it been?"

"Almost ten years," I said, stepping out of his embrace. "I'm surprised you recognize me."

"You're hardly forgettable." He fully inspected me. "You look great. I mean, you really look amazing."

"You're embarrassing me," I said, looking down at my cut-off jean shorts, flip-flops, and "Girls Run the World" T-shirt. There wasn't much about me to rave about. "I didn't know you still lived in Georgetown."

"I've only just come back a few months ago," Quinton said. "How are your grandparents?"

"My grandmother is good, but my grandfather had a pretty bad stroke about a month ago."

"Oh, I'm sorry to hear that about Mr. Holland. I'll have to pray for him."

"I'd appreciate that," I said. "So where have you been living?"

"Columbia. Since I graduated from USC." He paused. He still seemed to be processing that he was seeing me. "Look, I'm running to get back to work, but I'd love to grab a bite to eat and catch up sometime." He reached into his pocket for his phone. "Can I call you?"

"Sure." I gave him my number.

"This was the best surprise." He smiled and began walking backward. I watched him get into an SUV. A nice, new-looking BMW that said, *I'm successful, Sabrina. I don't live in a van.* If it was true, I was glad for him. Quinton was always such a nice guy—friendly, helpful, patient, yet funny and so serious about the Lord. He was just perfect. I let that spin around in my memory for a moment and smiled because he wanted to catch up. It was something to look forward to.

Ten minutes later, I was back on the road when a text came through from Quinton's number.

Too soon? 😊

I smiled. I was surprised at how wide. It wasn't too soon. Before I could respond, a second text came through.

What about dinner tomorrow?

My first thought was who would babysit. Grandma had so much on her plate, and Mariah, well, Mariah would probably hold it against me somehow. She was already judging me. I hesitated . . .

I'm not sure about tomorrow. I need to let you know.

Bubbles showed he was texting, and then they stopped. A few minutes later, my phone pinged.

Don't blow me off.

At least he was thoughtful. Blowing him off was something I'd never been able to do. The memory of Quinton had always been with me, even through all I'd had with Kendrick. Whenever Kendrick and I broke up, which was far too often, my thoughts drifted to the "what if" of Quinton Rainey, that praying dude from VBS. But even though I thought about him, I didn't think I'd ever see him again.

Kendrick, while Christian, wasn't always, not in the beginning of our relationship. He was just cool. He talked about spiritual things in a sexy kind of way that drew me in. It wasn't until I'd been dating him for nearly a year that I realized he was struggling with what he believed about Jesus. He'd been reading books about other religions and combining them in some kind of self-created mess of a spiritual melting pot. Still, I didn't break up with him. I didn't know how.

We chose not to talk about our faith. That is, until the shift happened. His grandfather died, and the only thing that gave him comfort was his grandfather's Bible. He recommitted to the faith and even got rebaptized. I told myself on the nights we fought, the nights when he was at his lowest in terms of his testy temper and sharp-witted, cutting words, that if he and I ever parted, I wouldn't date a man who wasn't a Christian again.

I thought about my great-great-grandmother. Her love story was slowly unfolding in her letters. There was no mention of her marriage to a man named Joseph in our family history. I'd always assumed all her children had the same father, the one we knew. The more I read about Joseph, the more I could see my own choices. Great-Great-Grandma Tabitha and I had done the same thing—followed a charming man to painful places because we did not follow the Word. Rebellious behavior ran in our blood.

And there was Quinton occasionally skittering through my mind over the years, pressing into me in subtle, regret-filled ways.

I looked at my phone, replied to his text:

Blow you off? Never. I'd love to catch up. I'll let you know.

A thumbs-up emoji came through with a smiley face.

I would let him know, and I wouldn't make him wait long. But I had not dated in years. And because I'd cut off the few friends I had after Kendrick died, I didn't have anyone to remind me that *date* was something I was supposed to do. Until now. I could still feel the gentle press of Quinton's body against mine. It was a friendly hug, but I was so starved for affection that I couldn't help thinking about how it could be more.

Blow him off?

I guffawed and turned the steering wheel for a sharp right turn I'd almost missed in my musing. That wasn't happening.

My phone rang in a call from Ellen, and I pushed a button to turn on Bluetooth to receive the call. She greeted me and asked the same questions she asked about Grandpa every day: "How is he? How is the rehab progressing?" Today she added something else. "It seems there was no medical emergency."

"Not really."

"Well, why were you summoned in the middle of the night?"

It had not been the middle of the night. It was actually in the middle of dinner that I picked Kenni up, but I didn't argue with her. "My grandmother needs help."

A discernible grunt came through the line. "What about your job?"

"It's a temp job."

"Not at the bakery."

"I told them I needed family time, and since I'm kind of temp there, it's okay."

Ellen's aggravation was obvious. "I have Kenni's space at the preschool."

I gripped the steering wheel tight. Daycare . . . that was the real rub, and she was right. I owed her my timeline. "I'll be here for a month . . . at least."

She gasped. "A month?"

"I'm helping with the restaurant. We're renovating it, and I'm in charge of the creative vision."

"Creative vision?" Ellen's tone carried a sneer. She didn't say anything else, and neither did I for a long time. I just continued to drive, hoping one of her patients would need her so she would get off the phone.

"I feel like you're not telling me something."

I thought about the business license I was headed to get. I had made a decision that affected her. I *might* be staying here. I owed her to tell her, but today wasn't the right day. I'd seen Quinton, Mariah liked my ideas, and I was on my way to jump-start my business. Everything was good, and I wanted it to stay that way.

There was a voice in Ellen's background, and then she said, "I have to so see about one of my people."

Happy for the reprieve, I released my breath before adding, "I think you should let the preschool slot go."

Ellen ended the call without saying goodbye, but she heard me, because I heard her swear before the line went dead.

Chapter 12

June 1915

Tabitha

No one could have told Tabitha that she would ever just leave Mama, but the decision to take Joseph's hand had already been made for her because she had not bled in two months. She was with child. If she didn't go with Joseph now, she feared she might never see him again.

But still, she didn't need a carriage or horses. Regret carried her all the way from Georgetown to Charleston. As the city got closer, anticipation became a distant feeling in her heart. It was replaced with a heavy emotion she could not put a name to. Ambivalence was squeezing the happiness out of her.

Mostly, Tabitha felt guilty. She wasn't sure she wasn't making a mistake, but she couldn't go back. She'd made a hard bed.

She wondered how Joseph felt. Surely he wasn't born a thief—a man who stole another's daughter in this way. But Tabitha couldn't see anything in the side of his face or the set of his jaw that made him look like he carried regret. In fact, he slept part of the way like trouble had not found him.

It was late when she and Joseph arrived. Tabitha stepped out of the carriage to noise . . . people walking, horses whinnying, a car rumbling against the cobblestone, and a baby crying from somewhere. City noise. That's what she heard. And although they were less than a half mile from the port, there was no breeze, no smell of saltwater in the air. And the heat stole her breath, left her wanting relief from it.

There was nothing remarkable or unremarkable about her new home. The two-story building was painted a pale yellow, which looked faded against the deep red brick steps. A wrought iron door kept it closed to the outside. She and Joseph entered with his coachman behind them carrying her bag. Passing a pair of sweethearts in the lobby, they climbed the stairs to the second floor. The apartment was small—four rooms with a wash closet—but it was furnished and appeared clean.

Tabitha expected more. She couldn't quite reconcile why a man with Joseph's money lived in a place so simple. From what she could see, it was in a decent part of Charleston. Respectable enough, but far from the only part of Charleston she'd been to, which was Morris Street, where they'd traveled once for a church convocation. They had passed through a neighborhood with automobiles and polished carriages with drivers. All she saw here were wagons and working-class people.

"This is where you'll be for a while."

"Me?" Tabitha asked. "Just me?"

"Until we're married."

"And then?"

"We'll figure it out together," Joseph said.

Tabitha nodded understanding but still clutched her bag to her belly as she continued to inspect the front room.

"I'm glad we have a chance to be alone, Peach." Joseph put his hands on her shoulders. His eyes melted into hers. "I was tired of having to sneak around with you. We both deserve better than that."

Tabitha understood his happiness, but he'd lost nothing. She'd left her family, and she didn't even know anything about his. She wanted him to notice her lack of enthusiasm so they could talk about it, but he didn't. He didn't see because his own vision of how things were was filling up his eyes.

"Charleston is a big city. You can do whatever you want here."

"What will I do for work?" Tabitha asked. She was reminded she had abandoned the store without notice. That was added to the list of ways she'd disappointed people.

"You can do nothing."

Tabitha found that statement ridiculous, and her tone reflected it. "How can I do nothing?"

"I'll provide for you . . . rent, food, clothes. I prefer you not work."

"But how will I fill my days?"

"Making my baby." He lowered his hand to her belly.

"That's nature, Joseph. God is making the baby."

"Well, there's not much here to do that won't require you to work hard, on your feet, lifting things."

"What about in a shop?"

"That will be on your feet, and I'm afraid most shops in this city are family-run businesses. They don't have any need for an outsider."

"Well, perhaps . . ."

"No, Peach. There is nothing."

Joseph removed his coat and pulled down his suspenders. "I have to leave early tomorrow to go to Sumter."

Tabitha couldn't believe her ears. He was leaving her alone. "How long will you be gone?"

"Not long."

"I wasn't expecting you to bring me here and leave me."

"It will only be for a few days."

"But what will I do?"

"Learn the neighborhood."

Joseph undid the buttons on his shirt. He left her and walked to the washroom. After he came out, he went into one of the two bedrooms. Tabitha followed him. He opened a closet and pulled out a shirt.

"You have things here?"

Joseph slipped on the shirt and took to buttoning it. "I think it's obvious I have things here."

This was confusing to her. Joseph lived somewhere else, but he had clothing here. Joseph owned a carriage and had a driver and owned part of sawmills, but she was in a common neighborhood, in a small apartment. "Why am I here when you obviously live in a different place?"

"Things will change once we're married."

His response was not an answer to her question, so Tabitha pressed him for more. "Where do you live?"

"In Charleston proper, but I can't take you there until we're married."

Joseph continued buttoning his shirt. He treated this conversation so casually that it unnerved her. This was not what he promised. She was supposed to become his wife, but then she considered the reason why he delayed. She was probably too dark for his family. Charleston proper was full of high-yellow Negroes who rejected anyone darker than a brown paper bag, which she was by many shades, but that wasn't going to change. Keeping her here wasn't going to lighten her skin.

"Are you ashamed of me?"

Joseph frowned. "What's to be ashamed of? I've given you the best of me." He touched her belly. "You're not hiding, Peach. You are simply waiting." He smiled, and his countenance was full of charm. "There's a difference."

Tabitha felt some relief, but she still didn't like being left alone. "Can you take me with you?"

"No."

"I can stay in the room where you are just as well as I can stay here."

He chuckled with irritation not humor. "What's your problem with here?"

"I'll be lonely for days."

"You'll make friends. There are other women in this building."

"But . . ."

"Tabitha!" She'd never heard impatience carry her name so strongly out of his mouth. "That's enough. I know this is new to you and you are anxious, but you're worried about being bored, and you're not even bored yet. Try to take things as they come." He pulled her to him and kissed her forehead. "Let's go have dinner."

The next morning, Joseph left early. Left her alone to figure out her new life. She didn't understand how she got here. She was only eighteen, and she was alone, with child, and without her family. Joseph left her money. Enough to buy meals for a week and then shopping money if she wanted to buy something. Tabitha unpacked her things and looked for a place in the room where she could hide her own money. She'd brought her savings. Joseph knew nothing about it.

It was wise of her to keep her money hidden because her man had secrets. He was gone more than he was here. It wasn't long before Tabitha realized he was not going to marry her anytime soon. Whenever she brought it up, she was told the time wasn't right, to wait, and eventually to hush her mouth on the subject.

"I take care of you. You don't work or suffer to beg for bread, Peach."

And that was what Joseph said to her for three years, through two babies. There was no ring. No marriage. Tabitha did not meet his family. She lived in the tiny apartment, caring for her children and seeing him when it was convenient for him. She had not gone home. Preferring not to hear the sadness in their voices, she had only talked to Retha and Dot on the telephone a few times. She did not see Mama for years. She was ashamed, and she'd let that shame trap her.

Chapter 13

Present Day

Sabrina

When I told Grandma I ran into Quinton yesterday, that he wanted to have dinner, she volunteered to babysit Kenni. "He was always a nice young man. Nice family," she added. "I'll be home in time for you to make your date."

I fought the idea that it was an actual date by reminding myself that Quinton and I were old friends. We were catching up, but then I stood over my luggage, hating that all I had was one dress, a black one, and it was a rather dated thing that I considered all-purpose. How I wished I had something fresh in a summer yellow or pink.

Grandma liked to stay until Grandpa ate, but she insisted I be ready to walk out of the door when she walked in. At six fifteen Mariah arrived at the house. I heard her blaze a trail from the door to my bedroom like she was coming for some good gossip.

She stood in the door. "Where are you going?"

"Dinner with an old friend."

"Who happens to be in Georgetown?"

"Yes," I replied. I wanted to steer the conversation away from Quinton. "You know, I didn't ask you yesterday. How are we going to handle desserts?"

"We haven't talked about that yet."

"What about my cakes?"

"Tabby's has used that baker at Grandma's church," Mariah said, "for almost twenty years I think."

"Yes, sliced pound cake, chocolate, and key lime cake. That's boring."

"She's Grandma's friend."

"You said we were going to try new things, and if we're saving money—"

Mariah cut into my words. "I'm overthinking about the restaurant. I need to save some of my energy for your daughter. Grandma is running late. She asked me to get here so you could go."

I had one more protest on my lips, but as always, Mariah made her exit when she was done with what she had to say, and I felt even more insignificant than I did before she entered the room. It was her special talent—making me feel like nobody. I wondered if she knew she had that power, or was she so obtuse that she didn't realize how much she hurt me? I expected better from my sister, but this is who we'd been to each other practically our entire lives. I had no clue when it began because it was all I ever remembered. Me talking to her. Wanting something from her and then being covered in disappointment as if someone had tossed a bucket of rank water at me.

Shedding the emotions my sister drummed up, I traded them for new ones . . . anxious ones over seeing Quinton. I found Quinton sitting at the restaurant bar. I approached nervously and wished I hadn't put on makeup or this too-tight dress because I would be giving him the wrong impression. I had no idea if the man was married, if he had a girlfriend, or what. I was just some kid from years ago that he wanted to catch up with. People did that.

But his text was curious yesterday. Too soon? That sounded flirty.

I weaved my way to the bar and stopped at the stool behind him. "Hey," I said in the lightest, most carefree voice I had.

Quinton turned. He looked me up and down from head to toe twice, and then his lips split into a smile. "Hey, yourself."

"It's crowded in here."

"It just got crowded a few minutes ago. Seems like everybody rushed in at the same time."

"Well, I guess I should have been here a few minutes earlier, and we would have had a table easily."

"Don't worry. I expected you to be late."

My mouth dropped open. I was not late. "Is that a criticism?"

"No, you're right on time, but I did expect you to be late, you know, based on your history." He chuckled.

"What are you talking about, sir?"

He picked up his drink. "You were always late for Bible study."

"I don't remember that."

"You were late every week. I mean, it just became a part of your personality, which was adorable."

"I don't know if I like the sound of that."

"I lived in fear that you wouldn't show up and I'd have to do the whole thing," he said. "You caused me to have anxiety big-time." He raised his hand and flagged someone. "Let me get us a table."

A pretty blonde with a ponytail that hung down the center of her back was instantly at our service.

"We're ready to be seated," Quinton said.

The hostess smiled at me like she knew a secret and said, "Come this way."

We followed her to rear of the restaurant. Quinton turned to me and asked if I wanted to dine inside or on the patio.

"We're getting special treatment. I don't wanna be a choosy beggar," I replied.

"No worries. I already did the begging, so just let me know what you like."

Glad to have a choice, I said, "I'd like outside."

The hostess opened the door and led us out to the patio where there was one table available. It was a little warm and a lot humid, so I immediately regretted my choice. My hair was going to explode into an Angela Davis afro, but we were here now. I slipped into my chair.

Quinton already had a glass of sweet tea. The waitress dashed in as the hostess left us, filled our water goblets, and took my drink order before leaving us alone with our menus.

"The food is good. I eat here more times a week than I want to admit."

"No wonder you can get bumped to the front of the line," I said. "But multiple times a week at these prices? Don't you cook?" I reached for my water glass and took a sip to hide my embarrassment over talking about the prices like some country bumpkin who didn't get out. This was expensive but obviously not for Quinton.

He said, "I was spoiled growing up. My mother made all the meals, and when she didn't make them, my sisters did. I had meal plans in college."

"We're both a long way from college," I teased, putting my glass down.

"I know, but then after college I was in a relationship with a woman who made sure I was fed all the time." A hint of sadness washed over him. "I budget for dining out. And there are the occasional ramen noodles and scrambled eggs. I know how to fry bologna."

I laughed. "That is pitiful. And your mother did you a disservice, sir." I raised my index finger. "And I'm not talking about ya mama."

An easy smile slipped on his face. "You know mothers. They mostly get it right, but sometimes . . ." And then he froze on the last word.

"What were you gonna say?" I asked. I realized he'd read my face. When he said, "You know mothers," it occurred to him that I didn't have one.

"It's okay, Quinton. I wasn't raised by wolves. You know I had a stepmother for a long time—practically my whole upbringing."

"You're right. You did. I remember that, but it's been a long time. And I don't know how you feel about that. Relationships change."

Again, I thought that was sensitive of him. I liked that he anticipated my feelings and was careful of them. *This isn't a date,* I told myself. I'm not dating because I don't even know how anymore.

"What just went across your mind?" Quinton asked. "Something heavy. I saw it."

Now he was reading me. "It was nothing," I said. "Tell me about you being back in Georgetown. Are you here for family or the job?"

"I'm here for the job. I've been trying to get transferred from Columbia for the last three years. I wanted to be back in the low country—Charleston, Georgetown, Myrtle Beach . . . something down here. I don't like living inland, but it took a few years for a position to come up."

"Is it working out?" I asked, thinking of my own situation. I could stay here versus going back to Greenville.

"Absolutely. I've got a pretty good staff. My mother is getting older, so I like being closer."

"Your mother. What about your dad?"

"He passed four years ago."

I raised my hands to cover my mouth. "I'm so sorry."

"It's okay. There was no way for you to know that. He had a heart attack. It was hard losing him. Really hard on my mother because none of her children lived in town."

"I can only imagine," I said, but I could imagine a little. I'd lost Kendrick after loving him for four years. When people spent a lifetime together, it had to gut them. My parents skittered through my mind. My dad losing a wife after she delivered a baby. Me. I still saw sadness in his eyes.

Quinton was saying something. I gave him my attention.

"My parents were older when they had me. I was the last of the bunch and a surprise. My brother lives in south Florida, and my sister is in New Jersey. I'm the only one here in South Carolina, so I feel a little more responsible for Mom."

"I'm sure she's thrilled to have you here."

"I think she is." He emptied his glass before asking, "What about you? You said you were visiting your grandparents?"

"Like I told you, my grandfather had a stroke, and my grandmother needed some help from us—my sister and me—with the family's restaurant. You remember my grandparents own Tabby's."

"I'd eaten there a few times, but then it closed. I had no idea it was still in your family."

"Eighty-seven years."

"That's something," he said. "How's your grandfather?"

"In a rehab center working on regaining function. He's better. Thanks for asking."

"I'll pray for him." He bobbed his head to the seriousness of his words. "Is the restaurant still closed for renovations? I'm game to give you all some business."

I smiled at that. "It's still closed. My sister and I are here to get the place opened back up."

The server arrived with my sweet tea, and she put a basket of bread on the table between us.

"Are you ready to order?" she asked.

I realized we had jumped into talking so quickly I had not even looked at the menu. Quinton asked her for a few minutes, and we both opened the menus. He looked briefly, but I was sure he already knew what he wanted because he ate here multiple times a week. I picked out a pasta dish and a salad from right at the very top of the menu, which I didn't find particularly appetizing. Burgers and sandwiches and wings. Nothing really on the low-country order. What was the point of living down here and eating down here if there wasn't going to be some low-country cuisine?

Quinton waved the waitress over, and she came back and took our orders. I reached into the basket for a piece of bread.

Quinton joined me. He hadn't been particularly interested in it, but I guess he wasn't gonna let me make a little pig of myself.

"Do you have experience working in a restaurant?"

"No, but my sister does. She manages Clark's Diner in Hendley. Are you familiar with it?"

"Of course," he said, impressed. "That must be a nice spot for a restaurant manager."

"It's owned by her husband's family. When they first got married, the place was going out of business. Mariah turned it around. Turned it into what it is today." Admiration for Mariah pressed into my emotions. "She's good at what she does."

"I can see you're proud of her," Quinton said.

I was, but I also wished I was more like her . . . surer and more focused, more intentional, but I wasn't going to tell him about my insecurities. That was TMI. "If anyone can turn Tabby's around, it's my sister."

He smiled. "She won't be doing it alone. You have talents too. Tell me, what are you bringing to the table? Pun intended."

"Creativity and grit." I laughed. "Seriously, I'm just a gopher. Whatever she tells me to go for is what I do."

"Well, you must have some skills that your grandmother thought were valuable or she would have just called your sister to come."

"I don't know. My grandmother is always trying to get us together. Her dream in life is that we'll be closer."

"I remember you weren't close back in the day. She's a lot older than you, right?"

"You have a great memory," I said.

"For people who matter." His eyes and his words were definitely giving, *This is a date. I'm here to impress.*

I raised my glass and took a sip of tea before answering him. He'd sucked me into his vortex. "Six years," I said. "You're right about us not getting along. Nothing about that has changed—in fact, it's worse. I've prayed God would show me how to fix what's between us that's broken because I really don't know what it is, and I'd like it to be healed."

"I'll be praying with you," he said.

Warmth gushed through me. That was the second time he'd said he would pray. I liked a man who prayed. I'd seen Quinton do it in practice. He opened our Bible study with prayer. Even as a teenager, he was a powerhouse.

"So, if you're not in the restaurant business, what is it that you do?"

This is where it got complicated, I thought. He had a nice car, a budget for dining out, a staff. He was successful. I let those thoughts run around in my head for a few seconds before pushing them out. I did have a profession. It just wasn't successful yet or really established, but that was going to change. "I'm a baker. I make specialty cakes for parties and weddings and things like that."

"A cake designer?"

He'd called it correctly. I said baker, but I was a designer.

"Cool," he added. "Do you have any pictures of your work?"

I reached into my bag for my phone, swiped to the gallery, and held it up to show him a few of my most recent cakes.

"Wow," he said when he looked at the one I'd just done. "That's something. Did you go to culinary school?"

"No. I'm self-taught from YouTube, believe it or not."

"Are you serious?"

"Not to insult people who studied professionally, but yes, I'm serious." I giggled. "I didn't finish college. I did my first year and dropped out. I couldn't figure out exactly what I wanted to do, and I did *not* want to waste money."

"That makes sense," he said, and I could tell he meant it.

"When I dropped out, I started working in a bakery. I iced cookies and frosted simple cakes. They didn't do anything like what I do now. I've baked since I was a child, but I learned how things work at a commercial bakery on a large scale—how to use larger instruments. How to scale recipes, replace ingredients."

Quinton nodded. He was a good listener.

"And then I just started experimenting with different cakes for parties for people I knew. Eventually I started getting clients."

"That's cool. I like to hear when people get to follow their passion—figure it out organically."

"Well, following your passion has its ups and downs. Like I said, I'm in business, but things have been rough. It's not easy to get a cake business going when there's so much competition. And then people expect decorative cakes that are expensive to make, but they don't want to pay for them."

"I imagine they must be pricey with the amount of work you have to put in."

"Hours of time and expensive baking materials."

"But you're doing okay with it?" he asked.

I didn't think it wise to tell him how poorly I was doing with it on this maybe a date, catching up, dinner situation, so I shrugged through it. "Business is growing. I'm not sure if I'll keep at it though. I've got more bills some months than money."

The server arrived with our salads and placed them in front of us.

"I guess we should have said grace over the bread," Quinton teased. "We'll show the Lord appreciation now."

A tiny smile came to my lips. I closed my eyes. Quinton said a nice grace, thanking God for the food and the company. When he opened his eyes, he said, "It has been a desire of my heart to see you again, Sabrina. It really has."

And with those words, I realized I actually was on a date, the first one since Kendrick died. But I didn't feel date-type stress. Quinton and I'd always slipped into conversation easily. We talked for two hours straight—through appetizers, dinner, and dessert.

We exited the restaurant, walking and talking like we didn't want to let each other go.

"It was nice catching up with you."

"I agree. You know there's one question I didn't ask you though." He shoved his hands in his pants pocket. "I know things are uncertain, but do you have any idea how long you're going to be here?"

"I would say at least until my grandfather is out of rehab, which is a month or more. I'm not sure."

He nodded. "A month is enough time."

"Enough time for what?" I asked curiously.

"For whatever, you know." He smiled, and I was silly enough to believe I saw my future.

I laughed at myself. "You're being evasive."

"I'd like to get to know you better—better than I ever did when we were kids. Is my timing okay?"

I wanted to say yes. But what was I saying yes to? Escaping the house? A jaunt down memory lane where my life was simpler? Someone who didn't know me enough to judge me? "I don't know. I have a lot going on."

"What do you mean by that?"

"I don't want to talk about *what* that is tonight, and maybe I won't want to talk about it on a second date, but my life is complicated. I'm not seventeen anymore."

He took my hand, raised it to his lips, and said, "Neither am I, beautiful. And I don't want a seventeen-year-old."

I melted into a puddle right on the asphalt.

He looked at my hand. "I don't see a tan line on your finger or anything. You aren't married, are you?"

"I'm not," I replied.

"Engaged?" He shook his head. "Of course not. Any man who was engaged to you would put a massive rock on your finger."

"You flatter me, sir. The answer is no. I'm not engaged."

"Boyfriend?"

I shrugged. "No one."

"Okay, so it's not that complicated," he said. "What's complicated is me remembering you over the years and not knowing how to reach you."

I had that, too, but I wasn't ready to admit it.

He leaned over and kissed me on the cheek. "Thank you so much for having dinner with me. I'll text you about another date." Quinton looked off, stuck his hands in his pockets, took a deep breath, and let out a lot of confident energy. "Believe me, I'm motivated to help you uncomplicate your life." His eyes swept my body again. "I don't just pray. I work."

I laughed at his corny twist on the scripture. He laughed too.

"Thanks for a good time," I said. I stepped back. My head was swirling from his words. This guy knew all the right things to say. He couldn't help me uncomplicate anything, but it was nice that he wanted to. I'd been alone for years with every decision, every choice, every success, and every failure resting on me. That was lonely. So even the thought of someone sharing something with me caused a rush of emotion I couldn't describe with anything other than the tears that came to my eyes.

I hurried to the truck, got inside, and started it. As I pulled away, I waved goodbye to Quinton.

I drove down the street and pulled over. My eyes had filled with water. No one had listened to me since Kendrick—well, my dad, but he was so far away, and he was my father. He wanted to fix things, not listen to me figure them out.

I had an overwhelming desire to go home and read one of Great-Great-Grandma Tabitha's letters. Her story was resonating with me, and I needed to know what was next.

When I arrived home, the house was dark, except for the light in Mariah's room. I undressed and changed into pj's before walking to my sister's door. I wanted to knock. Like a teenager, I wanted to talk to her about my time with Quinton, but we were not teenagers, and we didn't talk like that. As I was leaving to walk away from her door, I heard a noise. I pressed my ear closer and realized it was crying. I raised a hand to knock and then thought better of it. Mariah would not want my help or my comfort. She didn't want to share her joy or pain with me.

I remembered my father's words to try harder, but it wasn't me. I wasn't the one fighting against the closeness. It was her, so I turned and went back to my bedroom.

Chapter 14

Mariah

It was Wednesday of the next week before Dante called again. I'd employed Google. I should have recognized him last week, but now that I knew who he was, I wasn't letting him get away from Tabby's.

"I'll stop by in few hours," he said. "I'd like to see the menu."

Tabby's did not have a website. I offered to email it to him, but he said he preferred to put his hands on it. I was glad he was looking forward to the work. We weren't opening soon, but I thought we might be able to find some catering jobs to bring in money.

Sabrina and I were making paint decisions when I let Dante in. He was carrying bags of groceries in one hand, rolling a cooler with the other. I introduced him to Sabrina. After she gushed over him being a South Carolina–famous chef, he walked to the table where we had all the design stuff laid out and asked, "What are you getting into over here?"

"Making decisions about our updated look for this part of the restaurant," I said, panning my hand around the space.

A loud saw ripped on, and Dante looked in the direction of it.

"Obviously our construction crew is working on the build for the new section," I added. "Did I tell you that was in the works?"

"You did," Dante said. "And there's that mysterious black tarp."

I picked up two pictures. One had dark walls and the other had light walls.

"I like the idea of going dark," Sabrina said, "and using a ton of lighting to bounce off glass and metal."

"Black just seems so permanent and hard to undo," I said.

Sabrina picked up another picture of the same room shot from a different angle. "I know it's drastic, but with the light blue and white trim and the right lighting, flowers, and accent décor, it'll be perfect."

I rotated it. "I do like this."

Dante sorted through the pictures and then returned his attention to the one in my hand. "She's right. That's fire."

"Okay. That's two votes to my uncertain one," I said. "We can start tomorrow."

Sabrina clapped her hands like an excited child. "I'll pick up the paint right after I drop off Kenni." Sabrina flipped her wrist and looked at her watch. Speaking of which, I need to go get her now."

"Ask Abel One about the number of cans we need."

"I already did. It was nice to meet you, Dante." Sabrina was out the door before he could reply.

"She's the creative one, and you're the business head."

"It takes creativity to run a business," I said, teasingly, "but the artsy stuff is her jam." I walked into the kitchen with Dante following.

I eyed his bags curiously. "What's all this?"

"A little surprise. Let's talk about the menu first. I want to see what you have in mind."

I grabbed my notebook and sat on a stool at the island with him. I showed him the current menu and then showed him a list of ten dishes I thought were good, cost-effective choices that we could rotate. "I was thinking about that langoustine pasta you posted on your Instagram last week."

Dante chuckled. "So she knows who I am now."

"Of course. Why didn't you just tell me? I was looking at you like you were a creep."

"Is that what that look was?" he asked, smirking.

My mind went back to the moment I'd blushed over his physique, and I blushed again. He was cooking up too much in here.

"Anyway . . ." I rolled my eyes. "You could have told me you were *Dante That Food Truck Chef*."

He smiled. "It sounds so corny when people say it, but it is catchy."

"You once came to Spartanburg. I was going to drive up to taste your food, but something happened—I don't recall what—and I couldn't make it."

"You see, last week you were looking at me like I was any old Stanley, and once upon a time you were trying to come see me."

I folded my hands over my chest. He wasn't wrong. "And I insisted you cook for me."

"Yeah, well, I'm still going to do that," he said. "Clark's Diner is a spot. You get mad respect for what you did with that place."

I was stunned that he knew who I was.

Dante's dimples stretched his cheeks. "You're not the only one who googles."

I cocked my head. "How many geniuses does it take to change a light bulb in a kitchen?"

Dante laughed, a hearty laugh full of his personality. "She has jokes too I see."

I walked closer and watched him unpack his ingredients. He reached into the small duffel bag he had with him and removed a case that held his knife collection. Chefs rarely worked without their special set.

I pulled an apron over my head and handed one to him. "What are we making?"

He walked over to me and placed a bundle of celery in my hand. "You can wait to find out, but I'd appreciate it if you would chop these as small as you can make them."

I washed the celery, reached for one of grandpa's knives, and walked to one of the cutting blocks. Dante did what all Gullah men do—start telling a story, a funny one about his restaurant. He had lots of stories to share. We found our rhythm working together. My job was to chop and fetch ingredients and his, commanding the pans over the fire. At one point, he tapped out a drumbeat on the bottom of a pan while singing an old Gullah spiritual. "So glad I'm here. So glad I'm here. So glad I'm here in my Jesus' name." I'd questioned his barely discernible Gullah accent, so he sang to prove his roots were deeply planted in Gullah culture, as he'd spent his summers on Sandy Island.

"I'm convinced," I said, laughing. "And you've got a nice voice."

"Thank you much. Oona got me makin' all this ruckus."

"You sound just like my grandfather."

He laughed and got back to his cooking. Dante's dark skin glistened with a light coat of perspiration as he moved around the kitchen with purpose and skill. He sliced meat and shellfish with delicate precision, and his long, nimble fingers worked quickly. His eyes scanned the unfamiliar kitchen for last-minute additions to the dish. A smile fueled by joy simmered just below the surface. His artistry was no different from that of a painter.

He battered and fried catfish nuggets and made red rice with sausage. Finally, he started a she-crab chowder, and I knew he was showing off. Crab chowder was my favorite thing. I watched as he added the butter and flour for the roux and then expertly added the cream and milk and broth and other ingredients. The kitchen had been smelling good for hours, but once he added the crab roe and crab meat, it produced a heavenly fragrance.

"You can turn on the oven now," he said, taking his dirty pots and pans to the sink. "Just enough to warm the bread."

I reached under the sink for the detergent and sprayed everything.

"So, how long are you going to be in this area?" he asked.

"My plans are kind of open. Certainly long enough to get things under control," I said, being vague.

"You have someone else to manage the restaurant up there?"

I cleared my throat. "It's fully staffed and able to run without me for a while."

"It's like a family-run spot right? Husband-and-wife team, if I'm remembering correctly."

I didn't respond to that. It was a statement more than a question, and he was right and knew it. He moved on quickly to his next question.

"So why you say your name is Holland?" A little Gullah had slipped back into his diction. Maybe that happened when he was not talking business.

I cocked an eyebrow at him. "Nosy much?"

His lips slipped into a broad smile. "Yeah, I actually am nosy, and your grandmother had already told me your name was Mariah Clark. How do you think I googled you?"

I reached for a sponge and turned on the water. "I feel like a Holland when I'm here."

His eyes showed he read my BS meter, but he didn't question me more. He returned to the stove, and I washed what was dirty.

With the bread out of the oven, Dante placed two serving sets next to each other. I sat while he plated the food. He reached into his bag, pulling out a strip of fabric.

Recognizing what it was, I said, "A blindfold?"

"I have some food that goes along with our dinner. I want you to try it and tell me what you taste." I quirked a questioning eyebrow, and he added, "The blindfold will help you focus more on the flavor and smell instead of what you see."

I let him tie the fabric around my eyes, found my stool, and pushed back onto it. "I don't often give permission for strangers to do this."

"That's probably a good thing," he mumbled.

I could hear him digging around in his cooler. I could also hear the opening and closing of containers and the sound of food being added to plates. Finally, I felt Dante moving toward me.

"I'm going to give you a spoonful of each thing. Let's see how sharp your palette is."

I was excited about this. I'd never tasted food with a blindfold on.

The first dish was creamy with tiny pieces of shrimp, bacon, and cheese in a savory gravy served on grits. "So good," I said. "That's shrimp and grits."

"Okay, easy one," Dante said. He put a glass in my hands. "Clear your palate."

I did as I was told and prepared for the next thing, which was the catfish nuggets, but there was something sweet on top of them. "Chopped pieces of fruit, onion, cilantro. I taste pineapple and mango. There's a little bit of lime." I thought on it for a moment before saying, "It's a salsa." I couldn't see him, but I raised my hand for a high-five. He slapped it. "That's delicious."

The last thing was fried, sweet, and easily recognizable as a fried green tomato. It was dipped in a creamy, citrusy, peppery sauce. "Geechee dip for the tomatoes. That is so good."

I removed the blindfold. Dante was pouring a small amount of sherry into the she-crab. He stirred it, then sliced some of the bread and served the chowder in a bowl next to it.

My mouth exploded with all the rich flavors of the chowder. This guy was talented, and I was stuffed. "This is the best food I've had in my life."

"And to think, I had to blindfold you to get the job."

I smirked. "You did not. I had already hired you in my head."

Dante sat down to eat. He was pleased with himself. "I know I am. Ya been salivating in here."

I snatched my head back. "Chefs. You guys are so cocky."

He tossed up his hands and smiled. "When you know who you are, no way can you show up different."

He had the right attitude. I'm sure it served him well throughout his career. "Tell me again why you're not working somewhere already."

"It's complicated, but let's just say I had a restaurant in Florida. My investors turned out to be shady, we lost the building, and I decided I didn't want to start over down there, so I'm in between spots."

"Are you planning to open another restaurant?"

"Once I find the right location, but I'm not in a rush."

"In Georgetown?"

"Not as long as Tabby's is open. People follow chefs. I wouldn't open something in this county, but I might operate my food truck in Charleston until I find the right spot."

He took some of the empty dishes to the sink. "What's your favorite Gullah dish to make?"

"I don't cook Gullah."

"A what you say, gurl? That doesn't make sense. Why?"

"It's a long story."

Dante folded his arms over his chest. "Shorten it up." He was determined to know.

I sighed and gave him the short version. "I had a chance to go to a cooking program once, and it fell through. Then I got married and started building Clark's. My husband needed me to focus on the business side."

Dante nodded, but he wasn't done with the topic. "Why didn't you learn from your grandparents?"

"I wasn't interested when I was a kid. I was too busy playing, and then once I became a teenager, whenever I came down here, I worked at a bookstore. They hired me every summer, so I just never got in the kitchen," I said frankly. "Is your curiosity satisfied?"

Dante had many smiles; the one that covered his face was playful. "Not nearly." He folded his arms over his chest. "You may not cook Gullah, but I noticed you have skills in the kitchen."

"I mostly cook soups and stews. They're popular in the Upstate because of the mountains."

"A pot girl. All right now. I like that." He did look impressed. "Most Gullah food is one pot, so you're Gullah in spirit and by blood. You just need teachin'."

"It's intimidating, especially after watching you today."

"You don't strike me as someone who is easily spooked."

I shrugged. "I cover well."

Dante nodded. "I can teach you some things."

I joined him at the sink. "I get to get your fancy education for free."

"I told you. I learned how to cook before I went to college. *That* I got for free too." He smiled, and my tension eased. "We need to preserve the culture. One more person knowing how to cook Gullah is one more archivist of our food ways."

His eyes were serious. I'd read up on him on a few blogs and watched some media interviews. He was intent on keeping the Gullah alive through food. I liked that. A lot.

"That's righteous," I said, and the admiration was real. "I can't wait for us to start serving the community again."

"I have an idea, something that will get you back in business faster than that paint can dry." Dante flashed me that million-dollar white smile. "I still have my food truck, Ms. Holland."

I laughed, surprising myself. He had no idea how close I was to becoming Ms. Holland again, but I didn't let the thought of it steal a second of my excitement about the truck. I raised a glass to him and said, "Now that, sir, is a good idea."

Chapter 15

September 1917

Tabitha

Joseph moved Tabitha to an apartment on the first floor of the building. It was still small, but being on the first floor made it easier for her to manage the children as she entered and exited the building. All the tenants were women. Some of them received their male guests in the sitting room at the entrance. They would play cards or listen to music on weekends. Tabitha tried to make friends, but they were unfriendly. In fact, she felt a coldness from most of them.

Some nights Tabitha would stand in the hall and listen to the conversations being held in the sitting room. There were hushed tones that ended in giggles and conversations that were on occasion about her—or at least she assumed they were about her. Tabitha was the only *she* in the building with a stroller and the only *she* who did not work. Those were words she heard them use.

One afternoon as Tabitha pulled the stroller in the door, one of the women jumped up from the sofa and held it open.

"Thank you so much," Tabitha replied, grateful for her kindness but even more grateful to be seen. "It's not easy to manage the weight . . ."

The woman's eyes stopped Tabitha's conversation cold. She dropped her eyes to Margaret and Amos and then raised them to Tabitha's. "You gon' have ten children by him if you don't help yourself. There are teas to stop babies from coming. You best get some. Miss Libby . . . upstairs . . . she knows the old ways. She can help you."

Tabitha was so shocked, she did not reply. The woman walked back to the sofa, picked up a magazine, and trotted up the stairs, leaving Tabitha standing there for many minutes to recover. She placed her hand on her bulging belly. It had occurred to her that the babies were coming quickly, yet the marriage had not. She feared the marriage never would, and she needed to hear the truth about why. Joseph owed her at least that, so when he came again, she asked him.

"I can't marry you. It's not that I don't want to. I can't."

As they were often these days, her hands were on her round belly. She rubbed, fighting to find space in her brain for the words Joseph had just uttered. For a fleeting second, she thought she had not heard him correctly. But there was nothing wrong with her hearing. That sentence, this moment, would forever be seared on her memory, even if she delayed processing it.

Joseph's lips moved again. "I've been married for ten years."

Tabitha looked across the room at the small dining table. The birthday cake she'd made for Joseph became the focus of her attention. She'd prepared a special dinner. Margaret was looking forward to singing to her father before eating that cake. Because he didn't arrive in time for dinner, Tabitha had to cut it without him and put the children to bed without their song.

She pulled her eyes from the table and looked at Joseph again. With only the light from one lamp on the table, the room was dim. A shadow from the moonlight divided Joseph's face with a diagonal line. Most of him was cast in darkness.

Married ten years.

Tabitha didn't know how she was supposed to respond to such evil words. This man had intentionally pursued her. He'd run her down, took her from her family, and made three babies with her when he already had a wife. She had a sudden revelation of a piece of the Bible. *The devil is a roaring lion, walking around, seeking whom he may devour.* Joseph was the devil.

Her fingers rolled into her palms until they made fists. Tabitha banged against her thighs on both sides. "No, no, no." She lunged at him and pummeled both fists on his chest with one hitting his chin. Joseph clasped her arms.

"Gal, now you get off me!" He pushed her onto the sofa.

She sat there, fists locked. Heat and pain mixed together in her blood and moved through her like fire. "Why would you do this?"

"Because I wanted you."

She didn't know how to process those words. Was that the only answer the devil had for her today? "You wanted me so you could make me into your whore. You promised me marriage."

"I know."

"You lied to me."

"I know that, Peach, and I'm sorry."

Peach. Tabitha felt disoriented and confused. He still thought it was okay to call her that.

"I'm sorry I put you in this situation."

No one was sorrier than Tabitha because she knew there was a reason he wouldn't marry her. She'd told him about the snickering in the hallway by other tenants. He assured her the other women were jealous. Tabitha had told Retha about it.

"What do they have to be jealous about?" Retha asked.

Retha's tone carried the tenor of worry more than curiosity. Tabitha didn't have to hear her sister's thoughts. Tabitha was a kept woman, and keepin' was never for a good reason. Though their conversations were on the telephone and by letter, the distance did not lessen the impact of her sister's questions. When Retha wasn't being subtle, she was being frank.

"Bitta, if he hasn't married you by now, he probably never will."

But Tabitha denied that lie. Rather than look more deeply at Joseph, she believed lies about herself. She wasn't pretty enough or light enough or worthy of being his wife. She believed he might be comparing her to his first wife . . . that he'd simply changed his mind about marriage but cared about his children too much to abandon them. She refused to accept anything but this. And now her silly thinking had trapped her here with the children like a rat who was being fed enough cheese to keep her beholden to him. She had no power, not even any to deny him her bed, which she wanted to do on many nights because the love and hunger she'd once felt for him she didn't feel as strongly.

"I left my family for you."

"I didn't have to beg you. You came willingly."

"Well, I can't go back with three children and no man!" Tabitha's words sounded so much louder than she intended, but the rage that had been building inside of her amplified her voice. She raised her hands to cover her lips. A sound escaped her throat, one she didn't even recognize. It was uglier than the grunt she made when she delivered all three of her babies, and it ended with sobbing. "Why would you do this?"

"I love you."

He'd carved a hole in her heart and called that love. He was a Judas.

"I know you don't believe me right now, but I do know how I feel. When there's something natural between a man and woman that can't be denied, you can't ignore it."

"The only thing between us is sin, Joseph."

The bedroom door opened. Wiping sleep from her eyes, Margaret padded into the dark room. When she met her father's leg, Joseph hoisted her to his hip. "What you are doing up, Maggie baby?"

"I want Mama," she cried, extending a hand in Tabitha's direction. Tabitha was too injured to respond to her daughter. Her tongue was stuck in the top of her mouth.

"Mama and I are talking. You have to go to bed . . ." Joseph's voice trailed off as he walked her back into the bedroom. He was gone for a few minutes before returning without her.

Joseph was a good father. Good enough . . . when he was here. But he was not a good man. Not at all. No matter how much she wanted to blame him for this mess, it wasn't all his fault. She'd waited four years—through excuses from everything like work interfering to money to trying to prepare his preacher daddy to accept that he had children before marriage. Excuses, all of them. This was why Mama wanted her to wait for Papa to see him. To do what fathers do for their daughters. Even if Tabitha was not Papa's daughter, Charles Cooper would have known who this man was and was not. Looking back now, she realized she should have trusted Mama. She should have trusted family. Family would have recognized the devil she couldn't. But now it was too late to depend on family.

Mama traveled to Charleston once when Papa was away. That visit was the only time she and the children saw Mama. Joseph would never take her to Georgetown, his excuse being that he'd sold his business interest in the mill. Tabitha held on to Mama so tightly, she didn't want to let her go.

She was tempted to get in the wagon with her and go back to Georgetown. Mama said, "You can come home," but Tabitha could tell by the strained way that Mama extended the invitation that Papa's house would not be home. Mama had a tell—tightness in her neck and clutched hands. She avoided looking Tabitha in the eye. Those were signs that Mama'd already fought with Papa and had not won. Mama never really won. She was one of those women who submitted under the strong thumb of a man.

Joseph's voice broke through her thoughts. Disappointment had so engulfed her that she'd forgotten he was there. "I need to tell you more of what's going on."

"Iffen you not about to tell me you're going to divorce your wife and marry me, I don't want to hear what you have to say."

"I can't say that, though I wish I could because she's . . ." Joseph hesitated. "She's unwell. I've been waiting for her to get better, but she's not better; she's worse."

"What kind of unwell?"

"She has fits and other things."

Fits. Tabitha had seen those before. Old Mrs. Rice down the road a piece from back home had fits and had to go to Bull Street in Columbia. Tabitha couldn't imagine Joseph's wife would be there. It was for the poor Negroes. "Where is she?"

"In a place for people like her. It's in Atlanta. Near her family."

Tabitha shook her head. This didn't change anything.

He added, "You can't divorce someone in a mental sanitarium."

A sick wife. So this was the truth that stole her happiness? The shame Tabitha felt did not decrease.

"I would prefer it if you didn't stay here tonight," Tabitha said. "If you do, I don't want to share a bed."

"You can't stay angry with me forever, Peach. I know this is not the way you wanted things, nor did I for that matter, but we are a family."

A family. She wasn't sure she agreed. "You should allow me time with my hurt. I never expected this."

Joseph nodded. He leaned into her, and though she turned her head, he kissed Tabitha's cheek. "I'll give you time." He placed his hat on his head, and after a final plea with his eyes, one that lacked lasting contrition, he left her.

Tabitha walked to the window. She watched him climb into his carriage. He had not dismissed his driver. He had no intention of staying or suspected he would not. She dragged herself away from the window. Standing at the table, she looked down at the cake. Her plans were spoiled, and not just dinner. Her plans for her life were ruined, and that hadn't happened just tonight. It happened the day she gave herself to him.

Tabitha placed her hands on her belly. "God, what have I done?" she asked, and then a more important question crept into her mind. *What am I going to do?*

Now that she knew he was married, sick wife or not, she didn't want to continue things the way they were. But Tabitha didn't have a choice. She had no skills, no one to help with her children, and way too much pride to go home and deal with Papa's bitter disdain. She was dependent on Joseph, but they were damaged forever like the broken leg of a horse. There was no way to fix their relationship and make them whole again.

Tabitha grunted. Joseph thought he was giving her time to get over it. She would never. She'd hate him always.

Tabitha baked a butter pound cake, and after putting the children down for a nap, she cut it in half, wrapped it, and made her way up the stairs with the words from her neighbor in her thoughts.

You gon' have ten children by him if you don't help yourself.

Her baby would be born any day now, and she needed to be prepared not to have another. She knocked, and the door opened. Tabitha had seen the older woman a few times. She was the newest tenant in the building and mostly stayed to herself. She kept children while their mothers worked.

She smiled and asked, "What can I do fa ye?"

Tabitha smiled back at her. "I'm Tabitha. I live in one of the apartments downstairs."

"I know who you be, sweetheart. I'm Miss Libby. You need me to look after your youngins?"

"I may, but first I thought we could get to know each other." Tabitha extended the cake to her. "We're neighbors."

Miss Libby looked at it and took it from Tabitha's hands; then she invited her in.

Tabitha counted three babies and a set of twin girls who looked about four years old.

"You have a full house," Tabitha said, sitting in the kitchen chair Miss Libby offered her.

"Can I make you a coffee?" Miss Libby asked.

Tabitha smiled. She realized this was the first bit of hospitality anyone had offered her in the years she'd lived in the building. Heat pricked the back of her eyes from the emotion of it. She shook her head. "My children are napping. I don't have time, but I made the cake and thought of you."

"That's kind," Miss Libby said. She got a knife from the counter, unwrapped the cake, and cut a piece. "I love a yallah cake." Tasting it was a joy for the woman and one for Tabitha to watch. She praised it far too much. "I ain't one to bake." She cocked her head toward Tabitha's belly. "When de babe be bawn?"

Tabitha was carrying so large, she wished it was now. "Soon. Maybe a month."

"Oona here fa tea?" Miss Libby asked. "Me na when I see oona in de door. I'll make it."

Relief washed through Tabitha. She was glad she didn't have to explain herself. "Thank you." She put her hands on her belly and rubbed, hoping her unborn child didn't think she wished she had the tea before. "I'll need some help with my children after the baby."

"I da ya," Miss Libby said.

Tabitha didn't know what it meant.

"I be here," Miss Libby said, "to help with the children." She smiled and took another bite of cake. "Oona come back tonight with the chillun'. Ima make dinner, and we can get to know each other."

"I'd like that." Tabitha stood. She turned to leave the small kitchen, and Miss Libby followed her to the door and pulled it open.

"Tabitha, him ansa for what he do," Miss Libby said. "Sooner not lader."

A chill slipped down Tabitha's spine. There was no malice in this women's tone, but it carried a surety that made Tabitha think Miss Libby had been born with a veil.

At 6:00 p.m. an excited Margaret knocked on Miss Libby's door. When it opened, Miss Libby smiled wide as if they were her family. She took Amos from Tabitha's arms and welcomed them inside. She still had one baby and the twins. Margaret made quick friends with the girls while Amos, new to walking, held on to Tabitha's skirt.

Miss Libby's meal was an oyster and okra stew and yams. They sat down to dinner, squeezing the other two girls in at the small table. Miss Libby was very good with the children, gentle, but also firm on table manners. Tabitha noticed something different about her. She waited until they were done and the children were in the front room to ask.

"You didn't speak your native tongue during the meal."

Miss Libby wagged a finger at Tabitha, seemingly pleased that she observed it. "Mamas don't want me to teach their youngin' Gullah. I speak as properly as I can in front of the children so they don't pick up my way of talkin'."

Tabitha nodded, further impressed with her ability to move in and out of it so well.

Miss Libby reached into the cupboard for a large, corked jar of dried herbs. "When your blood comes back, you drink dis, b'fo' day. It don' fail none."

Tabitha accepted the jar and looked at the colors of the different herbs. "Thank you," she said, and her heart burst with gratitude. She had something that she could use to take back some of her own space in the world.

"We women have to help each other. There ain't no way to make it alone in these times."

With the jar clutched under her armpit, Tabitha stepped toward Miss Libby and gave her a side hug.

Tabitha returned to her apartment and put the children to bed. Once she was alone, she picked up the jar of tea and examined it, hoping it held the answer to her prayer not to give Joseph McCoy another child. She was glad for her new friend. Community was what she was missing, especially since she didn't have the closeness of her family. But the words Miss Libby said about Joseph came back to her.

"Him ansa for what he do. Sooner not lader."

Her baby kicked—hard. Tabitha put down the jar and rubbed her belly, letting the feel of little feet push into her palm. He would be the last, and then with Miss Libby's help, maybe Tabitha could figure out a life that wasn't meted out to her by Joseph McCoy.

Chapter 16

Present Day

Sabrina

Mariah came home with all kinds of good food that Dante cooked. But more important than that, she was thrilled to share good news.

"He's going to let us use his food truck. We can set up outside on Fridays and Saturdays for a few weeks, but before that, he suggested we set up at the county fair next week and at the food truck festival and the Georgetown Fair. He has a huge following—or at least he did before he disappeared and went to Florida for a few years, but no matter. People will remember him. He'll cook and share the details about our grand reopening. He said we should collect names for our email list—give something free to people who follow us on our social media page. He's brilliant."

"Wow. You're excited about working with him."

"I am. Grandma knew what she was doing when she asked him to help us."

"She's not on social media. She may not know how popular he is."
Mariah's eye roll dismissed me for being silly. "Sabrina, the
man has been on all the TV networks and in *Essence* and *Black
Chef* magazines. Those are the two I know for sure because I
subscribe. He's from John's Island. Believe me, she knows, and
Grandpa Odell's old community is proud of him. You know how
the Gullah are."

The Gullah weren't the only ones impressed with him. I would
say my sister was pretty impressed too. I rarely saw her smile, and
she hadn't stopped since sharing the news. I fixed plates for Kenni
and me and then put the rest of the food away for Grandma.

Mariah disappeared upstairs but came back down while I was
washing our dishes.

"I'm going to do some baking," I said. "Kenni, you want to
help Mommy?"

"I want to watch *Doc McStuffins* first," she said. That was one of
her rituals, so I went into the living room and turned on Nick Jr.
I couldn't find her show, but she became interested in something
else.

When I returned to the kitchen, Mariah was making a cup of
tea. I located Grandma's baking pans and got my mason jars and
the box of cake ingredients I'd put in the pantry. I took everything
out of the box and turned on the oven. "It's going to get hot in
here," I said.

Mariah frowned. "What are you doing?"

I propped my hand on my hip. "Baking. I plan to sell cakes."

Mariah rolled her eyes. "Sell them to who?"

"I don't know yet, but I have to generate some income. I'm
not like you. You have a business and direct deposits hitting
no matter what," I said. "Speaking of which, how's Vince? You
haven't mentioned him at all since we got here."

Mariah continued to stir her tea. "Maybe we can figure out
how to pay you a small salary, so you don't need to do this."

"We're supposed to be saving money."

"We are saving money. We're not hiring painters or people to do interior design work."

"I don't mind baking, Mariah. It's what I do."

Mariah raised her cup and took a sip from her mug. "It's May. Am I going to have to put up with a hot kitchen every night?"

"Who said I was baking every night?"

"You're going to have to bake a ton to make some money," Mariah said more bothered than interested. "And then how are you going to sell them? You can't drive from place to place in your house van looking for customers."

Her mood had changed substantially. What did my van have to do with this? "I'll do whatever it takes."

Mariah pushed off the counter. "I said we could give you a salary. The idea of you selling sweet cakes is ridiculous."

She walked out of the kitchen. I followed. Grabbing her arm, I said, "Look, I know your life isn't perfect, but why are you acting like this?"

Mariah pulled her arm from mine. "What do you mean by that?"

"I heard you crying last night. What's wrong? What's going on with Vince?"

"So now you're snooping?"

"I couldn't help but overhear."

"You know what your problem is? You've never understood boundaries. You were born in the way." She marched up the stairs.

Mariah was gone, but that blow to my chest was still present.

Born in the way?

My eyes stung from upset. I had no idea what had just happened. We had an entire day of getting along and her not being nasty, but of course the sun couldn't go down without her making me feel bad. She was so mean. I was convinced she didn't think I deserved to live.

Forget her. I pressed the hurt out of my mind. I was going to give this business a go. Her not believing in me was her problem. It had nothing to do with me. I went back into the kitchen.

The next day, I took four jar cakes and put them in a cooler on ice, loaded Kenni in Grandpa's truck with some of her favorite toys, and drove to the daycare. Today was one of the first days that I was going to be useful at the restaurant.

I drove to the paint store with the color card we'd chosen last night and purchased five cans of paint and five cans of primer as per Abel One's suggestion. Then I drove to the restaurant.

Mariah had gone to the rehab center to see Grandpa, but she would come by to help when she was done visiting. Abel One was working with a few men on the build. They took the paint cans off the truck. I rolled the cooler into the kitchen and emptied my cake jars into the refrigerator. The refrigerator here was much larger than the extra fridge at Grandma's house.

I was putting the last jar in as Dante entered the kitchen. We greeted each other, and he pulled the refrigerator door open. "What are these?"

"I make cakes," I said, holding one up for him to inspect.

He took it from my hand and read the little tag I'd handwritten for each jar. It was a note that told the buyer this was my mother's recipe. It was made with love. On the back it instructed the buyer to refrigerate. "Sweet Cake. All right, but aren't all cakes sweet?"

"Most, but it's not named sweet because of the taste. Sweet was my mother's nickname when she was growing up. The cakes are her recipe, and the jars were her thing too."

Dante nodded understanding. "Great packaging. It's cool it's in a reusable container. People like that."

"The inside is pretty good too."

His brows crinkled with his smile. "I like confidence. Let me try one."

He walked to the area where the utensils were stored and got a spoon. He twisted the lid off and tasted, one spoonful, then another and another, moaning each time he pulled the spoon out of his mouth. I could see he highly approved. "This is all right." He nodded. "Yeah, that's a good cake. How many different kinds you got here?"

"Three right now, but I make like seven different flavors."

Dante nodded. "How are you going to sell them?"

"I figured I'd go to farmers markets and mom-and-pop spots."

He nodded again. "That's good. You need to make sure to use social media heavily. This is the kind of product that posts well."

"I will try to get my social media game up and do the #caketok and #cakestagram thing."

Dante gave me a thumbs-up. "So you're going to sell them on the food truck?"

I scratched my head. I hadn't talked to Mariah about it yet. "I'm not sure."

"You should. Your sister is trying to go with the easy option, some baker your grandparents have used for years, but I think having something new and different would be cool."

"You think?"

"I know." He picked up the jar he'd been eating out of, put another scoop in his mouth, and said, "This is good. How much do you sell them for?"

I looked at my jars as if I was expecting them to tell me what they were worth. "I guess these would be six dollars, but I make a smaller one that I could price at four dollars."

"Well, I think you could go seven or even eight, but you know, price where you feel comfortable." He paused. "Bring a combination of the big ones and little ones and see how it shakes out. Have a little sample for folks. Once they taste it, they'll buy. People are not going to deny their sweet tooth."

Dante took one more mouthful, closed his jar, and put it on the bottom shelf. He reached into his pocket, removed his wallet, and handed me a ten-dollar bill. "For you, Madam Baker."

I shook my head. "You don't have to pay me for a cake, not after all that good advice."

He took my hand, pulled it open, and put the money inside. "Yes, I do, and keep the change." He walked out of the kitchen and into the restaurant.

I placed my cooler on the side of the fridge and pushed my ten in my pocket. My first Georgetown sale felt good.

Chapter 17

Mariah

I entered my grandfather's room at the rehab center. Grandpa's broad, gapped smile sparked joy in my soul. He looked so much better than he had a few days ago.

"Grandpa," I sang his name as I walked to his bed.

A rumbling laugh rolled out of his throat. "Mariah, my favorite granddaughter."

I leaned in for a hug, and Grandpa gave me one with all the strength he had. "You say that to all your granddaughters," I said, sitting.

"Oona de only ones of dem I see. So you and Beanie be me favorites."

Beanie was his nickname for Sabrina. He didn't have one for me, but I didn't mind. I liked my name as it was. My mother named me after her favorite singer, so that was special to me too.

"You look good, Grandpa."

"I'm ready to get out of here. I think your grandmother is tired of me. She won't tell those folks to let me go."

I chuckled. "You need to behave, sir."

"I want to see what you're doing to the restaurant. Your grandmother told me you won't let her see."

"We want to surprise her—both of you. Besides, you know how Grandma is. She'll pick through everything, not knowing that sometimes things don't look the way you want them to look until it's all pulled together."

He grunted. "Well, I trust ya not to turn it into something too trendy."

"It will continue to have elements of classic Gullah style and culture." I stood and walked across the room, stopping at the windows and observing his view of a small grassy patio area.

"I'm sorry I haven't been by much. I've been trying to get some things in place. It's been a lot of work getting your books together." I wasn't being honest. The truth was I hated to see my grandfather in this weakened state. The thought that I could lose someone else was terrifying. It gripped me and kept me away from hospitals. Watching Vince's mother in her last days was difficult, and we weren't even that close. Seeing my grandfather in a weakened state was hard.

Grandpa had always worn his mortality as tightly as he wore his own skin. He was one of those people who stayed busy. It was ridiculous to think he'd live forever, but his father lived to be ninety-seven, so Grandpa should have another twenty-six years in him.

"I'm more cook than manager."

I folded my arms over my chest. "And definitely not an accountant. Back taxes are the number one thing that takes small family businesses out." If he had been well, I would seriously expect him to explain how they'd skipped paying taxes for two years.

Grandpa coughed, but it was more embarrassment than anything. He said, "Your grandmother and me . . . we have some money put up fa de tax. We can pay . . . I mean me no know what we owe, but oona can tell me, and we can see wa we can do."

I walked to the edge of his bed. Resting my hands on the metal footboard, I said, "Let's wait. I expect to get a lump sum from my divorce."

"That's oona money for the future," Grandpa said. I heard the pride in his voice. He didn't want to take money from me. "How you be with the Vince situation?"

"Waiting. In this state you have to be separated for a year before you can get a divorce. We have seven more months to go."

"All of who yo da is not who ya be with Vince."

I nodded but struggled with the idea that my marriage didn't define me. My career had been tied up in Clark's from the beginning, but I didn't argue with him. "Yes, sir."

"I teach oona young. Change is like cookin'. Te way te meat look from te start is not te way it look in te middle or at te finish. Heat fix it, you know."

I walked over and gave him another hug. "What if I burn, Grandpa?"

"Oona na burn. Oona know to move from te flame."

A knock sounded on the door. I walked to it and pulled it open. One of the medical staff sailed in. "I'm here to take you to therapy, Mr. Holland." He greeted me and reached into Grandpa's closet for a robe.

I kissed Grandpa on the forehead. "I'll see you later," I said.

He took my hand and put it to his lips. "Go be me best gal."

I blew him a kiss and left the room.

Dante called in a favor with a friend to get a last-minute slot for his truck at the annual Georgetown County Fair food court. My initial excitement about it turned to regret because it was so last minute. I hadn't had time to process the fact that we were doing a soft launch.

I woke with anxiety churning in my gut. I didn't do anything at the last minute. What if today was a bust? Hours later when Dante's food truck arrived on the grounds, I was still asking that question.

Dante's truck was a kaleidoscope of vibrant colors with graphic designs and murals painted on its sides. The artwork was bold and intricate, with cheerful decals and humorous bumper stickers on the back. The graffiti-style lettering was eye-catching, and the whole truck was alive with energy that matched Dante's. In no time, he had the truck set up.

The buzz of the engine, the condensation coming off the compressor, water dripping underneath, and steam from the vent were all welcome on this Saturday. The banners we'd expedited at the printer hung on the front and sides and read: TABBY'S MEATS & SWEETS FEATURING CHEF DANTE.

Music played from the food truck's speakers, intermingling with the rhythm of Dante's movements as he manned a stove, a grill, and a fryer. Outside, the sound of the other food trucks created a melody of people chatting above their own music. Sizzling noises came from all the kitchens.

My fears were alleviated early because the weather was beautiful. Customers queued up everywhere to order food, while the cooks and their helpers busily prepared the dishes. The traffic was great. By noon we had a line. A local TV news reporter stopped to interview Dante right in front of our banners, giving Tabby's publicity.

I reached into the cooler and pulled out more plastic-wrapped cake slices to put on the tray in the window.

Dante looked over his shoulder at me and asked, "Where's Sabrina?"

We'd been there since nine thirty, opening to serve at eleven, and my sister had not appeared. "She texted me this morning and told me she had something to do."

Dante frowned. "For real?"

"Sabrina changes her mind." I opened my phone and read a second text she'd sent a few hours ago. Call me if it gets busy and you need me. I'm not far.

Dante's frown deepened. "She was excited to sell her jar cakes."

"Well, that wasn't happening." I reached into one of the coolers and removed slices of the cakes for our dessert display. "I told her we had a cake vendor."

Dante turned all the way around, giving me his full attention. "A cake vendor? Why would you get your desserts from someone else when she bakes?"

"My grandparents have been using this baker for years."

"But this," he said, pointing his spatula at the tray of slices I was organizing, "is boring. Half the trucks out here have cake like this."

"And they go with the food just fine."

He hiked an eyebrow. "Not with my food." Then he grunted. "Always go for the different and unique, Mariah. You know that."

"I'll figure out something unique for next time. You don't know Sabrina. I can't count on her."

"I had a feeling your relationship was complicated, but sometimes people need a purpose to make them move. She'd be here if she could sell the cakes."

"Well, isn't that just about her and what she wants? This is our first paid event, and she's not helping."

"I don't need her help, and apparently you don't either." Dante's phone rang, and he tapped the button and took his call through the Bluetooth headset he wore around his neck.

More customers walked up, and I took their orders, but his words and his disappointment hung between us for longer than I would have liked.

I hadn't known Dante long, but I cared about his opinion. He was the opposite of my husband's family. They made me fight through every suggestion, and for every change I made at Clark's. Even after I'd long proven that my ideas worked, they continued to protest. Dante wasn't like that. Sure, he wasn't in charge, but I could tell he respected my knowledge and experience.

My phone pinged an alert. I kept it under the counter. I looked down at it. I could see the notification from the online Hendley newspaper with the intro to a story. The title: HENDLEY'S OWN VINCE TAYLOR HOSTS...

I removed my glove and tapped it open to read the rest of the title . . . COOKING SHOW ON ABC UPSTATE DAILY TV. I read the article, skimming it at first, but then reread it to absorb the reality. Vince had stolen my show.

My heart dropped into my stomach, low. Pain lingered there while I recovered from the blow. I looked out. Everyone waiting around the truck had already had their orders taken.

"I'll be outside for a minute." I exited the truck and walked around back where neither he nor our customers could see me.

They were continuing the show without me. How? Vince wasn't a cook. I was doing a show about soups and stews.

I didn't realize I was crying until a woman stopped in front of me and handed me a wad of tissue.

"Are you okay, honey?"

She had sweet, kind eyes. Kind of like Grandma's.

I wiped my face. "I will be."

She smiled. "I like the way you said that. I believe you will."

"Mariah, you got enough air?" Dante's voice bellowed out of the door.

I wiped my eyes one more time and reentered the truck, pushing my feelings down into that compartment in my belly where I always placed them until I could process them.

"Sorry," I said, my voice cracking.

I took orders from the customers who were waiting and clipped them on the clothesline we were using for sales slips.

Dante stole a peek over his shoulder at me. "You all right?"

"I'm good. What can I do to help with the food?" I washed my hands and waited for him to answer. He was looking through me like my "I'm good" wasn't working for him.

"I could use some onions sliced," he said.

I slid past him, glad to have them to cut. It would explain the tears I had to fight to mask.

It was almost two o' clock when Sabrina showed up. She was with some woman I'd never seen.

"Wow," the woman said, smiling. "This is a great turnout."

Sabrina introduced her friend as Tameka Avery. "Tameka rents a booth at the Choppe Farmers Market. We met in the craft store the other day, and she offered to let me share her space this week."

"I didn't have much inventory," Tameka added. "Plus, it was nice to have the company."

I fought hard to stop my eyes from rolling. My sister had apparently found a new hippie friend. "I didn't know you were going to the farmers market."

"I just decided this morning," Sabrina said. "I baked all those cakes, and I didn't want them to just sit."

"You could have told me," I said through gritted teeth.

"I'm sure I wasn't missed," Sabrina replied.

I looked back at Dante who was ignoring the conversation in favor of chatting through his Bluetooth earpiece neck thingy.

"What do you sell?" I asked Tameka.

"I make jams and jellies. Chowchow."

"It's so delicious," Sabrina added.

I cocked an eyebrow at my sister.

"Sabrina had a great sales day. Most of her cakes sold out." Tameka turned to Sabrina. "How many jars did you sell?"

"Thirty-four," Sabrina said, cutting her eyes away from me.

Thirty-four. In one morning? At a farmers market? I couldn't believe it. A sting of resentment settled around my heart. I didn't know why that bothered me so much.

Tameka looked at my cake tray and said to Sabrina, "The little jars would fit nicely at events like this."

Once again, my uninventive and un-unique dessert display was dissed. "Now that you're here, I'm going to run to the restroom right quick." I pulled my apron over my head and flew down the steps and away from the truck.

So Sabrina had cake allies. Of course Dante was on her side, but now she had a new little friend. I wasn't going to count on her for anything that would affect this business because no one knew better than I did how quickly she might change her plans.

When I returned from the restroom, Tameka was gone. Sabrina was standing inside, in my spot, and as I got closer, I could see three small jars of cake on the counter. I stepped in and took them down, white-hot anger fueling my movements. "I told you no."

Sabrina propped her fists on her hips. "Mariah, this isn't just your—"

I sliced into her protest. The success of Tabby's would rest with me. "Grandma trusts me with this. Not you."

"She trusts both of us."

"Let's step out so we can talk."

Sabrina looked at Dante like she wanted him to save her. He didn't say anything, just shook his head and continued to cook. Once she was out the door, Sabrina said, "Grandma asked me to come help with the restaurant the same way she asked you."

"Do you really think she asked us in the same way?" I shook my head. "Look at today. You showed up when most of the work is done."

"You didn't want me here anyway."

"Which is it, Sabrina? Are you here for Grandma or yourself?"

She didn't reply. I could see her eyes getting wet from the temper of tears, but I continued. "Our insurance doesn't cover your willy-nilly food creations. It's over nearly ninety degrees out here. Those jars should be in a cool space. If someone gets sick, it hurts the whole business, and you . . . you walk away to your next project while Tabby's is ruined."

"I would never hurt the business," Sabrina said firmly.

"There are health and safety standards."

"Oh, so I suppose you checked all Dante's recipes and processes against your standards."

I rolled my eyes. "Girl, please. Dante is already a brand. He has his own reputation to protect."

Sabrina threw up her hands. "But I have to start somewhere."

"Not here. Not today."

I walked around the front of the truck and put her jars back into her cooler.

I was expecting her to leave, but Sabrina stayed. The atmosphere in the truck was somber.

I offered, "I don't think all three of us can fit in here cleaning, so if you need to get Kenni, Dante and I can manage."

"They have an in-house carnival at the daycare, so I'm in no rush to get Kenni. Why don't you go? You started early. I can finish up."

Dante coughed uncomfortably. "I need one of you to choose. I've had it with the vibe in here."

Sabrina propped a hand on her hip again. I could see she was thinking about digging in her heels, but then I gave her the death stare, and she snatched off her gloves and tossed them in the garbage. She turned to Dante. "Thanks for trying to help me out."

He nodded, and she turned and left, rolling her little cake cooler behind her.

Dante continued to spray and wipe the grill. "I've got this, Mariah. I'm used to breaking down my truck."

I was emitting the vibe he didn't want to be around. "I'm sorry for the cake drama."

"You created it," he said without looking at me.

"You don't understand."

"You're right." Dante gave me his full attention. "I don't, and I don't have to. I want to help your grandparents—"

"And we need you," I said, feeling panic. He couldn't quit on me.

"I like you and your sister, but I don't do drama, Mariah. Don't make me walk away." He turned his back, and the conversation was over.

I peeled off my gloves too. "I'm sorry. I really am."

I was talking to his back. He didn't accept my apology; he just kept working. I opened the refrigerator and took out the container I'd packed for Grandma and left the truck.

My phone rang. It was Hope. I had no doubt Hope knew about the show. That's why she was calling.

"How was the food truck?" she asked after we greeted each other.

"Great. Fantastic. I'm leaving now." I slipped into my car and placed the bag of food on the seat next to me. "I saw about Vince." I figured I'd go ahead and get it out there so she didn't have to feel me out.

"I figured you might have. Are you okay?"

"I've been so busy, I haven't had time to really think about it, but I'm . . ." My emotions burst through. A tear flew from my eyes. I suppose the dam holding back my feelings broke. On a hitched sob, I said, "How am I here, Hope? What did I do so wrong to deserve this?"

"Honey, I don't know."

"I just . . . is it me? I'm never happy. Nothing is ever good enough for me."

Hope was silent. She knew my story. All of it.

"Vince can't even cook. How's he going to do the show?"

Hope was quiet. Way too quiet for my liking. She had bad news. "Hope?"

"His girlfriend is a chef. She's going to do the cooking with him."

"He's dating a chef? Is it someone I know?"

Hope sighed. "She cooked for you guys three years ago. Jess Daley."

Vince was such trash. "She's a kid. She can't be more than twenty-two."

"It's her."

I nodded. "I fired her. She told me it was what she needed to get her motivated to apply to culinary school. Now she has my husband and my diner and my TV show. Great." I should scream, but I wouldn't let myself.

Hope said, "Don't focus on her. She'll get what's coming to her soon enough, and so will Vince."

"Oh yeah, I've so seen life play out that way. People reaping what they've sown. I don't care what the Bible says. That's not how life works. What did I sow to deserve this?"

"I don't know. All I know is God is still good. He has good things for you, but you can't let this make you so bitter that you never get what God has planned."

"Are you about to tell me to forgive him? I know that's not where you're going."

"No," Hope said firmly, although I know she wished she could, because as a counselor in her church's mental health ministry, she believed that forgiving people was the answer to every conflict in her life. "I'm telling you, don't let it make your heart hard."

I nodded. "I need to get out of this parking lot. We'll talk later." I ended the call and dropped my phone on the seat next to me.

I wrapped my hands around the steering wheel and leaned forward, pressing my forehead into the wheel, holding on to it as if it were a life raft while the tears burst through again. I saw Sabrina's

cakes in my mind, and the familiar scent of cinnamon and straw-
berries wafted through my memory.

*"You have to trim back the cake so you have a perfect square to work
with."*

I saw my mother's hands slicing the top and sides of the cake,
pushing the parts aside that she wasn't going to use. The baked
hard parts she called them. *Caramelized* is the technical term I
knew now.

"Can I have the scraps, Mama?"

I always asked for them when she got finished shaving the cake.
I could taste the pieces of cake mixed in with my salty tears. I
wiped my eyes.

"All I have now is scraps, Mama," I cried, reaching into my bag
for a tissue.

A knock on the window startled me. I looked out to see Dante,
turned the key, and let the window down.

"Are you okay?"

I nodded. "I'm good." How I got that lie out I didn't know.

"I'm sorry I was hard on you a little bit ago."

I shook my head. "You were right, but these tears . . ." I blew
my nose and wiped it. "This has nothing to do with you." I rolled
my lip in and bit it. The image of those jars came back to me.
The taste of the cake was barely out of my mouth and memory. I
shook my head. "I'm going through a divorce."

Dante nodded. "Sorry. I didn't know."

"How could you? I didn't tell you. I haven't told anyone but
my grandparents and my best friend."

"Sabrina?"

I didn't respond, just answered with my eyes.

"You should," he said.

"She has her own problems."

Dante ground out the words. "And one of *her* problems is your
attitude."

I rolled my head back. "Excuse me?"

He shrugged. "Maybe she'll be more . . . I don't know . . . understanding if she knows you're going through something."

I released a long breath, a cleansing one that blew away my frustration with Dante's advice. "Like I said, I'm sorry for the drama."

Dante stood to his full height. "You have a bank bag full of cash. Go home." He rapped his knuckles on the roof of the car twice and walked back to his truck.

I turned on the engine and pulled out of the lot. Dante was good people, and I needed him. I was going to have to figure out how not to let my emotions get the better of me again or I'd lose him too.

Chapter 18

October 1918

Tabitha

It was the day before Joseph's birthday, which meant it was nearly a year to the day that he'd told Tabitha about his wife, when she woke up to the horrible press of dread in her spirit. She didn't care much about celebrating with him anymore. Those days were over for them. Only the children and his obligation to them occupied her mind. Joseph didn't see it that way, so he still pressed her for lovemaking when he wanted. He insisted he was a man without comfort and love because of his wife's illness and he was desperate to have something normal, but still, he'd stolen Tabitha's reputation with a lie. She resented him deeply for it, but she wasn't foolish enough to think she didn't need him. Thanks to Miss Libby's tea, she didn't worry much about having another baby. Tabitha also demanded more money from him. She figured if she was going to be a kept woman, Joseph was going to give her more for the shame of it.

Tabitha saved every penny she could. One day she'd have enough money to start fresh, and she'd leave his place and figure out a life on her own. That's what she told herself every night when she climbed into bed. That's what she asked God to give her. God still loved her—that's what the Bible said—so she took care to pray for deliverance from this sinful situation.

The dread she'd felt over Joseph's birthday this year continued to hover in the back of her mind. She had not heard from him or seen him. Tabitha checked her calendar and counted the days. It had been two weeks. By the time the days reached four weeks, the dread overwhelmed her. It did not help that the mayor ordered churches, theaters, and schools closed on account of the Spanish flu. It meant she and the children were trapped in the house, using only the food reserves she had. As the days went on, the city became more closed down, but Tabitha didn't think even that would keep Joseph away from them for so long. Something was wrong. She sensed it deep in the pit of her gut. By the end of the week, there was a knock on the door. Tabitha opened it to Joseph's driver. "Mr. Flynn," she said.

"I'm sorry it's taken me so long to come, but I had to travel to Atlanta . . ." He paused briefly and asked, "May I come in?"

"Of course. I'm so sorry." Tabitha stepped back, and he passed by her. Joseph and the maintenance man had been the only two men who had ever entered this apartment. The maintenance man was shorter than Tabitha was, so she wasn't used to anyone filling the height of the room except Joseph. Now Mr. Flynn did. "Can I get you something? I have water and tea."

"No, miss, I'll be taking my lunch down the street in a few minutes."

"Well, if you don't mind, I'd like to know why you're here instead of Joseph. I haven't seen him—"

He removed his hat and with it pulled down the veil of pain he'd been hiding under the rim. "Miss, I'm sorry to tell you this, but . . ." He swallowed deeply before finishing his sentence. "Mr. McCoy has passed on."

Shock clenched Tabitha's body like a fist, and she could not breathe through the jolt of pain that came over her. "Excuse me. I need—" Her words and air left her. It was his hands and then strong arms that kept her up before moving her to the sofa where she sat.

"I'm sorry. I should have had you sit before telling you."

"What . . . happened? How could he be . . ." Beads of perspiration popped out on her forehead. She was going to be sick to her stomach. "When?" she cried or growled. She wasn't sure. The sound of her own voice was foreign.

"It was two weeks ago."

Two weeks? That hit her in the chest hard enough to stop her heart. "Two weeks?"

"Mr. McCoy was attacked leaving a poker game by a man who owed him a debt. He went to the hospital. He was there getting better . . . but he came down with that awful flu, miss, and well, you know, lots of people are dyin' from it."

The flu? Something in nature that they couldn't even see had taken down a man as powerful as Joseph McCoy. That seemed impossible to believe, but she believed it because she'd prayed too many nights to be free of him. She hadn't meant it in this way. Never in this way. In the middle of all her mixed emotions, he'd been suffering. Tabitha sobbed for a long time. Her tears were from feelings of loss and guilt. When she was done, Mr. Flynn was sitting across from her. Margaret was on his lap. Amos was at his feet. Both looked terrified.

Tabitha wiped her eyes and nose with a towel he'd fetched from her washroom.

She raised her hand and motioned to Amos. "Come here, baby." Amos raced to her. She picked him up and put him on the sofa under her arm. "I'm so very sorry for all this."

"Miss, I understand. You have nothing to apologize for," Mr. Flynn said.

Margaret scooted down from his lap and joined Amos next to her. "Was he here in Charleston?"

"Yes, ma'am."

"He's buried . . . without me?"

"Buried a week after. I had to travel to pick up family for the funeral, which is why I'm just today getting here."

Family that was more important than her and her poor children. Tabitha looked at them. They absorbed her sadness but had no idea how much they'd eventually feel when they learned they wouldn't see their papa again and her baby asleep in her bed, would never know him. She had not asked God for that. "Margaret, you take your brother and go to your room while I talk to Mr. Flynn 'bout grown-up business."

Margaret picked up a doll she'd abandoned on the floor, took her brother's hand, and they disappeared into their bedroom.

Once she saw they were gone, Tabitha turned to Mr. Flynn and asked, "How was he hurt?"

"I think it's better you don't know."

Tabitha stood. "Better for who? I have three children without a father." She walked around the sofa and pressed her fists against the upholstery across the back.

Mr. Flynn released a long plume of air. "He was stabbed."

The thought of a knife in his body sickened her. She'd seen a crumpled body before. Not from stabbing, but her brother, Hank, lying in the road, bleeding as his life left him. Maybe he was right in assuming she didn't want to know. Tears leaked from Tabitha's eyes again. She wasn't sure if she was crying for Joseph or Hank at that moment. She reasoned both. She wiped her face again.

"Is there anything else you need to know?" Mr. Flynn asked.

"What of his wife?"

Mr. Flynn seemed shocked by that question. "What about her?"

"I know that she is unwell."

He hesitated, confusion etching lines in his forehead. "Mrs. McCoy is . . . she's fine. As fine as she can be."

"I only found out about his wife last year," Tabitha offered, needing him to know she hadn't chosen to be a woman who couldn't attend her own man's funeral.

"You didn't know he was married?"

"No. What kind of woman would . . ." Her words trailed off. "I never knew. I was demanding he marry me, and he wouldn't, so he finally told me."

"I'm sorry, miss. I didn't know you didn't know about Mrs. McCoy."

"I wouldn't have made myself a married man's mistress. I'm abandoned here. I have nothing." Tabitha dropped her head back and closed her eyes for a minute. An ache inched its way up her neck to her left temple. She opened her eyes and looked at Mr. Flynn again. "I don't even know anything about this place. The rent. Who to pay. When it's due."

Mr. Flynn was quick to answer. "Mr. McCoy owns—or owned—this building."

Now Tabitha felt even dumber.

Mr. Flynn continued, "I believe you probably have some time before his family will insert themselves into his business affairs."

"They know nothing about me. Nothing about his children." Tabitha pushed her fist deeper into the back of the sofa. She needed to be alone now with her grief and stupidity. "Thank you for coming here to tell me."

"I can't say it was my pleasure." He walked to the door, paused, and reached into his pocket. "I almost forgot." He stepped back to her and handed her a piece of paper. "This is my address. If you have anything urgent, you can send me a letter."

"Thank you. I appreciate your concern so much."

"Mr. McCoy was a good employer. I know he cared for you and these children a great deal."

It was Tabitha's turn to sigh. "I suppose."

"Miss, he did. I know he did."

"Having a sick wife is no reason to deceive someone, but . . . I shan't speak ill of him while he's in his grave."

Mr. Flynn stepped through the door, and she closed it behind him. The gravity of grief pulled her down the door until she landed on the floor. Miss Libby's warning about Joseph came back to her.

"Him ansa for what he do."

Tabitha stuck her fist in her mouth and fought howling again. She didn't want to scare the children. She had enough fear for the whole lot of them, because with Joseph's death, she would be kept no more. She had to take care of her own family.

On the morning of Saturday, December 7, 1918, readers of the *Southern Reporter* woke up to good news.

FLU EPIDEMIC DYING HERE, a headline on page 2 of the newspaper reported. *Only Thirty-Five New Cases Reported Yesterday.*

Thirty-five cases in all of Charleston. This pestilence was nearly gone. It was far too late for Joseph, her children, her life. It had only been a month, and already Tabitha was pulling up the floorboard and reaching into the metal box for the money she'd hidden there.

It had grown some, as she was in the habit of saving a little of what Joseph gave her. Not trusting him meant she was always preparing in her mind to leave him and this life behind. But even with what she put back, she only had a hundred and ten dollars. That would last her some time but not long. A landlord would eventually come looking for rent.

Tabitha sat at her table with the money in hand. She needed a job, she needed help with the children, she needed the life Joseph had promised, but Joseph was gone and so was that dream life. Tears prickled her eyes, just as they had every day since Joseph's passing, but the time for crying was over. Joseph might not have been able to legally marry her, but surely his family would want to know his children. Determined, she grabbed some paper and a pen. It was time to be strong for her children. It was time to come out of the shadows. With fire in her heart and the last glimmer of hope, she penned a letter to Mr. Flynn.

It was a little over a week before he appeared at her door again, and he was none too eager to fulfill her request to be taken to the McCoy house to meet Joseph's mother, but he realized she was determined.

Once the carriage stopped, Tabitha waited for him to open the door.

"It's just over there," he said, pointing to a large redbrick house on the corner of Queen and Johns streets. "I can't take you to the front. Someone could see me." He took her hand and helped her down.

He took the children out, too, and impressed upon Tabitha a final warning. "I know these people. This is not a good idea."

"I have to try." Tabitha thanked him, gathered the children, and made her way down the street.

Standing outside the estate of Lady Charlotte McCoy was intimidating but necessary. The house was a large Victorian. It appeared to be at least three floors and had enormous bay windows on each side. The pitched roof was covered in gleaming red tiles. The yard was pretty and neatly trimmed with a garden in the front. Tabitha steeled herself and pushed the doorbell.

The door opened, and after she looked Tabitha and the children over thoroughly, a maid asked her business.

"My name is Tabitha Cooper, and I would like an audience with Mrs. Charlotte McCoy."

"Lady McCoy," she said, correcting Tabitha with intensity, "is not expecting a visitor."

"I am aware. I could have written, but I—I thought it more impactful if I came directly."

The maid only pitched an eyebrow at that statement. "How do you know Lady McCoy?"

She hefted the baby on her hip. "I knew her son."

The maid's eyebrow came down. She looked at the children, and Tabitha could see she knew. "I will check to see if she'll receive you." She closed the door, leaving them on the porch.

Minutes later, the door opened again, and Tabitha was shown into the house. The first thing to capture her attention was the staircase. It came down on two sides. The entryway was huge and airy with hardwood doors to the left and right leading to rooms. Dark hardwood floors contrasted with the white walls.

A woman stepped into the entrance of a sitting room just to the left of the door. Her height, statuesque like a queen. Her light brown skin glowed in the light coming from the bay window to her left. An elegant black tea dress wrapped well around her frame. Tabitha knew she was Joseph's mother. He had looked like her.

Her eyes fell on the children briefly, and Lady McCoy said, "Mae, will you take them into the kitchen?"

"I would prefer they stay with me," Tabitha said.

"I will not discuss your business with small ears present."

The matter was settled. Mae was already at Tabitha's side.

She leaned over and told Margaret and Amos to mind themselves, then put baby Tom in the maid's waiting arms.

"I don't have much time," Lady McCoy said. "Come in."

Tabitha followed her into the room. Fresh flowers were in vases all over the room. The strong scent of honeysuckle and lilac perfumed the air.

"My maid tells me you knew my late son."

"Yes, ma'am."

Lady McCoy walked to one of the two sofas in the room, took a seat, and motioned with her hand for Tabitha to take a seat on the chair opposite her. Once she was seated she said, "I do not receive visitors that I do not know."

"And I apologize for the intrusion."

"Many of Joseph's schoolmates and business associates have called over the months, so I've tried to be flexible to accommodate people who loved him."

"That's kind of you in your personal time of grief, ma'am."

Lady McCoy cocked her head. The suspicion in her eyes came across in her voice. "You asked for an audience with me so that you could be *impactful*. How did you know my son?"

Tabitha didn't want to shock this woman, but there was no way to say this and have it not be shocking. There simply was not, so she cleared her throat and spoke. "I was . . . Joseph and I . . ."

"Joseph and you what?"

Tabitha wiped her sweaty palms on her skirts. "Those three children are his."

Lady McCoy didn't move at first, didn't even blink, and then she chuckled uncomfortably before standing. "That's ridiculous."

"It's true."

"It is not." She said the words firmly as if she was as certain as she was that the sun would set and rise again.

"If you'll look at the children, you'll see some of your son in their faces. My oldest boy looks just like his father."

"Your son looks like half a dozen darkies I've seen on the street in the last week." She stepped close to where Tabitha was sitting. "I do not believe my son would lie with the likes of you and sire children."

Darkies. The likes of me. Tabitha struggled to keep calm. "Then you didn't know him."

"And you knew him so well, did you? My son was a married man."

Tabitha shook her head. "I did not know that at first. It wasn't until last year that he told me about his wife."

"So are you in the habit of having children with men who aren't your husband?"

"No, ma'am."

She continued, "Even if the first child was an accident, you had two more children."

Tabitha hated the way she towered over her. It made her uncomfortable because she had to look up at her to take in the nasty words she was saying. "We were a family. He said he couldn't divorce his wife on account of her condition."

Curiosity shifted Lady McCoy's features to confusion. "Her condition?"

Something within Tabitha shifted too. Her voice, the tone of it when she posed the question, was a sound like a warning whistle letting her know more disappointment was coming. She lost confidence and, because of it, lost her words for a minute.

"Explain what you mean," Lady McCoy said.

"Joseph told me she was not well in her mind . . ."

Lady McCoy grunted. She walked to the door, reached for a rope, and pulled it. The maid reentered the room. Lady McCoy called her close and whispered something to her. Tabitha took a deep breath. She could hardly bear this. It was too much, and she wanted to make sure her children were all right in that kitchen.

The maid left, and Lady McCoy said, "You were saying."

What was she saying? She cycled back and remembered she'd been speaking about Joseph's wife. "He said she was unwell and it was not something he could legally leave her for."

Tabitha saw nothing in Lady McCoy's placid face, so she kept talking. "Joseph said it would be difficult and immoral to divorce her."

"Unlike having three children out of wedlock."

Tabitha had been prepared for this. No one could make her feel worse about her affair with Joseph than she could herself. "I'm not the first woman to fall in love with a man and accept his lies, and I won't be the last."

"Don't sass me, gal."

Gal was a smack to her face. She swallowed and calmed herself before speaking again. "I'm only saying I didn't come here to be shamed. If there is shame, he and I both own it."

"Do not speak ill of my dead son."

"Any harsh words I have are not because I wish to speak ill of him. I loved him . . ." Tabitha's voice failed her. She hadn't loved Joseph in a long time. "He didn't expect to leave here like this. Joseph would never have left me without some way to take care of his children."

"Which is my evidence that those are not his. He would have made a will. Had a letter of some kind. There is nothing in his things, and he was sick for weeks before he died."

"Still, I'm sure he did not expect to die." Lady McCoy didn't seem fazed by Tabitha's statement. "He would have married me if not for his wife."

"I don't think so." If Lady McCoy could have cut her with her eyes, she'd be bleeding. "Joseph knew fully what was expected of him . . . the kind of woman he should marry and have children with."

Tabitha took that dig. Lady McCoy probably meant light-skinned like his mother. Educated. Well-bred. "His driver knows me."

"Don't bring my employee into this, young lady."

"But he does know."

"What he may know is that my son visited you—perhaps in an indecent way, but I won't embarrass him with such questions."

"I live in his building on Calhoun Street. I only ask to continue to live there without rent and to be given some small allowance to help with food and childcare for the children while I work."

"That's all," Lady McCoy said, the hint of a chuckle in her voice.

Tabitha heard heels clicking on the floor in the entry. Expensive ones that did not belong to a maid. A woman entered the room. A beautiful, tiny slip of a woman in her late twenties. She was nearly the color of cotton with big, dark eyes and silky black hair that she wore pinned in a severe bun. Her dress . . . black. Her face . . . drawn from sadness.

This visit had been a kind of hell, with Joseph's mother's evil disregard, but Tabitha had a feeling it was about to become worse. Lady McCoy had not called this near-white woman into the room for no purpose. The sneer on her face evidence that she was intent on hurting Tabitha.

"This is *Mrs.* Evelyn McCoy, my daughter-in-law. As you can see, she is very well."

"What is this about, Mother?" Evelyn's voice floated across the high-ceilinged room like a song—sweet and pretty. Her voice was void of trouble.

"It is about nothing, my dear. This young lady knew Joseph. She needed to see you, but I told her we don't have time for a visit today. We are expecting friends for tea."

Tabitha opened her mouth. She wanted to say something, but Lady McCoy's eyes silenced her. "I'll join you in the library in a few minutes."

Joseph's wife left the room without so much as a goodbye to Tabitha, who understood why his mother didn't believe her. Evelyn and she couldn't be more different.

Lady McCoy spoke. "I am a generous woman, but I will not be conned by you, young lady. You will not be the only one to make this claim. Of that I am sure. These things happen when men of Joseph's stature die. They happen all the time."

"You speak like you know your son's character was above me, but he didn't just die. He was stabbed in a brothel where he played cards, which means it was not."

"I thought you loved him and would not speak ill of him." Lady McCoy's words came through gritted teeth.

"That was before I found out he played me for a fool. That he lied to me about his wife's illness." Hot tears burned the back of her eyes. She felt faint, like she didn't know if she could stay on her feet. "I have no money. I've spent all he gave me and what I saved. I have no way to feed your grandchildren."

"My grandchildren are at school." Lady McCoy walked to a desk, opened the drawer, and removed something Tabitha could not see from her position. Then she rang the bell again. When the maid entered, she handed her an envelope. "Give this to Miss Cooper and see her out appropriately." She left the room. Left Tabitha with the maid without the courtesy of a goodbye, in the same way her daughter-in-law had gone.

The maid pushed the envelope at her and said, "Miss, there is nothing for you here septin' this."

Tabitha opened the envelope to find a ten-dollar bill. In all the grand splendor of this house, this woman handed her ten dollars for the entire future of her grandchildren. Tabitha's heart sank to the floor. She felt tears burning in her eyes.

The maid took her to the kitchen. The cook, a kind-looking woman, handed her a small rag with some biscuits, jam, fried chicken, and a few pieces of sliced salt pork with a ball of rice in a smaller cloth. "For your trip home with the children and your supper." Then she turned and resumed what she was doing.

"Thank you," Tabitha whispered to her back. She gathered her baby, and with Margaret and Amos at her side, she turned to leave the same way she came, but the maid said, "Miss . . ." She opened the back door. "Godspeed."

She wanted to be strong for her children, to not cry in front of them, but these tears she could not stop. Her heart ached so that she felt it in her back, a sharp pain dead center that radiated up into her shoulders and neck.

"Lord, keep me," she cried. She had nothing. What was she going to do? She steeled herself in the same way she had before she entered that awful house and put one foot in front of the other until she was walking down the street. But to where? She had no idea how to get to a streetcar or trolley from here. She wished she'd left the children with Miss Libby, but she thought she would need to present them to Joseph's family as proof of their relationship. Her foolish heart never expected to be turned out this way.

"Miss Cooper." The voice came from behind her. She turned quickly. It was Mr. Flynn. He hadn't left her. "If you'll walk down to the Nazarene Church"—he pointed—"I'll pick you up at the steps on the side of the building and take you back to your apartment."

Tabitha turned in the direction he pointed and, seeing a steeple in the distance, thanked him and walked. She arrived at the steps to the massive church and sat with the children. It was only a few minutes until the carriage arrived and they were safely inside. The visit to the house had not solved her problem, but at least the smaller problem of getting back to her flat was resolved.

The next day, she left the children with Miss Libby and went to see a lawyer. He had the reputation of working with Negro women on all types of legal issues.

With no appointment, she waited until he could see her, which was hours after she'd come in.

"I'm sorry to hear you lost someone to the flu. My sister-in-law was quite ill. Fortunately, she recovered," he said, sliding into the chair behind his desk.

Tabitha sat in front of him and told him her story. She ended with the question, "What do I do if his mother will not give me their inheritance?"

"Was there a will?"

"Not that I know of."

"Are all three his children?"

"Yes," she said somewhat insulted that he'd think she had children with yet another man.

"Well, a husband's property is willed to his wife. Your mother-in-law may want to keep it, but—"

"I was not his wife."

"You weren't married?"

"That's what a not-wife is, sir." Tabitha hadn't meant to be so sharp. She closed her eyes and dropped her head. "Forgive me for my sharp tone."

He continued with his questions as if her nasty comment did not matter. "Has the family acknowledged the children before? Publicly. Ever?"

"They met us yesterday. I don't believe his mother or wife knew we existed. His mother seemed quite surprised by my visit, and she was angry."

He paused for a few seconds, surveying her, possibly judging her, but then he pressed his pen to the paper he was writing on and asked, "Do you have any letters, photographs, witnesses?"

"He was very careful not to . . ." Tabitha started. "No."

"Surely, there's someone."

"His carriage driver, but he's employed by his mother now."

"You have children but no proof that they are his, no witnesses at all who will come forward?"

"I don't believe so."

He put his pen on the desk and clenched his hands together. "I'm not sure I can do anything for you. Perhaps you can find out the pastor of his family church and speak with him."

"What will the pastor do?"

"If he believes you, he may ask the family to hear you again."

"That's it?" Tabitha spread her arms. "Their pastor? He was a lying adulterer, and his mother is godless. I don't think they listen to man or God."

"I'm afraid it's my only suggestion." His eyes softened when he asked, "Miss Cooper, do you have family?"

"None that want me."

"There must be someone."

"There isn't. My stepfather didn't want me without children. I–I humiliated my mother." I summed up my thoughts on the situation. "She is always his wife first. Always."

"The path to redemption is not as narrow as we think, Miss Cooper." He leaned back against his chair and studied Tabitha for a minute. "Are you sure you're not being prideful?"

"I'm sure I'd rather die than face that rejection, sir."

"But you wouldn't rather your children suffer the consequences of that decision with you." He let those words sit between them for nearly a minute before standing. "I wish you the very best."

Tabitha thanked him for his time and left for her walk home.

The next day, she was surprised by an unexpected knock at the door. It was Mr. Flynn again.

She let him in, and he removed his hat. They got the formalities out of the way before Tabitha had him sit. "I have something for you, Miss Tabitha."

He reached into his pocket and removed an envelope and placed it on the table between them. She opened it and found money, over a hundred dollars.

"I don't understand."

"Mr. McCoy had me take a silver watch for repair. I picked it up on the morning of his death, and I have sold it for you."

Tabitha looked at the money again.

"No one at the McCoy house knows about the watch," Mr. Flynn assured her. "He won it in a poker game a few weeks before he was . . . hurt. The man owed him more than a hundred dollars, so he offered the watch."

Once again, Tabitha's eyes filled with tears. For every disappointment, she had the joy of a kindness bestowed on her by the McCoy servants.

"Thank you. This will carry me for some time."

"Enough time, I hope."

He handed her a piece of paper. "I'm moving into the main house next week to become the full-time driver for Lady McCoy. She has purchased an automobile for me to learn. This is the address of a close friend. You may write to me if you need something urgent. I don't know if I can help, but . . ."

Tabitha took the paper. "Your first name? I don't know it."

"Micah, miss."

"Micah, I will forever be in your debt."

"It's Christian charity, miss. The kind the McCoys lack."

She nodded.

"If I can make a suggestion . . ."

"You just saved my life. Surely you can say anything to me."

"You should go home. If you need help doing that, I can see what I can do to assist."

"You are aware of how I left my family?"

"I drive in this city every day. My eyes see things I wish they hadn't. A single woman with no family is prey for many troubling situations."

Tabitha gave him a tiny smile. "I will consider everything you have said."

He tipped his hat and went on this way. She had been warned by the lawyer and now Micah Flynn, but she trusted the voice in her heart. She only failed when she didn't listen to it. She had enough money to make a new start right where she was.

But their warnings stuck in her mind and sat heavy on her heart for a while. She found *prey* to be such a peculiar word choice. Prey was a creature that was living its life one moment and hunted the next. That was how life shifted, moment by moment. She thought *victim* to be easier to digest, but she understood. He was trying to give her a firm warning. He wasn't wrong for it. She'd lain in bed on many a night and wondered what made her such easy *prey* for a man like Joseph. He lured her away from her plans and her family. Her children were not a source of regret, but her stained reputation was. And she had no real explanation for her folly other than infatuation. Until she had something better, she could not go home. She would not go back with regrets and no reason. She was in this city now, and she would figure out a way to survive in it.

Chapter 19

Present Day

Sabrina

The sound of Mariah's car in the driveway got me off the sofa. I'd spent this week avoiding her, doing what I needed to do at the restaurant without uttering a word to her, but I couldn't live like this. It was too stressful. Mariah had not made a single attempt to apologize for what she'd done last weekend, and I was going to confront her about it.

I barely let her get her feet in the house before I ambushed her. "I want to talk."

Why she looked like she'd been out on a bad date, I don't know, but she did.

"I'm tired." She kicked off her sneakers and moved them into the foyer shoe rack.

I folded my arms over my chest. "I don't care that you're tired."

Mariah looked at me, curious now. She almost looked amused for half a second. Exhaustion came back down on her heavy.

"Kenni and Grandma are already asleep. This is a good time."

Planning to ignore me, she took steps toward the stairs, and I reached for her arm, stopping her. "Now."

She looked down at my hand, and I removed it.

"I've had a horrible week."

"So what? You likely caused whatever it is that made it so bad."

I'd stunned her, but she did not say anything.

"You humiliated me last week."

"You strolled up at two in the afternoon for an event you were supposed to open with us."

"You didn't want me there anyway. You don't want me in Georgetown, in this house, possibly on the planet."

Mariah flashed an irritated look at me, and this time she was the one folding her arms over her chest. "So much drama. Always."

"I'm being dramatic? You didn't have to do that in front of Dante."

"I told you we were not selling your little projects."

"Projects? What is wrong with you? Why are you so mean and controlling and toxic?"

Mariah dropped her arms and turned to go into the kitchen. She threw words over her shoulder. "I told you no."

I followed her and watched her get a glass and pour water into it. After she drank, I said, "Dante told me to bring my sweet cakes."

"He should have talked to me about it."

"But this restaurant isn't yours. You don't have the only say."

Mariah looked totally unfazed by this. She rolled her neck and put a hand on her hip. "Are you done? The event is over. I couldn't give you your little moment back if I wanted to."

I spent my life trying to understand my sister, but she gave me no space to have that grace anymore. "Why do you hate me so much?"

She put the glass in the sink. "I don't hate you."

"Yes, you do." I took a deep breath, looked down at the floor and then back into Mariah's eyes. I wanted to see her face when I said this. "It's because of mother. I killed our mother. You should have had her instead of me."

Mariah's nostrils flared, and she looked away before giving me her attention again. "I don't hate you."

But she did. She struggled to even say the words just now. "You don't think I have guilt? I never had her. How do you think I feel about that? You're not the only one who has pain."

"Are we going to start swapping our stories?"

"Why not? We are the only two people in the world who shared her."

Mariah bit her lip. I could see her eyes getting wet.

"You had her for some time. You got to touch her, smell her, hear her voice, feel her presence. What memories do I have? All I have are pictures and videos."

Mariah's lashes fluttered wildly in disbelief. "I was six, Sabrina. You think I remember all that? Do you know how hard I struggle to remember things about her? Don't romanticize my memories and accuse me of being blessed to have more time. All time did is taunt me by stealing her. That's worse than not having her."

"Easy for you to say when you don't have my perspective." I took a deep breath. "I wish we had more than this between us because this is sad and pathetic."

"We had a chance to have more between us," Mariah said. "You ruined that."

I shook my head. I had no idea what she was talking about.

Mariah's eyes narrowed with a grim concentration on the facts. "The cooking trip, Sabrina."

I pulled my head back. She was talking about the trip we were supposed to take ten years ago. "The cruise?"

Mariah tossed up her hands. "Where else? It's the only thing you and I planned to do together in our entire lives, and you bailed on me."

"Mariah, I—"

"What? Didn't know how important it was to me? I couldn't go when you backed out. I needed you to pay your part, and I lost money I worked hard for."

"But you said it was okay."

"What was I supposed to do? Cry and beg you? I said that to you so you wouldn't know how much you disappointed me."

I went back to that in mind, but before I could think of something to say, Mariah spoke again.

"I don't want to talk about this."

"But we should. I didn't know—"

"Sabrina! I have problems that are bigger than this conversation," Mariah said. "But if you want an apology for embarrassing you. Fine. I'm sorry I embarrassed you, but that's not going to change anything about the sweet cakes. We're not selling them. Baking was her thing with me. Not you. I won't let you keep dragging those old feelings up."

We forgot where we were, having it out like this. We were sure to have woken Grandma. She was a light sleeper, but she didn't come out of the room. Maybe she, like me, thought it was time to have it out with Mariah. Get the accusations and angry feelings on the table so we could decide what we were going to keep.

I followed my sister out of the kitchen and up the stairs. Once she reached her door, I called her name . . . low enough not to wake anyone, but firm enough to get her to stop moving.

"She wouldn't want you to feel this way."

"How would you know? You never met her."

If she had stabbed me in the heart, those words wouldn't hurt more. I felt tears wet my eyes. I sniffed hard to fight crying.

"If you want to do your *thing* at the markets, do it. I can't stop you, but you won't do it around me. I mean it. I'll leave and let you figure out how to save Tabby's on your own." She opened her door and closed it behind her.

Once she was gone, I slid down the wall and sat for a long time, feeling the sting of the words she'd said about our mother and the cakes. That hurt so deeply, I wasn't sure I would recover from the wound. But more than anything, I realized my sister was messed up. Angry and mean. I thought about her words: *"I have problems that are bigger than this conversation."*

Something was going on with her and Vince. She didn't mention him. But more than anything, there was the cruise. She was still upset about that all these years later, and I had no idea she was angry about it.

I dropped my face in my hands. I'd wanted a confrontation, and I got it. Now that I'd forced Mariah to talk, I wished I'd let her be.

Chapter 20

Mariah

The argument had stolen my sleep. I lied to myself . . . made
myself believe that I was immune to feeling hurt about how
messed up my relationship was with Sabrina.

My mind was spinning with all the things that kept us apart.
They were like pictures inside of glass balls moving around in my
head. She didn't even look like she remembered the cruise, and
yet some days it was all I did remember about her. I still hadn't
forgiven her.

I threw the blanket off my legs, got up, and went downstairs.
I liked having it to myself. The only sound was the ticking of
the vintage grandfather clock in the foyer and the slight hum
of the refrigerator. I flipped on the light and walked to the
stove. Sabrina had done some baking. I touched the still-warm
surface with both hands, dropped my head back, and soaked in
the heat. I loved the feeling of a warm stove. I loved the quiet
of a kitchen at night. It was my happy place. When Mama died,
I slipped out of my bed, went down to our kitchen, and sat at
the table, imagining that she was there with me cooking or

baking a cake. It was my safe place to remember Mama until Daddy sold it away from me. When he sold the house, I lost that space.

I opened the refrigerator. Although it was two o' clock, I wasn't likely to fall back to sleep just because I got back in bed. I decided to make my grandfather a nice healthy vegetable soup. He would love it.

I removed stock, cream, carrots, celery, collards, and butternut squash. I loved putting squash in my soup. I got my herbs together and grabbed some onions and potatoes and began chopping and loading up my pot. Just as I put it all on simmer, I heard feet on the stairs. Grandma entered the kitchen stating the obvious. "Somebody can't sleep."

"I think that's two somebodys," I said. I washed my hands. "Can I get something for you? Water, decaf tea?"

"Oh no. I'll spend the night in the bathroom. I don't need anything but a little talk with you." She sat and pulled the thin cotton lapels of her robe together.

I sat across from her. "I'm making vegetable soup for Grandpa."

Grandma smiled. "He's going to love that. They don't like for us to bring outside food in. He has dietary restrictions, but I ain't studin' them folks. I told them my husband will get better enjoying the foods he's used to."

I raised an index finger and inserted my but: "Minus a little salt."

Grandma chuckled. "Yes, minus some salt. I told your grandfather that with his blood pressure and diabetes, he's not built to be able to just eat all the salt he wants."

"I made sure to use all the herbs and some other tricks. He'll love it."

Grandma smiled. "Well, I know you love your grandfather, but I'm pretty sure he's not the one keeping you up." She placed both hands on the table and extended them so I would put mine in hers, and I did.

"I have a lot of things on my mind." I sighed. "So much."

"I have a feeling that one of those things might be your sister." Grandma pursed her lips. "You two had some heated words."

I nodded. Once again, shame tiptoed around me.

"I heard you say something about a cruise. Were you two supposed to go on a vacation?"

I shook my head. "Grandma, it's a long, old story."

"It can't be that old. You yelled it less than five hours ago."

I stood and walked to my pot, stared down in it at the mix of vegetables, and then stirred, unnecessarily at this point, before turning around and leaning against the counter. "Sabrina and I were supposed to go on a cooking cruise some years ago, and she backed out on me."

Grandma frowned. "What is a cooking cruise?"

"A summer culinary tour. We were going to travel to Haiti, Jamaica, Panama City, and Xalapa in Veracruz, Mexico." I still felt excited about the itinerary. I realized I was talking about it like it was happening in the future. I sighed and reeled back that emotion. "In each location, I would learn to cook African-influenced foods indigenous to the countries, and Sabrina was going to learn about the local baking culture. It was really special, Grandma. A once-in-a-lifetime opportunity to travel with two world-renowned chefs."

"Sounds expensive."

"It was. We planned it my last semester in college, but the trip wasn't until the following spring. I worked every part-time job I could find, from grocery delivery to sorting packages in a warehouse, to save the money. I was paying my half and some of Sabrina's."

"Seems like I remember some mention of this. You didn't come home for any holidays."

"Right," I said. "I worked all the time."

"Where was your sister's part coming from, because I don't ever remember hearing that she was doing all that?"

We chuckled together before I replied, "She had money she'd saved from birthday, holiday, and graduation gifts she had over the years. Plus, you know Daddy was giving her an allowance. The money wasn't the problem."

"What was?"

"Sabrina backed out. Nearly at the last minute. She'd met Kendrick. He wanted her to travel to the Grand Canyon with him, and she decided that was more important. The Grand Canyon that would always be there, with a man she'd only been seeing for a few months. I couldn't go alone. I couldn't come up with the rest of her money plus spending money in a month."

Grandma pulled her hands into her lap. I could see understanding in her eyes.

"I was heartbroken. I needed that trip. *We* needed it. Three weeks on a ship, touring islands and cooking together away from the worries of the world would have fixed a lot of things between us. *I* was finally ready to fix it." I wiped a rebellious tear that found its way down my face and sat.

"Baby, I'm so sorry she did that to you."

"I feel silly still being angry about it. It's been ten years."

"Well, sometimes yesterday feels closer than we'd like, especially when it's a matter of the heart."

I was glad she understood. It made me feel less silly. "I never really told anyone this, but I had dreams of becoming a food expert and culinary writer. I was going to create my own podcasts and videos about Black cooking, including Gullah of course. The cruise was going to be the kickoff of my career. The video footage would have drawn viewers to my platform."

"Your sister didn't stop that, Mariah."

I sniffed and nodded. "I know. I mean, I was dating Vince, and he wanted to get married."

"You both did."

"Yes, we did." I sighed. "Once upon a time." We sat there for a moment with neither of us saying anything until I added, "I found out that Vince is going to go on with the cooking show without me."

Grandma looked disappointed for a few seconds, and then she squared her shoulders and said, "So what? You young people are always talking about the YouTube app. Well, I been looking at it some. I see all kinds of people teaching stuff and holding classes and cooking and baking. They're not letting television networks stop them from creating their own thing. Why can't you create your own show? You got one of them fancy phones just like they do. You can use Tabby's as your base. You can make an opportunity."

I hadn't considered this. It sounded like a lot of work, and I was so broken from disappointment, I couldn't see my way clear to being that creative. Not after all I'd given to Clark's.

"Mariah, I see you wilting right before my eyes. You can do it."

I heard my grandmother with my ears, but not my heart. I didn't have any interest in thinking about this right now, so I told her what she wanted to hear. "I'll think about it."

"*Umm-hmm,*" Grandma said. "Now, on the matter of your sister, I know you don't want to hear *this*, but you need to forgive her. Honey, this bitterness is not serving you."

I sighed and turned my head from her eyes toward the blue and orange flame under the pot. My emotions were like that pot, on boil. The bitterness I was carrying had never served me well, yet I didn't know how to let it go.

"You're the oldest, Mariah. Your sister is afraid of you. She can't handle your sarcasm. She's also intimidated by your success. She doesn't think you need her, but I know you do. God brought the two of you out of the same womb for a reason."

Grandma stood. "Forgive her and get to know her before it's too late." She opened her arms, and I stood and walked into them. Grandma gave me a snug hug, the kind I needed to push the hurt

I was feeling out of my skin through my pores. Because making this soup, my usual stress reliever, had not worked. I kissed my grandmother's cheek.

"Don't stay up too late."

"I won't."

She left the kitchen, and I walked to my pot. I looked down at the ingredients through tear-filled eyes. I could barely see them. My grandmother was right. Hope was right. Dante was right. My father was right. Everyone was right about me and Sabrina. But I'd been here for so long, settled into this toxic relationship with her from the time she was born, that I didn't even know how to fix it.

Chapter 21

March 1919

Tabitha

*T*he *Charleston Chronicle* listed advertisements for cook jobs. Tabitha spent her mornings going to each one. No one would give her a chance. They wanted someone with more experience than dishing food at a general store. The final place where she inquired was near the docks. She was rejected there too. Once she exited, the fresh sea air pulled her off the street to the boardwalk.

Tabitha plopped down on a bench and opened her lunch sack. She had a biscuit with sweet muscadine jam that was no longer warm, but it was still a treat. It was nearly as nice as the breeze that floated by her. She took in the quiet minutes—minutes in which she owed no one anything, but they did not last. Worry about her situation settled in her mind like a piece of driftwood. She'd received a note from the building manager telling her she had to pay rent on the first of the month. Although she had been disappointed in the ten dollars Lady McCoy had thrown at her, Tabitha appreciated the three months she'd had of free rent. That must have been given on the word of Lady McCoy because the woman knew she was in Joseph's building. Tabitha had told her so. She had to find a job.

Tabitha left the boardwalk back to East Bay Street for her walk home. A loud thud caught her attention. An older man was putting a hunk of wood with the word *Closed* etched across it in red paint in front of a shop door. She looked above him and read the name of the establishment—Hank's Place. Thoughts of her brother entered her mind, causing a pinch of pain in her heart. If her Hank was alive, so much would be different about her life. He had been her best friend, and she was sure he would be her protector now.

Curious about the kind of establishment that bore her brother's name, Tabitha crossed the street and headed in the man's direction, approaching him just as he reached through the open door for a broom. He spotted her. With the first swipe across his stoop, he said, "I'm closed, miss."

Tabitha could see a counter and tables and chairs through the windows. It was a restaurant. She clutched her purse and lunch sack together in front of her and asked him the question on her mind. "It's almost the lunch hour. Isn't this the busiest part of the day?"

He stopped sweeping and inspected her before replying, "My wife is sick. I need to go see 'bout her."

"Are you the only cook?"

"This is my place."

"You're Hank?"

His eyes narrowed. He was losing patience with her. "I just said it's my place."

"What if you didn't have to close?"

Hank started sweeping again. "Young lady, you holdin' me up."

"I'm . . ." She gathered her courage to face possible rejection again. "I'm a cook, a good one, and I need work."

His eyes settled into hers. "I'm not looking for help."

"It's obvious you should be, sir."

His brows knit together ferociously. She could see he was not a man who liked to be told what he needed.

"Forgive me. You said your wife is sick. And I don't know you, but I have a sense about people. This is not an isolated sickness. Your wife is not well in general."

He regarded Tabitha now, letting his eyes inspect her in a way he hadn't before when he was trying to dismiss her as a pesky fly. "What makes you say that?"

"You carry it in your face, in your movements . . . I see the burden." Tabitha stepped closer, just enough to close the gap in their knowin'. "If you had help, you could spend more time with your wife."

Her words stirred his thoughts, but then he shook his head. "If I was going to take on some help, I wouldn't want a woman."

Now it was her who regarded him. "May I ask why?"

"'Cause don't nothing come in here but rough men. A man would be easier to deal with."

"I need you to give me a chance. I have three children and their father is dead. All I know how to do is cook."

"That ain't no reason for me to get myself tied up with a young gal in here."

"I grew up with brothers. I can handle myself."

He grunted. "You sound too educated to be able to handle anything."

"I'm most educated about farming and preparing a meal. Please, let me fix lunch. Test me . . . for free."

He sighed, long and bothered—thought about it for what felt like hours to Tabitha. Sweat beaded on her temples along her hairline as she waited.

Finally, he said, "I'm probably going to wish I held to my no, but you come at ten tomorrow, and I'll let you cook the midday meal."

Tabitha contained the joy enough to keep herself from leaping at him and hugging his neck.

He raised a hand and shook his finger at her. "I don't want no youngins underfoot."

"No, sir. I have help."

Without a goodbye, he stepped inside the door and closed it. That closed door was the open door Tabitha needed. She looked up at the sky and whispered, "Thank you, Jesus."

The next day, Tabitha arrived at nine thirty and waited for Hank. Once inside, she was given the space to work. The meat for the day was chicken. She decided on a chicken bog because she grew up on boggy rice and cooked it best. She boiled the chicken in garlic, pepper, basil, and onion, and once it was done, she pulled the meat into strips and seasoned it some more. After an hour of going in and out of the pantry and icebox, the kitchen smelled of her success.

By eleven thirty, the men came in from the docks, noisy and hungry. Hank had just lifted his face from the bowl she'd given him. Tables filled, and Hank took the food she dished and served it to men, table by table, collecting his money along the way. Tabitha held her breath in anticipation of their satisfaction. As they ate, she asked Hank, "Why are we only serving one thing?"

"Because it's easy for one person to do. Most of these men don't have no wife. They eat what I cook and don't complain on it. This is the best meal they get all day." He put his bowl and spoon in the sink.

When they were done, some of the men told Hank they knew he didn't cook and that he should hire Tabitha right away. They ate fast and left just as quickly. Within two hours, the restaurant was empty again.

"You are hired," Hank said. "You can work four days, and I'll pay you a dollar a day."

Joy filled her heart so that she had to fight crying in front of him. Though they would be tears of happiness and relief, men didn't like cryin' women. She'd already had to get him to overlook her being a woman.

"Thank you, sir. I'll see you tomorrow."

Hank grunted like he wasn't sure this was a good idea, but he extended his hand for Tabitha to shake. "It's a trial basis—week by week."

She shook his hand and went into the kitchen to clean up.

The next day, Tabitha came in ready to take over Hank's kitchen. Salt pork and okra were on the counter in the kitchen. Hank's old woodstove was burning hot. Two large pots of lima beans were already cooking.

"Lima beans, okra, salt pork. I cooks it every Wednesday. They like it fine."

Tabitha nodded and got to work chopping the okra and onion to add once the beans were ready.

"I have an idea," she said.

"Already?" Hank asked.

Tabitha smiled. "I think it might be more efficient if we had the men form a line to the counter rather than take the bowls to the table."

Hank frowned. "What makes you think that?"

"Well, for one, I won't be passing their tables and tempting them to be ungentlemanly, and two, it'll save you and me walking back and forth. I noticed your knee was bothering you at the end yesterday."

"Where you get this idea?" Hank grumbled, moving his weight from his left to the right knee as if it pained him already.

"That's the way I served the dinner meal at the store I worked in."

Hank rubbed his hand over his head. "I would think you would do things my way the first day."

"I will do whatever you want. These are your customers. It's only a suggestion, sir."

Hank grunted. "I shouldna hired you, but since I did, I guess I gots to treat you like I would my daughter. We can try it." Hank pushed the front door open and walked outside.

Tabitha smiled and went back to her cooking.

At the end of the week, Tabitha stepped onto the railcar with four dollars in her pocket. She would be able to pay her rent and the care for her children. Her heart was full. That night when she pushed her head into her pillow, she thanked God for blessing her.

Chapter 22

Present Day

Sabrina

I set Kenni up in front of the television in our room, locked us in so she couldn't wander, and climbed back into bed. I slept on and off for as long as my daughter would let me, and then I pulled myself together and got out of bed. I wasn't going to let my sister ruin another day of mine. I couldn't believe she actually threatened to leave, to disappoint our grandparents over the sweet cakes.

I received a text from Quinton inviting me to a barbecue. I enjoyed spending time with him, but he needed to know about Kenni. I decided if today was going to be a bad day, I could add him to the list of things I had to bemoan. I texted him back.

I have a four-year-old daughter.

His response.

Bring her. There will be kids there.

So he wasn't going to reject me because I had a child? I smiled. He was still on my list of likable humans.

I stood. Kenni was sitting cross-legged staring at the television, mesmerized by Barney the dinosaur. "Are you hungry?" I asked.

She looked at me over her shoulder and said, "I want pancakes."

I dropped to my knees and crawled toward her. I pulled her to me and walked my fingers up her belly until she giggled. "Pancakes? You always want pancakes."

"I love pancakes, Mommy."

"Let's go down and make some." I popped up and unlocked the door. As we walked to the stairs, I looked at Mariah's closed door.

"Is Auntie here?" Kenni asked, obviously following my eyes in that direction.

"I don't know, honey."

"Is she feeling sick like you was?"

I was hoping Mariah was feeling regretful. "I wasn't sick, baby. I think we're both tired. We worked hard yesterday."

I took her hand, and we walked down the stairs.

Grandma wasn't back from church yet. That didn't usually happen until two o'clock or so, and it was just one. With Kenni's help, I fixed pancakes and then relaxed with a cup of tea.

I went to my TikTok page. This was easier for me to use because there were no ghosts on TikTok. The videos I'd taken as I shopped for supplies had a lot of views. I was so excited about my TikTok results, I popped on Instagram to see my results there. I had comments to respond to, mostly people who'd been following me for years. I remembered the advice from the social media expert I'd found on YouTube: *"You have to engage with some of the people. Not all, but at least a few, or people will unfollow you."*

When I was done answering comments, I resisted the temptation to visit Kendrick's page, instead putting my phone down. I didn't need to look. I knew every line and curve of his face. I had memorized every word he said, the inflection in his voice, the essence of him.

He's gone.

I'm here.

Kenni is here.

It's time to stop mourning and live.

I didn't know what living looked like these days, but I was going to find out.

Kenni and I bathed and dressed. Just as we were about to leave to meet Quinton, Mariah emerged from her bedroom.

"Where are you two headed?" She was not contrite at all; in fact, her tone was chipper.

"Out," I replied.

"I can see that. I was hoping I could take Kenni to the circus. I got free tickets yesterday."

I felt the tug of Kenni's hand on my shirt before she squealed, "Mommy, I want to go to the circus."

Just like that, Mariah had hijacked my daughter, which was fine. The circus trumped a barbecue with strangers for someone her age.

Mariah and I did not exchange any other words. I'd said everything I had to say to her last night. If she thought treating Kenni to an afternoon out was going to make up for what she'd done, she was wrong.

Quinton and I agreed to meet in the Walmart parking lot. Once I arrived, he popped out of his car and came over to the truck. "Where's your daughter?"

"My sister stole her. Circus tickets."

"That's too bad." He looked disappointed, which made me smile inside. I was glad he was interested in meeting my daughter and not just pretending he was. "Next time we'll entice her with more." He smiled. "I need to make a stop on the way. I volunteer for an organization that helps farmers keep their land during disputes."

"I've heard of that. Heirs' property disputes."

"Right. We had a protest downtown today. I need to stop by it for a few minutes to help pack up things, if it's okay with you."

It was okay with me. I was his for the afternoon, no matter what he had in mind.

We settled into his beautiful BMW with its new-car smell, polished woodgrain trim, and butter soft seats. I liked the luxury, a lot. It made me wonder how many cakes I'd have to sell to own a vehicle like this. He asked me a few questions about Kenni—what she was like—and to see a picture. I had tons of those. He didn't ask me about her father. I was glad I didn't have to get into that. I was struggling with all my emotions today—anger, disappointment, grief, and fear. Mariah felt like the enemy. Kendrick seemed to be haunting my thoughts, and this Georgetown startup cake business was scary.

We had a brief lull in our conversation after talking about Kenni. I picked it back up with, "So you're just packing up? You didn't participate today?"

"I was there all day. I left to meet you." He took his eyes off the road just long enough to smile at me. "I show up, but that's not where the cause needs me. I handle paperwork. I make sure land deeds are right. That taxes and other county expenses are understood so people don't lose the farms because of paperwork shenanigans."

"That sounds important," I said, but I was thinking it sounded complex.

"It's rewarding," he replied.

We reached downtown. After Quinton parked and left the car, I took my phone out and googled Georgetown heirs' land and then reclamation of stolen land and read enough to be somewhat knowledgeable. Knowledgeable enough not to look like I lacked consciousness. Once I had a quick and dirty on the details, I put my phone down and looked out the window to see what Quinton and his people were getting into.

About fifty protesters were assembled. Most were men—young and old—but some women and children too. They carried picket signs that read: STOP STEALING OUR LAND, RETURN OUR LAND, and BLACK FARMERS MATTER TOO.

Two police cars were parked nearby. Most of the people walking by looked like tourists.

A reporter from a local TV station interviewed a man who appeared to be the leader. He even asked Quinton a few questions. Then Quinton and a few other men loaded coolers and tables and some other boxes into a van, and Quinton came back to the car. Just like that, they were done. It was all very anticlimactic. I didn't see the point of it all, so I asked, "Was this a good protest?"

"It was a great one," Quinton replied. "We got media coverage and donations. Anytime we do that, it's all good, and no one got hurt."

"Do people get hurt often?"

He shrugged. "Depends. Not here, but sometimes in other places."

We headed out of the city and turned off the road to a gated property with a huge sign that indicated it was private. I marveled at the tremendous farmhouse at the end of the long driveway. "Whose house is this?"

"It's the family home for one of the organizers," he replied. "A friend."

There was a beautifully appointed bottle tree in the front. It was the largest I'd seen. I took a picture of it because it was so pretty.

People from the protest were here—along with what looked like their families. The backyard was made for entertaining. There was a barbecue pit, comfortable-looking furniture, and a retractable canopy over the patio. Tables covered in picnic tablecloths were set up at the end of the patio. And there was food. Lots of food. Off to the side was a man working a second open pit grill.

The gathering was all it was intended to be—festive. There was as much food as there was joy in eating it. Quinton and I fixed plates and found a table of our own to eat at. Once we were done eating, we joined some conversations. Quinton took good care of me but also gave me space to meet other people. He spent a good deal of time huddled in a conversation with a group of men. They were looking at maps and notebooks and papers.

Quinton kept looking back at me, but then he'd get pulled back into the conversation.

My phone vibrated, and I saw it was a text from him: Sorry. There's an emergency with some land we've been advocating for. I'll just be a few more minutes.

I appreciated the fact that he realized I was still here, because the meeting looked intense. I got myself involved in a teenage spades game. I'd never learned, and that was a secret. Not being able to play spades was a crime in the Black community, nearly punishable by the loss of one's Black card. The teens didn't hold it against me.

When the sun went down, the music got louder. Couples danced, and the kids disappeared into the theater room inside. I was out of sorts. Being uncoupled was unnerving. I had gone from never having a man to always having one, and now I was back to having no one. Some would believe this thinking was problematic, but I liked being in a relationship. That was my truth.

Quinton gave a fist bump to the guy he was talking to and walked toward me. "This is the worst date ever, isn't it?"

I laughed. "Not ever."

"I'm sorry. I've been talking business. Maybe I can redeem myself a little. Would you like to dance?"

Anticipation bubbled in my chest, but I kept my face calm. I loved to dance. Something about Quinton made me think he would be a good dancer. He had an athletic body, and he walked to the rhythm of personal theme music playing in his head. The brother had an unfair amount of swagger that went with his good looks. But I still shook my head no.

"Okaaaay, a brother can bounce back from rejection. I've got something better than public dancing. I want to show you something." Quinton walked to a table. He grabbed a blanket and a small picnic basket and waved me to him. I followed him around the side of the house.

"Where did you get that stuff?" I said pointing.

"I had plans for you. My friend hooked me up."

He was trying hard. I liked that. We entered an area where the hedges were as tall as he was. We walked on a long, winding cobblestone trail that ended at a small building on a lake. It was gorgeous.

He unrolled the blanket, popped it open, and let it settle on the ground. I followed his lead and sat. "Let's see, we have some grilled shrimp and oysters, fresh mango slices, and plain old water because that's your preference."

I scrunched up my nose. I was full, but I loved oysters and mangoes. Quinton put them between us, and we snacked.

"Your friend must be really successful to own all this on a lake."

"Actually, he's a fifth-grade teacher. His wife has the bag. She's a corporate lawyer. A real savage in court."

I nodded. "Must be nice."

"If that's who you want to be," Quinton said, taking a sip of his water.

I took a few pictures of the lake. The moon's silvery glow cast a light across the water that stole my breath. We sat there finishing the food. "I understand why you brought me here. It's pretty."

"I'm glad you like it, but it's not the only thing I wanted to show you." He put our empty food containers in the basket, and we stood. He folded the blanket. When he was done, Quinton cocked his head toward the building and started walking. I followed.

The building was all windows, but there were closed shutters on the inside. It was made out of the same tan brick as the main house.

"Is this a cottage or something?"

"No." Quinton put in a code that released the lock. He pushed the door open and flipped a switch on the interior wall. The room was flooded with a warm incandescent light.

It was an artist workshop. There were paintings on easels—at least twenty—and more hanging on the walls. In the corner a table and cabinet held paints, brushes, and empty canvases.

"Get out of here," I said, walking to the first easel. It was a painting of two women sitting on a dock shelling oysters. I moved to another painting. The second was of a woman standing in the marsh, seagrass all around her. I moved to each canvas, becoming more and more emotional over the beautiful depictions of Gullah life until I couldn't even see for the heavy tears that filled my eyes. I wiped them and turned to Quinton. "Who is this artist?"

"The corporate lawyer."

I chuckled. "Are you serious?"

"This is her hobby."

I let my eyes scan the walls, taking in each of the paintings until I was done. "This is not a hobby."

Quinton shrugged. "It is for her."

"She should have a showing. Open a gallery."

She doesn't have time. She's too busy making the big money. And she lets fear tell her she's not good."

I shook my head. "That's nuts. She's like ridiculously gifted."

"Kind of like you."

I frowned. "What are you talking about?"

"Your cakes. You can make it as a baker. It might not give you savage money, but God will make sure you and Kenni don't want for anything. Follow your passion."

"You brought me here for that pep talk?"

"No, I brought you here because you love art and . . ." He walked to the table, took out his phone, and tapped on it a few times. "I don't handle rejection well." I recognized the intro music to "Satisfy My Soul."

I pulled back my head. "Bob Marley?"

"I sat on the sidelines rocking to the new-school music, but I'm old school, baby." He threw up his hands and swayed to the music.

"I haven't heard this in a long time."

He cocked an eyebrow. "It doesn't remind you of another dude, does it?"

I laughed. "No."

"Good. Now satisfy my soul, and show me what you got." If Quinton had any inhibitions, I couldn't tell. He was into this song, moving to it using his arms and torso and footwork that didn't miss a beat.

I slipped in closer to him, and we danced in unison, imitating each other's moves, mostly humorously at first. That was us working out silly nerves. By the time "No Woman, No Cry" came on, we were more than comfortable with each other. Quinton pulled me closer, and I followed his lead to the slower music. I loved this song. He didn't know it, but it was one of my favorites. I closed my eyes and let the music take me far, far away but still allowed myself to be connected to this man who was making such an effort to entertain me in ways that I enjoyed.

Quinton pulled me even closer. We rocked together. My head was flat against his chest. I could feel his heart pounding against my ear. He wrapped his arms around my back, and his chin touched the top of my hair. He kissed my hair and wrapped his arms around my body at the shoulders. This was getting way too sexy. The instant closeness was too good to be true. The pounding of his heart . . . too intimate. I hadn't experienced that sensation—a man's heart beating and belly rising and falling—since Kendrick. I spun out of his grip.

"We need to slow this down."

Quinton frowned. "Is something wrong?"

"I feel like you know me, like you know what I need and what I want."

"Is that a bad thing?"

I tossed up my hands. "It's too much all at once."

He stepped toward me. I stepped back—anxiety making it hard for me to believe this chemistry was real. I'd had this before. People didn't experience this twice. You only got one soulmate.

"It's just a dance, Sabrina. I promise I'm not trying to steal your soul or anything." He threw up his hands palms out like he was surrendering. He was amused, and I could see he was fighting not to laugh. He started chanting the lyrics, "Everything is going to be all right" over and over with the song. When that part of the song was done, he laughed.

I shook my head. "You see that, timing—you're a magician or a warlock or a rootworker of some kind."

Quinton shook his head. "A rootworker?" He reeled in his amusement. "I am a man with a good memory. I remember that you like reggae. We talked about it way back in the day. And that you like art—paintings specifically. That you love the water—oceans, rivers, lakes. That your favorite fruit is mangoes, and your favorite shellfish is oysters." His face became serious. "I remember you."

I nodded and said, *Okay*, wordlessly. I got it. He *did* remember.

Quinton started rocking to the beat again. "Are you gonna dance with me or what? This is the seven-minute version."

I laughed and took his hand again. This time when he pulled me close, I let him.

The party broke up. Quinton and I headed back to Walmart. More music was our company on the ride. Once we arrived, he parked the car, but neither of us made a move to get out.

"I appreciate you thinking of me today."

"It was my pleasure to spend time with you. I hope Kenni had fun, but next time"—he turned to the side so he was looking directly into my eyes—"I want to meet her."

My tender mommy heart appreciated his interest. "Maybe the next time you will."

A beat of silence passed. Quinton raised his arm and rested his elbow on the steering wheel. "I'm curious about her father. Is he in the picture?"

I was surprised it took him so long to ask. "Deceased. Before she was born."

His eyebrows hitched. He wasn't expecting that answer. People never do. "I'm so sorry."

"Yeah. Us too."

"How are y'all coping?"

"Better since being here in Georgetown. There might be too many reminders of him in Greenville. I don't think I realized how many until I came here and stopped seeing them every day."

"Maybe you should relocate."

I shrugged. "Maybe I should."

"I'm sure your grandparents would love having you."

I shrugged again. "Maybe they would."

Quinton smiled at me. He was amused by the game I was playing with my words.

"Her paternal grandmother would miss her."

Quinton stated the obvious. "She can visit. Or you can take Kenni to her."

"The same way my father did with us. He brought us to Georgetown for summers."

Quinton smiled. "And that's how we met."

"Seems like a hundred years ago." My eyes drifted to the window where the view of the cloudless sky confirmed the vastness of . . . everything. I returned my attention to Quinton. I refused to believe he was as perfect as he felt, so I nudged him. "Are you sure you don't mind that I have a child?"

"Why would I mind?" he asked. His eyebrows came together again. Quinton's face hid nothing. I remembered that about him. He hadn't changed. Not that way anyway.

"Because some men don't date women with children."

"Some women don't date men with children."

I pursed my lips and teased him. "I'm one of them, so do you have kids?"

He laughed. "No. I'm just saying it goes both ways. Anyway, I'm not like *those* men. Children add to your life, not take away." He was quiet for a few seconds, thinking before speaking as he always did. "I'm sorry she doesn't have a father. I'm sorry you both lost someone you loved."

I'd heard that so many times from family and friends, but the words still stung.

"I like you, Sabrina. You know that. I have always thought about you. You could have six kids, and I'd still want to get to spend time with you."

This time I was the one who laughed. "Now that . . ." I shook my head. "I don't know."

Quinton chuckled. "I mean I'm glad you don't have six, but I'm serious. I've wondered about you for years. Where is she? How is she? I searched for you on social media."

"I don't have a page in my real name."

"I know. I thought that was weird." He laughed again. "And that made me even more curious. I wanted you to be okay . . . so badly," he said. "I prayed for you . . . often."

I reached for his hand. "Thank you. I needed someone standing in the gap for me." Tears wet my eyes, and then the first one flowed. I swiped at it with my free hand.

Quinton leaned across the seat. He raised his hand and wiped a second tear that trailed down to my lip.

"Are you going to kiss me?" I asked, anticipating he was.

"I want to." He hesitated a beat, and when I didn't say *no*, he leaned in and pressed his lips against mine, gently, not lingering long, but leaving enough heat to imprint his touch on my memory. He smelled spicy. His cologne had clove, cedar, and some kind of floral note. It mixed with his perspiration and created a heady, warm scent that made me wish the kiss was longer.

"I want you, Sabrina."

"What?" I asked, heart and eyelashes fluttering.

Quinton leaned back. "In my life." He smiled. He could see he'd shaken me a little. "I say how I feel. Always. So, my intentions are . . . serious. But everything about us is on you. Your timing. Your way."

His words made me feel good. All of them. Desire and patience—I needed and wanted both. "Okay."

Quinton tapped out a little celebratory beat on the steering wheel. He nodded, and it was plain to see satisfaction filled his chest. "Okay."

I thanked him again for getting me out of the house. He walked me to the truck, and after a quick hug, I slipped in and drove home.

My phone started pinging, and I looked at it. I had a series of text messages from Ellen. Once I pulled into the driveway, I read them.

When are you coming back?
You never said this was permanent.
I need to hear from you.
We need to discuss this.

Ellen was not a texter. She seemed to have gone off the rails, so I called her.

"Ellen, what is all this?"

"You have been gone for weeks."

"I know how long I've been gone. I told you—"

"I know what you told me." She cut me off. "But it's time for you to bring her home."

Home was with me, or didn't Ellen understand that? Her house was temporary, but I needed to offer her something. She was really upset. "I'll put her on FaceTime in a few minutes."

"She should be asleep!" She screamed so loud her voice petered out at the end.

I snatched my head back. "Ellen, you don't need to yell at me. I'm not a child."

"You aren't? Sometimes I can't tell."

That was nasty. I didn't need to match her tone, so I counted to five before replying. "I'll call you tomorrow."

"We need to settle this now."

"We need to settle it when you have a calmer head." I pressed End and put down my phone. My heart was jackhammering out of my chest. I'd never heard Ellen sound so angry, not since the night Kendrick died. After the shock of the news about the accident, Ellen's anger was directed at me because he'd been on the road because of me.

I closed my eyes. I shouldn't have hung up on her. Not Kendrick's mother. We weren't going to fight over Kenni, not ever. We agreed. I rang her back but got voicemail. I tried again and still . . . voicemail. I didn't know what to say, what I knew would make her happy. I *was* staying here much longer than I anticipated. I felt good about what I was doing, and I wasn't going to apologize for it. Not to her. Not to anyone.

Chapter 23

Mariah

Jordy, my little neighbor back in Duncan, was on my mind. Spending time with Kenni made me think about him. I'd been gone for weeks. I wondered what Jordy was eating now that he'd grown accustomed to me feeding him a few times a week.

I sent Hope a text message: Call me when you can.

I went downstairs to the kitchen. Sabrina and Kenni were still in their bedroom. I made a pot of grits and cooked some bacon. Sabrina didn't eat much meat, but she never passed up bacon. The smell quickly drew them downstairs.

"I was hungry, so I made breakfast," I said.

Kenni dashed to the table, and Sabrina stood there, shock gluing her feet to the floor. I could literally knock her over with the tip of a teaspoon, so I fixed them both a plate and placed them on the table. Kenni went right for the bacon.

I crouched down next to her. "What do you have planned for today?"

"I have ta go ta school," she said, popping a piece of bacon in her mouth.

Sabrina sat, and I stood. "Thank you," she said.

"Enjoy," I replied. I left the kitchen and returned to my bedroom. I dropped down on the bed. I was perspiring. That had been hard. Something was wrong with me.

My phone rang in a call from Hope. "What's going on?" she asked.

"You know that kid I've been giving extra food to?"

"You mean the one you've been cooking for. Mr. Call-me-Jordy-cause-I-ain't-a-river?"

I smiled thinking about that. "He's been on my mind. I haven't been feeding him because I'm not there."

"So you're just remembering your kid needs a meal? I need to open a child welfare case on you." Hope laughed. In her job as a family and children services community partner, she had many open cases.

"Very funny," I said. "I want to get some food to him."

"How are you going to do that?" I could see the expression on Hope's face in my mind. The question made sense.

"I don't know. I don't have a relationship with his mother, but I was thinking . . ."

Hope grunted and said, "Go on."

"I was thinking I could order something for them. I don't know if she can cook, but maybe I can get some prepared foods delivered."

"Girl, that's a lot."

"I know."

"And are you sure she's going to be good with that? I mean it's one thing to make her think you're sharing leftovers; it's another to send her food from somewhere else."

"She'll take it. She's never sent anything back to me."

"That means she's in need."

"And maybe too prideful to get help," I said, thinking about how she never even thanked me. I assumed it was her pride keeping her from doing so. No one's manners were that horrible.

"I tell you what, Zelle me some cash. I'll go and pick up some food and deliver it to her. While I'm there, I'll talk to her, see if I can get her linked to a service that will provide her with food to fill in the gap between her paychecks. Sometimes people don't know what's available."

I loved what Hope was proposing, but this was asking a lot. "I don't want to make you work after you clock out. You're busy enough."

"Girl, please. There's always some neighbor or church member asking me questions. I'm rarely off the clock, and the truth is, I kind of don't want to be. If I can help somebody, especially a child, I want to. Text me what to get him. I'm not trying to figure that out."

"You are amazing."

"I know. You don't have to remind me." She laughed. "I have a meeting. Call me later. I need an update on what's going on down there."

I nodded. "I will. Love you."

I ended the call just as a knock sounded on the door.

"Come in," I offered, and Sabrina opened it and walked in.

"I'm sorry. Did I interrupt you and Vince?"

"Vince?" I asked.

"I heard you say you loved him or someone."

I put my phone down and waited for her to come all the way in the room.

"I have something for you," she said. She pulled her hand from behind her back and handed me a stack of old envelopes. There was no name outside of any of them.

"What are these?" I asked.

"Letters that Great-Great-Grandma Tabitha wrote."

I processed those words slowly. Letters from our great-great-grandma? Where had they been? I opened one of them. "The paper was yellowed with age, the ink faded to a brownish hue, the paper brittle with the folds of time. There were three pages, and on the last, I saw her signature—Tabitha Cooper—in the neatest cursive script that I'd ever seen.

"Where did you get these?"

"Grandma gave them to me the night we arrived. I've been reading them."

"Why haven't we seen them before?"

"She said she was waiting for the right time. And now that I'm reading them, I think I understand that it's the right time for me." Sabrina's words made me more curious. "Maybe it'll be the right time for you too."

I found that statement curious. I counted five of them. "What was she writing about? Who were they for?"

"They're addressed to her mother, but I think she was writing for us," Sabrina said.

"Us?"

She nodded. "You'll see what I mean. They're in order. As I finish more, I'll leave them for you."

A faint smell was tickling my nostrils. I raised the letter to my nose, expecting it to have some hint of mold. I was caught off guard by a familiar scent.

"The box she kept them in has a sprig of dried lavender," Sabrina said, obviously realizing I was trying to figure that out. She continued, "I was thinking you might have to leave soon. If I hold on to them until I finish, you'll have to wait until you come back."

I looked down at the letters. I hadn't read a word, but I knew I would find the vulnerability of my great-great-grandmother's heart. For that reason, I felt compelled to be vulnerable with Sabrina. There was no point in pretending with her anymore.

"I won't be leaving. Not anytime soon," I said, placing the stack on the nightstand. "Vince and I are separated. He's filed for divorce. I'm no longer living at the house or working at Clark's."

Sabrina's mouth dropped open. She sat on the end of the bed. "I'm so sorry."

I shrugged.

"Are you two sure? You've been married a long time."

"It's over. There's no way for us to come back together, and after the way he's treated me, I wouldn't want to."

Kenni's voice sounded from the bottom of the stairs. "Mommy!"

Sabrina stood and walked to the door. "I have to get her to daycare before she takes herself."

A little laugh bubbled in my chest.

Sabrina hesitated for another beat before saying, "I'm so sorry about Vince and Clark's."

I could see she was. "Thanks. I'll be okay."

"We'll talk later," Sabrina said. "Thanks again for breakfast."

I nodded. I almost smiled, but then Sabrina turned and walked out of the room. I heard the gentle pounding of her footsteps as she took the stairs, and then minutes later the opening and closing of the front door. She and Kenni were gone.

I released a long breath. That hadn't been so bad—breaking the sheet of ice between us.

I reached for the stack of letters. As I delicately unfolded the fragile, century-old paper, a rush of emotions overcame me. This was a bridge between eras. The weight of my great-great-grandmother's ancestral roots and the legacy of my family settled upon me, and for some reason, Dante crossed my mind. He was a man who wanted to keep our history. He would really trip over these letters. I sat down and read. A little over an hour later, I had one left. I was so filled with emotions I couldn't bear to read it yet. My heart ached for her, and it ached a little for myself. We were a century apart, and DNA wasn't the only thing we shared. She had the disdain of Charles Cooper, and I had Lorraine, my shady ex-stepmother. The enormity of that was something I needed to sit with for a while.

The next day, I was up before the sun, standing on the porch with a mug of coffee, taking in the morning sounds and the earthy smell of the marsh.

The door opened, and Grandma stepped out with her mug. "You're up early."

"I couldn't sleep anymore."

"I suppose you have a lot on your mind," Grandma said, sinking into one of the rocking chairs.

"More than I'd like." I raised my coffee mug to my lips. "I've been reading Grandma Tabitha's letters."

Grandma nodded.

"I ripped through the ones I have. I have to go back and read them again." I was having an experience with Great-Great-Grandma Tabitha. The way she took over Hank's and found a way to survive all alone in Charleston was unbelievable. I'd always said Harriet Tubman was my shero, but Tabitha Cooper was a baddie. She left me with zero excuses for failing at anything.

Grandma's voice pulled me from my thoughts. "Your sister told me you made her and Kenni breakfast."

"Yes, ma'am. It was grits and bacon."

"It was a big deal to her. She saw it as an olive branch."

I took another sip of my coffee. "Maybe it was."

"You know, you girls have me looking at YouTube all the time now. I have a sign-on and everything."

I laughed. "Grandma, what?"

"I've been searching for stuff I want to know." She giggled and took a sip from her mug. "I like it."

I covered her free hand with mine and squeezed it. "I'm glad. Sometimes a distraction like that can be good."

"I ran across this video the other day from one of those Bible study teachers. I forget her name . . . Jackie Hill or Perry something."

"Jackie Hill Perry?"

"Yes, that's her name. She was talking about Christians needing therapy. She was sharing her own journey."

I put my mug down. "She talks about that quite a bit."

"So, you've heard her?"

"I have. I follow her on social media."

We were quiet for a moment. Grandma was trying to steer this conversation to my mental health. My grandmother, advocating for therapy? I never thought I'd see the day. I inhaled deeply and released a slow breath, reminding myself that my grandmother always meant well. Always.

"You and I have talked about you talking to someone," Grandma said. "You know this is a big thing for me to suggest. People in my day didn't know anything about therapy. If Jesus couldn't fix it, it couldn't be fixed." She smiled. "But I am wise enough to know that everything we believed wasn't right."

I set my gaze on my mug but then eventually closed my eyes to the pain and confusion I was feeling.

"Every generation does the best it can with what it knows."

I opened my eyes and looked at her. I figured my grandmother had to think something was really wrong with me for her to keep suggesting therapy. Hope kept the message on repeat.

"I can't help but think the migraines you have come from bottled-up stress."

"I haven't had one since I got here. Maybe the air in the lowcountry is better for me than the air in the Upstate."

Grandma's eyes grew wistful, then sad. She added, "And you not getting pregnant . . . that could be stress."

"I didn't try to get pregnant." I shrugged. "Every woman doesn't want children."

Grandma threw up her hands. "Okay. Forgive me for assuming. I never knew that. I'm just on the hunt for more grandbabies."

I pushed my back into my chair and sighed a little. "It's for the best that I never got pregnant. Look at us."

"Your marriage ending is not hindsight."

"My having a child would just be another thing Vince might be trying to take from me."

Grandma frowned in worry. "Let's not focus on Vince right now. This conversation is about you. You have had to deal with a lot. Losing your mother, and then my son could have done better when he remarried. By the time I realized how bad things were with Lorraine, you were almost in high school, and your father . . ."

"Had surrendered his power." I completed her thought. We both knew what it was. Hot tears crept into my eyes. I wanted to fight the idea that I needed help, but I knew it wasn't true. I was angry and controlling and bitter. I couldn't deny that I saw myself and didn't like what I saw. But it was all scary.

"Are you listening to me?" Grandma's voice rose an octave, and I drew my eyes back to her. I was listening. Kind of. "Baby, this isn't just about your sister."

"What if it doesn't help or it makes things worse?"

"How would it make things worse?"

"I don't know. But I'm scared, Grandma. I'm afraid of what I might find out about myself." I pressed my hand against my chest. "What if the safe space I've tucked my feelings into explodes and I need to get my feelings back in the box and can't anymore? I may be limping, but I'm coping. I get up every day and do what I have to do. Therapy could disable me."

"You are not going to live your life not taking action because of fear." Grandma put a hand under my chin and turned my face to hers. "If you had a lump in your breast, you'd be scared, but you would go to the doctor. We don't avoid help because the treatment might be hard."

Grandma let go of me. Nothing anyone had ever said to me made more sense.

I sighed heavily and whispered, *Okay,* in my head and then let it come off my lips.

Grandma said, "Okay."

I wiped my tears. I was tired of crying.

Before my anxiety overtook sound thinking, I made an appointment with a local therapist grandma's pastor recommended. She accepted my insurance, so I figured she was a good place to start. I wouldn't have my insurance for long with the divorce pending, so I might as well get some use out of it.

The doctor's name was Johnson. She had a cancellation this afternoon. I tried to put it off, but the next opening for a new patient wasn't for three weeks. Getting started couldn't be delayed. I had to commit before I talked myself out of it.

I still didn't know how I felt about therapy, but it was time to try something new. My joy was gone, and it was time for me to stop wanting to be accepted the way I was when the way I was might be wrong.

I reopened the text I'd kept from Hope, the one I had not completely read.

> Therapy is an opportunity to get strategies. It doesn't mean you're unwell. It just means you need a little help coping. It's no different from going to a medical doctor for a physical health condition.

If I had a lump in my breast, I wouldn't ignore it. I would go to the doctor immediately. If I started bleeding from some orifice I wasn't supposed to, I would get help. I would run to the emergency room. The things I told myself made sense, but reconciling the sensibility of it all was difficult. It seemed natural to be able to take care of my own feelings. But then . . . there was nothing natural about my life. Nothing had been natural about how my mother left this earth. Growing up without a mother was unnatural.

I stepped out of the car into the swelter that was summer heat in Georgetown and walked into the building.

Dr. Johnson was tall and slim with gorgeous skin and an elegant neck that reminded me of a swan. She moved with the confidence of a model on the runway, and she was just as attractive. She looked so beautiful and so strong. I admired her immediately.

After our initial greeting, she put on dark purple reading glasses and tapped on an iPad. "In looking at the paperwork you filled out online, I see this is your first time trying therapy."

I nodded.

She pushed her back into the plush leather chair and crossed one long leg over the other. "Tell me, what brings you in?"

I wanted to say my grandmother and my best friend, but the truth was Dante's assessment of my situation with Sabrina hung in my mind more than anything else. When he'd said one of her problems was my moods, I felt convicted, and that conviction hadn't lifted. It sat in the middle of my chest like a heavy rock. Dante didn't know us, but he'd observed us enough to know or feel comfortable saying I was the problem.

It was funny how little triggers could move us when big triggers froze us. Sabrina and I had been fighting our entire lives, but I'd never felt moved to do anything about it. Now Dante, someone looking from the outside, saw me, and I took action. I wasn't one of those women who was only moved to action by men. That wasn't my story. I think he could have been anyone I respected, right?

Lord, stop.

I was already spinning. I raised my eyes to Dr. Johnson's and said, "I'm angry and mean. I have headaches and . . . the people in my life see my behavior."

She nodded. "Tell me what you're angry about."

"Everything." I summed it up with that word but ran down the list, which included my divorce and losing my role at Clark's, the house I'd been living in for nine years, and my television show. I mentioned my daddy issues, and then I finished with, "I have a complicated relationship with my sister."

Overall, it was a getting-to-know-you type of meeting. We talked about the HIPAA stuff and confidentiality. She told me what she was required to do by law if I was thought to be a danger to myself or someone else. She asked me how I felt about medications. Had I tried breathing exercises? How did I cope with stress? She talked about her part of the process. She was not a fixer. Her role was to help me deal with my problems and create new strategies for coping. She would never be judgmental or critical and would not give me unsolicited advice.

Dr. Johnson probed, but it was all harmless and unintrusive. It didn't make me feel terribly uncomfortable. I ran out of gas and didn't say much beyond yes and no to her questions. Saying what bothered me had stolen the air in my lungs. By the time we were done, we had determined I did not sleep well, I was somewhat antisocial, I had OCD, and I had anger management issues. I basically knew all that, but it really sucked to hear someone else say it.

Later that week, I was back for session number two. Dr. Johnson began with questions about my career. She wanted to know why I chose to study hospitality.

I imagined it seemed a contradiction for someone who was as antisocial as I was. Antisocial people weren't hospitable, but I hadn't always been this way. I tried to remember the moment I'd selected my major, but I couldn't. "I don't know really."

"If you could go back in time, would you change your major?"

"I don't know."

"Base your answer on how you feel about your work, not your current situation with your ex-husband."

"I like my work."

"Tell me what you like about it."

I sucked in air and let my mind search for the answer. "I like the order in kitchens. There are systems. If a kitchen is organized, it will run efficiently. Everything has its place and is always put back in its place at the end of the night. Kitchens"—all the kitchens in my life passed through my memory, including Tabby's—"are polished, shiny, and clean. A well-run restaurant's kitchen holds no surprises." Feeling vulnerable, I wrapped my arms around myself. The thoughts that fueled my OCD were showing, and I didn't like it. I shut down before the session was over. I was tempted to quit already.

At my third session, I decided I was going to try harder. My copay was fifty dollars. I wasn't a fan of wasting money, so I wasn't going to come here and act like any part of this session was free.

Dr. Johnson opened with, "Is there anything you want to begin with today?"

"Like what?"

"Tell me how things are going with the restaurant."

I replied, "Better than I expected. Working from the food truck until we can reopen was a brilliant idea. The truck is getting busy already."

"And you're open how many days?"

"Thursday through Saturday evenings."

She nodded. "Nice. You seemed anxious about the actual building last week."

"Was I?" I didn't recall being anxious about the building.

She nodded; a little affirming noise escaped her throat.

"The renovations are pretty much done. The rebuild is coming along faster than I anticipated. With the code inspection, we should be able to open in three weeks. I'm happy. I'm doing a good job."

Dr. Johnson smiled a little. "Does it surprise you that you're doing a good job?"

This is what therapists got paid the big bucks for. To ask questions to make you reflect on your answers.

"No," I replied. "I usually do a good job at anything I do."

She nodded and made a note. Was she documenting I was a narcissist?

"Why is it that you think that you usually do a good job?"

"I think because this is my skill set. This is what I've worked on for the last nine years of my life. Not necessarily a rebuild per se but running a restaurant. Understanding the heart and soul in the guts of it. There's more to it than cooking and serving. There's atmosphere. There is the very paint on the walls. The soul in the tables and chairs. There's so much more than just the food, although the food is amazing."

Dr. Johnson said, "I hear your passion. Are you cooking?"

"A few things here and there." I told her about Dante. "He's a total artisan. He completely understands the gastronomy of the region's food. His ideas for the menu are already attracting millennials." I realized I'd gone on about Dante quite a bit. Even to me I sounded like he was perfect.

Dr. Johnson said, "I have an assignment for you. I want you to get a journal. It doesn't have to be anything fancy. It can be a seventy-sheet notebook from a dollar store, or you can get something fancier if you need to. I make my own." She held up a pretty notebook with applique and whatnot. My mind went right to my sister. I would never think to decorate a notebook that way. I might look for a pretty one, but change an existing one? No.

"It's up to you, but I want you to start right away. Don't let the instrument keep you from doing the work."

She knew me a little better than I knew myself. That I would let the hunt for a journal get in my way.

"What I want you to do is make two lists." She held up two fingers. "The first is of twenty things you've accomplished in your career. Push yourself if you have to, but get to twenty. Do this list first." She put one finger down. "The second list . . . what you've accomplished personally." She dropped her hand in her lap.

I nodded. "Is that it?" I shrugged.

It was her time to nod. "That's it." She picked up her iPad. "I see you've committed to biweekly sessions."

"I don't know how long my insurance is going to last. I kind of want to fast-track this."

She chuckled. "Understandable, but I have to caution you, there's no magic timeline here."

I nodded again. I did a lot of nodding with her.

"Dig into the homework and that'll help." She stood and walked me to the door. She handed me a sheet of paper, which I looked at. It was the homework assignment. "I'll see you on Friday."

Friday came, and we didn't talk much about the list I made—not as much as I expected anyway—because she went another route. She asked me about my friendships and social life; then she sent me home with more homework. This time I was journaling about my personal relationships. She wanted at least a page about the people closest to me: Vince, my father, my grandparents, and Sabrina. Dr. Johnson wasn't wasting my copays. This was about to get real.

Chapter 24

July 1920

Tabitha

A smile set in her heart and on her lips as Tabitha entered Hank's to begin the day. She noted as she passed the pantry that the supply shipment they should have received had not been delivered. It would cost more if she had to go to the market to stock up. She put her things away, washed her hands, and donned her apron. She found Hank sitting outside in the back, drinking coffee and smoking a cigarette. Hazy smoke and the harsh smell of tobacco lingered in the air.

Tabitha coughed and fanned the cloud away before coming to the reason she was invading Hank's private time. "What happened to the supply order? I need flour, and our rice barrel is getting low."

After a reflective minute, Hank took another sip from his coffee. "I didn't order."

Not needing to ask because he would tell her, she waited for his explanation.

"I'm closing this place."

Hank had mentioned this before several times, but this was the first time he delayed the supply order.

"Ruby's going to die if we stay in this wet city. Her lungs are too weak. The doctor says she needs a dry place."

This news was not surprising, just unexpected . . . today. "Where will you go?"

"Tennessee. I have family there."

Seeing he had given this decision thought enough to fire off replies, Tabitha straightened her back. This was not just talk; it was real. "When will you go?"

"Soon."

Panic filled her chest, but she kept her emotions out of her voice. "When did you decide this?"

"I've been deciding it for years."

"Years of maybe." She sighed. "You could have given me some notice on the supplies."

"You've got a good name now. One of the restaurants will hire you."

"I don't want to work for *one* of them." She'd thought about it many times because Hank was always mumbling about leaving. Hank was known to make decisions impulsively, like not ordering supplies without telling her, so it was time to speak her mind. She didn't want him to make plans before she had her say. "I can take over *this* place."

"By yourself?"

"Of course by myself. You know I have the gumption, the ideas, and the back for the work."

"This isn't a place for a woman to be alone. Some of the new ones working the docks . . . We don't know them."

"I keep my pistol in my skirt, and Sam is in and out." Though Tabitha did not know how much weight to give Sam. He was Hank's wife's cousin from Tennessee, so he always behaved himself, but still they did not get on well. On Tabitha's suggestion, Hank hired Sam to wheel a food wagon down the dock. There were Negro men there who couldn't walk this far on their short lunch break.

Hank shook his head. "Gal, I'd fear God if something happened to you."

She stepped closer to him, cocked her head, and forced him to look her in the eyes. "*God* is my keeper. I've learned that the hard way, and I don't want to work for anyone . . . other than you."

Hank laughed, the smoker's crackle making it sound less jovial. "You don't work for me." He finished his coffee and handed her the empty tin mug. "I can't guarantee the landlord won't want more rent. He's been trying to raise it."

"Maybe we can keep the arrangement you have with him for a while," Tabitha said. "This is your place. I can still pay it in your name."

"My name."

"It's Hank's Place. That don't have to change. Not right away."

"You know business, Tabitha. Long as you can keep these men off ya, you gonna do all right."

"All I need is a chance." Tabitha smiled. "And flour and rice."

He nodded. "What you makin' today?"

She relaxed some. Hank was in agreement, and it hadn't been hard to convince him. "I'm going to use that pork meat. I figure hash, rice, and corn bread."

Hank dropped his cigarette, stood, and stepped on it. "I'll go to the supply store while you cook."

Tabitha raised a hand to his shoulder, squeezed, and kissed his cheek. "Thank you, Hank."

He grumbled and went on this way to the store. Tabitha sailed back inside, put his mug in the sink, and gathered the things she needed. She walked out of the kitchen and looked at the dining room, inspecting every foot of it. This was going to be hers. Now she understood why she was in Charleston. It was so she could have her own little corner of the world.

Two weeks later, Hank was gone. His exit brought a change in her relationship with Sam. He didn't try to hide his disappointment that Hank hadn't left the place to him. Tabitha didn't know why he thought Hank would. He couldn't cook, not well. Selling off the wagon was all he knew.

One of the first small changes Tabitha made was to put a bell over the door to alert her when someone entered.

Brady Moore, her neighbor on the left side of her building, entered carrying the day's newspaper and a small sack. Tabitha knew without opening it that it contained candies for her children. Brady operated a store that sold newspapers, leather goods, men's twill clothing, and shoes appropriate for the work they did on the docks. He also sold penny candy and soda water. He'd been open for a few months, bringing the business with him from Savannah. But he'd been gone for a few weeks, visiting his sick father in Columbia.

"You will ruin the teeth of my children."

"*Aw*, a little candy never hurt teeth. It's not brushing that ruins them." He placed the sack and paper on the counter.

"You've missed a great deal since you were gone."

Brady's brows rose with interest. "Have I?"

"Yes, but first, how is your father?"

Brady slipped onto a stool. "Healing well, thank you."

"And your mother?"

"Tired of my father but well also. Now please, you know I sell the paper. I want the news."

With his easy wit, Brady pressed a smile out of Tabitha every day. She went into the kitchen to fix his plate. She'd made his favorite dish, stewed chicken and Hoppin' John rice. Once she returned with his bowl, she told him of Hank's departure as he ate.

"So you own the place now? That's impressive. You'll do a fine job." Brady's smile was a welcome light in the early part of the day. Everything about him was welcoming, and she had to keep her fondness for his looks a secret so as not to make a fool of herself with someone she had to see so often.

Brady was tall and broad shouldered, his skin as deep as hers after the sun toasted him for the season. His eyes . . . intense and thoughtful. His voice . . . deep but soothing at the same time. He was often slow to speak, deliberate instead of ready with a word for everything. Being intentional made him more trustworthy. She had no use for men who spoke fast on all subjects. That was how Joseph had been. That kind of way about a man was like a bitter root in her mouth.

"I would not be a good neighbor if I didn't tell you to keep your eyes open. With Hank gone, some of the men might try you." He frowned through those words. "I'm next door and available to help with anything you need, Tabitha."

"I appreciate your offer," she said.

His easy smile teased her again. "Keep a broom handle or something handy behind the counter, so you can bang on the wall."

"I will." And with the suggestion, she really considered him to be her protector.

Brady put money down and left with his bowl. He always returned it at the end of the day. She hadn't noticed he'd put down twice as much. She rushed out the door after him. Just as he reached his store, she called to him. "You put down too much money."

A slow smile spread across Brady's face. "I believe they call that a tip. You should put a jar on the counter. Let the men give you a little extra. Pennies add up to dollars." He stuck his key in the door and disappeared behind it.

Tabitha was frozen in place for a few seconds. She was one heartbeat short of a swoon. At first the little tug in her belly felt good. By the time she reached her kitchen, her stomach turned over and fear crept into her chest. She did not know what to do with a man other than make babies, and she didn't need any more of those until she had a husband, if that was ever to be.

It wasn't long before Sam entered with the bell ringing over his head.

"That sound is gonna make you a looney one," he said, twirling his finger around by his ear.

"Good morning to you too," Tabitha said. She'd already loaded his food on the wagon.

"You got it ready?" Sam asked.

"Of course." Tabitha noticed he was avoiding her eyes. "Are you settling the account?"

"I'll take care of it when I come back," he said. "I'm running late. I best be going, or I'll have wasted food."

Wasted free food, Tabitha thought, but didn't say. She didn't want to delay him. If he was going to go without paying her, she'd prefer he make the going quick.

Sam walked out the back door, and seconds later Tabitha heard the squeak of the wagon wheel as he dragged it away. She pulled the back door closed and locked it. He had not paid her. The arrangement he had with Hank was to transfer to her. Sam was supposed to pay for his meals on Friday for the following week. But last week he paid on Wednesday, which put Tabitha in the position of giving him food with no payment. Now she had to see what he would do this week as it was already Wednesday and he'd given her nothing. Hank was concerned about the men taking advantage. The only one doing that was the troublesome cousin he'd left behind.

She didn't like this. She didn't like him. Never had, but now that Hank was gone, he was doing things he hadn't done before, like not even washing the rags they wrapped the food in. The rags had to be washed daily or at least every few days. Sam had always done some of that wash. Now, he didn't even bother to put the rags in the wash pail. He left them in the wagon or brought them inside and dropped them on the floor near the pail. Sam was treating her like she worked for him, and he was a bad boss. Tabitha didn't know how things would end with Sam, but for sure they would. She just hoped no one got hurt in the ending.

Tabitha and Brady stood outside her place and looked over her door.

"Tabby's Place," Brady said. "That has a nice sound to it."

"You don't think I was too ambitious to get it done? Hank's only been gone two months."

Brady shook his head. "He's gone, and he's not coming back. Everyone knows this is your place, Tabitha. Your name should be where it is." He gave her a pat on the shoulder and walked into his store.

Tabitha went inside Tabby's. She pulled biscuits from the oven and rolled butter over them before slicing them in half and stuffing each with pork meat.

The bell rang over the door, and she looked out.

Sam.

He was early enough to argue his situation for longer than normal. She readied herself for the conversation and said a prayer in her head for strength.

"Morning, Sam," Tabitha said, wiping her hands down her apron.

He hung his jacket and went to the wash sink to clean his hands. "Those biscuits smell good. Meat too."

"Thank you. How was your Sunday?"

"Quiet," he said, inspecting her as he wiped his hands on a towel. "I went to Toby Dillard's place down at the end of the pier."

She pitched an eyebrow. "Did you? That's far."

"The ports are going to be taken over by the city."

She'd been hearing that and wasn't sure if it was good or bad news. She wasn't as political as she should be. Charleston had a lot to be political about. She found it confusing sometimes.

"Things should improve. The business going to Savannah will come back through here. There will be more dock workers. I was thinking I should wagon further down."

Tabitha continued to work without replying to him.

"Whatcha think?"

She raised her eyes. "I don't know. That's more cooking for me."

"Well, the business grows."

Tabitha kept her tongue, focusing on slicing the meat for the biscuits he would be carrying out.

"You ain't gonna tell me what you think? I'm asking you."

"That's more cooking."

"Well you is a cook, ain't cha, gal?"

Tabitha's anger flared. Being called gal by him warmed her up good. "I cook when it makes sense. This don't make sense for me."

"Why not?"

She placed a hand on her hip. "Because I'd be cooking more for no money."

Sam frowned. It was that same frown he gave her every Monday when she didn't say what he wanted to hear. "What you mean no money? I pays you."

"What you pay me just covers the cost of the food. I don't make anything from your wagon."

"Now whatcha mean by that?"

"I mean what you give me doesn't add money to my business. All it does is make me have to cook more. I can't cook any more than I'm already doing without coming earlier and leaving later. I won't do either."

"This is the least you could do. You won't make me a partner."

Tabitha walked to the counter and put the containers of jam and butter on it. "Sam, we have gone 'round about this partnership thing. I don't want a partner. I don't need one. Now I lets you have the wagon—"

"Lets me. Woman, is you out of your head? I walk and sell this food—"

"For yourself! Not for me. Why can't you see that I have nothing to gain with the wagon? You were more fair with Hank. You are taking advantage of me, and I'm not dumb. I know it."

Tabitha walked back into the kitchen. Before she reached her pot, she felt a hand on her. "You flappin' mouth, woman." He pulled her by the neck of her dress and then shoved her against the icebox. "This why you ain't got no man. Besides being too black, you think you know everything."

He turned her loose, and she pulled the neck of her dress to fix the collar. "You should go."

"Go?" Darkness filled his rough features. "I ain't going nowhere. This is my family's place."

"Hank and I made a deal. It's no longer in your *family*. If you have a problem with that, talk to Hank."

"I don't have to talk to Hank."

"Well, you done talking to me. I want you gone." She pointed toward the door. "You paid through last week, so I don't owe you nothing."

He stepped toward her saying, "You raggedy—"

Tabitha reached in her pocket and pulled her revolver out. "Don't you move." She raised her other hand to support it. "I've been shooting birds since I was seven. You'll be a lot easier to hit from five feet away."

Sam froze. The corner of his mouth tipped up. It was a smile but not friendly. "So, you gonna shoot me?"

Tabitha fought to keep her voice sure and firm. "You handled me first."

The door opened with a jangle that was most welcome.

Sam and her eyes locked. She whispered, "No more wagon. This business is done between us."

"Tabitha . . ." Brady's voice carried into the kitchen.

Tabitha put the revolver in her pocket. Sam turned and walked out of the kitchen. She followed him, watching him walk past Brady without a word until he reached the door. Once it was open, he yelled. "You ole sow. You gonna be sorry you crossed me." And then he left.

"I been sorry," she said to his back. Once he was gone, she nearly collapsed on the counter. Brady came around and pulled her into his arms. He held her for a minute, rubbing her back in circles as she counted in her head to ten twice, trying to calm down.

The temptation to stay under Brady's comfort was strong, so she slipped out of his arms.

"You're trembling. What happened?"

"We are done with our business together."

Brady nodded. "That's probably for the best, but now you need to be more careful."

"I know."

"I mean careful, Tabitha." Brady locked eyes with her. "Coming in and leaving. He's not a good man."

She nodded, her heart rate returning to normal. "I know. All this has been building since Hank left."

"It was probably building before that."

The bell rang, and the first of her customers entered. She grabbed Brady's hand and squeezed it. "Thank you."

Tabitha was thanking him for so many things—caring to help when she needed him, the comfort of his arms, and the reminder to watch out for Sam. She could not put his kindness out of her mind. Still, she worked the entire day with a knot in her stomach and throat. Once she was done serving the last of the supper run, she locked the door and cleaned up faster than she ever had.

She picked up the bag with her children's meals and pulled the back door, locking it. The red wagon leaned against the wall, reminding her more than she needed to be reminded that she had an enemy.

The alley behind the store was narrow but short, and Tabitha chastised herself for never putting a different door on the front of the restaurant, one that she could lock from the outside to enter and leave from. She would take care of that as soon as she could.

Tabitha stepped around the corner and was startled when she saw a figure standing there. Her heart caught, froze, and then relaxed.

"Brady, you almost gave me my death."

"I didn't mean to. I was waiting for you."

"You've been closed."

"A little while." They both knew that wasn't true. His work-days ended at four o' clock. "I'm going to walk you to the rail."

"That's not necessary. It's right up the road two blocks."

"That'll be two blocks we'll share." He took the bag of food from her hands, and she fell into step with him as they walked to the trolley car.

The trolley rambled toward them. "I can ride home with you."

"No, I–I'm going to have to get used to watching out for myself."

His kind eyes filled with sincerity and warmth. "Maybe just for the week."

Tabitha felt her insides melt. This familiar feeling unnerved her. It reminded her of Joseph and what she felt when he came around. "I'm a big girl. I can take care of myself, but I thank you." She reached for her bag, touching his hand and squeezing it just below the wrist before removing the bag. Again, there was that tug she'd felt before. Blood rushed to places all over, and she gathered herself before stepping onto the trolley car.

As it pulled back into the street, she caught a glimpse of Brady standing there, still, watching her car move away from him.

Tabitha's heart swelled with a feeling that was deeper than gratitude. Deeper than friendship. She felt protected, and that was something she had not felt since her brother died. A tear streamed down her face, and she reached into her bag for a handkerchief. She missed him, and she missed Mama.

Chapter 25

GEORGETOWN, SOUTH CAROLINA

Present Day

Sabrina

I hadn't heard from Quinton all week. Not even a text message. I was feeling some type of way about being ghosted. The last thing I needed in my life was a *trash* man, especially one I'd likely run into. Georgetown wasn't Greenville. The city of Greenville was bigger than all of Georgetown County.

That's what I thought, until Quinton arrived at Grandma's door carrying a dozen pink peonies. Peonies were my favorite flower. It was just like him to pick the right kind. Adrenaline rushed through my veins, stirring conflicting emotions I didn't want to feel.

"Showing up without calling," I said. Sarcasm felt like my friend in this moment.

"It's the South," he replied.

No he didn't. The grunt I made said everything I was feeling about his answer. "Thank you for the flowers." I waited for him to speak. This was his moment.

"I hope they convey that I'm sorry." His voice cracked uncomfortably, and I winced. "I apologize for going dark this week."

"Going dark?" I snorted. "We're not living in a spy movie."

"I know that."

I couldn't keep my frustrated sigh in. "If that's the case, what do you want?"

"A chance to explain."

"My life is a little too complicated for me to have to work around *inconsistency* right now."

"And I didn't want to put my problem on you, but I need to tell you where I've been."

"You don't need to tell me. I get it. I'm a single mother. Some men don't want that life."

Quinton was shocked, so shocked that it was easy to see he wasn't faking. "What? No." He shook his head. "Your daughter has nothing to do with anything."

Suddenly, I felt silly for thinking that's why he'd disappeared on me. I sat, put the flowers on my lap, and waited for him to explain.

"I told you I had an ex . . . Alicia. We were engaged. Alicia has a drinking problem. Sometimes she has a drug problem. When she gets desperate, she blows up my world."

Now it was me who couldn't hide my surprise. The fluttering of my lashes was involuntary. "In what way?"

"She shows up places. My apartment. My mother's house. When I was in Columbia, my job. My church. She keeps up a lot of drama." He sighed. "She needed to get into a program. I found one and drove her there. It's in High Point, North Carolina."

I was speechless. I should say something, but my tongue felt like lead.

"Exes are supposed to be in our past, but she has no one else. She's alone except for her mother, and she's not well. She's finishing cancer treatments."

Empathic feelings washed over me. I had way too much experience with being alone. Needing someone didn't make anyone a bad person, but being willing to help added to his good qualities. "Quinton, I'm so sorry."

"I know I have to figure out a way to close that door, but I keep thinking, we started as friends. I don't give up on friends."

"You don't have to explain that," I said, thinking about how hard I'd always gone for Kendrick. How I would never abandon him if he was sick. I took Quinton's hand and pulled him down on the two-seater chair with me.

"I *do* have to explain, but this is it. I'm done. I told her this is the last time." He continued, "I like you, Sabrina. I always have, even before her. I'm not letting guilt or drama or even an old friend come between me and what I want right now."

"Are you sure you're going to be okay with that?" I asked.

"I've considered her to be an assignment, but that's not what this is. Alicia is a burden. I don't have to carry her. She's *not* my wife, and she never will be."

I released a weighty breath. "I appreciate you being honest with me, but I feel bad. I thought you were avoiding me because of my daughter when you were dealing with a whole rehab situation."

Quinton frowned. "Why would you think I'd have a problem with your daughter?"

"I don't know." I shrugged. "The timing."

Quinton's frown deepened. "I would've called, but I didn't want to project that energy on you, and I needed time to think and pray on the ride back from High Point. My mother traveled with me."

"Is she close to Alicia?" I wanted him to say no. I didn't want Alicia to have very many pieces of his life.

"Not really, but taking her was more to get my mother out of the house and honestly to have another person in the middle, you know?"

I nodded. I understood. Things could get complicated between exes. I'd been there during my own on-and-off again situationship with Kendrick. It took us a long time to settle into being a real couple.

Quinton sighed. "All I want right now is to spend some time with you . . . today if you don't have plans."

"I think there's room on my social calendar for a needy friend," I said teasingly.

"This friend is in the mood for a milkshake. My favorite spot is in Charleston. You up for a ride?"

"To Charleston?" I scrunched up my nose. "For a milkshake?"

"Charleston for some real time with you."

I smiled. I felt him. I looked down at my flowers. "I'm going to put these in water."

I stood. Before I could move, I felt Quinton's hand on my arm. I waited for him to speak. He seemed mesmerized by the connection of our skin. He sighed again, more loudly than he had the last time, and dropped his hand. He looked up at me. Quinton's honest eyes always told the truth. Whatever he was about to say was coming straight up from his heart.

"Sabrina, your daughter is"—he paused, considering his words—"probably the best part of you. If I want you, I want all of you, especially the best part. I would never not want you because of her."

Quinton's words burrowed into my chest and spiraled right down into my belly. How sweet was that? I was speechless.

"I'd like to meet her . . . when you're ready to introduce me to her."

I nodded. "I'll let you know."

Quinton smiled, and aside from the stress crinkles around his eyes, he seemed okay. I, however, was not okay. I didn't want to be a cliché, but as a single mom, a man who said the right things about my child was winning. Kenni was my heart.

I found a vase for my flowers, put on a little makeup, and joined Quinton in the car. One of the things I loved the most about Georgetown was its proximity to the coast. The ride down Highway 17 didn't provide constant views of the water, but when the ocean appeared, it was everything I needed in my life. The water, the sun on my face, the smooth jazz on the radio, and Quinton's warm hand on mine massaged my soul to satisfaction.

We arrived in Charleston and immediately merged into traffic. The city was alive with street vendors and shoppers. Musicians and dancers. Tourists and locals. The people-watching distracted us from the fact that we were crawling down the street.

"I haven't been to Charleston in six years," I said, recalling the last time was a weekend getaway with Kendrick.

"It's a hike from Greenville."

"My last trip was for a weekend birthday celebration," I said, continuing to enjoy the view out the window.

Quinton didn't ask for details. I suspected he didn't want to hear if I was with a man. "I hope you can eat, because I'm hungry," he said.

We parked his car in an area that looked more residential than commercial. He fed the meter, and we walked the short distance to Hannibal's Kitchen, which was famous for its soul food.

It was crowded, but we only had to wait fifteen minutes to be seated. Having Dante cook for us spoiled me, but I was always down to try another Gullah-Geechee soul food spot. I ordered the crab and shrimp fried rice and shark steak. Quinton had the rice with oxtails but then begged until I gave him some of my fish.

Once we left, we went down East Bay to King Street, stopped in a bookstore, and walked through the City Market. Quinton picked up a pound cake from Fergie's Favorites, and I picked out a beautiful bouquet of flowers fashioned from sweetgrass. Sweetgrass symbolized harmony, love, peace, strength, positivity, and purity. I needed any symbol of those things that I could get. I also thought they'd be a nice peace offering for Mariah. I'd give her a few.

We walked to Kaminsky's for dessert. I had their berry cobbler with ice cream. It was served in the ceramic dish it was baked in. I liked the coziness of eating out of a baking dish. The ice cream tasted homemade. The strawberry syrup exploded on my tongue. I didn't make pies, so whenever I had dessert out, I got pie. Quinton had his favorite milkshake and took key lime pie and bourbon pecan pie to go for his mother.

Quinton groaned as he fidgeted with his seat belt. "I don't know about you, but I ate entirely too much."

"You're right, you did. You ate my fish and my dessert."

"I swear I'm not like that all the time. You just know your way around a menu, girl."

I smirked. "Don't try to con me. I can tell you're one of those people who has to have what everyone has."

We laughed. "You spend more time in the gym than me."

Quinton popped on his sunglasses. "I'm glad I could help you stay fine, but I'm kind of ashamed of myself."

"Although I'm not a hundred percent convinced you have any shame. I'm in the restaurant business and I'm a baker. I like to see people eat."

"Yeah, well, when this sugar high comes down, I'm going to need a nap."

I laughed and opened my phone to take a quick look at the pictures we'd taken. I held my phone so he could see the usie of us having dessert. We both had whipped cream on our lips.

Quinton glanced at the picture and then me. His eyes weren't readable through his dark sunglasses, but the combination of the way he nodded his head and pushed out his lips spoke before he did. "We're making memories." He pulled out in traffic and added, "Again."

I pulled my phone back into my lap and looked at the rest of our pictures. We were . . . making memories. I was about to close my phone when I saw a video Mariah sent me of her and Kenni.

They were singing "I Smile" by Kirk Franklin. It was Kenni's favorite song.

I laughed at the silly expressions they made, especially Mariah. She was so good with her.

"What's up?" Quinton asked.

"Kenni and my sister were hamming it up in a video." We were stopped at a light, so I held the phone up for him to see.

"She's beautiful," he said. "She looks like you."

I admired the video for a moment. She did look like me, more and more as she got older. I closed my phone. "I'm glad she's close to her aunt. I know she's only four and might not remember, but the memories I made visiting Georgetown are the best from my childhood."

"You'd be surprised what some people remember, but I don't recall anything before like five," he said.

"Same," I said, buckling my seat belt. "Except I do I remember getting shots in pre-K and seeing the dentist who visited our school."

"You remember the medical stuff. I remember holiday potlucks in the classroom."

"You would remember the food," I teased. I looked out the window and enjoyed the view as we moved through traffic. It struck me. I was on Market Street in Charleston. I'd seen it mentioned in my great-great-grandma Tabitha's letters. We weren't far from the location she had for Tabby's Place. I closed my eyes, trying to focus on what she said about it. I recalled Market Street. Near the docks. I pulled up maps on my phone to see how close we were.

Quinton looked at my phone. "Did you want to go somewhere?"

"Yes. Would you make a right here and take this down to the port?"

We reached the port, and Quinton parked. We stepped out, and I stared, looking at the different modern buildings, hoping to catch a glimpse of something that would signal Tabitha Cooper had been here.

"What are you looking for?" Quinton asked. "Waterfront Park is in this direction."

I explained to him about Great-Great-Grandma Tabitha's first restaurant.

Quinton did a thing with his mouth when he was impressed. I recognized it from when he was a teenager.

I pulled my eyes away from his rather good-looking lips and made myself focus on why we were on this street. "Her restaurant business goes back to 1920."

"That's powerful."

"It is. I've been reading letters she wrote from that time. She was doing the doggone thing."

"Well, I can see she passed her resilience down."

He couldn't possibly *see* resilience. I hadn't done anything to demonstrate it to him, but I didn't want to tell him what he saw in me or hoped for me.

We drove over to the area I thought might be where she'd been, that is, if the streets weren't changed. There were so many restaurants, it was impossible to figure it out. I tried to imagine what this area must have looked like a hundred years ago, but I couldn't. What I did do was feel something, an energy that made me think I'd passed an ancestorial marker or something. I don't know, I felt a presence. It quieted me.

"Tell me, Sabrina. What are you thinking?"

"Just about all my ancestors did for me . . . for us. Times aren't great now with respect to race issues, but Jim Crow was a horrible time. They survived that, and we're the ones who are benefiting."

Quinton nodded. "I think about that all the time too. It's cool that you have letters. I've been using the ancestry site, trying to build a family tree, but it's time-consuming."

"Probably worth it though, right?"

Quinton agreed with a smile. "Based on what you know about this spot and your gran's history here, definitely worth it."

We left Charleston and headed back up Highway 17. Once we entered Georgetown, Quinton pulled off to the right and headed in the direction of the water. We rode along the access road for a stretch, and then he parked. We sat there for a minute before getting out of the SUV, Quinton following me. We stared at Winyah Bay—together—watched the sun disappear over the water.

Quinton reached for my hand. I looked down at the two of them clasped and then back up at him.

"You've been quiet."

"Reflective," I replied. "I can't help but think things would have been different if I grew up down here . . . with my grandparents."

"Thinking you and Mariah would have been closer?"

"Something better than what it is," I said. "But then I think like that and feel bad because all roads lead to Kenni, you know?"

"I can't exactly relate because I'm not a father."

"Yeah, you can," I said. "I bet there are days—or let me say seasons—when you wish you'd never met Alicia."

He frowned, and then his face relaxed.

"It's the same thing. It's wishing you didn't have the burden of whatever a thing is. We want to clip out the parts of our lives that bring us pain, but if we didn't have that pain, how would we grow? What would God use?"

"Don't give up on Mariah," Quinton said, putting his arm around my shoulder.

I closed my eyes and let the intimacy of his touch soothe me. I hadn't been touched like a lover in years. This felt too good. I moved out from under his embrace, but Quinton reached for my hand again. He wasn't going to let me go. "I better get back. I want to beat Kenni home. She might be full of sugar. No one deserves a cranky four-year-old."

We held hands as we walked back to his SUV. Once he opened the door, I started to step in but then turned back around. I didn't even realize I was leaning toward him until I kissed him. It was just a peck on the lips, but it was sweet. "Thank you for inviting me."

"Thank you for coming with me," he replied. A smile settled in his eyes, and it drew me back to him.

The second time I leaned closer, I was aware that I craved a real kiss. I raised my hand to his chest and felt it rise and fall beneath his T-shirt. Quinton met me the rest of the way. His lips brushed against mine, flooding my senses with warmth. He was gentle as his hand slid up my arm, over my shoulder and across my collarbone. His free hand slipped around to my lower back, where he applied just enough pressure to pull us together. It seemed like it took forever for his mouth to fully cover mine, to deepen the kiss, but once it did, it became hungry, irresistibly so. I moaned against his lips, and in return, he growled. I pulled back, but our faces were still inches apart. The racing of my heart matched his. Our ragged breathing matched each other's. "This might be too much, Quinton."

"Too much?" He released me, stepped back, and scratched the side of his face like he didn't know what to do with himself. "I've been wanting that kiss all day." He chuckled nervously. "And I was just getting warmed up."

What? A whole shiver traveled up my spine. He already had my senses all fuzzy. Now he was messing with my head. I gathered myself, crossed my arms over my chest, and said, "I'm lonely."

Quinton nodded. "Me too. But we don't have to be. Not anymore."

The vulnerability I'd just confessed unnerved me but freed me at the same time. I felt compelled to be honest with him. If he was really a man of God, he would help me keep us from finding out how warmed up we both could get.

I looked past him at the massive sky. The clouds painted their final picture before disappearing into the stars. My loneliness had been a small piece of who I was, but it was strong. Stronger than I knew. I dropped my arms and slid into the vehicle.

We arrived at my grandparents' house. Quinton walked me to the steps and said his goodnight with just a peck on my cheek. I lingered until he drove away.

Before I turned to enter the house, I noted a woman getting out of a car across the street. She powerwalked up the driveway, approaching with purpose.

"Can I help you?" I asked.

She was still moving in my direction. I stuck my hand in my bag, my finger on my pepper spray.

"Are you Sabrina Holland?" she asked, stopping at the bottom of the steps.

Before I could say yes, she pushed a manila envelope at me. "This is for you." Then she took a picture with her phone. "You've been served."

Chapter 26

Mariah

"You should *not* accept that offer from Vince," Hope said.

I opened the back door and stepped onto the screened porch. Sabrina was in the backyard spray-painting mason jars white. The intensity in her face told me this project was not about creating but escaping.

"This woman is obsessed with mason jars," I said.

"What?" Hope was thrown off by my inserting what I was observing in the middle of what she was saying.

"Sabrina is spray-painting jars."

"Her ability to take something and make it more beautiful is a gift," Hope said.

Hope was always an advocate for my sister's artistry, maybe because she used to dabble in art herself, but it got on my nerves. Sometimes I just wanted an ally. Someone to say, *"Girl, she's doing too much."* But Hope was always Hope. She was honest to a fault when I wanted a lie.

I suppressed a chuckle. Dr. Johnson would ask, *"What do you think that alliance does for you? What does a lie ever do for us?"* Did

I need therapy? I was getting good with the questions. I could analyze myself.

"My mother never painted the jars. You have to be able to see the cake inside to want it."

"Sabrina is doing it her own way. Maybe making them fancier makes them more of a keepsake," Hope replied. "And you are focused on the wrong thing. Have you talked to your attorney about that sorry offer Vince made you?"

"I'll call today."

"No, you won't." Hope let out an exasperated groan. "You're dead set on letting Vince rob you."

I was no longer focused on Sabrina. Hope had snatched me fully into our conversation. "Why would you say that?"

"Because this is what you do."

"Greenville is not like Turnin County. You don't know how small counties work. His father, before he died, hunted with two of the three judges for thirty years. His cousin *is* the third judge."

"Maybe the lawyer could get your divorce dealt with in another county."

"A change of venue for a divorce? You watch too much television."

"And you have way too little faith in God."

I rolled my eyes. "That's a leap. How did we get all the way to my faith?"

"I'm not wrong. It's been more than a week since you received that email with that pitiful offer. Call your attorney and stop acting like you don't have any power."

Hope didn't give me a second to say a thing.

"Losing everything to him will only give you something else to mope about. You already have a long list."

That hurt. She didn't have to be so honest. "Wow, Hope. And just why are you friends with me?"

"Because I love your crazy behind. I've loved you since those folks at South Carolina State made us roommates freshman year."

I felt a tug of nostalgia, but still, she wasn't showing me any mercy right now. "I can't tell right now."

"Because I'm holding you accountable? Please." She chuckled, sending the message that she was sick of me. "Look, I have a meeting with my boss, so I have to go. I fully expect an update, or I'm driving to Georgetown this weekend and kicking you in the butt."

My heart warmed a little because she'd do just that. "I wouldn't mind seeing you."

"You're looking at me right now," Hope said. She wagged her index finger in front of her face. "Show up for yourself. You're the only one who can."

We ended the FaceTime call. Kenni and Sabrina were playing now. Kenni was chasing Sabrina with a water hose. I watched them for a while. They had such a fun, carefree nature about their relationship. I loved that for Kenni. Children deserved joy.

I turned and walked into the house. It was Monday afternoon; therefore, it was time for yet another therapy session. Hope wasn't giving me enough credit. I was trying to work out my issues, but this stuff was like a crusty oven. It took time to get the baked-on crud off. That's what I told myself; however, as I sat in Dr. Johnson's office, I realized I was already weary of this process. I didn't want to do this anymore. She had pushed one of my buttons—a big one called Lorraine Holland. Lorraine was not a Monday session kind of conversation.

It's said that body language is more than 70 percent of communication, or some high number like that. As a therapist, Dr. Johnson would know that, and if she was reading me the way I knew she was, she knew . . . I was over it.

"Let's take this conversation in a different direction. Tell me something that was good since the last time you were here."

I cleared my throat and sat up straighter than I had been sitting. The first thing that popped into my mind surprised me. It wasn't the fact that we got all the flooring in and it looked fantastic or the fact that the new windows arrived and were ready to be installed or that the installer was coming tomorrow instead of next week like he originally told us. Or even that we had a 50 percent increase in sales on the food truck over the weekend. It was Grandpa—he walked three feet without his cane yesterday—and Kenni—she drew a stick figure of me surrounded by sunshine and flowers. I was not a sunny person, but she saw me that way.

I told Dr. Johnson both, and the corners of her mouth tipped up like I'd said the right answer. But we both knew there were no right answers, so I wondered.

"You smiled a little," I said. "What made you do that?"

"You found the joy quickly."

"That's improvement?" I asked, stating the obvious.

"Do you feel like it is?"

I let out a wry chuckle. "Of course. I've struggled to see . . ." I stopped talking, remembering how Sabrina was always telling me I saw glasses as half empty, and then a memory surfaced strong in my mind. It was of me in the kitchen with my mother. Me on a stool at the island, arms folded watching her pour ingredients into a bowl from glass mixing cups—large ones and small ones, all the cup sizes. She used flour, sugar, cocoa powder, and other ingredients.

My mother was trying to teach me to make a cake. She was always showing me and giving me cooking tips, or maybe she was talking to herself, enjoying her craft while using me as her audience. It reminded me of someone narrating a recipe on a cooking show.

"See, I sift the dry ingredients first."

She mixed them with a whisk until it looked like she was tired of doing it, and then she reached for the cup that held the yellow milk.

"*Buttermilk is heavier than regular milk, so I use a little less water.*"

"*A half-empty cup,*" I offered.

"*No, the cup is half full.*" Mama smiled and tipped my chin up. "*It's always half full, not half empty.*"

"What are you thinking about, Mariah?"

"My mother."

"What about her?"

"She and I spent a lot of time in the kitchen."

Dr. Johnson looked curious. "Okay, and . . ."

I shifted in my chair. That memory. It was my last one. "My father's favorite cake was my mother's chocolate, and it was the last cake she baked."

I wanted to get back to the topic. "You asked me if I thought finding the joy faster was an improvement. I was going to say . . . Sabrina sees glasses half full, and I see them half empty. But my mother told me glasses were always half full."

"Go on."

"Mama didn't have to tell Sabrina that. She figured it out on her own."

"And?"

"What would my mother think if she knew I was down here seeing life through the wrong lens? At six, she was telling me that it's always half full."

Dr. Johnson made a note.

"You told me last week that the brain processes information whether it's real or not."

Dr. Johnson nodded. "I did."

"I see half-empty glasses everywhere, Dr. Johnson. I have lived my life being negative, being afraid, never believing I would have abundance. Even when I had it, I didn't expect it to last, so I have gotten exactly what I have believed in."

I thought about Hope's words about my faith. She'd been so right. I hadn't followed up with my divorce attorney, using the excuse that I had time because in this state you had to be separated for a year, but that was no reason for me not to have my demands in writing.

I cocked my head and looked at Dr. Johnson. "I accept half-empty glasses."

"You're here, Mariah."

Tears streamed down my face, a river of hot, salty ones that I could not hold back.

Dr. Johnson gave me a minute before she said, "How are you and Sabrina doing?"

"I think she has something going on with her. She seems sad or stressed. She and Grandma have had some hushed conversations."

"Have you thought about asking her if she's okay?"

I shook my head. "I don't think I've ever asked my sister if she was okay."

"Maybe you can give it a try."

"She'd probably faint from shock." I chuckled bitterly.

"Find something nice to say to Sabrina. Maybe about something at the restaurant that she's done."

I reached across the desk for a tissue. My nose was still running a little from the crying.

"Remember, Sabrina is a creative person. She's not as practical as you are. That doesn't mean either of your styles is wrong. It just means she probably appreciates a compliment about something she's used her creativity for."

"I like what she's done with the décor."

"Then *tell* her. It'll be a nice way to enter into a conversation with her. Remember, you have to do the work at home too."

I was out of time. The session was over.

"Do I have homework this week?"

Dr. Johnson stood and walked me to the door. "Yes. I want you to make a list of things that trigger sadness. Chocolate cake might be near the top. If you feel like you can't do it, we can save it for a session."

I nodded. I already felt triggered by writing the trigger list. I supposed the homework was supposed to get harder.

"Don't dwell on the list as you make it. Don't try to psychoanalyze yourself." Dr. Johnson smiled. "Don't get stuck in the crossfire of inner talk. Sorting through the whats and whys can be polarizing. Give yourself grace."

I didn't want to ask anyone for a recipe for chocolate cake, not Sabrina or Grandma or even Dante, so I found a recipe on the internet. I didn't want anyone to know I was making it, so much so that I purchased all the ingredients and took them to the restaurant to bake on Tuesday night when no one was going to be there.

I measured out all the ingredients, set the temperature on the oven, and then stood there looking at everything. I knew this was going to be hard when I shopped for the ingredients, but now it felt impossible. Dr. Johnson did not tell me to do this, but I didn't need her to tell me everything. Baking was a trauma trigger.

Some triggers could be avoided. You don't have to go to certain places if you were traumatized there. If you almost drowned, you don't have to go near a pool. If you were attacked by a mugger while jogging, you don't have to jog the same trail or run at all. But a trigger that you had to meet needed a solution. Restaurants had baked goods. Confronting this one was necessary.

I poured the flour in the mixing bowl, then the sugar, baking soda, and baking powder. I continued until I had the batter complete. By the time I put it in the oven, I was perspiring, feeling nauseous, and in general wanted to escape. By the time the cake came out of the oven, I had one of my headaches.

"This was a bad idea."

My phone rang. I glanced down and saw Dante's name and face flashing. I answered.

"Are you okay?" he asked.

I felt oddly seen. "What, are you psychic?"

"No. I'm outside wondering why you're inside at this time of night."

I sighed. "I'm fine."

"Are you sure?"

"I'm positive."

"You still haven't told me why you're in there."

"It's personal."

"Are you on a cooking date or something?"

I smirked like he could see me. "I don't date."

"Well, then I'm coming in."

"Don't," I cried.

"Too late," he said. I heard the key in the back door, and seconds later he was standing there. "A what gwan on in me kitchen?"

I chuckled, glad to see him. I was always glad to see Dante. He was like the brother I never had. Younger but older at the same time, because if someone could be blessed with the gift of wisdom, he had it.

Dante squinted like he had to be imagining the scene in front of his eyes. He walked to the island. "You baked a cake?"

I took a deep breath. "I'm minding my business."

"I thought you didn't bake."

"I'm in therapy. Baking is apparently something I need to do."

Dante rubbed his hand over his head. "Why is your relationship with cake so complicated, Mariah?"

"Sir, I pay someone to ask me that question."

"Okay, so this is some kind of serious." He leaned against the island. "I'm sorry I interrupted." He looked like he meant it, but still, he didn't move.

Neither did I. I propped my hand on my hip and looked down at my flour-dusted shoes. When I was done calming my inner enemy, I raised my eyes. "My mother was a baker."

Dante nodded. "This I've been told."

"And I've had a really complicated relationship with chocolate cake."

"And de jar cakes too," Dante said, infusing his Gullah tongue. I liked when he did that. It reminded me of my grandfather, but not quite, because Dante's Gullah was kind of hot.

"It's just the jar cakes baked by my sister."

He nodded. "That explains a lot—I think."

He did not look like I was making sense to him, so I continued, "You've seen me be crazy about it."

Dante's facial expression was downgraded to a frown. "Don't use that word. It's not right."

"My therapist told me that. I think it's a habit."

"A bad one."

"On the list of *others* I have to break on this journey to being a better human."

Dante pushed off the island and came closer. He stood right in front of me, raised his arms, and said, "Bring it in, boss."

I hesitated before stepping forward, but then let myself be hugged. I closed my eyes. Allowed him to tighten his grip. He squeezed in the right places. It felt good to be hugged by someone strong. It also didn't feel brotherly, which was a bit concerning.

Dante smelled good, like cinnamon and lavender with hints of orange and something spicy. My nose was sharp. The ingredients were food, but they came together and gave off a heady scent that was sexy.

Dante let me wiggle free. I swiped a tear off my cheek and got myself together.

"You're good," he said. "At least you will be."

I nodded and released a cleansing breath.

"So," he said, looking at my cake, "we gwan cut this or what?"

I stared at it for a long moment before realizing what I needed to do. "Or what." I picked up the plate and turned it upside down over the trash.

Dante frowned. "It probably wasn't that good anyway."

I laughed, loud and strong and gut clearing.

He shrugged. "I'm just saying. You ain't baked in almost thirty years."

I laughed some more.

He sucked his teeth. "Wastin' food like it grows on trees. That's not the Gullah way."

"It's cheaper than my copay with the doctor."

He raised a finger and said, "Ah, I see what you did there. Smart woman." Dante pulled the trash bag out of the can, tied it, and tossed it near the door; then he rolled up his sleeves. "Let me help you clean up my kitchen." He took the plate from my hand and walked to the sink, carrying my burden with him.

I was wrong. This was a good idea.

Chapter 27

July 1920

Tabitha

Tabitha woke with a headache. Dread crawled up her body before she tossed back the blanket, readied herself for the day, and left her apartment. The last time she'd felt this way was when she found out about Joseph's death. She stepped off the trolley, steeling herself for a long day. She kept her eyes sharp and her hand on the pistol in her pocket.

She'd tossed all night, questioning the decision to stand up to Sam. It was bad enough she sometimes had to fight off the men who came into the restaurant, but now she had to watch for Sam. She didn't need the extra bother. Maybe it would have made sense to let him have what he wanted, but then she reasoned, she was delaying this end. They were eventually going to come to this place. If she waited, he might want more.

Tabitha rounded the turn to the back of the buildings and saw a figure by the back door. Relief washed through her when she saw it was Brady, not Sam.

"Good morning, sir. What are you doing out here?"

"Waiting for you, miss."

She stuck her key in the lock. "You can go now," Tabitha said, knowing he needed to be in his own store. She pushed on the door. Instead of it falling open, it got stuck on something. Tabitha pushed, and the sharp sound of metal scraping sent a shot of alarm through her. She pushed again, and this time she had to put her weight on the door to move it a few inches.

Brady looked as alarmed as she felt. "Let me try."

Tabitha moved aside, and he pushed hard until he finally opened it all the way open. Tabitha wished it was still closed.

The wagon was what was in the way. It was broken into pieces. She stepped in past it, further into the kitchen and restaurant. Everything was strewn about. The chairs and tables were knocked over. Rice and flour were spilled. Brady was at her side inspecting the wreckage too.

Rage rolled through her. Sam didn't have time to follow her. He was busy destroying her place.

"Why does he have to be so evil?"

Brady didn't reply. It was a question with no answer. A conversation that didn't have to be had. He was evil because he was angry.

"He means to intimidate you," Brady said. "He's probably done. He knows he can't try to talk to you again."

Tabitha put down her bag and went to the closet for the broom. Brady picked up two of the wagon's wheels and took them outside; then he came back in for the other two and then more pieces until the entire thing was out of her kitchen. Tabitha wasn't sure what to do first. She put the broom aside and decided to pick up the tables and chairs, praying the whole time none of them were broken, especially since they were so old.

"I think you should report this to the police."

"For what? What would they do?"

"You can make them aware that you've had trouble so if . . ."

"If what?"

"If he comes back, there'll be one account on the record."

Tabitha supposed he was right, but she couldn't imagine he'd come back again. "This business is all I have. This is how I feed my children." She shook her head. "He's not just hurting me."

Brady reached for the broom. "A man like that don't care about his children or yours."

She walked to the front door. It was there she discovered how he got in. A broken piece of the pane.

The broken glass and openness made her feel exposed. She placed a hand on her churning stomach. "You should go." She whispered the words. There was no way for Brady to hear her, so she repeated myself . . . louder.

"I'll help you get this cleaned up."

"No." She crossed the space to where he was. "I'll do it. I'll open late or not at all." Her thoughts of what Sam had done raced through her mind and emotions. "I need to see about the wood to cover this window and a better door." The money she hid under the floorboard in her apartment entered her mind, bringing more irritation with it. She glanced down, leaned over, and picked up a splintered piece of wood from one of the broken wheels. "And the wagon. I can't operate without something to tote supplies."

"There's a man, Herbert, over on Market Street. He works wood. I can go fetch him."

"No." She spun toward him. "You have your own store. I'll leave this one closed, and I'll walk over."

"He'll come right away if I ask him."

Tabitha walked to the sink. She dipped a cup in the water pail and took a sip. Tension left her parched. She walked back to an overturned chair and picked it up. "Are you saying he won't come for me?"

"Not right away," Brady said. She could tell he was disappointed to say it. "You're a woman."

"That's a reason to not want my money?"

"It's a reason for him to make someone else more important than you."

She sighed. "Why must men make the entire world so difficult to live in?"

Brady swept some of the flour into a pile. Then he reached into the closet for the dustpan, pushed the pile onto the metal plate, and emptied it into the trash box. He looked at her, but he didn't reply.

Brady was not a man who made anything difficult. She imagined he didn't like being lumped with Sam, and she should improve her statement, but the knot in her throat and chest swelled as her eyes roamed the destruction. "I will open today. Even if it's late. I won't fail on account of him."

Brady picked up a second pile of rice and flour and pitched it in the trash box. She took the broom from him before he started making the next pile.

"I'll finish this. If you can get this man to fix the window and door, please go for him."

With Brady's help, she did open that day. And she opened the next and the next without seeing or hearing from Sam, but he had not gone away. Tabitha found that out on the fourth day—the day after she cooked her okra stew—because that was the day many of the men who ate at her restaurant became sick.

Word spread that Tabby's Place served bad food, and she lost her customers overnight. All of them.

Rain poured down in sheets as Tabitha pushed open the door to the restaurant. With the horrible sales she had each day, she should have stayed in bed on this dreary morning, but her hopes and dreams wouldn't let her. She would not fail. Not this fast.

Hopeful she would get her customers back, she continued to cook each day. A few wandered in, nowhere near what she needed to live. She was going to have to do something to save her business. She had to figure out what.

Tabitha pulled eggs, salt pork, and grits from her stores. One meal would have to do for anyone who gave her their patronage. Once she was done cooking, she sat with her bag and removed a paper and pen. She'd been so distracted by the weather, she'd forgotten she'd grabbed the newspaper on the way out of her building. There was an advertisement for The Young Women's Christian Association Colored Branch of Charleston.

She'd heard of this YWCA many times. They trained girls by teaching them domestic homemaker skills but also fed them and prepared them for work. Tabitha hoped to one day be able to donate money to the cause. Mama had taught her to be generous with charity when she could, but Tabitha had not given a dime to anything since leaving home. Not really. Maybe that's why she wasn't blessed. She had planted nothing. If she hadn't learned anything over her lifetime, she'd learned no seed, no harvest.

She fixed a plate for Brady and walked it over to his store. She hadn't seen him since he'd stopped in for a biscuit earlier. He was busy sewing a man's pair of pants at the waist. He did tailoring on the uniform pants he sold, and he'd told her he had a few pants to get done for a pickup order this afternoon.

Even among the thread, buttons, and fabric scraps, finding a place to set the plate was easy. Brady was neat and his counter was long like he'd fashioned it for a store that would have ten men waiting in line at once. Tabitha had never seen it busy, not even close, but like her, this man had dreams. She sat next to Brady, scanning the pages of the *Chronicle*. She favored it over the other three Negro newspapers. There was a story about the YWCA and their need for food donations.

"I'm going to close and take the food to the YWCA."

Brady's brow wrinkled. Keeping with what he was doing, he asked, "That on Coming Street, right?"

"It is. The rain has stopped. It'll be a fair walk, but I want to do some good with what I have."

Brady raised his eyes to hers. "I'm sure the women there will appreciate your charity."

"I'm glad not to waste it."

She left Brady to his work and his worry. He still didn't like the idea of her moving about with Sam's discontent in the air, but what was she to do? She had a living to live out, and she'd fail her children if she let Sam steal her faith.

Her route to the YWCA was the same as the one home. She went up Concord Street, turned on Market, and headed straight until she came to Meeting, and then turned on Calhoun, except she continued to Coming to reach the YWCA. Tabitha parked the wagon on the grass and knocked on the front door. After a minute, a woman opened the door.

"My name is Tabitha Cooper. I own a restaurant on Market Street. My business was slow today. I have this food. I didn't want it to go to waste."

The woman was cautious, inspecting Tabitha first and then her wagon. "Where on Market?"

"Six, ma'am. Tabby's Place."

"Six. Is that by the docks?"

"Yes."

"It's early. Why is your day over?"

"Business is slow. I only serve lunch most days and dinner three days a week, depending on the loads the men have."

The woman continued to ask questions, obviously disbelieving Tabitha had good intentions. Tabitha reached into her pocket and pulled the mailer out and showed it to her. "I received this just this morning. I thought this sounded like a useful cause. I haven't donated much to charity." Looking back at the wagon, she said, "It's enough for quite a few."

"We have thirty-one girls here."

"Well, this should feed most of them if they don't eat much."

"I wish I could accept it, but I can't. We're already preparing dinner for this evening. Perhaps they could use the food at Emanuel Church. They are always in need in the soup kitchen and don't have to be as choosy."

Tabitha nodded. Disappointed, but then also feeling silly for thinking that they would take food for the girls from a stranger.

She turned to step off the porch.

"But, Miss Cooper, is it?"

"Yes, ma'am."

"We could use help with cooking instruction. Might you be able to teach a cooking class for us?"

"A class?"

"Our current cook is fine but not gifted in instruction." She smiled for the first time. "Some of our young ladies are sensitive to her tone."

"I would be happy to assist."

"That's good. What would be the best day for you?"

"I could come on a Saturday afternoon. I'm usually done by three."

"Fine. What should I make sure to get at the market?"

"I can make do with whatever you have as long as you have some basics. I can cook without meat if I have to."

"Really?"

"Yes, ma'am. Cooking is what I do."

They agreed on Saturday, and Tabitha left for Emanuel. The church was most appreciative. She repeated the same the next day. On the third day, she needed change. Mama always said three days of nothing was long enough. Jesus got up on the third day, and any child of hers needed to be able to make a decision in the same way.

Tabitha stepped outside the restaurant, looked outward to the small slit between buildings where she could see the water, and wondered where the men were eating. There was nothing close for Negroes. She had to figure it out before they got used to eating wherever that was.

The next day, she served the few customers she had and closed up. With Brady at her side, she went to the docks to find answers. Tabitha found some of her former customers, standing and sitting around on the boards, eating sandwiches. She approached, went directly to a man name Ferg whom everyone knew and respected as the unofficial spokesman for the Negro men on this dock.

He gave Brady a courteous tilt of the head and then gave her his attention. "Miss Tabitha, what can I do for you?"

"You can help me get my business back."

"Why would I do that when you 'bout killed some of us?"

"I did not."

"We were sick from your stew. I ain't never paid to be sick," Ferg barked. "I just got to feeling better."

Another man, Rosebud, spoke up. "I missed two days of work behind that. I might be short on my rent."

"I don't have a dirty kitchen," Tabitha said. "It was Sam, the man who used to work for me. He was trying to run me out of business."

They didn't look like they believed her.

Brady spoke up. "It's the truth. He made a firm enemy out of himself. I was there. I overheard his threat."

Tabitha placed a hand on Brady's arm. She appreciated his help, but this was her problem. She was tired of men thinking they could do what they wanted with her life.

She said, "My own daughter was ill. I swear to you on her life that Sam put something in that meat, and he tore my whole restaurant up trying to scare me. You see I got a new door. I had to buy it to keep him out."

"He had been telling us you didn't keep no clean kitchen."

"You know Hank wouldn't do that to you."

"Hank been gone," Ferg barked again.

"But I was cooking for the last year. All of you know that, so why would I change?"

No one replied.

"Where are you getting your meals now that you've abandoned me?"

One looked over her shoulder, and she turned to see a sandwich shop down the walk. White owned. She knew of it. "You can't tell me that you're paying for food out the back door of a white man's shop."

Again no one spoke.

"I will feed you all for a week without a cost, build your confidence back up in me, if you will tell the others about what Sam did and convince them to come back."

Rosebud was thoughtful for a minute and then said, "I don't much care for these fat ham sandwiches he sellin' us."

Ferg smirked. He was apparently tired of the gristly ham too. "I'm sticking my neck out here for you. You best make good or you really will be finished."

Relief filled Tabitha. She nodded and, with Brady by her side, went back to the restaurant.

"You did good making your case," Brady said.

"I've never been so afraid of failing, but I'm tired of being treated like nobody. It's happened too many times in my life."

Brady's brows creased. He put a hand on her shoulder. "You are the strongest young woman I know. My prayers are with you."

Tabitha placed a hand on the one on her shoulder and looked down at it. The connection between them was warm and strong. "Thank you for being with me," she said. "And I accept all prayers."

Brady looked at her like he was seeing something in her for the first time. Their eyes locked and held for a long time before he left and went back to his store.

The next day, Tabitha cooked chicken and rice. By eleven she saw a line of men walking from the dock. At least twenty strong. Blood rushed into her heart. She skirted into the kitchen and began to scoop out their dishes. The aroma of garlic and other herbs greeted each of them as they crossed the threshold. Mixed with the hot buttered corn bread she served, the warmth of the food made them all eager to get their helping.

That lunch period she had a lot of eyes raised to hers as they checked her face for sincerity before walking away with their dish, but they'd come, and she sold out with only one plate remaining. Her last was for Brady.

Chapter 28

Present Day

Sabrina

Ellen had lost her mind. I didn't call her for a few days. I was too angry to talk to her. However, I knew I couldn't go on like that forever, so I dialed her number.

"Hello, Sabrina." Ellen's voice held no special inflection. She didn't sound like someone who was suing me for custody. "How is Kenni?"

"She's fine."

"I haven't talked to her. Is she there now?"

"She's in the garden with my grandmother."

"How is your grandfather?"

I cut through the small talk. She did not care about me or my family or she wouldn't have done what she did. "Why are you suing me for custody?"

"Because it would be best if Kenni was here in Greer."

"And you feel that way because . . . ?"

"Because she's been with me for almost a year. I offer her a stable home and a nurturing environment."

"Ellen, Kenni has not been living with you. You've been babysitting her."

"Is that what you've told yourself?"

"She's not your daughter. She's mine."

"She's my granddaughter. I want what's best for her. That is not you, Sabrina."

I struggled to believe we had reached this point. Ellen and I always got along. "How would you have felt if someone said you weren't the right person to raise Kendrick?"

"I'm a different kind of mother. No one would have said that."

Those words sliced through me. What she thought of me was coming out loud and clear. "There isn't one way to parent."

"No, but there are better ways. Better ways like not living in a van. Better ways like not coming and going when it suits you. Better ways like taking her for her medical well checks and shots on time—"

"You know how I feel about the immunization schedule, how rushed it is. You and I talked about it."

"I let you ramble about it. She was attending a good preschool. You've taken her away from it now for over a month."

"It was daycare, Ellen, and daycare is not required."

"But she was enrolled, required or not. I was paying for it. Now she's lost her space."

I didn't want to fight with this woman, but her insistence that she was better for Kenni was way out of pocket. "Ellen," I tried to keep my voice even, "Kendrick wouldn't want this."

"Kendrick would want what was best for his daughter."

I held my tongue again before responding. "He would believe that to be her mother. Whether you can handle it or not, he was different from you. He wanted us to get an RV and homeschool her on the road. Those were the things your son and I talked about—"

"Stop it! We all have ideas about what we want to do for our children, and then we have them and figure out some of this child-rearing is more practical than fanciful. And you will not use my son against me. It's your fault he's dead."

I inhaled a deep breath and forced myself to remember who I was talking to. "Ellen, it's not fair for you to blame me for Kendrick's death."

"It's true, and you know it, and I will not let you raise his daughter any old kind of way. Now I want Kenni back here. I'll give you a week, or I'll proceed with the case."

She hung up on me.

I heard a noise at the door and looked. Grandma was standing there. "What is going on?"

"Oh, Grandma, what's not?"

I filled her in on the details. I didn't want to burden her, but she was the only person I could talk to.

Grandma groaned. "You never let another woman keep your child like that, especially a woman who's grieving the death of her only child."

An *I-told-you-so* wasn't what I needed, but I understood. I hadn't thought this through from the start. "I never thought she'd do something like this."

"We never know what people are capable of until they're caged. She believes she's fighting for her grandchild's future."

"I'm not unstable."

"I know that, but baby, living in a van is different." Grandma sipped coffee. "I heard you say Kendrick's death wasn't your fault. Why does she blame you?"

"Because I sent him out that night. For ice cream."

"I don't understand how that makes you guilty of anything."

"It doesn't. Ellen is wrong, but she's not wrong at the same time." I dropped my face in my hands before raising my eyes to her again. "I didn't even want ice cream. Not really. I wanted that scene; you know, in the movies where the woman is pregnant and she tells her husband she's craving something, and he goes out in the middle of the night to get it for her because that's how you love a pregnant woman and the baby?"

Grandma was so still. She didn't blink at my statement.

"I wanted Kendrick to prove he wanted our baby and me because . . . he wasn't happy about being a father. He had to grow into it. And I wanted to be sure so . . . I tested him. I made him go for nothing."

"Kendrick died in a car accident caused by the other driver. That man fell asleep."

"But—"

"Sabrina, no buts. Ellen is wrong, and that's all there is to it. Brother Hambrick from the church is a family court attorney. He can tell you what to do. I'm going to call him."

I nodded.

Grandma pulled me into a hug and squeezed tight. "We're going to fix this, baby." She pulled back and grabbed my hands. Shaking them, she said, "We are going to fix it together."

She left my room, and I collapsed on the bed.

The attorney, Mr. Hambrick, fit us in at the very end of his day. As we sat in his office, the memory of Grandma Tabitha's visit to the lawyer came to me. It was not lost on me that we were both single mothers trying to navigate issues with people who had more money and power.

Mr. Hambrick went down the notes he'd taken on a legal pad. "Kenni was sleeping overnight at her house for five months. You had almost daily visitation with the child. You were still the primary decision maker. You have text messages to prove some of that, and she willingly handed her over to you for the trip here, which in itself demonstrates that she believed Kenni would be safe in your care."

I had been sitting with an elbow on my knee and my jaw propped on my fist. I sat back and looked at Grandma. "Right. All that is true."

He hunched his shoulders. "She would have to prove abuse, neglect, or abandonment, and without something egregious, that's difficult."

I nodded.

"If she won't drop the case, I'll get it thrown out. If for some reason I'm unable to do that, you should be prepared to play hard ball with her."

"What does hard ball look like?"

"You let her know if she proceeds with this and wins, you'll still have visitation. If she loses, it will impact your relationship with her, which in turn will impact how much she gets to see Kenni."

"You mean like make her think I'd keep Kenni from her?"

He shrugged.

"I'd never do that."

"This is not about what's true. It's about what she believes. Grandparents have some rights, but she certainly has no right to interfere with you moving to another county in the state or even out of state for that matter."

I thought about it. It was a strategy. Lawyers had a reputation for being slick. Now she understood why. "Will court be here?"

"I can get the case heard in the county the child resides in. You'll need a Georgetown address. Change your driver's license. Start to receive mail. Get a library card. Anything that will establish you live here."

I nodded. "Of course. I've already changed the address for my bank statements."

"Good," Mr. Hambrick said. "Do the things I mentioned and your vehicle registration, voter's registration. You can't overdo it."

I nodded again.

"I have to warn you, custody cases can be expensive—very—but unless there is some reason she can ascertain that you are unfit, I can have a judge recommend mediation."

I covered my face with my hands for a few seconds and then wiped them on my pants. I was glad this wasn't going to drag on. "You're sure?"

"I'm certain. Like I said, if there's nothing in your past that she can use, this won't be difficult."

I rolled my lip in and swept my eyes between him and my grandmother, wondering if he thought I had something hidden in my past.

"What are the next steps?" Grandma asked.

He told us about the paperwork and confirmed my contact information. We stood.

"Mrs. Holland, I need to speak to Sabrina alone."

Grandma looked a little put off by that, but she patted my arm and said, "I'll be in the lobby." She extended a hand to Mr. Hambrick. "Thank you for fitting us in so fast."

Once she was gone, he walked around the desk and closed the door. "Miss Holland, please have a seat."

I sat and watched as he reclaimed his chair. He picked up his pen again and rested his hand on the legal pad he'd been using.

"It's important for clients to have the privacy to divulge details without the judgment or even upset of their relatives and friends."

I swallowed and tried to keep my face even, tried not to cry.

"Do you have any questions for me that you didn't want to ask before, or is there anything you need to tell me—something you might not want to say in front of your grandmother that I need to know?"

I raised my hand to the side of my face and rubbed my temple. An ache was settling there. It had been building all day. I looked down at my shoes. When I raised my head, my eyes were burning from the tears I was fighting.

"Is this case just about what's been going on this year since my mother-in-law has been babysitting overnight?"

Mr. Hambrick reached for a tissue box on the credenza behind him and put it on the desk in front of me. I reached in for one and caught a tear just as it fell.

He folded his hands in front of him. "No. It's not just about this year. It's about the moment you told her you were pregnant and potentially before that."

I let out a long breath. "Okay." I nodded nervously. "Then I have something to tell you, and I think it's probably pretty bad."

Mr. Hambrick unfolded his hands and picked up his pencil. "Start at the beginning."

I took a deep breath and told him my story.

When I was done with him, I met Grandma in the lobby.

"That took longer than I thought," she said.

"He had to repeat all the client confidentiality stuff and a few other legal things."

Grandma humphed, but then she fell into step with me as I left the building.

"The next time you're struggling—if there's a next time—you reach out to me, you hear?" Her tone was more than a little firm.

"Yes, ma'am," I replied.

"I wish I could go by the restaurant," Grandma said, settling into the passenger seat of the truck. "How are things looking?"

"Good. The work in the old part is done. The new section should be done in a few weeks."

We'd told Grandma this, but I think she was nervous. She tended to ask questions when she was nervous.

"Sabrina," she said, and I knew she was about to probe, "there's nothing in your past that Ellen can use against you, is there? You need to be sure."

I turned to my grandmother and looked at her. She'd managed to raise three children, more if we counted the years she and Grandpa took in foster children, official and unofficial, or helped out a homeless family here and there from the church. I could trust her with anything, but sometimes I felt so inadequate in her stead.

"She doesn't have anything." I started the truck and backed out of the space. Guilt came over me. I'd never lied to my grandmother before. I felt terrible about it. Not telling the truth didn't change what the truth was. I had a secret. Ellen knew it, and now Mr. Hambrick knew.

Chapter 29

Mariah

I made a chocolate cake."

Dr. Johnson's expertly arched eyebrow hitched. "Really. What prompted that?"

"The list."

"Explain more."

"I can't be triggered by cake. I run a restaurant where baking is likely going to happen because . . . Sabrina is going to bake, and she has a . . ." I was going to say she had a right because she did, but I wasn't ready to acknowledge that. Not yet.

Dr. Johnson could tell when I wasn't ready to flesh something out. She didn't press me. "How did you manage to get around the baking cake thing at Clark's?"

"All desserts were contracted. My idea of course."

Dr. Johnson nodded. "Okay, so tell me more about baking the cake."

"It was hard. I felt sick. And I threw it away when it was done."

"What did throwing it away do for you?"

"Nothing. I didn't want to eat it. I didn't want to give it away. I think it was too soon for me to bake."

"Hmm," Dr. Johnson said. "Knowing that is good, Mariah. Very good. Part of this process is taking emotional risks but also knowing when it's too early and being okay with waiting."

"The last time I was here, I told you that the chocolate cake was the last one my mother made, but there's more to that story."

Dr. Johnson cocked her head the way she always did when I was about to tell her something deep.

"My mother made a few extra layers and made jar cakes out of them." I looked down at my shoes. I'd been tapping my foot and didn't even feel it. I stopped. "After my mother passed, one of the women from our church put them in the freezer. I told you my father sold the house four months later. After he married Lorraine." I took a deep breath. "When she packed up the house, she threw them away. She threw my mother's last cake in the garbage. She had no right to do that. I tried to stop her, but she wouldn't listen."

"Why do you think she did it?"

"To be mean. To erase my mother from my father's life, his memory, his . . . I don't know, but she should have thought about me." I raised my hand to my chest. "That I would want the cake."

Dr. Johnson looked so sad for me.

"Do you know why your father and Lorraine's marriage ended?"

"No." I swiped tears from my eyes.

"Are you curious?"

"It makes like zero difference to me why it ended."

"Why do you say it that way?"

"Because he stayed married to her long enough to ruin my life. He never should have married her, so I don't care why they're divorced."

"Maybe you should ask your father. There may be an answer there that you'll find helpful."

I considered that, but I couldn't imagine there could be. Talking about Lorraine without screaming was going to take a lot of restraint.

"What are you thinking about, Mariah?"

"How much I hate Lorraine. And I know I'm not supposed to hate anyone, but I do."

"She's an emotional enemy, and *hate* is just a word. Don't beat yourself up for thinking it. It's not like you're acting on the emotion."

"I expected you to say I'm supposed to forgive her."

"You don't need me telling you who to forgive. Maybe you'll find a way to forgive her one day. But I do think you should consider finding out your father's truth."

"His truth?"

"The actual reason his marriage failed. It could be one of those questions you have to drill deep to get the answer to. His natural response may be to just say irreconcilable differences, but that's never really all there is."

I grunted. "That's what my petition says."

"There's more to why you and Vince aren't together anymore. You're not a catchall legal term. None of us are. If your brain is going to recognize something, it might as well be the truth."

I nodded.

Dr. Johnson continued, "But remember there aren't always clear paths to the truth. People don't always participate in your process, especially if they're suppressing their own pain. The best you can do is challenge them to share, but then accept if they won't or can't."

"I'm not sure I'm up for that."

"Think about it, Mariah. It's your choice. No decision is wrong."

Talking to my father about his divorce felt invasive, especially since I spent so little time talking to him at all. We were on FaceTime. Gray was coming in at his temples, but he hadn't aged much over the years. Sabrina had his whole face. That's what Grandpa Odell would say in Gullah. It was a good thing for her. My dad was as handsome as she was pretty.

I'd asked him about Lorraine, and he'd hesitated to answer.

"Lorraine never liked me."

"That's ridiculous. She liked you."

I rolled my eyes. He was always telling that lie. "I lived an experience with her. Please don't dismiss how I felt I was treated." I paused and added, "I reminded her too much of my mother. She resented me for it."

My father was quiet. Processing truth, I supposed, so I continued.

"Why did your marriage end?"

He grunted. "A lot of reasons."

"Tell me what they were."

"Mariah," he frowned, "it's complicated and—"

"And what? Personal? Dad, I'm in therapy. I'm trying to work through some things."

He pitched an eyebrow. "Therapy. How's that going?"

"Slow, but I'm learning things about myself . . . good and bad." I rolled my neck to work out the tension this conversation was bringing on. "My therapist advised me to find out why your marriage ended."

"Why would she tell you to do that?"

"I guess because the marriage itself was such a huge source of pain for me."

My father groaned. "Mariah, I'm sorry I let you down . . ."

"Dad, please. This isn't about you or your failing. Not right now. It's about me and what I need to know, so can you just tell me?"

He pressed his lips together firmly. "Lorraine was hard to live with. She'd become increasingly narcissistic and paranoid. She accused me of being unfaithful and wouldn't believe it wasn't true. I got tired of the witch hunt. By the time I filed for divorce, I'd already given up on us."

This time I grunted.

"What was that sound?"

"Vince gave up on me. I'm trying to figure out how it's different. I don't think we expect our partners to give up on us."

"We also don't expect our partners not to try to be their best selves." He sat back. "I'm kind of overtalking about this."

"It's okay, Dad. I have your answer. She was mentally unwell."

We were both quiet for a while, and then he asked, "How are things with the restaurant?"

I gave him an update.

"Sabrina sent me pictures. The refresh looks great."

"The food truck business is solid, so I think we'll do really well with the restaurant."

We talked about a few more things and ended the call. I didn't feel the way I usually did when we finished talking. I wasn't as angry as I normally was, but I was still feeling some bitterness.

Dr. Johnson told me that anger was normal. All negative emotions were normal.

"It's a primary emotion that protects us. Don't let anger or shame trap you. We can't think our way out of our emotions. We have to process through them."

I took a deep breath and another. And I let it be okay that I was angry. I put down my phone and sat there for a few minutes. After practicing my breathing exercises, I meditated on my thought for the week, which was "Focus forward." I spent way too much time in the past looking at half-empty glasses, so this was an important mantra for me.

I opened my journal and looked at one of the notes I put there.

I can overcome anxiety, fear, and depression. After all, David slew Goliath.

I let that sit with me for a moment and then said it out loud. "David slew Goliath."

An alert popped up on my phone. Another one about the show Vince was going to do. I laughed instead of crying this time. David slew Goliath. Hope's words came back to me.

"Show up for yourself. You're the only one who can."

I deserved more than a hundred thousand dollars and a car that would only be good for another few years. I deserved to have a savings and a house of my own since I was sure not to want to live with my grandparents forever. My settlement needed to give me all that.

I closed the alert and sent a text message to my attorney.

I want to get every possible dime I can get from Vince.

A thumbs-up emoji came back with the words: I was hoping you would fight.

Chapter 30

September 1920

Tabitha

When Tabitha returned to the YWCA on Saturday, she learned the woman's name was Miss Ada C. Baytop. She showed Tabitha to the kitchen and dining area where thirty teenagers were waiting for her. Most of them were scrawny and dark like she'd been at their ages, except the wideness in their eyes was a combination of excitement and fear. It was that look that said, "I don't know what's next." She knew it well. She'd seen it in the mirror many times after Joseph died. It was a wild-eyed and desperate look with a halo of hope dead center.

Tabitha introduced herself and then had them follow her to the pantry and let groups take turns inside while she showed them what they had to work with. "Tell me what you want to learn," she said, putting on an apron.

The responses were a variety of things from fried chicken to cakes and pies. Tabitha decided she'd start with basics—what she deemed were foods every woman should know how to prepare for herself and her children no matter how much money they had.

"In lean times, we need to know how to make things from flour and meal. Let's start there, and if Miss Baytop has me back, we can learn some meats and eventually some cakes.

"Being able to cook in one pot is how we cook. This is the way our ancestors have cooked for generations."

One of the girls raised her hand. "What iffen you have two pots?"

"If a kitchen has more than one pot, they can cook in them, but many don't have more than one, and when you cook on the fire or cookstove, there's only one space."

They made biscuits and hoecakes and a tomato and corn stew. Miss Baytop was appreciative of her time and said so. She wanted her back the next week.

Tabitha arrived at her building and went directly to Miss Libby's apartment to pick up her sons. She found things in disarray. It looked like she was packing.

"What's going on here, ma'am?" Tabitha asked.

Miss Libby handed Tabitha a piece of paper. "They say I have to go by Monday."

Tabitha looked around the room and then looked at the paper. "They must give you notice of some kind."

"I had that paper before. I didn't know what it mean." Miss Libby reached into a drawer and pulled out two other notices. She'd been warned about being late and not having her full rent. Miss Libby's eyes filled to the brims with tears. "I learn to talk as good as I can, but mi nebbuah laa'n mi letters."

Tabitha took in a deep breath. She didn't understand. During the week, there were always five or six other children in her care. Tabitha paid her two dollars a week herself. Surely with the other mothers, there was enough for rent and food. "Maybe I can settle the account for you. Do you have money?"

Miss Libby shook her head. "I have nothing. Some moddas nebbuah pay."

"What you mean they don't pay? If they work, they have to pay you."

"I know. They no'count." She shook her head again. She normally talked to Tabitha in the best English she had, but her emotions had her slipping into Gullah. "Tem is not like oona, but I still uh he'p dem with tem chillin."

"They are using you. I wish I had known this. I would have helped." Tabitha hated to talk about what should have been, but in this case, it was necessary. "You should have been paid before you did the work."

"I na tink of that."

"I understand. You expect people to be decent." Tabitha's eyes roamed the room again. She looked at her own children. They were aware of the tense situation. She could see it in their little eyes. She stepped closer to Miss Libby and lowered her voice. "Where is your family?"

"No family."

"No one?"

She shook her head.

Tabitha considered asking the landlord for more time for her, but the answer would be no. The woman who ran this house was firm on being paid, and based on these due notes, she had been generous with Miss Libby.

"I still need you. I have a business and no one I can trust with my children." Tabitha walked around the room and looked at the few things the woman owned. "Margaret, get your brothers." She looked at Miss Libby. "I will not see you on the street. You come with us."

The tears hanging on the edges of Miss Libby's lower eyelids fell. It was as if Tabitha was offering her a grand house in Charleston proper. She took Tabitha's hands in hers and kissed them. "God bless oona."

"He has," Tabitha said. "Let's go. I should prepare us dinner."

They moved Miss Libby's belongings into the apartment, and she settled into a room that was not really a room. It was tiny, nearly a closet with no window. Tabitha stored food there.

"We'll find you a bed of some kind as soon as we can. Until then, the children will sleep with me."

Miss Libby's hands trembled. Tabitha could see her busting with gratitude. "Oona a good Christian woman."

Tabitha grunted. "I suppose. No matter what anyone says about me, I try."

"I have lived more than twice oona years, and I know people talk what they no live."

Tabitha took her hands. "No matter what has happened between you and your family or whomever"—Tabitha thought to say a man but decided it might not be best—"God is always God. He always cares."

Miss Libby nodded. She looked around Tabitha's apartment. "I'm standing in His care."

Tabitha smiled, turned the woman's hands loose, and went to make a meal for her family.

Later that night, she lay in bed with the boys at her back and Margaret under her breast. She thought about the warnings she'd received about staying. Retha would have a fit to know this woman was in her house. She would certainly delay telling her. But now she understood what people meant when they said it was hard for a woman to survive in this city without family. Miss Libby had no one, so being put out at her age left her to beg on the street.

She recalled Mr. Flynn telling her that single women were prey for troubling situations. Between her trouble with Sam and other things she had seen, she couldn't deny that was true. Taking in Miss Libby was the right thing to do, and Tabitha decided she liked doing what was right. She always met Jesus there.

CHARLESTON, SOUTH CAROLINA

February 1922

In the same way Tabitha knew something bad was going to happen, she sensed when something good was going to happen.

The bell rang over the restaurant door, bringing the good she'd been expecting. Mama, Retha, and Clifford stood in the door, and a rush of warmth flooded her body. She had not seen Mama in years. The first press of the hug had an awkwardness about it, but then Mama wrapped her arm around her shoulder and pulled her tighter for a long moment before letting go. "You look well, Bitta."

Every space inside Tabitha filled up with love for her. "So do you." Tabitha hadn't seen her dressed this nicely since her graduation, but then she realized she hadn't seen Mama at all. She'd let years get between them. Retha filled the gap, carrying greetings and stories from each side to the other.

They talked a little first, and then Tabitha showed them around her place and seated them at her nicest table, one by the large window with the view of the water through the slip of street that led to the pier.

Brady popped in, and Tabitha introduced him. He sat with them through an early lunch before her crowd came. Her family lingered at their table, observing as she ran her business. Afterward Tabitha served chicory coffee and lemon cake and rejoined them at the table.

"You have a young man."

At first Tabitha didn't know who Mama was speaking of, but then she realized it had to be Brady. "I don't. We're friends. He helps me here as a neighbor."

Mama reached for the scarf at her neck. "I have eyes. He is not *just* a friend."

"But he is," Tabitha said with meaning, but unconvincingly. "I know what you must think of me after the way I left with Joseph."

"I think nothing of you other than you were a teenage girl influenced by a man many years older than you. A man who lacked good intention and character." Mama leaned forward in her seat. "I'm not here to rehash the past, Bitta. I have some hard news."

Tabitha pushed her back farther against her chair and waited for whatever was to be said.

Mama didn't speak, didn't seem able to, so Clifford took the lead. "Papa Cooper passed."

A knife sliced through Tabitha. She raised her hand to her mouth. "My goodness," she sputtered. "When?"

"More than a month ago," Clifford said.

"A month." She felt as if she hadn't heard correctly. Her eyes fell on Retha. "Why didn't someone tell me?"

"He died while traveling. He was in Chicago." Mama's eyes filled more with each of those words. She reached into her purse for a handkerchief. "He became sick and . . ." She covered her mouth with the handkerchief for brief seconds before continuing like nausea stalled her. "I received word, and it was too late to travel. He was already buried."

"Buried how?"

"George and Robert took care of him," Retha said.

Tabitha didn't know how to process this. George and Robert were in Chicago, obviously. She'd always thought her brothers had passed, but if Papa went to see them, they could not have. But this wasn't the time to dwell on her brothers. She took Mama's hand and squeezed it. "I'm so sorry."

"Sorry for all of us." Mama dabbed at the corners of her eyes. "He was your father too. The only one you had."

"Of course," Tabitha said, her chest tightening with her mixed emotions on the subject.

Minutes passed with them sitting there quietly, and then Clifford seemed to stir the air in the room with a cough before speaking. "You've done fine for yourself, Bitta. I'm impressed, but not surprised. You always had what it takes to build something."

Although her words could not come out above a whisper, Tabitha thanked him. She was grateful for his assessment.

"You've done exceptionally well." Mama looked around again. "Your own restaurant in Charleston. Simply amazing."

"You have managed to survive without starving, even after the children's father died, which is admirable," Retha added. Tabitha could hear a "but" in her sister's tone. She didn't talk this formal-like with her.

Tabitha's eyes rested on each of them. Their measured words sounded like practiced parts of a speech. This visit had a purpose. Retha and Clifford's eyes darted away and then back to Mama. Tabitha supposed her part of the speech was next.

Through a smile that was merely a lifting of the corners of her lips, Mama said, "I would like for you to come home."

Tabitha pitched an eyebrow and squeezed the fabric of her skirt under the table.

Clifford added, "It's not safe for a woman to be in this city by herself."

Were they not aware that she had lived in this city for years? "This city is my home."

Mama shook her head. "It's not."

"I own a business." Now it was Tabitha who looked around her space. "One that I enjoy."

"It is crowded and filthy. It's not safe," Mama said.

"It is not filthy, and I'm not by myself. I have people."

Retha spoke next. "They are not your family. We're concerned for not only your safety but that of the children. All the changes in people have reached Charleston . . . the music and dancing."

"How can you talk of the renaissance like that? Negroes expressing themselves through literature, art, and music is not a bad thing."

"I've seen the dancing. It's not Christian, and it's overtaken this city. We read the papers," Mama said.

"Everybody is not Christian. Judging them for it won't get them to be."

"I would say you learned to sass me while being away, but your mouth had been smart before you left home." Mama's chest heaved up and down heavily.

Tabitha regretted talking back as she remembered one of their last conversations. When she *told* Mama she was going to take up with Joseph. Her words had haunted her over the years. "I apologize for my tone, ma'am."

No one said anything. Everyone seemed to be recovering from the tense moment. Then Retha broke the silence. "Mama has started a sewing business—needlework. She could use your help. Your creativity and ideas."

This time when she spoke, Tabitha was slow and deliberate enough not to sound contentious. "You are sitting in my creativity and ideas." Tabitha cut her eyes from Retha's to Mama's. "I've never been good at sewing."

"I lost Hank and now Charles. I cannot lose my daughter. I know you've made your own way . . ." Mama let her words trail off. Tabitha wondered if she thought her own statement unfair.

Tabitha sucked in a deep breath and released it on a long, hard wind. "Catherine is in Savannah. George and Robert are obviously in Chicago, although no one hears from them."

Mama snapped, "Don't talk against your brothers."

"They left you, and unless something has changed, they don't write or call. You're grieving, and they're still not here." Words about her brothers seemed to injure Mama even more.

"I am not here to talk about your brothers," she said, standing. She circled her chair. "I was not happy about them going north or even about Catherine going to Savannah, but they weren't tethered to children. You've got to do all this and manage three babies with nobody but paid help."

Tabitha didn't remove her eyes from her mother's pale hands. Her fingers were red from their tight clutch on the wooden chair back.

"My help is not paid. Miss Libby is a dear friend," Tabitha said. "Can't you all see I'm managing very well?"

Mama banged her fist on the top of the chair, asserting her authority. "No more. No more. This doesn't make sense."

She was ordering her. Did Mama think that would work when she'd left home at eighteen without her blessing? Retha swallowed loud enough for everyone to hear. "What I think Mama means is—"

"I hear our mother just fine," Tabitha said, cutting Retha off. "I will not leave."

Retha looked at Mama, waiting for some signal of some kind. Were they going to tie her up and take her back? Was that part of Clifford's role, to provide the muscle?

"Your mother has another solution that will ease her nerves," Clifford interjected. The tension in the room was heavy.

Tabitha waited a beat. She wasn't sure she wanted to hear any solution. She'd made up her mind the minute it was suggested she leave, but she looked up at him, nodding to encourage him to have his say.

"If you won't come"—Clifford paused and then continued— "let the children come."

Tabitha's gasp was audible. "What?"

Clifford raised a hand to halt her protest. "Just listen. You let the children come where they'll be cared for, safe, and you won't have to have them underfoot and using strangers to take care of them. You can work and do what you need to do without—"

Tabitha was on her feet now, cutting Clifford's words off. "Without my children. Why ever would I want to do that? I'm working for them."

"You're working for yourself," Retha said, shaking her head. "I think we've established that."

There was disappointment in Mama's eyes. She was proud but not proud at the same time. Whatever that quandary of emotions was called, it made Tabitha feel bad enough for tears to prick at the back of her eyes. "I *am* building this for them."

Mama shook his head. "This is not your land, Bitta. You are never building anything on someone else's land. I don't have much, but I own the property my house sits on." Mama sat again. She placed both her palms down on the table's surface.

"What do you mean you own the property?" As far as Tabitha knew, they rented. They'd always rented.

"I've moved." Pride carried Mama's words. "I purchased a house and have bedrooms ready for them and you. Let the children come with me. I could use their comfort."

"They'd be too much for you."

"You don't know her, because you haven't been home, but Miss Fran's nieces came to live with her shortly after you left. They are 'bout grown. They live with me now. They cook and clean. They're a big help."

"Where's Miss Fran?" Tabitha waited but knew the answer. She could see it on Mama's face.

"She passed too. A few months ago."

The word *oh* stuck in Tabitha's throat. She was still wrestling with her feelings about Papa's death. That he could be gone so suddenly. But she pulled her thoughts from him to Miss Francine. She'd been good to her, allowing her and her brothers and sisters to sit with her during the times when Papa was too drunk to be around.

Mama continued. "My new house is down a piece from the new school at the church. Margaret wouldn't have to walk far."

How Mama could afford to live near that area was a question that needed an answer, but it wasn't the time. Tabitha was still in shock, and Mama was noticeably struggling with her grief.

"Think of them, Bitta," Mama said. "What kind of life do they have being couped up in a flat all day with a stranger?"

Tabitha left them at the table. Going into the kitchen, she took a moment away from them while she stirred a pot that didn't need stirring. Papa was dead. She felt so much and so little at the same time. He had never fully been a father, and she had never fully been his daughter. She'd never gotten over that conversation she'd overheard as a child.

"We can leave her with Fran."

"I won't leave my child, Charles."

"I'm not going to last much longer," Papa said.

There were muffled words she didn't hear and then more of Papa's insistence.

"I'm right." Papa sounded defeated by his words. *"And you can't make us all pay for a mistake."*

"Charles . . ."

He cut Mama off. "Think about it. But know this, I've decided about the boys."

He was willing to leave her with Miss Fran. To go where she had no idea. Mama had stood up for her. So now how could Tabitha send her own children away?

"What kind of life do they have?" Those words sat heavily in her chest. Miss Libby was too old to even take the boys to the park down the street, and on days when she considered it, she changed

her mind because she was afraid she'd lose them, so they were cooped up.

Life outside of the city had been beautiful and free for Tabitha and her sisters and brothers—most of the time.

She gathered herself and walked out of the kitchen. The decision was made between the first and the second step closer to her family. She would let them go, but she would not give up Margaret. She had to have someone here with her. "Margaret is already in school. She's involved with charity work with me."

Mama released a long breath. "Fine."

Tabitha closed the restaurant early. She didn't want her family to travel back to Georgetown in the dark. Packing up her sons was one of the hardest things she'd ever had to do. They didn't have much, but she was planning to keep a few things rather than send it all.

"We'll pack everything," Retha stated, helping her. "This isn't temporary."

"You understand this is hard for me," Tabitha said. The boys were in the front room with Clifford and Mama, giggling and running and enjoying them, accepting their new station in life before they even knew they had one.

"I can only imagine," Retha said. "I would not want to be without my children."

Tabitha struggled with the ache that cut her from the center of her chest on down into her gut. It did not stop the dryness in her throat or the wetness fighting to surface in her eyes. It did not stop the question swirling around in her mind— was this the right thing to do? She didn't know, but she kept packing and praying, hoping God would give her peace about it. And there was Papa's death. Would Mama really be okay to care for them? She could hardly imagine her mother's world without him.

"Why didn't you tell me about Papa?" she whispered.

"When I mentioned calling you to Mama, she asked me to wait so we could tell you together . . . in person."

"But a whole month, Retha?"

"He'd been away for almost half a year. You know that. I don't know how to explain it, but I felt like the last time I saw him was going to be the last time."

Tabitha grunted. She did understand. Every time he left, it felt like he might not come back. It was a weird kind of coming and going over the years because it never made sense. The story about why he stayed so long never sat right in her mind.

"How did she buy a house?"

Retha shrugged. "There was money after he died. I don't know the details. She will not discuss it."

Tabitha frowned. "How could there be enough for a house?"

"I don't know," Retha said firmly. "All I know is she has no note. She has money. She is quite comfortable."

Tabitha placed a hand on Retha's forearm. Their eyes locked. "There's a secret here."

"There's always been a secret, Bitta."

"Don't you want to know what it is?"

Retha pulled her arm free. "Of course. Now that Papa's gone, I'm sure she'll tell us . . . in her own time." Retha seemed sure of that.

Tabitha had no choice but to accept it as well. She reached across the bed for the rag dolls the boys slept with. She pressed them to her chest and then looked down at them before looking back up at Retha. "I'm sorry you lost your father."

Retha wrapped her arms around Tabitha and squeezed. The emotions of the day melted into a pool around her feet. Hugs healed. "He was your father too."

They pulled apart, and Tabitha swiped her wet eyes. Charles Cooper was gone now. There was no point pondering who he had been to her. He clothed her and fed her. That was what fathers did, but still, she ached for a connection she'd never have. "I've always had you."

Retha smiled and squeezed her hand. "And you always will."

Shortly after, Margaret was in from school.

They all sat down for a meal while Tabitha told the children what was happening. Amos was four. He understood. Little Tom simply clapped his pudgy hands.

Margaret stood and rushed to her side. "I want to stay with you, Mama." Tears filled her eyes.

"You are staying with me," Tabitha said, stooping and rubbing her arms. "We girls are going to stick together."

Margaret grabbed on to her and squeezed.

An hour later, Clifford's automobile rolled away from the front of her building. They'd taken most of Tabitha's heart with them. Tabitha and Margaret sat by the window, with Tabitha praying without ceasing that her children were not crying for her.

Miss Libby came out of her room. She sat on the sofa. "'Iffen oona no mind, I wantuh say something."

Tabitha was tired of people talking, but she sent Margaret to the bedroom to do her math tables, giving Miss Libby the courtesy of her attention.

"I love you, Miss Tabitha, oona knows I do, but you being foolish."

"Foolish?" Tabitha never expected that.

"Oona have a home. People who love oona and wan' be with oona. Instead of gwan der', you stay here all dese years. Raisin' your chil' 'round low-class men and women like me . . .'bout po'."

"My family is not rich."

"The car cost a lot of money. Mi 'no how your family shows up in de world—"

"I—"

Miss Libby raised her hand to stop her. "I'ma have de whole of mi say if you let me."

Tabitha nodded. "Go on."

"It's a good ting you sent your sons, but oona and Margaret could have a better life too."

"There's nothing wrong with my life. There's nothing wrong with you, and some of the men here have saved my life."

"A life that needed savin' from the men they work side. Ain't no life in danger where dat fancy car be goin'."

"You don't understand. Being here is important to me."

"Oona sure you not lettin' shame keep ya?" Miss Libby asked. "Ya modda lose her husband, and she beggin' you to come back. She not tinkin' on what happened before." She paused. "I know 'bout shame. I come from people on Craig Island. Tem' use shame heavy. We had a whole ceremony fa' see make you feel like nobody. They say it was in the name of savin' a soul." Miss Libby grunted. "But I watched my sister be shamed so, she walk into the ocean and never come out."

Tabitha's heart sank. Today was filled with grief. "I'm so sorry."

"Tis be the reason I leave de island. Tis why I has no family," she said. "De devil use shame to hurt us. He like to get us alone with our tinkin'. He like to make us tink we don't have choices. Your modda gave you a choice, and her heart was pure when she did. Oona should go home before you too old to find you a new man." Miss Libby stood. "Don't end up alone like me."

Tabitha cleared her throat. She appreciated Miss Libby's impassioned plea, but "What would you do if I left?"

"Get work in a house caring for chillin. White folks like old round women like me with dey young ones."

Tabitha shook her head. "I don't want you thinking the boys leaving changes anything here."

"It's okay if it do. Oona been good to me. On the scariest day of my life, you gave me the gif'of time. I would neva want oona not to have God's best 'cause oona was tinkin' on me."

Tabitha touched the woman's forearm. "I appreciate that, but I still need you for Margaret. I'd like to keep things the way they are."

Miss Libby smiled. "You a good woman. I'll leave you ta ya own mind."

She did leave Tabitha thinking, pondering really. What was God's best for her? Brady slipped into her thoughts. She tried to push him out, but he would not leave, and that scared her. That scared her a powerful lot.

Chapter 31

Present Day

Sabrina

Quinton was going to have to see the whole of me in order for us to move forward. I didn't keep secrets. I didn't have time for judgment. Any man who was going to be with me had to accept me for who I was. So, I showed him my van.

"That's my grandfather's pickup I drive," I said as he inspected it inside and then out.

"I assumed that. It's kept like a man's truck."

I suppose it was with the fishing tackle box and tools on the rear floor in the back part of the cab.

"I don't see you buying a plain gray truck for you and Kenni. You're much too . . . colorful for that." He smiled and then returned his attention to the van.

"I know this is a lot to take in."

He stuck his hands in his pockets and sighed. "It's different."

"That's it? That's all you have to say?"

"I mean, what do you want me to say? I feel bad that you had to live in a vehicle. It just seems you've had a hard time of things."

"I'm not the bright-eyed ambitious teenager from ten years ago."

"You thought you were bright-eyed and ambitious?"

I smirked. "I assumed. You tell me what I was."

"More like doe-eyed. Cautious, contemplative, and unsure."

"Why are you using three words that mean the same thing?"

He fell back against my van and shoved his hands in his pockets. "Driving my point home."

I sighed, seriously. "Have I changed?"

"You've completely evolved."

"For the better, I hope."

"Oh yeah, in good ways." Quinton smiled. "For one, you're a talented cake designer. You own your choices and your words. You're sure. Quite decisive."

"Am I?"

"Yes. I mean you don't linger on decisions. You let your no be no and your yes be yes, all the time."

Quinton sensed my anxiety. He pulled me closer, raised his hand to my hair, and pushed it off my face while planting his eyes on mine. "Timing is everything. Don't let this van situation make you question your purpose."

"I think my purpose is to be a mom."

"It's one of them. Sometimes one takes precedence over the other. You've been raising a small child and not as able to manage your cake business, so your finances suffered."

I pulled away from him. "But I haven't been raising my child. Not alone."

Quinton frowned, waiting for me to go on. I told him about Ellen. How I had Kenni for the first three years because I could live off Kendrick's life insurance, but once that ran out, I couldn't afford the rent. "And I let it run out," I said. "I saw the end coming, and I still couldn't make myself figure out how to keep us together. I'm so ashamed of that."

"You were depressed."

"My great-great-grandmother had the same situation. Her children's father died. He left her with nothing. All she had was a small savings. Instead of wallowing in her pain, she carved out a restaurant business and a life for herself. During Jim freakin' Crow." I could feel heat in my eyes about what I was going to admit to him. "I didn't do that. I gave Kenni to his mother, and now she's suing me for custody."

"Wait a minute. What?"

"She's angry I'm here and not in Greenville or Greer where she lives. She's used to having Kenni close." I was hesitant about sharing everything I thought, but I'd told myself I was going to be completely honest with him. "The thing is . . . I wonder if Kenni isn't better off with her."

Quinton pulled me into his arms again. He kissed the top of my head. "No, babe, she's not better off with anyone except you." He held me back and stared at me. "Why do you question your motherhood? You love your daughter. I can see that."

"Is it enough? Am I loving her in the right way? I don't know. I didn't have a great example. I mean my stepmother adored me, but she treated my sister bad . . . As I got older I could see it, so it was hard to receive her love." I closed my eyes. I hated seeing that truth about Lorraine, but if I was ever going to understand Mariah, I had to.

"I want Kenni to feel secure. To have self-esteem. Not to struggle with those things." I pressed a hand to my chest. "I still struggle. I can't give what I don't have."

"Sabrina, you're being *really* hard on yourself. What's going on?"

"People who grow up without mothers do this. We question if we can be good mothers. I'm a textbook case. I don't feel like I'm on solid ground." I looked at the van. "This was my home for almost a year." I stepped back. "I don't want to fail Kendrick's daughter. Despite his complaints, his mother did a good job with him."

"Just because she did a good job with her son doesn't mean she gets to raise your daughter," Quinton said. "If it was just the homeless situation, I get it. That's temporary. Let Kenni stay with family. But if you're delaying getting yourself a stable place because you're delaying being a mom full-time, don't do that to yourself. Don't do it to her."

Quinton and I stood there with inches between us, looking into each other's eyes. I liked that we could do that and not look away. I liked that I saw no judgment from him. "If the only issues you really have are living in this van and a pending court thing, let me help you." He shrugged. "I have money."

I stopped him right there. "I can't take your money, but this understanding thing you've got going on is attractive, sir."

"It's real."

"I know. You're a good man. Everything I remember about you as a teenager is still true."

I folded myself into his arms. I was glad to have his comfort and his respect. He knew everything, except that one thing, and if I could, I would probably take it to my grave.

"You have done such a good job with the social media," Mariah said.

We were standing in Grandma's kitchen. I was making macaroni and cheese. Mariah had just come in from the restaurant. If being knocked over with a feather was a real thing, I would have fallen.

"Thanks," I said. "I learned everything I know from YouTube videos and Dante. He's a social media wizard."

"You took the time to learn. You took the pictures and came up with the captions and used the hashtags. And it's working," Mariah said. "I don't know where we'd be if it wasn't for the work you've done on social media."

"Dante's a great chef."

"People had to learn he was here." Mariah reached into the refrigerator for a bottle of water. "That's all you."

She opened her drink, and then she reached into the junk drawer for a pair of scissors and cut through a small box the mailman left earlier. She smiled, removed a business card, and handed it to me.

Tears came to my eyes as I read, *Tabby's M & S Diner.* It listed the address and phone number and then our names together with our new website.

"I figured we might need them for something."

I wanted to hug my sister, but I thought better of taking this emotional moment too far. I fought letting the tears fall too. She'd always accused me of being sentimental. "Thank you."

"We've both worked hard." Mariah pulled a stack of about twenty cards out and gave them to me. "I'll put the box in the office at the restaurant." She turned to walk in the direction of the living room and then turned back. "Something is bothering you," she said. "I sense it."

I took a deep breath. I wasn't used to this Mariah, and I had to gather myself around that fact.

"You should tell me," Mariah pressed. "Maybe I can help."

I nodded and decided to take a chance. Quinton accepted me for who I was. Maybe it was time to trust Mariah too. If things were ever going to change between us, we had to share our lives, not just business cards. I dismissed the little voice in my head that taunted me—made me feel ashamed—and told her.

"Ellen is suing me for custody of Kenni."

This time it was Mariah who could have been knocked over. I told her the whole story, which ended in tears for me . . . my sister, anger.

I raised my hands to dab at the water in the corner of my eyes and sniffed. "She's not budging. She wants me back in the Upstate."

"What makes her think she can control where you live?"

"She's not thinking. She just wants her way. She also thinks she has something . . ." I paused and reached for my bag. I put my cards in the interior pocket.

Mariah was waiting for me to finish. "You were saying?"

"What?"

"You were about to finish a sentence. Ellen thinking she has something. What does she think she has?"

"It's not something I really want to talk about."

"Let me help you."

I folded my arms over my chest. "You? Since when?" I hadn't meant to say it. I wanted to take the words back. Mariah didn't look fazed.

She shrugged. "Since therapy, girl."

I cocked my head. "Therapy?"

"I've been going for weeks. Haven't you noticed a change in me? I just gave you a compliment on the social media and purchased business cards."

I examined her claim by thinking about recent events. "I did notice some changes, but I thought you'd just . . . had a good day and that you'd snap back."

"To being a witch."

"Pretty much." I dropped my arms as I laughed.

Mariah pursed her lips before saying, "Well, I'm not. I'm working out my issues, so tell me more about this Ellen thing."

I sighed. I didn't want to ruin the beauty of the last ten minutes. I didn't trust my sister. "I get that you're trying to be better, but how am I supposed to believe you're not going to judge me as soon as it comes out of my mouth?"

Grandma walked into the room. "Because no one is going to judge you in this house. I overheard a little of what you've been saying. I know you've been whispering with your lawyer. Tell us what happened so we can know how to help you and so I can know what to pray about."

I dropped into a kitchen chair. "You're asking me to share the saddest and most painful day of my life."

"Yes, we are," Grandma said.

"Does this have to do with Kendrick?" Mariah asked.

"No. It's about Kenni." I took a deep breath and paced myself as I talked. "You know she was a beautiful baby, and we started off so good." I looked at Grandma. "You remember when you visited us after I had her? She was breastfeeding, but that didn't go well. A lot of it had to do with me being depressed. My milk supply was low. I started giving her formula, which she had problems with. She got gassy and colicky. She wouldn't stop crying."

Grandma reached for my hand.

"I wasn't getting any sleep. I didn't want to eat. I was grieving. Everything was wrong. Everything." A tear slid down my face. "I took Kenni to Ellen and told her I couldn't keep her. I told her I didn't want her. I didn't understand her. I literally freaked out. Ellen thought I was a danger to myself because I talked about not wanting to live without Kendrick. I was having a moment." I tossed my hands in the air. "She had me put on a seventy-two-hour hold."

Grandma and Mariah's eyes told how heavy the pain of this story was for them. I kept going. "When I was discharged, I didn't go get Kenni." I shrugged. "I was tired. I couldn't bear to deal with the crying, so I left her there. I felt like she was better off without me. I didn't call or check on her for a month. Ellen applied for guardianship to be able to take her to a doctor's appointment."

"Oh, chile," Grandma said.

"I was scared of how I felt around my own daughter. I was afraid I was going to hurt her. I sat in my apartment in the dark for weeks. The mail was piling up. Someone called the police to do a wellness check. I ended up going back to the hospital where I had Kenni. They did a full assessment and diagnosed me with postpartum depression.

"Once I got treatment, I went to get my daughter. Ellen was glad to give her to me. She wanted me to be well enough to care for her."

"So that's what she's holding over you—abandonment?" Mariah asked.

"Kenni was five weeks old when I left her. I was so messed up."

"You don't have to explain yourself to us," Mariah said. "PPD is a real illness. The judge is going to understand that."

"But I don't want Kenni to ever know that happened. If we go to court, there'll be documentation in a file that I said I didn't want my daughter."

Grandma tightened her grip on my hand. Suddenly, I felt a hand on the opposite arm. Mariah said, "We're not going to let Ellen run over you."

"Custody fights are expensive. She has money. I can't fight her. I might need to go back to Greenville."

"You don't need to go anywhere you don't want to go. She's not going to hold you hostage," Grandma said.

"I have money," Mariah said, "and I'll have more once my divorce is settled."

I turned my eyes to my sister's.

"Money from Clark's, and there will be much more, so you tell your lawyer you're in for the fight."

Grandma's face broke into a smile.

Mariah squeezed my hand. "I should have been the one you came to when you were struggling with Kenni, but you couldn't because"—she shrugged—"I was not a good sister. I'm ashamed of that. But I'm not going to stay ashamed."

"The devil likes to use shame," Grandma said. "He uses it because it works, but not when you resist him."

"When you resist him, he will flee," Mariah said.

"Great-Great-Grandma Tabitha dealt with shame. It kept her away from her family for years," I said.

"It sure did," Grandma said. "Things like shame can be strongholds that pass down like a spirit affecting each generation."

"Not anymore," Mariah said. "We are breaking this curse on us. Shame will not work against me. It will not work against you, and it will never work on Kenni."

"Thank you, Jesus, for healing up in here." Grandma lifted her hands in praise. "Glory!"

Mariah and I smiled at our grandmother's loud exclamation of joy.

My sister said, "You couldn't count on me then, but you can count on me now. I've got you."

I never thought I'd hear those words come out of Mariah's mouth. I stood and wrapped my arms around her and hugged her like I'd been wanting to do my entire life.

Chapter 32

Mariah

Vince and I were permitted by the courts to mediate virtually. The first thing he said to me was, "You look good. Are you planning to stay in Georgetown?"

I hadn't seen him since that day he handed me the divorce papers. He was wearing some kind of bronzer on his skin that made him look greenish in the lighting. His hair wasn't as gray at the temples. Hair dye? He looked awful.

"I'm not sure about my plans."

He nodded. "Hendley's such a small town. There are lots of restaurants in the low country."

"You don't need to concern yourself with my job prospects, Vince."

"Excuse us." My attorney muted the microphone. "I think it's best if you don't engage in small talk. He's bound to say something to make you angry."

The mediator's face appeared on the screen. She introduced herself and stated the reasons the parties were present and that mediation was required for divorces in South Carolina. After ascertaining that divorce was the wish of both parties, she quickly moved on to property because there was nothing else. Since Vince was the plaintiff, his lawyer began. He started by listing the assets, which included the Clark family land, the house, personal property, our vehicles, and of course Clark's Diner and financial holdings from Clark's merchandise.

By the time we were done, between the mediator's questions and the lawyers' back-and-forth, we came to the end of the meeting. Vince was offering me a hundred thousand dollars, of which he'd already given me ten, and seventy percent of all royalties for existing contracts with Target stores.

In his words he was doing this to finish the business without angry feelings. I suppose he meant without angry feelings on his part, because surely he wasn't talking about mine. One of the things I'd learned in therapy was not to let other people decide how I should feel.

A month ago, I would have taken this offer. I would have felt sorry for myself, unworthy, and I would have let him rob me, but I was no longer that woman. If Clark's Diner was a glass, I had filled it with blood, sweat, and tears.

"My client is not willing to accept this offer. She has documentation that she turned Clark's Diner into a regional brand. Does your client have a more reasonable offer for us to consider?"

Vince's attorney looked at Vince. They hadn't discussed it. I almost laughed at the lunacy.

Whatever that crap was Vince had on his face looked like it was gonna slide down onto his dress shirt. Vince had known me for nearly all of my adult life, and he fully expected me to accept his offer because that was what I'd always done. But I'd changed. I was a powerful woman, and now I was harnessing that power and using it. Therapy was the truth.

"We're done until we hear back from the plaintiff," my attorney said, and the mediator went through the steps to end the mediation.

She was just about to end the Zoom when Vince barked, "What do you want, Mariah?" His lawyer tried to stop him, but Vince continued. "You must have a figure in mind."

The mediator reminded him the session was over, but I was as rebellious as Vince. "I do have something in mind. You can wait for the paperwork. You know, how you gave me the paperwork."

"I'm willing to settle this divorce with irreconcilable differences. Don't make me bring up the ugly issues," Vince said.

"What, your heavy-handed-with-salt girlfriend?"

"No, the real reason I don't want to be married to you anymore." He shook his head. "You know what that is, and quite frankly, *no one* is more unfaithful than you, Mariah, and you know it."

"We're done now," Vince's attorney said.

The mediator added, "I'll be in touch with a summary."

The Zoom camera went off. Seconds later, a FaceTime call rang in from my attorney. "Well, that went well," I said.

"Reasonably, but is there something I don't know?"

"There is something. Something I didn't think that he would use," I replied.

My attorney sighed and said, "Let's discuss it."

I walked into Dr. Johnson's building still carrying the irritation that the drive over had not fully taken away. I purposely scheduled therapy to follow mediation because I assumed I was going to need to talk to somebody about it, and I'd been right.

We opened with Dr. Johnson's questions about my week, and then she moved to the mediation and my feelings.

"I'm angry. I've seen movies and read books about how couples become during divorces, but you hope you're never in this situation. I feel like Vince is stabbing me in the back over and over again, and I can't get the knife out." The first of my tears spilled. "What makes him think he has the right to have everything?"

"Is this taking of everything a part of his personality?"

"Oh yeah. I mean, he's a jerk. I think even he knows that, but he wasn't that way in the beginning."

"What was he like?"

"He considered my feelings. My thoughts and opinions. He told me he was lucky to have me—he'd married up."

"How did you feel when he said those things?"

"I felt lucky. I thought I was lucky to find someone who wanted to spend his life with me."

"Why was that luck?"

"Because." I curled my fingers around the chair's cold steel arms. Hot tears burned the back of my eyes. I swallowed, pushing my emotions back down into my belly.

Dr. Johnson sat back. She waited a beat before she pressed me. "Because what?"

"Because I'm always surprised when people love me." I wiped my nose. "I didn't have anyone to love me when I was a child. My father put his wife first, and she didn't love me. My grandparents were far away. I know it's juvenile to say this, but *that* felt like a betrayal. I needed them."

"Cousins?"

"Not really, and the few I had lived here. My father traveled a lot for his job, so we didn't get to Georgetown often . . . only for some holidays."

"What about Sabrina?"

"Six years is a big gap between children. I told you, Lorraine pitted us against each other so much and for so long that I didn't connect with her, but . . ." I paused. "We had a breakthrough the other day. A good one. I offered to pay for an attorney for her. She's being sued for custody of my niece."

Dr. Johnson smiled a little. "That sounds great."

"It is. We hugged. I know that I have a lot of work to do. I'm not romanticizing one conversation, but Sabrina is not my enemy."

Dr. Johnson's lips ticked up. "I'm glad to hear that."

The smile dropped from my lips. "But I do have an enemy," I said. "Vince."

"How did mediation go?"

"I want more of what I built, and he doesn't like it. I'm fighting him."

"Good. You sound proud of that."

"I am. He's cheating. I can get evidence. That'll help my case."

Dr. Johnson got a look on her face that I'd seen a hundred times. She was about to probe. "You haven't really mentioned his infidelity much. You've talked more about the money. The loss of the television show."

"That matters to me more."

"Why not your marriage?"

"Because it changed a long time ago."

Dr. Johnson cocked her head. "How did it change?"

I looked up at the clock to the left of her. I had twenty minutes left in this session. I was tired of talking, but even I had to admit talking was helping. This process . . . it was working, so I answered. "We were a couple in love, and then we became a couple falling out of love. His mother got sick. It took a year for her to die. And then it was just him and me again, and we didn't have anything left."

Dr. Johnson made some notes and then looked at me again. "There's something you're not telling me about your marriage. Why did you fall out of love? What changed it?"

"Me, I suppose." I hesitated, took a deep breath, and grappled with my thoughts before admitting them out loud. "I didn't want to have children."

"Okay. That's something to talk about."

"I never wanted to have children. Vince did from the beginning. After we got married, I turned the diner into our child. Keeping it out of bankruptcy was a whole thing.

"I worked sixteen-hour days. Once it became financially sound, I started trying to figure out ways to market it outside of Hendley. It only took a few years before I had a publicist pitching it to food shows. Do you know we have merchandise in Target?"

"I didn't know that."

"We do." I raised my hand and pointed at my chest. "I did that." I sighed. "But the whole time, Vince wanted us to start a family. He was happy about the business, but he wanted children more than he wanted to be with me."

"What were the conversations about children like?"

"Well, at first I said we were young and let's wait, and then later I pretended I was trying. Vince wasn't as daft as I thought he was. Married people have sex, and a lot of times children result, so when they don't, there's usually a reason. He found out I was using birth control. When he confronted me about it, I told him I was never having a child."

I inhaled deeply and let it out, processing the memory in my mind as I was telling it. "The way he looked at me . . . I'll never forget it. There was a cellular shift in his affection for me. Then his mother died, and he was done. She hadn't had grandchildren, and that was my fault."

Dr. Johnson gave me a minute to process through that. Tears ran down my face again. I cried every week in this place. I used to hate it, but now it felt good.

"Why didn't you want to have children?"

A heaviness came down on me like I'd been drugged. I could barely lift my head. "For the same reason other women don't want to have children."

"I want to hear your reason, Mariah. Why didn't you want to have children?"

"Vince told his mother about the birth control, and she threw it in my face . . . her disappointment in me. How could I rob them of this? What kind of woman deceives her husband? She wanted grandchildren. But this is *my* body."

"It certainly is. But you're avoiding answering about why *you* didn't want children."

"Oh, I hate this. I'm answering you. What do you want from me?"

"Mariah, healing won't start until you figure out what's actually hurting you. You can't recover until you know what you're recovering from."

I still sat there, not responding. The fear was so deeply imbedded in my body that it was intertwined with my arteries and veins. This is what I'd been avoiding. This question was why I didn't want therapy.

Dr. Johnson's voice sliced through my self-analysis. "I'm trying to help you see where you need to get. I want to know if you have unhealthy thoughts about childbearing. Is the reason you don't want children because you're afraid that what happened to your mother is going to happen to you?"

"Of course I am!" I snapped, and then I sobbed like I was emotionally unstable, one minute, two, three minutes of nonstop crying with hyperventilating in between. At some point, Dr. Johnson stood and handed me a wad of tissue and then returned to her chair. When I finally calmed, I said, "You lose a mother to childbirth, and the idea of being pregnant and delivering a baby is horrifying." I reached for more tissue, but I didn't have any more tears. "Having babies is natural. It's supposed to be beautiful. But it's not always beautiful." I was crying again. I thought that was done. "You know the scariest part isn't dying, Dr. Johnson. I've died in my mind a hundred times." I covered my hands with my face and then dropped them. "The scary part is leaving a baby alone in the world without a mother. Who they stay behind with is not always someone who makes the right choices. People don't always do what's best."

Dr. Johnson was looking at me with deep compassion. Her normally stoic face and composure were broken by my brokenness.

"My father didn't handle things right. He married the first woman he met, and she was looking for a husband, not a six-year-old. And I felt that." I pointed at my chest. "Every day I felt her resentment until the day I left for college. That was the happiest day of that witch's life."

"But it wasn't like that for Sabrina?"

"Nooo. Lorraine couldn't have kids of her own, so she worshiped Sabrina. Sabrina was like a new penny. Pretty and shiny. No attitude. She could pretend that Sabrina was hers because she was a little light-skinned baby. I was too dark for her perfect picture. I stood out among the four of us like a sore black thumb."

I rolled my head back to release the ache and stood.

"How could my father marry a woman like that? He should have chosen better. Or not at all." I wiped my nose and tossed the tissue in the trash. "I won't have a child and leave them behind."

Dr. Johnson nodded. Now she understood, and on a deeper level, so did I.

Chapter 33

October 1922

Tabitha

Tabitha examined herself and shushed pride away as she inspected her high-heeled boots, wide-brimmed hat, paste pearls, and a yellow flapper dress with elaborate floral embroidery across the hem and down the sides. She hadn't been to church in a long time. She missed it, and more importantly, she needed Margaret to experience more than she had exposed her to.

The streets were quiet on Sunday morning, making the walk easy. Once they entered, they found a seat, and minutes after, Margaret pointed. "Mama, it's Mr. Brady." Tabitha grabbed the child's hand and pulled it down. "I've told you it's rude to point at people."

Margaret apologized. Tabitha fought the temptation to look in that direction, but once she did, she saw Brady sitting two pews behind them. His Sunday best suit was a nice crisp black color, made of a fabric with just the right bit of sheen. He was handsome in it. A ripple of warmth erupted and spread through her. She contemplated her thoughts of Brady. Lately she'd had too many. She didn't really want to imagine her days without seeing him. Mama had seen what she didn't even know she felt.

Brady caught her staring, and she blushed when he tipped his head at her. Then he smiled, and her entire insides smiled back.

After service, Brady was quick to move in her direction. He complimented her on her dress and then did the same about Margaret's new pink dress.

Once they stepped outside, Brady put on his hat. "I'd like to take you ladies to supper. A cook deserves a meal out."

Margaret pressed into Tabitha's body, and Tabitha knew she was itching to remind her of the fact that she had somewhere to be. "Margaret has rehearsal for a play at the YWCA soon."

Brady was thoughtful as always and then said, "Let's take her to the rehearsal and you and I have a meal while we wait for her to finish."

Tabitha fought to keep her breath even. A meal with Brady outside of Tab's was a date, wasn't it? She had no good reason to say no, so she said, "That sounds like a good plan."

Brady released a breath on a chuckle. "Good," he said happily, nearly eagerly, and the three of them walked to the YWCA building.

Once they arrived, Tabitha had Margaret sit on the steps and eat the biscuit and pork chop sandwich she'd packed for her.

"I know this area a little," Brady said. "There's a place just around the corner."

"Good. I don't like to go far."

Brady smiled. "I imagine you don't."

Margaret finished and went inside. She and Brady fell into step as they walked. Tabitha said, "Margaret knows the phone number to the house for emergencies. I made sure she learned it. It's sewed in her dress hems too."

Brady smiled again. "Mothers think of everything."

"We try."

"Do you have your own phone now?" he asked.

"No. It's the same one we've had for the house. In the common area. We all contribute a little to it."

"Same at my building. Phones are nearly necessary." Brady took her elbow and ushered her around a broken piece of rock she had not seen. In her heels, she might have fallen.

"I thought about getting one so I could talk to my family about my boys, but the expense doesn't make sense. Some months I'm barely scraping by."

Not being on the docks made a difference in their step and the conversation. They were more intentional with each other and, unfortunately, awkward in small ways. It reminded Tabitha of how she was when she met Joseph.

She had learned a lot about Brady over the past two years, but never had she known about his love for music or that he had a year of college before he ran out of money and had to stop.

After they settled into chairs at a table in a small place with good smells coming from the kitchen, Brady continued the conversation they'd been having. "I wanted to learn business in college and move north. So many people I know went north. Columbia had a big exodus."

"People are still moving," Tabitha said. "The YWCA has to do a lot to help the women with boarding in the North. The women there write letters of request all the time to the YWCAs up there."

"I wonder if our people fare better if their dreams come true the way they expect them to."

"I don't too much see anybody coming back. My brothers left a long time ago. Neither of them have come back . . . not even for a visit," Tabitha said, lifting her teacup for a sip. She felt a little shame about that, but she'd already said it. "It must be gold streets up there for them to not come see our mama."

"The North may not have Jim Crow laws, but they have systems that make it hard for Negroes." He sighed. "The streets are not made of gold. Not at all. I'm sure they've learned that."

"My brothers are much older than me. They were gone one day with just a hug and a goodbye."

Papa's words to Mama came back to her. "*I've decided about the boys. I'm sending them north.*" That didn't make sense to her, but she figured if Mama accepted it, she had to as well.

Tabitha took another sip of her drink. Brady was easy to talk to. He listened to her. "Sometimes people want things so badly they'll do anything to get them."

Brady looked into her eyes with a deeper intensity. "What do you want?"

"Me?" Tabitha gave him a tiny smile. "More customers."

He shook his head. "No, I mean what do you want besides Tabby's?"

She was quick with her answer. She'd always known what it was. "My own restaurant in a building no one can take from me."

Brady smiled again. "That's not too big to ask of God."

Tabitha put down her cup and traced her finger around the saucer. "I can't even save for it. Most weeks I'm just making my due bills."

"Nothing is unattainable. I think we have to be patient about God's timing."

Tabitha and Brady fell into the habit of attending church together, and it wasn't long before they were courting. The more time she spent with Brady, the more she realized that being with someone was supposed to make her feel free, not trapped the way she was with Joseph.

And though she burned for Brady in the same way she had in the beginning for Joseph, he was a gentleman . . . always. He never made her feel silly for wanting to be decent and modest. And so this gentle courtship continued through the winter and into the early spring, when Tabitha thought the beginning of the new season might bring a new beginning for her and Brady.

Tabitha was humming a tune, setting up for a new day of cooking and serving. She remembered the picture show she and Brady saw the night before, and the way they held hands in the dark of the theater, when the bell rang over the door, bringing Brady through it.

Her heart quickened when she saw him, but then froze when she noticed his countenance. For a second she thought he was sick. Knowing he only ate what she cooked, she wondered if she had once again become a victim of tainted meat. Though she was careful about who she chose to buy from, the fear of that was always with her. Sam's action had forever added a level of fear.

She walked to him cautiously. "What is it?"

"My father died."

Tabitha gasped and put a hand on his arm. "I'm so sorry."

"I have to go home for the funeral. They think it was his heart," Brady said. He cleared his throat. "I'm locking up, but I was hoping I could store some more expensive things in your back room since you'll be here every day."

"Of course. You fetch them while I make room."

Brady left and then came back with a pile of leather hides. He made a few trips before he was satisfied he'd secured his most important goods. When he was done, she handed him a bag with sandwiches and cake for the trip.

"Thank you for this, Tab." That was his little name for her.

"It's the least I can do. I can't imagine what you're feelin'."

"It's a cuttin' pain for sure. I'm already worried about how my mama will fare without him. They are like one person."

Tabitha nodded. She understood. Mama and Papa were the same in some ways.

"Is there anything else I can do for you to help you lock up?"

Brady shook his head. "I have everything done. I'll get the train soon and be on my way. Unless Mama needs me for something, I should be back by the middle of next week. If I delay, I'll call the phone at your place."

Tabitha nodded. Brady didn't move. Neither of them did. Her chest expanded more every second they stood there. They didn't have words, only feelings between them.

"I know this is not a thing I should rush, but Tab . . ." He got down on one knee and pulled her hand to his chest. "I want us to get married. I love you."

Tabitha nearly fell over. "What are you . . ." She hesitated. "Are you in shock about your daddy?"

Brady stood. "I want you to know how I feel and what I want. Maybe that has something to do with my father's death, but not in the way you think." He paused. "When I heard about my father, one of the first things I saw in my mind was you. You being there for me, traveling with me, holding my hand, comforting Mama. It was like a picture show in my mind. I thought you were my wife, I would have you . . . all of your tenderness and all of your ways. All of the things that make you beautiful."

"That's a fine way to think about me." Tabitha was a bundle of happy emotions. This was love, the love she read about in books. It was real.

"If you'll consider it while I'm gone, I will get a proper ring and travel to Georgetown to ask your mama, but let me know your yes or no when I return."

"What if I told you now?"

"I could not bear a no, and I will not assume you have a yes in your heart. I know you have children to consider. Besides, if you say yes, it might be a sympathy yes." He chuckled. He leaned in and kissed her on the cheek. "Be safe. I'll see you when I get back."

Brady released her hand, and she realized his palm was wet, sweaty like the sheen she noticed on his forehead. "You are perspiring, sir," she teased.

He removed a handkerchief and wiped his forehead. "The business of marriage takes nerve." He chuckled again. Then he kissed her hand and breezed out the door.

Within seconds she missed him.

Tabitha was aware that if she didn't fight for her life, she would not have one. She had no friends. She was isolated here. There was no one who would check on her, because the only other person who cared was in the room across from her, and she was just as sick. If she had a church family, someone would come by, but she didn't. She'd let her bitterness and shame keep her from choosing a church home, preferring to be a visitor with no accountability to anyone.

She was like a heathen . . . she and her daughter, living near the docks with rough men and unrepentant women. She'd spent years reading the Bible on most Sundays with no real teaching. She only started going to church regularly because of Brady. She'd let all those years get between her and her faith, and she needed it now because she was going to die.

All this condemnation made its way in and out of her mind as she struggled with fear and weakness that glued her to a bed wet from her sweat and possibly some of her own waste. Mama had warned her. She'd told her to come home.

A cool cloth touched her forehead. *Bless this child*, she thought, and then she turned to Margaret, whom she wanted to stay away from her lest she catch this disease too. What she saw was not her daughter. It was an adult woman wearing a cloth around her face, but the eyes she recognized. Her sister.

"Cat?" She croaked her sister's name across dry, cracked lips. "Oh glory." God still loved her.

Catherine squeezed her hand. "I'm here."

Tabitha's head pounded like a thousand cows trampled on her skull. "How?"

"Margaret called Mama."

Tabitha tried to express her gratitude, but she couldn't speak anymore.

"I have soup warming, but I'm going to force some water into you first. I also have some medicine we been using at my hospital. It helps, but you must have something on your stomach."

It wasn't long before Catherine was spooning broth into Tabitha's mouth. After the third spoonful, she asked, "Miss Libby?"

Catherine's eyes dropped, and she shook her head. She looked back at the door. Tabitha let her eyes follow. There was nothing there except the door that led to Miss Libby's room.

"Bitta, she didn't make it."

The pain in her chest sliced through to her back. She gagged, threatening to throw up what she'd eaten.

"No," Catherine said. "You must keep this down. You're de-hydrated."

Tabitha's lip trembled. Miss Libby dead. How could this be? How had flu stolen someone else from her? Tears ran down the sides of her face.

"Older people can get better if they make it to the hospital. This Spanish flu kills the young ones . . . like you. That's why I'm here. Mama was determined to come. I couldn't let her." Catherine raised the spoon again. "I don't know if I'll have a job when I get back. We have so many patients."

Tabitha wanted to say she was sorry. All she could do was try to swallow. Try to keep it down.

"I'm right on time to keep you from . . ." She stopped, choosing her words. "You don't want to leave this world. You have to let me help you. Grieving won't make you feel better, so try to put Miss Libby out of your mind."

Tabitha nodded.

"Focus on your children."

"Margaret?" Tabitha asked.

"Healthy. Eating a chicken I brought. It's good you have a full icebox. But the child has been keeping herself alive on cold food." Catherine looked at the plate next to the bed. "I see she been trying to keep both of you alive too. She is resourceful for seven."

Tabitha should have sent her with her mama as her mama asked, but what if she had? Who would have called for help?

After she ate, Catherine changed her and the bedding. Then Catherine gave her some medicine, and she slept fitfully, waking up now and then to thank God over and over in her spirit for saving her life and not leaving her children in this world without her.

The next morning, Tabitha felt a little stronger. She heard noises in the room next door. They had come for Miss Libby's body.

Catherine entered her room and confirmed Tabitha's thoughts. "I was able to get some men from the church on the corner to come and take her. Does she have a church?"

Tabitha shook her head.

"Family?"

Tabitha shook her head again.

"We'll figure out what we can do for her."

Tabitha's eyes leaked again. The agony was still ripe. "She has a policy for burial. The papers are hidden. I know where."

"Okay. We'll find them when you have a bit more strength," Catherine said. "You're doing good. Now I'm going to clean that room."

Tabitha closed her eyes and once again drifted off to sleep, but not before wondering what had happened to Brady.

It was three days before she was strong enough to manage a little on her own. Catherine was replaced with women from the

YWCA. Tabitha's letters to her sister had noted her volunteer work with them, so Catherine took the chance that they would return the kindness, and they did. The women cooked and cleaned. They got Margaret to school with a proper lunch. They even made the arrangements for the body of her dear housemate.

Community. She did have it. She wasn't alone.

On the seventh day after her sister saved her life, Tabitha put on a sweater and made her way down to the phone to call Brady's building. No one had seen him since he left to bury his father.

Tabitha walked to where the mail was and looked at the calendar tacked to the wall and counted twenty-three days. That was too long for him to be gone with no word to her. Not even a phone call.

Is he sick too?

She remembered how he'd been perspiring the day he left. His hands were sweaty, which was not like him. Later that same night, Tabitha felt like a trolley had run over her. The sickness came fast and hard. Miss Libby tried to take care of her, but within days she was sick as well. Had Brady given her this flu? If he did, he had it too.

She closed her eyes and prayed, "God, please do not take him from me."

Tabitha turned to take her weak body back up the stairs but then thought to check her mail slot. Catherine had gotten the few pieces of post she had, but there was something in there for her. A small slip of paper was pressed against the wall of the slot that was easily missed because it was a brown color that blended with the wood grain. She pulled it out. It was dated ten days ago in an unfamiliar hand. It read:

Bradee brother call you. He still in Columbia with the flu.

Tabitha's heart sank lower than it had ever sank in her life before. Her worst fear was confirmed. Brady was sick.

Over the next few days, Tabitha made multiple calls to Brady's building, where she was told over and over that he had not yet returned from burying his father. The man who took the calls was a friend of Brady's.

"Brady told me about you, Miss Tabitha. I checked on your restaurant. When I saw you wasn't coming, I boarded both the store and your place so no one would steal anything."

"God bless you a thousand times. Please let me reimburse you for the wood and your time."

"Miss, Brady is my friend. I'm concerned about him same as you. It's the very least thing I could do."

Brady's family did not have a phone, but someone in their community did because Brady would call and leave messages for his parents. Tabitha wished she had the foresight to get the number of that family before Brady left. She wished his brother would call with an update on Brady's condition. Now she would have to send a telegram and hope to receive word back.

Even though she was better, the women in the building were afraid of her. Tabitha imagined that watching men remove the body of everyone's beloved Miss Libby haunted them. Still, money made things happen. She was able to pay someone to carry her message to the telegraph office.

The response of nothingness kept her heart in a vice for the days that followed. Finally, she was strong enough to travel to her restaurant. With prayers on her lips, she hoped their businesses fared well.

By trolley car, she arrived at her second home. Brady's friend had boarded both fronts just as he said. She went to her back door and used the hammer she'd brought with her to loosen the nails, and then she pulled the boards. It took more than the strength she had regained since being ill. It took the help of God to get the boards off.

Inside, her precious business was as she had left it. A stench rose, rotten meat no doubt, but other than that, every table and chair was in place. She went to the back room where Brady's leather goods were hidden in flour bags under real flour and rice bags in disguise. She pulled one free and ran her hand down the leather, then pulled it to her chest.

"God, the same way you gave me favor, please have given it and continue to give it to Brady."

She did not weep. She would not allow herself to. She emptied the icebox, wiped it clean, and walked out the back in the same way she'd entered, nailing the door closed again as best she could. She would not open until she had word about Brady. She had not the strength to do so, and it wasn't just the flu that weakened her. Her entire chest area was filled with fear, sorrow, and mourning that she could not push out no matter how hard she tried.

She traveled to the school, got Margaret, and then went home, stopping at someone else's shanty because she didn't have the strength or mind to cook. Her bed was all she would find tonight. The pain in her heart was one she could hardly endure. It was so much deeper than the loss she felt for Joseph.

Margaret was just as sad, but for her it was that Miss Libby was gone, so they bathed with a little disinfectant in the water to keep more flu from finding them again and crawled into a freshly changed bed together with a book. For the first time since Mama had taken her sons, Tabitha was glad they were gone. She didn't have to care for them. Margaret didn't require much of her energy. Tabitha had space to be still. She could rest and pray and rest and pray some more.

Save the traffic outside the window, her daughter's quiet breathing was all she could hear. Her little chest rose and fell in an even rhythm that only healthy chest walls could produce. Tabitha scooted out of the bed with the intention of going to her own bedroom. On the way, she stopped at the front window and looked out. There were a million stars in the sky. It was so beautiful. She could hardly believe she had to look at such beauty on a night when she was so troubled. She let her eyes fall to the street below, where a few people moved about. It was quiet for a Friday night with such fair weather and brilliant natural light.

Just as she was about to turn from the window, a figure caught her eyes. It was a man walking in a familiar way. She squinted, thinking her eyes created the vision she wanted to see, but then he stopped in front of her building and looked up like he could see her.

She opened the door and dashed from the apartment and down the stairs just as the front door to the building opened.

Brady.

Alive.

Well.

Home.

Just in time to stop her heart from breaking for the thousandth time today.

"I will marry you," Tabitha said. He took her hand and pulled her into his arms.

Chapter 34

Present Day

Mariah

Between the hours of 11:00 p.m. and 8:00 a.m., I had my phone set on Do Not Disturb. The only people who could get a call through were my father, sister, grandparents, Hope, and anyone who called repeatedly, so when it rang, waking me at 5:00 a.m., fear gripped me. The call came from an Upstate area code.

"Is this Mariah Clark?"

My heart raced. "Yes."

"Vincent Clark is your husband?"

Soon to be ex-husband, I thought. "What's happening?"

"I'm calling from Greenville Regional Hospital. Mr. Clark has been in a serious car accident. We need you to come to the hospital right away."

Once my brain processed the accident, I could think clearly. I offered them the information they needed. "He has a girlfriend. Her name is Jess Daley. Have you been able to contact her?"

"Miss Daley has been here, yes, but you're still legally married, and we need someone who can make decisions about his medical care. Unfortunately, that is not her."

"Why isn't that her? She lives with him."

"Legally we cannot release his health information to her."

My shock gave way to confusion. "Can't he give permission? He just has to sign a HIPAA release, right?"

"You're not understanding, Mrs. Clark. Your husband isn't in a position to give us anything. He's not conscious."

Then I realized this was bad. They'd said "serious," but I didn't equate that with unconscious. "Are you expecting him to wake up?"

"At this point, until we have some identification from you, and we know who you are, I can't continue to talk to you about his health condition. If you could, please come to the hospital."

"I'll be there as soon as I can, but I'm in Georgetown. I'm four hours away, and that doesn't include the traffic that'll pick up after seven."

"The sooner the better. The doctors and surgeons need to make some very serious decisions for him."

"Surgeons?"

"Yes, ma'am."

⁓

My anxiety was high as I drove to Greenville. I might need a hospital bed before this was all over with.

I called again when I was halfway there to see what his status was and was told they were prepping him for surgery.

How was I supposed to make the life-or-death decision for him when we'd never talked about living wills? I tried to have those conversations with him. He would not talk about it. He felt like doing so would be giving in to the idea that something could happen.

His mortality was something that he was horribly afraid of. Now here we were with me not knowing exactly what he'd want me to do. I had to figure it out for a man who put me out of my house and business. Karma was something else.

I called my lawyer. I needed to know what my liability was from a legal standpoint.

"You are his legal proxy."

"I don't want to be. Can't his girlfriend do it?"

"With his consent and some paperwork. The hospital will have it."

"He's not conscious."

"That's why they called you. They have to defer to you."

"I hate this. I hate that he's hurt. I don't mean to make it just about the legal stuff, but you're my lawyer, so I have to talk to you about the legal stuff."

"It's fine, Mariah. I know you were married to him for nine years and you're sad for him. What questions can I answer for you?"

"If I give them instructions, can his family sue me if things don't go well for him?"

"They can sue. Anyone can sue for anything, but they won't have a case. It's all your call. You are protected by the law."

I had a few more questions, but she assured me that I was okay and told me to keep her posted on his condition.

My phone rang. It was Sabrina. "I got your note. Are you okay?"

"I'm fine. Vince is the one who's not." I filled her in on his condition." She promised to take care of the last-minute details for Tabby's opening and we got off the phone.

I arrived at the hospital and went to the main desk. I was directed down the hall to a waiting area. I was there for about ten minutes before a man who introduced himself as Dr. Warren appeared.

"Mrs. Clark, thank you for getting here." He took me into a private room down the hall. It was one of those cubbies that belonged to no one in particular—basically, the room where news was given to families.

He tapped on an iPad and said, "So, as you know, Mr. Clark was in a serious automobile accident early this morning. When he first arrived in the emergency room, his condition was grave. It took several hours to stabilize him. He has a broken pelvis, a leg broken in two places—the shin and the femur—multiple broken ribs, and a broken right hand."

Trying to take it all in, I played with the strap of my bag.

"He also has a head injury that we don't yet know the extent of. We won't know until he wakes up."

"When do you expect him to wake up?"

"We're hopeful, Mrs. Clark. He was having seizures. We put him in a medically induced coma to stop them."

He said many more things. Stuff I didn't understand. Things that sounded simply awful. I was overwhelmed.

"I just saw him last week."

"I understand that you're separated?"

"Yes. He has a girlfriend."

"Miss Daley. She lives with him. She completed the paperwork. She left."

"She left?"

"She got scared and didn't handle it well. Her exact words were 'Let Mariah take care of this.' She's the one that told us who you were."

"Of course." I sighed. "Vince and I are going through a divorce. I don't think I'm the right person to make medical decisions for him."

"You're the only person. According to Miss Daley, he doesn't have parents or siblings."

"He has a few cousins here in the county."

"Unfortunately, we can't reassign consent until he wakes up."

"I don't want this responsibility. What if I choose wrong?"

"You'd be asking these questions if you weren't going through a divorce. It's natural to be anxious. What I can tell you is we will try to give you as much information as we can in lay language so you're not overwhelmed."

The doctor continued, "If Mr. Clark does recover, he's going to require months of therapy, physical and probably occupational. He will need multiple surgeries, and we've already had one. And like I said, his head injury could affect all outcomes.

"Right now, he's in surgery. We had to take him in to relieve pressure on his brain. We need to know if extraordinary measures are necessary, what are his wishes?"

"Vince is too much of a narcissist to go out without a fight. I give you consent to do everything necessary to save his life."

The doctor left. This was too much. I wasn't doing it. And I definitely wasn't staying here in Greenville to deal with Vince's health issues, not when Tabby's was opening this weekend.

The only reason he was still my husband right now was because by law we had to wait twelve months for a divorce.

I sat down and thought long and hard about what I was dealing with here. I couldn't just abandon him like Jess had, but I also couldn't let him back into my life. I for durn sure wasn't going to spend a single day taking care of him. I'd already taken care of his mother. I had nothing else for the Clark family. I'd worked too hard on my mental health for that.

I opened my phone and did a search for the courthouse in Turnin County. After getting a clerk on the phone, I asked for Justice Sharon Clark. I was given the runaround at first, but I finally told them her cousin was having a life-or-death medical emergency.

"Mariah, this is Sharon," her smooth, cool voice came through my speaker. "What's going on?"

"Vince was in a car accident."

"What? When?"

"After some bar closed, so 2 a.m. He's at Greenville Regional. He's in a coma. They're trying to keep him alive."

Sharon muttered a bunch of words that shared her confusion. I waited for her to process. "Are you at the hospital now?"

"I'm on my way back to Georgetown. You should get over here right way. He's in surgery, and they asked me about his living will."

"Wait a minute. What do you mean on your way back to Georgetown?"

"Vince is not my responsibility."

"Yes, he is. He's your husband. You're not divorced."

"Yeah, but I'm not going to let that ruin my life. You signed the order to have me removed from everything owned by the Clarks. You're a judge. Sign the papers to make yourself his medical proxy. You'll be much better at it than I will."

I ended the call. I wasn't sure if that was the right thing to do, but it was all *I* could do. Dr. Johnson talked about there being no right or wrong decisions. I was certain this fell into that category. I waited for forty minutes. That's what it took for Sharon Clark, her mother, and her brother to come rushing into the waiting room. Once they reached the desk, I slipped out. Vince was in good hands. He was in the hands of people who still loved him.

I went to my apartment for the first time in almost three months. Everything was as I left it. I had no plants, no pets. Nothing needed care.

Except me. I needed care when I was here.

I undressed and stretched out on my bed. I missed it, but the one at my grandparents' house was of better quality. Then I called my lawyer and told her what I'd done about Vince's medical emergency.

"You left him in good hands," she said, and I felt good about my choice.

Finally, I texted Hope and told her what was going on with Vince. She was busy at work and couldn't talk but sent me a thumbs-up for making a decision that was about me and not what others expected.

I felt peace. A perfect peace that I hadn't felt in a long time. I didn't want Vince to die. I hated the thought of him being physically incapacitated, especially if he was alone, but he'd chosen to give up on us in a shady, spiteful way, so even though I wasn't perfect in our marriage, the nasty conclusion was not my fault.

I texted Sabrina and Dante to let them know I'd left Vince with his family and I'd be back in the morning. Both gave me thumbs-up. Sabrina's text included hearts and flowers. It felt good to be supported and not judged for not staying.

There was a knock at the door, a familiar one, and I sensed it was my special little friend. I opened the door, and he flew into my body. "Miss Mariah," he said. "I miss you."

I pulled him back. "I miss you too. How's your summer been?"

"Good. I go to camp."

"Wow. Camp is cool. How's your mom?"

Jordy smiled. "She's good. She's not home."

"Who's with you?" I asked.

"Jordy?" a voice called from outside.

Jordy ran to the door and opened it. A college-aged student was on the other side.

"Jordy, what are you doing in this apartment?"

I walked to the door. "I'm Mariah," I said, giving her my hand. "I've been away. We were just catching up."

She sized me up like that meant nothing. She looked down at him. "You have to go get ready for your grandmother's call."

"Has he had dinner?" I asked.

The sitter looked at me like I had two heads. "Of course."

"I always have dinner now," Jordy said. And my heart felt like it would burst.

I looked at his sitter. "Can I have three minutes?"

She thought about it for a few seconds. "Leave the door open."

"That's fine," I said. I walked to the couch, and Jordy followed. I sat. "Look. I have news that you might not like."

"You're moving?"

I looked at him curiously. "How did you guess?"

He shrugged. "You've been gone a long time. Where are you moving to?"

"Georgetown. It's down near the ocean."

Jordy nodded. "I won't have your soups anymore."

"No," I said.

"I guess it's okay now that Mom has food."

My heart smiled. "I bet she makes really good food."

He shrugged again. "Not as good as yours, but she's learning."

I laughed and stood. "Well, make sure you always compliment her for trying. Women need to be appreciated."

Jordy wrapped his arms around my waist. "Thank you, Miss Mariah. I'll miss you."

"I'll miss you too," I said.

Jordy walked through the door. I followed and closed it behind him. He wasn't hungry anymore. I thanked God.

Once Jordy was gone, I decided to pack. I pulled another suitcase out of the closet and packed my favorite outfits. Once I had everything I wanted, I parked my suitcase next to the door. I cleaned out the refrigerator and took the trash out. Then I showered and made a cup of tea and sat in my favorite chaise by the bay window in the living room. It was the best feature of the tiny place, and I missed it.

I reached across to the bookshelf and picked up my photo album. I flipped through the different pictures of my family. Warmth spread through my chest in a way that it previously had not done. Even when I came to my dad's pics, I felt a certain way, but not as negative as I had in the past. At the back of the album was a picture that triggered emotions. My grandmother gave it to me when I went to college. It was a picture of my mother and me.

I was perched on my knees on a stool, holding a spoon. The look on my face held anticipation of what was to come next. My mother was standing at the kitchen island behind a mixing bowl. One hand was on my shoulder and the other on her rising belly. So it wasn't just a picture of her and me. It was a picture of her and her girls.

I sat with that one for a few minutes, tracing the lines and absorbing the beauty of the few memories I had with her. Memories that Sabrina never had.

I turned the page, and the next photo was Mom standing behind a table full of her jar cakes. I remembered the wide smile in this picture and the soft, happy eyes. These cakes were her specialty. I'd allowed losing her to make me resent what she loved.

I flipped back to the picture of the three of us. Mom loved her baby. She'd traded her life for her. And yet while I was successful at Clark's, my sister was spiraling from the loss of Kendrick. She was living in a van and had given Ellen her daughter. All she needed was a little help, and I had not been there for her. I needed to make that right. I put the album down. I needed to right a few things. I picked up my phone.

Chapter 35

CHARLESTON AND GEORGETOWN, SOUTH CAROLINA
June 1925

Tabitha

Tabitha Moore, nothing else is going to fit on this wagon." Brady pushed the last box into the bottom of the wagon bed and pressed it closed. "Not unless you are planning to catch another wagon."

Tabitha stood there holding a bag of shoes and dresses that she could not fit in the trunks. She inspected the items. She would not ride all the way to Georgetown with these things on her lap.

"Can we take these to the YWCA?"

Brady removed his hat, wiped his forehead around the hairline, and put it back on. "Woman, the YWCA was supposed to be done."

Tabitha knew his protest was less about the time it would take than the simple fact that Brady was tired. He'd gotten a ride to Georgetown yesterday to retrieve the wagon from Mama and ridden it back. Now he was going to have to make the trip again.

They were leaving Charleston. The economy shifted, and with it, many of the businesses in the city suffered. As it was everywhere in the city, Negro men lost their jobs on the docks first.

"Where is Margaret?" she asked, looking around for her daughter.

"Here," Margaret said, coming down the steps carrying a book. One would think she was summoned for a funeral. She did not want to leave Charleston. It was the only home she knew. She had friends and activities here; Georgetown would be slower paced and quieter. Rather than see it as an opportunity to enjoy more peace, Margaret anticipated boredom.

"Let me help you." Brady helped Margaret climb into the wagon bed where he had put quilts and other bedding to make the ride more comfortable for her.

"Does it feel like you're leaving home?" Tabitha asked, looking back at the building they'd moved into after they married two years ago.

"Home is where you are." Brady kissed her cheek and lingered close to her.

Tabitha lifted his hat and wiped his brow with a handkerchief. "Are you sure you're not upset that we're going to Georgetown instead of Columbia?"

"There isn't much for me in Columbia but farming. Farming don't feed anybody these days."

Brady shook his head, but she knew he hated starting over. There was no plan for Georgetown. All they had was shelter and food at Mama's house. He'd always worked for himself, and now he would have to find a job. The newspapers did not paint promising prospects of that. South Carolina was suffering. The four-year drought and two years of the boll weevil destroyed harvests of food and cotton. More than thirty thousand farmers and many more sharecroppers walked away from their land. Negroes went north to manufacturing jobs, away from Jim Crow and its vagrancy and other oppressive laws.

Brady helped Tabitha into the wagon. Carrying their first child, she was more belly than anything else these days.

She didn't have to ask Brady to ride past the docks. He wanted to look at them for the last time too. They passed their boarded-up businesses but carried the ache of their loss with them. At first they combined stores, moving his business into hers, but doing that didn't help. There were no Negro and very few white dock workers to sell food or goods to. Without cotton, there were no textiles or exports, which meant there was nothing to ship.

"We have each other, Tab." She tore her gaze from the buildings and found Brady's beautiful brown eyes. She'd rode into this town carrying Margaret. It seemed a lifetime ago, but as her daughter was only nine, it had not been. Tabitha placed one hand on his thigh and the other on her belly and trusted that *each other* was all she would need.

October 1936

"A papermill is coming to Georgetown." Tabitha turned the folded newspaper around so Brady and Amos could see the headline.

Brady didn't seem much fazed by it. He was too busy packing their son's lunch pail. "I saw that. What about it?"

"I'm thinking the men working there will need lunch. I could start up a lunch wagon."

Brady chuckled. "You're trying to resurrect Tabby's Place."

"I won't be resurrecting anything. I like new things and new plans, sir." She shimmied her shoulders at him.

Their son Brady Jr. entered the kitchen and put his books on the table.

"Where is Tom?" Tabitha asked.

"He likes a girl, so he's dressing slow." Amos cackled. It was hard to believe this was Tom's last year of school. He was the book smartest of her four children. He would have already graduated, but the schools weren't always open during the Depression. She hoped to have money to send him to college.

Amos had already eaten breakfast, but he reached for another piece of salt pork and popped it in his mouth. "I can help make cakes," he said.

Amos had become a pretty good baker. He made ten cakes for his high school graduation. At the reception, everyone complimented him. Since then, he'd baked quite a few for pay.

Brady Jr. added, "You can name the wagon Tabby's Meats and Sweets."

"Somebody was listening to grown folks' conversations before he came in here." Tabitha cupped his chin with her hand and kissed him on the top of his head. "I like that idea, but you, sir, need to get down the road to that schoolhouse."

He hugged his mother and his father, took the lunch pail Brady handed him, and left the house.

Tabitha picked up the coffee cup she'd abandoned and took a sip. She stared at the new announcement again. "If this country ever finds itself out from under God's heel, I will open another restaurant with just that name."

"I don't think God is much to blame for greedy men destroying the banks," Brady said, "but things will get better. Bad times don't last forever."

Tabitha nodded her agreement. "This article says eight hundred men will be hired to build the plant."

Brady cocked an eyebrow. "You think any of them will be Negro?"

"Whites need to eat too." She thought some more. "We should be able to get excess from the local farmers. They'll be glad to sell for something rather than waste the crops like they've been doing. All I'd need to buy is some meat."

"We'll see," Brady said, but it wasn't his vision. It was Tabitha's. She saw.

In February 1937 Tabitha, Amos, and Margaret set up a food wagon outside the construction site every day at lunchtime and sold out her purloo rice and whatever meat she could get. Amos sold slices of cake for dessert. Tabby's Meats and Sweets was born. As the heel of God's foot lifted, businesses in Georgetown started ordering food for their employee parties. Tabitha received orders from people having weddings, birthday parties, and holiday parties. She named her signature purloo dish Tabby's Rice. It became well known all over the county.

One Sunday afternoon after dinner, Mama said, "We need to go somewhere."

Tabitha looked at Brady. He avoided her eyes, and she couldn't help wondering if he knew what Mama was up to. The two of them were as close as mother and son. Brady replaced the two sons who had abandoned Mama with evil disregard.

Brady, Mama, Margaret, and Tabitha climbed into Mama's old Model-A Ford. It took ten minutes to reach their destination, which was a small building located on the main road. Once they arrived, everyone stepped out.

"What is this?" Margaret asked, walking to the door of the building. She leaned to the side and looked in through the glass.

"This is Tabby's Meats and Sweets," Mama said with pride busting from her throat. "It's time for you to expand your business."

Tabitha felt the tears welling up in her eyes. She glanced at Brady and back at her mother before stammering, "This is too much." Her eyes went back to Brady. Just as she thought, he knew about this surprise.

"I believe this is just enough," Mama said, stepping closer to the building. "When I first visited Tabby's Place, I felt a pride in me that I'd never known before. I thought, *My Bitta did this all by herself. Nobody to help her and with little children on her hip.* Then, when you opened the food truck at the plant, I was so proud . . ." Mama's voice trailed off. "You can make something of this, Bitta."

Tabitha rushed to Mama's side and hugged her tightly. "I will make rent every month, Mama. You don't have to worry about the credit."

Mama released a light laugh. "There is no credit. This is your building."

Tabitha shook her head. She heard the words, but she didn't understand. "But how?"

"How?" Fierce joy was the expression on Mama's face. "I have something to tell you." Mama took her hand, and Tabitha followed. They stopped just under a shady live oak tree behind the building and sat at an old table and chair set.

The serious look in Mama's expression deepened. "This is a secret I promised I would take to my grave." Mama looked at Tabitha as if she was still considering whether to break the promise she'd kept. "Papa's parents took him and his siblings and left the South after freedom. They lived as white people in Chicago for the last seventy years."

Tabitha wrapped her arms around her middle and let those words settle in her mind.

"His father opened a business. It was *very* successful. Whenever Charles traveled, that was where he went . . . to Chicago. He was going to see 'bout family business there and to get money. He had an allowance. His father passed right before you were born, and then his mother died in May of 1915, right after your birthday."

Tabitha didn't say a word. She was processing her mother's words and the timeline of events.

"You remember Papa got a telegram. That was rare. It was urgent, so he left. He didn't know he was traveling to his mother's funeral. It was a hard time for him. But that's why he left and stayed so long sometimes. He had obligations, and his family did not know he was down here living with a Negro woman. Well, one brother knew. He sent the telegram, but if the rest of them knew, they would have cut him out of the family."

Tabitha shook her head. She was still trying to let this sink in. Papa, pretending to be a white man . . . She could not imagine that. His skin was white, but he still looked Negro to her. All white-skinned Negros were still recognizable as Negro people. She'd seen plenty of them in Charleston. "What did his family think he was doing when he was with us?"

"Traveling. Seeing the world. That's what he told them. Negroes couldn't pass and then be with Negro people in other places. They had to leave the race behind. Mixing the worlds was dangerous."

"My goodness," Tabitha said. "This is so surprising."

"Let me finish because there's more." Mama took a deep breath and exhaled before continuing, "Charles knew that if something happened to him, I would have nothing . . . that his children would have nothing, so he sent your brothers to Chicago to live in his house, to get an education, join the business, and enjoy the privilege of his family's money."

"Who did his family think was the boys' mother?"

Mama shook her head vigorously. "Charles had a story. None of that matters now. Being his children, your brothers could inherit what I couldn't."

"That's how you bought the house after he died."

"That's how I bought the house. It's how we survived all these years of depression, and it's how I purchased this place." Mama pointed to my building. "They are very wealthy, Bitta. Charles made sure we got his share."

Tabitha raised a hand to wipe not only the sweat on her lip, but a tear that made a path through the perspiration. She had so many more questions, but the one that stuck in her mind, she asked. "He wanted you all to go north, didn't he?"

Mama looked at her.

"I heard him say it. He wanted you to leave me with Miss Fran."

Mama frowned. "I didn't know you heard us talk on that."

Tabitha reached for her mother's hand and squeezed it. "You stayed for me."

Mama nodded. "Of course."

"Did you ever have regrets?"

"No, baby. I don't regret anything about my life. Your father sacrificed too much for me to have regrets. He had to work at the mill to keep from being locked up for vagrancy. He hated that job. He drank because of it. That and fear that he would be discovered and ruin things for everybody."

Tabitha had thought little of Papa. She felt like no one because he was willing to leave her behind, but in truth, some of his motivation for wanting to leave was fear. It had to be. "I just thought he didn't care about me."

Mama was contemplative for a few moments. "It was resentment that he felt about you, but he got over that, and once you were gone, he missed you . . . missed your cooking." Mama laughed. "On his deathbed, he told your brothers to tell me to do something special for Bitta and tell her she's always been his giant."

Something exploded inside of Tabitha. It felt like a special kind of joy. The kind that made you feel worthy. Her voice cracked when she asked, "Did he?" If he did, that meant she was accepted, and that was all she'd ever wanted from him.

"That's why we're here," Mama said, smiling wide. "I wanted to give you this place when I came to Charleston, but I saw the way you and Brady looked at each other, and I knew you wouldn't come."

"Brady and I weren't a thought then."

Mama raised her eyebrows and reared her head back. "I could see what you two couldn't. And you deserved love after the way Joseph treated you. Anyway, by the time you two came to Georgetown, the economy was bad. There was no way I could buy a building. White folks and Negroes would question where the money came from, and no one was eating in restaurants. I had to wait for things to get better. For the Depression to end."

Tabitha turned and looked at the back of the building. "Life is funny, isn't it, Mama?"

"Sometimes it's funny, and sometimes it's sad. Everything we struggle through has a purpose. That's what God's Word says. We have to take the good and bad and the bitter and sweet."

Tabitha folded herself into Mama's open arms. "I love you."

Mama pulled away and looked into Tabitha's eyes. "I love you too, Giant."

Tabitha looked at her building. Her heart smiled, and for the first time in her life, she *was* Papa's daughter.

Chapter 36

Mariah

The ride from Greenville to Greer was twenty minutes fraught with anxiety. I didn't know what I was going to say to this woman. I barely knew her. I had no idea what motivated her. Still those twenty minutes were all it took for me to be standing in the driveway of Ellen Guthrie's house. Seconds later, I was taking her stairs two at a time. The door opened before I could knock.

I hadn't seen Ellen in years. Suddenly, this impromptu visit felt rude, and Ellen's face showed she thought it was too. She did, however, open the door.

Her face brightened, and she looked past me. "Is she with you?"

She had to be talking about Kenni, not Sabrina. Kenni was the only *she* this woman wanted to see. "No."

"Is she back from Georgetown?"

I pulled my bag up on my shoulder. I didn't want to have this conversation on the porch. "Ellen, can I come in?"

"Not if you don't have my granddaughter."

"I need to talk to you."

She frowned, but she let me in, though not without a warning. "It's after nine."

"I'm just in town for the night. I'm sorry to come unannounced."

She was thoughtful for a moment. "Is Kenni okay?"

"She's fine."

"What are you doing here? I thought you were opening your family's restaurant."

"I am, but my husband was in a bad car accident this morning, so I had to come here to give the doctors medical consent."

"Oh no. I'm sorry to hear that. I'll pray that he recovers."

"That's kind of you," I said. "It's very serious. He'll need every prayer he can get."

She walked into a home office right there at the door, and I followed. If she was sitting at that desk, that's how she knew I was in her driveway. She had a clear view of anyone arriving. She directed me to a chair in front of her desk while she sat behind it.

"You work from home?"

"I run a personal care home for the elderly."

I looked around the room at the different paintings and framed certificates and pictures of her late husband and son. From a large frame on the credenza behind the desk, Kenni's happy smile reminded me why I was here. Ellen folded her arms on the desk. "I don't know you, Mariah, not at all, so I'm really surprised you've come."

"I don't know you either," I said. "I'm surprised myself."

"My lawyer told me not to talk to Sabrina about anything other than Kenni, but I suppose you aren't Sabrina. What do you want?"

"I want you to drop this court case. If you pursue it, you'll destroy the relationship you have with my sister."

"I have carefully considered this. My concern is not for our relationship. It's for Kenni's well-being."

"Kenni is safe in her other grandparents' home with her mother. She attends a nice daycare at the church. She is happy. You've seen how happy on FaceTime."

"Today, but what about tomorrow? Your sister is the very definition of unstable. Physically and mentally."

"She had postpartum depression. She was treated for it, and you know that."

Ellen didn't say anything.

"And as far as the van . . . Sabrina is poor. That's not a crime. It's certainly not a reason to lose a child."

Ellen's nostrils flared, and she swallowed visibly. I continued, "She asked you to help her with Kenni. She didn't have to do that. She could have moved to Georgetown at any time. She was trying to keep her near you."

"I noticed you didn't say she could go to Hendley with you and your husband. You two aren't close. You shouldn't be here speaking for her."

"We are close," I replied. "We're close now, and that's all that matters."

"You live up here. She should come back here."

"She *could* come back. If she did, I would help her. I would help with her rent and with her business, and she would be okay, but she wasn't happy here. She was sad and lonely and depressed. There are too many memories of Kendrick, and she's too isolated from her biggest support system, her family."

"I'm family too. She can't just take her away." Ellen slammed her fist on the desk. "Kenni's all I have of Kendrick."

I felt sorry for this woman. She had buried a husband and her only child, but neither loss justified her behavior. I tempered my tone for the harsh reality check I needed to give her.

"I realize you are used to having Kenni so available to you, but respectfully, Ellen, Sabrina could move to Ghana if she wanted to. Kenni is her child. Not yours. You would do well to preserve that relationship and count your blessings that she's still in South Carolina."

She edged her chin up. "I have rights."

"Some, but not as many as you think. I looked up that ambulance chaser of an attorney you hired. He settles every case he gets out of court. He's never been to trial, and he's handled very few family matters."

"I'll hire another one."

"No one reputable. I suspect you've already checked." I was assuming based on what Sabrina told me her lawyer said, but I could see Ellen's fight deflating with each argument I made. "I know you love Kenni. I'm so sorry for the loss of your son. My heart breaks for you, but I will not let you hurt my sister. She's suffered enough—never having our mother, losing Kendrick . . . not having my support the way she should have." I peered into her eyes, tried to show her I was serious. "But I'm here now, and I'll fight with her so that she can do what our mother couldn't, and that's give Kenni a mother's love."

Ellen slumped back in her seat. I leaned forward and reached across the desk for her hand. "Let's be family. That's what Sabrina wants. That's what Kendrick would want, wouldn't he?"

Ellen squeezed my hand back and whispered, "Forgive my grief."

I understood those words. I stood and walked around to her. I enveloped her in an embrace and let her sob until she didn't need my arms anymore.

Forgive my grief.

Those words told it all and fixed it all. I needed to say them to my sister, but first I needed to look in the mirror and say them to myself.

Chapter 37

Georgetown, South Carolina

Sabrina

I removed the last of my cakes from the oven and closed the door. After setting it on a cooling rack, I walked back into the restaurant.

"Thirty minutes to cool, and then I can cut them up."

"It's late. Are you going to finish them tonight?" Dante asked, referring to the jar cakes I was making.

"Yep. The only thing I want to have to do tomorrow is get dressed for our big day."

"How many do you need?"

"Five dozen total," I replied. "Selling at the local farmers markets has been good. I sell out all that I have every week, but this is a special order that came through this morning. I even had a big order from a small business. Word is getting around."

"I hope you charged more," Dante said.

"I did." He and I raised palms for a high-five.

"Your sister would be proud," Dante said. "You're going to have to sell them here too. I mean it is Meats and Sweets."

"Only if Mariah and I agree. I realize that it's not just about the cake for her. I have to respect that she's working on trying to feel good about her memories of our mother." I sighed. "In any event, it's time for me to scale up. I could get my jars at some other local supermarkets. Once I start making specialty cakes, the combination of that revenue could give me enough income to take care of me and Kenni for real, and I don't mean in the van."

I placed the last of the tags I'd written for my jars in a pile next to the ribbon I'd cut. Then I did one more check of all the décor on the tables and walls. I turned on the lights to make sure none of the bulbs had gone out. I was desperate for everything to be perfect. This reopening was our day to shine.

"With all the buzz on the social media page, we should have a full house," I said. "Even if only a quarter of the people who responded to the event page come, we'll be pretty packed."

"Yeah, it'll be good," Dante agreed.

"That's because of you. Everyone wants to eat Chef Dante's food."

He shrugged and said, "There has to be some advantage to putting up with me."

I laughed with him. "No, you are legit the best."

I made a few social media posts, finished working on the handwritten tags for my jars, and then went back into the kitchen.

I stored all sixty jars I'd made in the refrigerator. I had to deliver them tomorrow at noon.

I met Mariah as she was arriving at the house. She greeted me as she pulled shopping bags out of her trunk.

"I have a surprise for you," she said.

"In that bag?" I asked.

She smiled, and I really couldn't remember my sister looking quite so light. Therapy was good. Maybe I needed to go.

Once we were in the living room, she opened one of the shopping bags. She removed two gold lamé cocktail dresses and one sweet little gold dress for Kenni.

"The Holland girls are going to be fancy tomorrow night," Mariah said, handing me mine and Kenni's.

I examined the sleek and sophisticated cut. It would definitely show off our curves. Intricate beading along the neckline and the edges of the capped sleeves added more glamour to the design. The fabric shined in the light. We would sparkle like diamonds in the restaurant with all the lighting we installed.

"I've never had anything like this. I can't wait to step out in it." The heat of tears formed in my eyes. "Thank you," I said, the emotion in my voice coming from my heart.

Mariah hunched her shoulders like it was no big deal, but I could see she was choked up herself. "It was my pleasure."

This is what it felt like to be sisters. To share and do things for each other. To look forward to celebrating the sweet moments in life.

"I have something else for you," Mariah said. "I almost forgot."

"More than the dress?" I wiped a rogue tear that streamed down my face.

She bobbed her head up and down like an excited puppy. "I went to visit Ellen last night. She's going to drop the custody case."

My mouth gaped open, disbelief pinging through my veins. "What? How? What did you say to her?"

"I told her that you deserved to raise your daughter." Mariah's eyes got full. "I let her know that I would fight with you to make sure Kenni got to have what we didn't . . . her mother's love. By the time I was done, she understood."

I put my dress down and slipped closer to Mariah. I wrapped my arms around my sister's neck and hugged her. I didn't let go until I had my fill of the hug I'd been missing for twenty-nine years, and Mariah let me have it. Not only didn't she shrink away; she hugged me back.

"I love you, sis," I said.

"I love you too," *my* sister replied.

The next day, Kenni woke with a tummy ache.

Over our morning coffee, I said, "I need to text this number and tell this woman I'll bring my delivery later."

"No," Mariah said. "You stay with Kenni. I'll deliver the cakes."

I had entered the twilight zone. Mariah handle cake jars?

"Are you sure?"

"I'm positive," she said. "I have a couple errands to run anyway. Just give me the address, and I'll drop them off." Mariah left the room. I sat there with Grandma. Both our mouths were open.

"She's come a long way," Grandma said, a proud smile on her lips.

"You did this," I said, taking her hand. "You set us up."

Grandma grinned. "I did no such thing. All I was trying to do was save Tabby's."

I pursed my lips. "Uh-huh." I pushed my chair back and stood. "I'm going to check on Kenni."

Grandma continued to sip her coffee. Her face shined with joy and contentment. I left her with her happiness and went into the family room with my daughter.

Hours later, Kenni was better. All three of us were dressed for the grand reopening. The only person missing was Grandma. We called her, and she told us to go ahead.

"But Grandma, we wanted to make our entrance together," I said.

"You girls did the work. I'll be there soon enough," she replied.

I was a little disappointed, but the three of us got into Mariah's car. We arrived at the restaurant. Cars were already in the parking lot.

"Giveaways and door prizes will get you early turnout every time," Mariah said.

We walked around front and I spotted Quinton. He was talking to a small group of people. I figured they were his employees. He was treating them all to dinner tonight. Holding Kenni's hand, I walked to where he was standing and slipped my hand under his arm. He turned and gave me a kiss. After a quick inspection, he said, "You look amazing." He looked down at Kenni. "And so do you."

Kenni blushed and said, "Thank you. I have almost the same dress as Mommy and Auntie."

"You all are triplets," Quinton said.

I interjected, "The dresses are a gift from Mariah."

"She has good taste."

I looked down at it. "She does, doesn't she?"

"She had a good body to buy for."

"You think?" I teased.

"The best shaped woman in town."

I laughed and so did Kenni. I put a hand on his arm. "I'm going inside."

"I'm with you," he replied.

Once we were inside, we greeted Dante and the staff we'd hired to help tonight. The kitchen smelled amazing. Mariah and I were both blotting our eyes, trying to keep our makeup from smearing.

I looked around at the wonderful change we'd made in the old section of the restaurant. Something caught my eye. I hadn't noticed it before, but now . . . I gasped, walking toward it. There was a new refrigerator near the counter . . . tall and thin with shiny glass doors and nice chrome handles. Inside, at least three dozen of my mason jars. Over the refrigerator, there was an enlarged canvas photo of our mother standing at a kitchen island with sweet cake jars in front of her. A sign in front of the picture read: *Sabrina's Sweet Cakes*.

I looked at Mariah. "Now my eye makeup is really going to be ruined. You ordered the cakes under another name."

"Actually, it was one of Quinton's employees who helped me out. I needed a middle woman."

I turned and looked at Quinton. "You are good at keeping secrets."

"Not really. She didn't give me much information until just the other day."

"I wasn't sure I could trust him. You two have been joined at the hip," Mariah said. "I wanted to surprise you, but I needed cakes to make it right. I didn't want you to have an empty case on opening night."

My lips trembled so that I could hardly speak. I took a wad of tissue someone handed me and patted my eyes.

"What's wrong, Mommy?" Kenni asked.

Quinton scooped her up and said, "Mommy is very, very happy."

"With cryin'?" Kenni asked.

"That's what women do," Dante said. "It doesn't make sense, does it?"

Kenni laughed and shook her head.

"Our mother would be proud of you," Mariah said. "She would be so proud."

I thanked her and hugged her again. "You are officially *the* best sister in the world."

Mariah laughed. "I have to show up strong. I've got like twenty years of making up to do."

"You're not the only one. As soon as Sweet Cakes hits it big, I owe you a cruise."

Mariah bit her lip and shook her head. "No you don't. Owing each other for the past is over."

I wrapped my arms around my sister and squeezed tight. "I love you, but I need a vacation."

Mariah laughed. "Baby sis, you've got a date."

The opening of the doors interrupted our moment. The crowd entered. People toured the space, ordered food, won prizes, took pictures, and danced to music in the spacious new addition.

Just when I was about to get concerned, I saw Grandma enter. Someone held the door behind her, and Grandpa Odell followed. He was using a walker, but he was here.

Mariah and I rushed to him and hugged him and Grandma. Mariah and Quinton helped Grandpa to the table we reserved for family.

"This is why you were missing," I said to Grandma.

"I have a few surprises in me too. How do you like your new display?" Grandma's eyes shined with tears of happiness.

"It's beautiful." My heart was still full. I looked back at the picture of my mother. "I can't believe Mariah did this for me."

"She loves you," Grandma said. "She always has, but first she had to find some love for herself."

"We are strengthened when we are healed." I wrapped my arms around her neck and whispered, "Thank you for saving our relationship."

Grandma pointed up. "That was all Him. I just trusted what prayer led my heart to do."

Then the photographer said, "I need to get family pictures. Everyone outside."

We went out. I noticed Dante couldn't take his eyes off Mariah. He was touching her at the small of her back, on her arm, and whispering in her ear.

Quinton eased up behind me.

"Do you see what I see?" I nodded at Mariah and Dante.

"No doubt that's going somewhere."

We formed a line for the pictures. I took Mariah's hand and said, "We need one alone right under the sign."

Mariah agreed, and she and I stood under the *Tabby's Meats & Sweets* sign for photos.

"I can't wait for that one," I said.

"It's going to be the best," Mariah agreed.

When we were done, a server offered us all glasses of champagne.

"We did it," Mariah said.

"We did," I agreed.

"And because *you* did it, this place is all yours," Grandma said.

"What?" Mariah and I asked the question at the same time. We chuckled together and gave our grandmother our attention.

"We gon' set down fa good," Grandpa said. "We glad fa see oona take it."

Mariah and I stepped in front of the sign one more time. We raised our glasses, and Mariah said, "To you, Great-Great-Grandma Tabitha. Because of you, *we* have something of our own."

We clinked our glasses together and celebrated with a sip of sweet success.

Epilogue

Mariah

Six Months Later . . .

Sabrina stuck her head out of the sunroof. Seconds later, Kenni's head popped up too. Sabrina whispered something to Kenni and the two of them threw up their hands and yelled, "Road trip!"

"Greenville or bust." I placed my suitcase next to theirs and tapped the button to close the automatic liftgate of my new SUV, then stepped up on the running board and hopped inside.

Sabrina and Kenni dropped back down into their seats.

"Want a snack, Aunt Mariah?"

I looked back. Kenni extended a bag to me, and I took it. "Edamame beans." I turned up my nose. "Do you have anything normal?"

Sabrina reached into the back seat and pulled a shopping bag into her lap. I reached over and stretched it open in my direction. There was trail mix, seaweed sheets, protein bars, and chickpea puffs.

"Where's the good stuff?"

Sabrina scrunched up her face. "This is the good-*for*-you stuff."

I craned my neck in Kenni's direction. "Didn't I tell you to fight for regular chips?"

Kenni giggled. "Trans fat is bad, Auntie."

I pursed my lips and looked at Sabrina. "Trans fat is bad," she said, snapping her seat belt.

"You are such a hippie. Do not deny my niece Doritos."

Sabrina slipped on sunglasses. "Let's get this show on the road."

I pushed the ignition button, and just as I was about to pull away from the curb, I saw a familiar vehicle turning around in the street. It pulled behind me.

Sabrina lowered her sunglasses and looked out. "Seriously. He is behaving like you're going to Mars."

"Oh, and like Quinton wouldn't be here if wasn't working?" Mariah rolled her eyes. "That wedding of y'all's can't come fast enough."

"Girl, mind your business about Quinton," Sabrina said, looking down at the enormous, whole-year's-salary diamond she had on her finger.

Dante stepped out of his car. My heart melted and pooled into my stomach. He reached back in for a shopping bag before coming to my window.

"I got you some snacks," he said, handing me the bag. He looked in the back seat. He waved at Kenni. "Hey, Kenni girl."

Kenni covered her eyes and smiled shyly. She loved Dante. He played with her like he was her age, and she adored him.

I looked inside the bag and found all my favorites, including Doritos and a Slim Jim. I pulled the bag to my chest. "You are the best."

"I figured Sabrina was going to do you dirty."

"Whatever," Sabrina said. "You all need to try something new. You might like my snacks."

"Thank you, sir," I said, recapturing his attention. "I'm going to miss you."

"For three whole days," Sabrina added, extending her neck so she could see around me. She waved. "Don't fall into a depression while we're gone."

Dante laughed. He leaned out of the window and said, "I'm not going to hold you. Come back free."

I nodded. "I plan to."

I watched him walk back to his car and get in.

"Lord hammercy dat man." Kenni giggled.

Sabrina and I looked back at her and then at each other. "You are no longer to check out your bae in front of my daughter."

I waved Sabrina's words away. "Girl, please. She needs to know how to pick 'em."

"We'd be looking for a new chef by now if you two weren't cooking up love in the kitchen," Sabrina teased.

She was right, and that was why I couldn't get on the road fast enough. I pulled the car away from the curb, and we were on our way.

Four hours later, I pulled into Ellen's driveway. Ellen was on the porch and taking the steps before we even got out of the car.

"Nana!" Kenni screeched. Sabrina undid her seat belt and let her rush to her grandmother.

Ellen kissed Kenni five times, and then she wrapped her arms around her and squeezed her like she hadn't seen her just last month when Sabrina and Quinton brought her to visit. "I'm so glad to see you."

"I'm glad to see you too, Nana."

Ellen looked over Kenni's shoulder at me and Sabrina. She greeted us. Sabrina took her purse and snack bag out of the car and walked to Ellen who put Kenni down, and she and Sabrina embraced. The hug was warm and loving and long.

"You look good," Ellen said, squeezing Sabrina's forearm.

Sabrina smiled, "So do you."

I stepped out of the SUV, pulling my jacket together. The weather in the Upstate smelled like snow, which was always welcome during the holidays. I gave Ellen a proper greeting. She invited me to stay, but I had an early dinner date with Hope.

Sabrina waved, and I watched the three of them walk into Ellen's house.

I got back in the car, and just as I was about to back out of the driveway, I received a text message from Hope that read: My mom asked me to stay a few extra days. I'll see you next time.

My shoulders slumped. I was looking forward to hanging out with my bestie while I was here.

I sent Sabrina a text. Not seeing Hope, so don't bother with an Uber to the hotel. I'll pick you up when you're ready.

Through the glass door, I could see Sabrina remove her phone from her pocket. She swiped the screen, looked back at me, and blew a kiss in my direction.

"Have fun," I whispered. I backed the car out and headed to my old apartment building in Duncan. I noted the late model Chevy that belonged to Jordy's mother in the driveway. I pushed the button to open the liftgate, removed my sunglasses, and stepped out. I slid a box forward and hoisted it on my hip, walked to the door, and rang the bell. Seconds later, the door opened.

"Miss Mariah," Jordy exclaimed.

"Hey, stranger," I replied.

Jordy's mother, Rose, whose name I only knew from the packages, appeared behind him. "Jordan, let her breathe."

He stepped back.

"I had to come to town to handle some business . . ." I looked into the food box, ". . . and I had a bunch of frozen stuff . . ." I let my words trail off.

"As if the meal delivery service and other things you've done for us wasn't enough," Rose said. "Let me take this from you." She reached for the box.

"I miss your soups," Jordy said. His smile was all teeth. He'd gotten taller, and he was no longer as thin as he used to be.

"All your favorites are in the box," I replied. "Just in time for the cold."

Rose stepped back. A welcoming smile filled her eyes. "Please come in, Mariah. I'd really like to get to know you."

Jordy pulled the door open wider, and I walked into their home.

The clicking of my heels on the vintage marble floors was the only sound in the corridor at the Turnin County Courthouse. I'd only been here once before, and as I had the first time, I noted the historically rich interior, walnut paneled walls, massive wood beams, and ornately carved chair rails and benches. There was only one courtroom, and it was behind a set of tall double doors made of glistening mahogany wood. It was obvious that the janitorial staff took pride in polishing the brass handles. Their shine matched the crystal in the chandelier that hung in front of it.

Today was the day I put Vince behind me forever, and the reason I could smile about it was because everything was settled. We were only here to sign papers.

I slipped into the chair next to my attorney. She turned to greet me and then gave her attention back to the bailiff. They were looking at each other's pictures from their children's soccer games.

A dull rhythmic tap on the hardwood floor got everyone's attention. It was Vince . . . on a set of forearm crutches. He was thin and gaunt. His health had diminished. He'd aged. He didn't look like the same man who asked me for a divorce a year ago. The Hendley gossip grapevine spread the word that he was not expected ever to walk again without assistance. The rumor reached Hope's ears, and she, of course, told me. I felt horrible for him. Although he hurt me, I'd forgiven him. Bitterness wasn't my portion, not anymore.

Vince made it to the plaintiff table. His attorney whispered to him, and then Vince looked at me. We exchanged a nod. We were the only ones in the courtroom. The Clark name carried power. Vince's attorney requested a private proceeding to ensure no one in Hendley had spectator seats.

The bailiff stepped into place and said, "All rise for the Honorable Judge Hughes." The judge's presence filled the room with an aura of command.

Judge Hughes gave us permission to sit. She put on a pair of reading glasses, and the clerk called our case. All the preliminary steps were taken, and then the judge began, "Vincent and Mariah Clark, the court has reviewed your divorce settlement. By signing it, both parties agree to the following . . ."

She went through a list of our properties and assets, awarding Vince his family home and me a secret cabin in Tennessee that Vince purchased three years ago. That was discovered when my attorney did a deep dive into his assets. I received half of our retirement accounts and ten percent of revenue generated from Clark's Diner for the next seven years. I also received all the proceeds from merchandise agreements to date and was entitled to 50 percent of any deals negotiated for the next seven years. He even had to pay my attorney fees. And finally, I was to be paid a percentage of profits from any television show Vince negotiated, although now it seemed unlikely he would have one anytime soon. He was still healing, and his young chef-girlfriend was gone.

I got more than I expected, which was at least half of our marital worth and Clark's future worth. Although Vince tried to drag in the fact that I lied about trying to get pregnant, it didn't matter. He'd been hiding assets from me for years. But the thing that really hurt him was his infidelity. That's the way it was in South Carolina.

When we were done, I turned to Vince and said, "Take care of yourself."

He pressed his lips together and replied, "You too."

My attorney and I walked out with my being over three hundred thousand dollars richer, and that didn't include the value of the cabin. I was winning in ways I never dreamed I could. I was living proof that sometimes you need Jesus and a good therapist to make it through and then to make it better.

I left the courthouse. It was time to pick up my sister and niece so we could get back to Georgetown where we'd continue to enjoy this sweet season God had given us.

A Note from the Author

One of the things I love about being a fiction writer is that I get to make things up—all day, all the time. I've always written stories about women in crises. Some of those crises were worse than others, but my work will resonate with people who enjoy reading stories about women with real problems—complex issues that don't have one solution. That's the case for all the women in *Bitter and Sweet*.

Once again, I have relied on my own family history to bring to life characters in the past and present. Tabitha is a combination of several of my aunts who left home for various reasons and ended up trapped with men God never intended for their lives and the belief that there was no home to return to. My maternal grandmother died in childbirth, leaving three small children behind to grapple with her death even into adulthood.

The rate of maternal death in the Black community in the United States is a deeply concerning and escalating health care crisis, with disproportionately high numbers of Black mothers experiencing adverse outcomes during pregnancy and childbirth. For obvious reasons, maternal death is an intensely sensitive subject for our family. Although this is not my mother's story, I felt inspired to write about the potential aftermath. The children who are left behind during this health crisis are in my prayers.

My family's history laid the foundation for the women, but then there were the parts I got to have fun with—the complex Cooper history. I've heard stories of people adjacent to my ancestors who disappeared to live in a White world, never to return home, or, in one instance, only for his mother's funeral. They passed.

Passing is the decision to change one's background and social identifiers in order to gain benefits—access to better education, career opportunities, better neighborhoods, and elevated financial status—and then, of course, freedom from racism. Here in the United States, it's most commonly done by people pretending to be White (Hobbs, *A Chosen Exile*). I've always found this phenomenon fascinating but have also thought about how difficult that choice must have been for them. So, in writing this story, I wanted to turn the truth of passing on its head, and that's where the idea of making all of Charles's family a people who were passing for generations, and then Charles's choosing to show up daily as a Black man came in. Because of all he'd lost in leaving the world his family had built, including his family themselves, Tabitha's birth complicated it all the more.

I wish I could have incorporated the beauty of Upstate South Carolina in this story. Mentioning the names of cities such as Greenville, Greer, Duncan, Simpsonville, and Spartanburg was not enough, but I hope one day I'll find a story I can set in that part of the state. Hendley and Turnin County are fictional places that sit in a fictional strip of land between Spartanburg and Union Counties.

And now that I'm writing women's fiction in dual time, I get to do one of my favorite things—research. I found the Avery Research Center in Charleston, South Carolina, to be an invaluable resource. From their archives, I stumbled upon letters written by the women at the Coming Street Colored branch of the YWCA, including its founding charter. Miss Ada C. Baytop was a real person. She was the secretary at the Coming Street YWCA. Reading her correspondence to pastors, attorneys, local retailers, and YWCA staff in the Northeast was so enjoyable that I got lost in the letters for an entire afternoon.

In my research, I found there are parts of Charleston that erase the presence of Black people, making statements like: *There weren't many African Americans living south of Calhoun Street.* Primary sources aren't always available for our research, but I found a repository of restaurants owned by Black cooks south of Calhoun Street, and if that wasn't validation enough to support Tabitha's comings and goings in that area, there were the Black churches established in those areas. Churches are planted where the people live.

As with many Southern cities, Black people had a constituent and integral hand in building them—in creating the rich history, architecture, and texture that we enjoy today. Charleston is no exception. Black people were everywhere they dared to place their feet in Charleston, and some *real* woman, who looked and cooked like Tabitha, was a resilient woman who dared. I have told her story.

Here are some of the sources I used:

Bartels, Virginia B., ed. "The History of South Carolina Schools." Center for Educator Recruitment, Retention, and Advancement.https://www.teachercadets.com/uploads/1/7/6/8/17684955/history_of_south_carolina_schools.pdf.

Carolinas Integrated Sciences & Assessments and the National Integrated Drought Information System, "Carolinas Precipitation Patterns & Probabilities: An Atlas of Hydroclimate Extremes, 1920s Drought." https://www.cisa.sc.edu/atlas/events-1920s.html.

"Churches, Theaters, Lodges and Schools are Ordered Closed." *Charleston News and Courier*, October 6, 1918, 10. "Health Officer Explains Order," *Charleston News and Courier*, October 9, 1918, 8.

"City of Georgetown Historic Resources Survey Final Report," May 2002. http://nationalregister.sc.gov/SurveyReports/HC22002.pdf.

Fultz, Michael. "Charleston, 1919–1920: The Final Battle in the Emergence of the South's Urban African American Teaching Corps." *Journal of Urban History* 27 (5): 633–49. https://www.scpronet.com/modjeskaschool/wp-content/uploads/2016/04/Charleston1919-1920-17-pgs..pdf.

Gidick, Kinsey. "In Honor of Black History Month Here Are the Names of Every African American Restaurateur in Charleston from 1880 to 1920." *Charleston City Paper*, February 2, 2017. https://charlestoncitypaper.com/2017/02/02/in-honor-of-black-history-month-here-are-the-names-of-every-african-american-restaurateur-in-charleston-from-1880-to-1920/.

Hemmingway, Theodore. "South Carolina." In *The Black Press in the South*, 1865–1979, edited by Henry Lewis Suggs. Westport, CT: Greenwood Press, 1983.

Hobbs, Allyson. *A Chosen Exile: A History of Racial Passing in American Life*. Cambridge, MA: Harvard University Press, 2016.

Lange, Fabian; Alan L. Olmstead; and Paul W. Rhode. "The Impact of the Boll Weevil, 1892–1932." Davis, CA: University of California–Davis, 2008. https://faculty.econ.ucdavis.edu/faculty /alolmstead/Working_Papers/BOLL%20WEEVIL%20.pdf

Poliakoff, Eli A. "Longshoremen's Protective Union Association." In *South Carolina Encyclopedia*. Columbia: South Carolina Humanities. Accessed February 16, 2024. https://www.scencyclopedia.org /sce/entries/longshoremen%c2%92s-protective-union -association/.

Schultz, Rebecca L. "Pandemic! Charleston, 1918–1919." City of Charleston Records Management Division. December 4, 2020. https://www.charleston-sc.gov/2534/Pandemic-Charleston -1918-1919.

Shields, David S. *The Culinarians: Lives and Careers from the First Age of American Fine Dining*. Chicago: Chicago University Press, 2017.

Smith, T. W. "Changing Racial Labels: From 'Colored' to 'Negro' to 'Black' to 'African American.'" *Public Opinion Quarterly* 56 (4): 496–514. https://doi.org/10.1086/269339.

United States Census Bureau. "Quick Facts, Union County, South Carolina." Accessed February 16, 2024. https://www .census.gov/quickfacts/fact/table/unioncountysouthcarolina /PST045222.

———. "Quick Facts, Spartanburg County, South Carolina." Accessed February 16, 2024. https://www.census.gov/quickfacts /fact/table/spartanburgsouthcarolina/DIS010221.

Acknowledgments

First giving honor to God for all these stories and the right mind and heart to share them.

The rest of this is hard! There were so many people who loved and supported *The Thing About Home*. Special booksellers: Kenyatta with Riches with Reading, Valinda with Turning Page in Goose Creek, Vanessa at Books-a-Million Sumter and others who let me show up and talk about *The Thing About Home*. Libraries: Charleston County at Dorchester (Gerald and Maya) and Clarendon County Library (Holly). My new friends at the Sumter County Museum (Annie and Tracy) and the Pat Conroy Literacy Center. Every reviewer, bookstagrammer, booktoker, blogger, YouTuber, and other social media influencer, I appreciate you all.

Casey Kelley, you opened your heart to *The Thing About Home* and blessed me with things I didn't conceive would happen—like viral videos and access to readers who would have certainly passed my book by. (I know what it is out there.) That DM I sent to you in the middle of the night was seed planted in *good* ground.

The Collective Curates: Casey, Jen, and Sierra. Y'all are my favorite book people in the world. Thank you for bringing me on stage at the *Essence* Festival of Culture. I cannot express how amazing an experience that was for me. Like there aren't words, so I'm going to leave it at "Muah!"

The team of Hear Our Voices Tours made the month of July beyond special for *The Thing About Home*. Thank you for all you did for "my" voice. Also thank you Marcie with Brown Girl Collective, Angela Anderson at the Literary Café, and Nikesha Elise Williams at Black & Published for the fire interviews.

Books need endorsements and I'm humbled that so many awesome authors took the time to read *The Thing About Home*. Victoria Christopher Murray, Kimberla Lawson Roby, Vanessa Riley, Emily March, Vanessa Miller, Tia McCollors, Piper Huguley, Jacquelin Thomas, and Preslaysa Williams, I appreciate you all. Thanks to the rest of my author-friend crew: Sherri Lewis, Felicia Murrell, Michelle Stimpson, Michelle Lindo-Rice, Pat Simmons, Tyora Moody, and especially Unoma Nwankwor because she listens to every version, moan, grumble, whine, and complaint about all my stories. To my dearest author-friend, Lorna Lewis, I would not be here today without you. #receipt

Much love to author Colleen Coble for those doors you opened. You are kind and generous, *girlfriend*! If I could post a review, you'd get five stars. Highly recommended in the Kingdom.

Sharon Blount of *Building Relationships Around Books* holding that beautiful award for Christian Fiction Book of the Year was special. Thanks for all you do to make authors visible.

Thank you to my agent, Emily Sylvan Kim of the Prospect Agency, and everyone at Thomas Nelson for supporting me through the production and promotion of this novel, especially my very patient editor, Lizzie Poteet and other editorial team members and Nekasha, Margaret and your teams too. I appreciate it all. LaTasha, thank you for being there with me in New Orleans and for all your help with the indie stores and other guidance.

Last but never least, my family: Parents—Jimmie and Bessie McKnight; Sons—Aaron (Tamaria) and Micah; Siblings—Cynthia and Kenneth; Other relatives—Aunt Delores, Aunt Nell, Aunt Dot,

Etta and Donnell for the extra support when *The Thing About Home* came out. Friends: Heather and Desmond, Janice, and Jackie—the way y'all love me is everything, even when I'm missing-in-action *all* the time.

My readers—You keep reading, I'll keep writing. Love ya!!!

Discussion Questions

Please note that the following discussion questions contain some spoilers. I recommend not reading ahead if you want the story to unfold in front of you.

1. In the story we meet Mariah and Sabrina who are both at difficult places in their life. Mariah is grieving the loss of her marriage and business and Sabrina is grieving the death of her fiancé. What emotions did you feel as you met them? Why do you think their relationship is so complicated?

2. Mariah's grief was compounded by the decision her father made after his wife died. She lost her mother, her childhood home and then was subjected to an unloving stepmother. Are you surprised at how cold she was to Sabrina? Do you think her father should have shouldered more of her resentment?

3. Mariah carried anger with her from the cancelled cruise. Sabrina was barely out of her teen years. Should Mariah have given her sister more grace?

4. Do you think Ellen was justified in filing for custody or did she go too far in her attempt to get Kenni back to Greer?

5. Therapy plays an important part in Mariah's story. Therapy continues to be stigmatized by many. What ways do you believe therapy can help people? If you're not a fan, do you

think differently after seeing how the typical therapist would interact with a patient?

6. In the end, it was important for Mariah to fight for Sabrina. Were you surprised by her actions? What do you think motivated her?

7. Tabitha's story was even more complicated than her great-great granddaughters. Why do you think she was such easy "prey" for a man like Joseph?

8. Do you think it was foolish of Tabitha to stay in Charleston after Joseph died when Black people and women had so few rights, or was it courageous of her to forge her own path? What do you think of Miss Libby's advising her to go home when she had not returned to her own family? Were their situations different?

9. The Cooper family secret was interesting for me to write. I've always been fascinated by the phenomenon of passing and the complexities of it. What are your thoughts on this part of the story and all the pain that the lifestyle caused for the family? Were you surprised by Charles' generosity toward Bitta in the end?

10. The ancillary romances in the story were intended to leave the hopeful message that God will give us beauty for ashes (Isaiah 61:3). What are your thoughts about this with respect to the story and real life second chances that you've seen?

11. Food is an important part of the story. Discuss ways in which food empowered the Holland women.

12. What were some of your favorite scenes from the story. Which character or historical bit interested you the most?

About the Author

Photo by Alex Johnson III Photography

Rhonda McKnight is the author of several bestselling novels, including *The Thing About Home, An Inconvenient Friend,* and *What Kind of Fool.* She is the winner of the 2015 Emma Award for Inspirational Romance of the Year. She loves reading and writing books that touch the heart of women through complex plots and interesting characters in crisis. Themes of faith, forgiveness, and hope are central to her stories. Originally from a small coastal town in New Jersey, Rhonda writes from the comfort of her South Carolina home.

Visit her online at rhondamcknight.com
Instagram: @authorrhondamcknight
X: @rhondamcknight
Facebook: @BooksByRhonda
Pinterest: @rhondamcknight1